A SUMMER IN THE CATSKILLS

A Novel
by
Richard Mangan

A Summer in the Catskills

Published by Wheatmark
1760 East River Road, Suite 145, Tucson, Arizona 85718 USA
www.wheatmark.com

ISBN: 978-1-62787-369-7
LCCN: 2015959145

rev201601

This story is fictional, as are all of its characters. Any similarity in description or name to a real person is coincidental.

Dedicated To
Cecilia B. Sullivan
1891–1983

I

Begin your tale, O Narrator, at whatever point you will.

— Homer (adapted)

The geologic cataclysms that convulsed the North American continent eons ago, whelping from the Paleozoic surface the towering peaks of the Sierras and Rockies on the western continent, had little strength remaining from this vast construction to duplicate as powerful a formation along the eastern seaboard. And in its fatigued state could only muster enough energy to sire a mountain chain of modest heights and rounded peaks called the Appalachians, whose beauty is no less compromised and its appeal no less majestic by its lower stature. A stretch of this chain traverses New York State, where it is known as the Adirondacks. In contrast to the western mountains that stun the eye with muscular ridges which scrape the sky, the Adirondacks evoke a sanguine warmth with its rolling ranges and forested highlands.

Cradled within the Adirondacks is the Catskill Mountains, so named by early Dutch settlers who tilled its stony soil before the American nation was conceived. It is a picturesque area engraved with enchanting woodlands, meadows, and sequestered hollows that undergo a scenic metamorphosis with each season: In summer, the blue-green highlands, heavy with humidity respired by its diverse foliage, yield to the crisp air of autumn that is flavored with the aroma of variegated hues, emblazoning the countryside with a thousand shades of orange, brown, and crimson. By late November maples and birches have shed their leaves, and the complexion of the landscape pales beneath slate-gray skies announcing the start of winter. Soon, hills are cloaked in ermine snow; brooks are frozen; waterfalls are silenced into curtains of ice; and wildlife retreats into hibernation.

Come April the warming sun distills winter into spring, as droplets of mountain snowmelt form trickles that grow into rivulets, then swell to rushing torrents which cascade into alpine streams meandering through sodden fields and dales. As receding snows uncover pastures flecked with granite outcroppings, maple trees bud leaves of tawny yellow, and meadows sprout carpets of goldenrod empurpled with crocuses. Squirrels emerge from tree hollows, woodchucks awaken from their burrows, and blue jays and sparrows return from their winter havens. Spring soon ripens into summer—foliage is abloom, and hillsides turn verdant; wildlife roams the woods, and streams flow with trout—thus completing another cycle of seasons.

That the region has preserved its bucolic virtue is a significant triumph, given that the Catskills swell with summer vacationers from New York City, a three-hour drive away. Here, thousands flock to its seasonal resorts to escape the congestion and noise of city life. In my boyhood my parents took me and my siblings every summer to the Catskills, for these mountains are a natural setting for the Welsh, whose ancestral homeland bears a similar topography and semblance. A century earlier my forebears left Wales for West Virginia, where they lived most of the time underground working in Appalachia's coal mines, earning a pittance for slaving fourteen hours a day and dying of black lung disease by age forty. In 1900, many miners left that impoverished area to seek opportunity in New York, constructing the city's new subway system. There they toiled beneath the avenues of Gotham, excavating tunnels through which subways rumble today. Among those subterranean workers was my grandfather, who remained and settled in New York after the subway was completed.

In 1972 in the early summer of my twentieth year, while awaiting my final year of study at the university, I, Byron Rutledge, was utterly bored and listless from want of occupation. I spent many a hot and muggy afternoon knocking on doors of merchants and offices, pleading for work of any kind. Other days I hung about the house like a vagrant, for I had not a single thing to do and no one to visit. Everyone was doing something except me; my college buddies were traveling abroad and others had summer jobs. My sister had just left for Europe, and would be gone two months. Even my ten-year-old brother was occupied swimming, playing baseball, and going to the movies with his friends. I had succumbed to youth's most painful malady—boredom.

Boredom is a torture rack that stretches days into weeks. It atrophies the mind and bewitches the senses with chaotic thoughts to the point that one wants to dash his head against the wall to rid himself of the demons haunting his brain. It causes minor incidents to grow to gargantuan proportion, and trivialities plague the restless mind like a snake biting at the heel. Eventually the weary lobes of the brain dispels its disquieting thoughts, and the mind regains its rationality; but alas, the respite is only brief before more chaos rushes in and the cycle of confusion begins anew. By the end of June the misery of inactivity grew insufferable, and my indolence and self-pity had made me an intolerable nuisance in the house. With little coaxing I had my parents loan me their car and fifty dollars, so I could go to the Catskills for a few days to invigorate my spirits and distract my mind.

I was a bit nervous on the Saturday morning of my trip, for I had never driven beyond the city limits. My mother gave me endless exhortations to drive safely, which seemed more directed to the welfare of the car than to me. The Chevy sedan was the only automobile my parents ever owned, and it was like a family member. As I was about to enter the car I noticed a foreboding look on my mother's face, as if she were visualizing the condition of the car upon my return—a battered heap of scrap metal on wheels. Then she hugged me and kissed me; my father shook my hand; and, as for my kid brother he begged me to be on my way, pretending concern that I might be caught in traffic if I tarried any further. But he wanted to be quickly rid of me so that he could play my music records, wear my shirts, go through my bedroom drawers, and other devilment that a young scapegrace can contrive. Without further ado I tossed my suitcase into the trunk of the car and drove off, waving to my family who waved back, as I watched them recede from view in the side mirror of the car.

A few minutes later I was driving across the Whitestone Bridge, a steel-span bridge linking Queens with The Bronx. The bridge unfolds a spectacular vista: On the right lies the glistening waterscape of Long Island Sound with its bucolic inlets and coves; on the left stretches the length of Manhattan where the morning sun turns skyscrapers of steel into pinnacles of plated gold, hugging the banks of the East River so tightly that the city appears afloat on a sheet of water. But this remarkable panorama abruptly ends when I enter The Bronx, where urban decay sears the eye like a burning laser. The Bronx is a sad testament of how political corruption and social decadence can level a community as efficiently as a marauding army. At one time a thriving town, its post mortem reveals hollow shells of burned and looted buildings, standing shoulder-to-shoulder on a devastated and scarred landscape. After twenty minutes I crossed from The Bronx into the residential townships of Westchester County, where I felt like I had entered Mohammed's Paradise after fleeing Dante's Inferno. Further on I crossed the Tappan Zee bridge, where the chiseled headlands of the Hudson River known as the Palisades, rise perpendicular from the water to precipitous heights.

A short time later I was on the New York State Thruway driving through the Hudson River Valley, a storybook setting of Washington Irving tales and rolling pastures marked with Dutch farmhouses. After driving two hours I stopped at a roadside restaurant, where a pretty waitress with buttermilk hair and hazel eyes served me lunch. She was sweet and friendly and asked me where I was heading. I told her I was en route to East Durham to escape the city for a couple of days. My summer was depressing, I confided, and I could not wait until September arrived when I would be back at the university. "Why don't you look for work in the Catskills," she suggested as she filled my cup with coffee. Finding a job in the Catskills? The thought hadn't occurred to me.

A hundred miles north of the city, I exited the thruway and turned west onto a two-lane highway that would take me to my destination thirty miles hither. The road was carved into mountain wall, snaking through shadow and daylight; one moment I was curving into a mountain recess veiled in darkness, and a moment later bursting into sunlight that revealed a patchwork of woodlands, apple orchards, and dairy pasture quilted into the Knickerbocker countryside. The road gradually descended where it wound through gentle vales and meadows dimpled by ponds. Aided by a little imagination one can summon scenes of Indian warriors, when the five Mohawk tribes ruled the entire Hudson River Valley north to the St Lawrence River. Listen! Tune your ear! Hear the distant beat of Iroquois war drums, and the crack of musketry from the French and Indian wars which dyed the soil red with blood. All is quiet and serene now; time has rinsed the land of its turbulent past, and sylvan forests belie the bloodshed that once stained this inviting landscape.

When I reached East Durham it was early afternoon, and the shrill of cicadas echoed through the countryside marking the heat of day. I turned off the main thoroughfare and drove a half-mile along a gravel road that dipped into a hollow where Brookhaven resort lay, a lodging comprised of a dozen modest cottages scattered over 200 acres of undulating pasture. Ten years earlier, resorts like Brookhaven were packed during the summer with working-class immigrant families, mostly Irish, Germans, and Italians, who traded the sweltering boroughs of New York for the coolness of the Catskills. For two weeks in July each year my family vacationed here, where my days were spent swimming, hiking, tossing horseshoes, and playing softball. But in the 1960s when air travel to Europe became very affordable, families could visit their homeland for little more than the cost of a Catskill vacation. A growing number of resorts were no longer in vogue, and languished during the week for want of guests except for weekend getaways.

Brookhaven was run by Trudy Van Krent and her forty-year-old son. It was said they were descendants of early Dutch settlers, and at one time their family owned all of the land that is now East Durham. As generations passed the land was parceled and sold-off, until all that remained of the family estate was the acreage on which Brookhaven now rests. The Vans' antics were legendary. While other resorts bent over backwards to attract summer visitors, mother and her bachelor son scared away what few guests they received. Every night Mrs Van Krent and her boy got stone drunk in the lounge where they would shout curses at each other. Other times, they would insult and rage at their guests, who became so frightened at their madness they would run to their rooms, pack their belongings, and flee in their cars.

Several years earlier when I was visiting here with my family, Mrs Van had gone into a drunken schizophrenia and locked an elderly man and his wife in their guest room, claiming they had stolen all the money from the office safe. The police were summoned; they found that no money was missing, and persuaded Mrs Van to release the couple. The cops did not file charges against Mrs Van, for they had long known of her lunacy.

The scarce number of guests who did come every summer were the same who had been coming to Brookhaven year after year, because room rates were low and they found the Vans' quirkiness an added attraction. It was not unusual for a chef who had prepared afternoon lunch to quit or be fired before dinner, or a bartender to be sacked while he was on duty. Yet, however drunk the old lady got each night, she was as sober as a nun the next morning and ready to take on a full day's work.

When I rang the bell at the front desk, Mrs Van emerged from the back office. "I've a reservation for tonight and tomorrow," I said.

"Name?" she asked sternly.

"Rutledge."

She removed a large ledger from beneath the counter, blew on its leather cover raising a cloud of dust into the air, and set the ledger atop the counter. Then she put on her glasses which hung from a chain around her neck. "Let's see," she mumbled as she followed her finger down the page to the line where she found my name. "Yes, here you are. Rutledge, Byron. Hmm, I know that name. Ever here before?"

"Five years ago with my family."

"I never forget names."

The old *vrouw* was as sharp as a tack when not drunk.

"Thirty dollars, please."

After paying her she handed me the key. "Room B in bungalow 4. It's right off the shuffleboard court. You missed lunch by half-an-hour, but dinner is at 5:30."

"What are you serving tonight?"

"Cornish hen with stuffing and baked potato," she said as she closed the ledger book and set it below the counter.

My room was damp and musty, and spider webs collected in the ceiling corners. I opened the windows, and lay down in bed where I dozed for an hour. Then I went outside and strolled through the grounds. It was deserted. I will be bored to death here, I moaned. I sat by the swimming pool; the surface was littered with dead bugs, and I doubt if anyone had swum in the pool all summer. For a few minutes I dazed listlessly at the clouds as they floated westward over a distant mountain ridge, and wishing I were riding on their puffy, vanilla tops, carried away from life's cares and woes. I was snapped from my musing when I noticed an extremely fat young man, with a baby face and full beard standing a few feet away. He was skimming a nylon net fastened to a pole across the pool surface, gathering the rotting insects.

"Hello," he greeted me in a high-pitched voice that was in marked contrast to his bulky frame.

"Where did you come from?"

"Sorry if I startled you. Are you staying here?" he asked.

"For two nights."

"Great!" he cried. "Me and the others will have a job for at least a coup'la more days."

"What do you mean?"

"Brookhaven is a ghost town. There are only two old spinsters staying here now. The owner told us that if the resort doesn't get more guests soon, she'll close the place. Have you met the old bag who owns this graveyard?" he asked as he emptied the bugs from the net onto the grass.

"Yes. I've been here a few times over the years."

"And you've come back?" He looked at me as if I howled at full moons. "Then you probably know Van Krent's crazy son, too."

"I met him last time I was here—a tall, heavy man."

"What's your name?" he asked.

I told him.

"My name is Stubby."

His name, like his voice, contradicted his stature; it was like nick-naming a pet elephant 'pygmy.' "Stubby?" I repeated.

"That's right."

"Tell me Stubby, who else works here?"

Using his right hand as an abacus, he counted his fingers with his thumb. "Four. They're all asleep; they partied last night until dawn."

Stubby told me that two waitresses, a bartender, a cook, and himself comprised the entire work crew. As for Stubby he cleaned, swept, painted, mowed the pasture, and did other odd jobs. He was nineteen, and as I found later he had never gone past fifth grade in school.

At 5:30 a cowbell rang announcing dinnertime. The dining hall had twenty tables, and all were vacant but for the table where I sat and the one where the spinsters ate. I said "hello" to the vinegar-faced ladies as I walked past, but they returned a cold look, bearing the natural suspicion that barren wombs have against youth. I met both waitresses; they were sisters, one looked to be no more than eighteen and the other about a year younger. Good looks had been absorbed by the older sister; the younger was homely. Both were groggy and bleary-eyed, and were struggling in the aftermath of last night's bacchanalia.

The prettier of the two waitresses served me. When she set a plate of Cornish hen before me I thought I would break the ice and ask her name. "Beth," she answered dryly.

Occasionally, the owner's son would step from the kitchen, cast a glaring look around the dining room, and pass a sarcastic comment at the table servers. He was a tall, awkwardly-built man with an enormous belly supported on a pair of ostrich legs. The waitresses were glum and leaned against the wall with their arms folded waiting for us to finish our meals, so they could leave and catch up on their sleep. When I finished, Beth sleep-walked to my table and collected my plate, and asked if I wanted more coffee in a voice barely audible.

"No thank you," I muffled as I wiped my mouth with the table napkin. Then I rose from my chair and departed.

After dinner I returned to my room, feeling depressed. Boredom followed me like a gloomy shadow even in the Catskills. At half-past six I went to the lounge for a beer. The place was designed like an Iroquois longhouse, and at its entrance stood a totem pole bearing the carved images of Dame Van and her son in Indian headdress. The lounge lay conveniently next to the Vans' cottage, enabling them to safely stumble home blind-drunk each night.

I saw no one inside when I entered. "Hello!" I called out.

"I'll be right with you," returned a voice from a storage closet at the far end of the bar. A moment later a young, scrawny man with a ruddy complexion framed by mutton-chop side whiskers scurried from the storage room, carrying a case of beer which he set atop the bar. "What would you like to drink, sir?" he asked in an Irish brogue.

"Pour me a draught, please."

He grabbed a mug from the back bar and filled it, and then set the frothy brew before me with the foam running down the side of the glass.

"Are you passing through the area?" he asked cheerfully.

"I'm a guest here."

"Staying here? You and who else?" he asked cautiously.

"Just myself." I began to sense the unfolding of something ominous. I felt like Jonathan Harker, the unsuspecting visitor who came to Count Dracula's castle as a guest, only to become his prisoner.

"You've met the owners, then?"

"The crazy lady and her son. Of course."

"Ah, you know about those two," he said as he ripped open the carton of beer that he had set atop the bar counter. "They scare everyone away," he continued as he placed the beer bottles in a cooler. "Mrs Van comes here at nine, and talks my ear off as she polishes off a quart of vodka. By the way, my name is Danny," he added as he dried his hands with a bar towel.

"Byron," I responded as we shook hands across the counter.

"I'm glad whenever a new face pops in. From the city, are you?"

"That's right. I came here for a change of scenery."

"Well, you've left one madhouse for another. What part of the city?"

"Queens. And from what part of the Emerald Isle do you hail?"

"Now, how did you guess I'm Irish, lad?" he chuckled. "I'm reading the law in Dublin and working here for the summer."

"Going to be a barrister?"

"Indeed. And yourself?"

"I'm entering my last year at the university."

"What are your plans after you graduate?"

"I'm not sure what I want to do. My academic studies are in the humanities which makes for intelligent conversation, but won't put food on the table."

"I assume you haven't been in the war?"

"Correct. Saved by a student deferment."

"A lot dying over there. I've a cousin in Brooklyn who was drafted right after high school. He returned from Vietnam in one piece, but his mind is in several pieces."

Danny's eyes were suddenly diverted to the front door, where Mr Van Krent had just entered. He walked to the bar, pressed his huge belly against the counter, and in a solemn voice asked for a vodka tonic. When Danny placed the drink in front of him, Van frowned at the glass and did not touch it.

"This is not a vodka tonic, Daniel," he said in a low, contemptuous voice.

Danny examined the glass with a puzzled look. "Sure 'tis, Mr Van. 'Tis vodka and quinine water I poured."

"It is not a vodka tonic until it has a lime," he sneered.

Danny took a sliced lime from the condiment container and placed it in the glass. Van raised the glass, took a sip, and then asked, "Have you finished setting up the bar, Daniel?"

"Yes, Mr Van, sir."

"Why is that on the counter, Daniel?" pointing an index finger at the empty carton.

"I was stocking the beer bottles when you came in," he answered as he removed the box and set it on the floor.

"The bar is not set up, Daniel."

"Sir?"

"Where is the coffee, Daniel? There should always be a fresh pot. If a customer were to walk in and ask for a coffee and brandy, do you think he would wait fifteen minutes until you brewed the coffee?" His tone was tense and level, signaling he was ready to explode any moment.

"I'm sorry sir."

"Don't you 'sorry sir' me, Daniel. Just make the coffee." Then he drained his glass as if it were water and left the lounge.

"He's a contrary arse, he is," said the bartender bitterly. "Did you hear him talk! 'Make the coffee'! he says. He knows darn well nobody but his loony mother will be drinking here tonight. He saw you sitting here, and he just wanted to make little of me in front of a customer."

"You must get terribly bored here," I said.

"My God, I'm at wits end. I've been here four weeks with absolutely nothing to do. And I still have to suffer this place for another two months. I'm so lonely that I'm actually looking forward to seeing Mrs Van tonight. Ah, I'm ready to jump off a bridge," he said disgustedly.

"Quit," I replied.

"Quit? I won't find another job; all the resorts are staffed. And if I'm not working, I'll lose my visa and get booted back to Ireland." Then he glanced at the coffee brewer on the backbar. "I better tend to the coffee before the ogre returns."

As he was brewing the coffee I heard him mutter, "A lime in his vodka, sure, I'd like to put arsenic in it." Then he took out a book and placed it on the counter. "At least I have time to catch up on Keats," he said as he opened the volume of verse to a bookmarked page. "Will you have another beer, lad?"

"No thanks."

"How about coffee?" he asked as he grabbed the carafe from the hot plate. "No one else to drink it."

Before I could answer he had filled a cup and placed it in front of me. He was desperate for companionship, and did not want me to leave. He talked and talked without stop, but in the moment that he paused to catch his breath, I managed to ask him about Beth the waitress.

"Beth's a pretty thing. Seventeen years old. She and her younger sister, Peggy, are from a broken home. Their father abandoned them, and their mother is an alcoholic who was judged incompetent to raise them. The county welfare agency got them jobs here, and appointed Mrs Van as their legal ward. They're hardworking girls, but Mrs Van—the drunken witch—is always threatening to fire them. And if they lose their jobs they will be sent to a foster home. The poor things are scared to death. I hear them weeping in their rooms most every night.

"Each of them wants to find a guy to marry in the worst way. If they marry they would be emancipated and no longer considered minors under the law, and be free to do as they please. And that's when their real troubles will start. They will each wind up marrying the first jackanapes who proposes to them, who'll get them pregnant and then leave them. That's the problem with humankind; they set their own traps. In a way I can't blame them. Maybe if I were in their situation I, too, might leap into the fire to avoid the frying pan."

He paused to refill my coffee cup and continued. "All of us working here is bound to this wretched place by an invisible ball and chain. We'd all love to flee, but we can't. Stubby, too, was dumped here by the welfare agency. A crazy guy, he is. Has a plate in his head, I'm told, from an accident. And the cook is a transient, who needs the job for his room and board. Ah lad, 'tis a sorry state of affairs here at Brookhaven."

II

A tavern is a place where madness is sold by the bottle.
— Jonathan Swift

That evening I drove to a tavern in town that is a popular watering hole, frequented by workers from surrounding resorts. Greeting me outside the entrance was a snow-flurry of moths zipping around the electric porch lights. Inside were about twenty teenagers; a few were standing around a loud-playing juke box, a couple were playing billiards, while others were at tables drinking grog. I went to the bar to get a beer, and spotted Beth and her sister at one of the tables, who were joined by a few others. Beth left the table and came to the counter right next to where I was standing and ordered a pitcher of beer. "Hello," I said.

"Hi," she replied with a quick glance, without recognizing me.

"You're Beth, aren't you?"

She squinted her eyes to recognize me. "Are you staying at Brookhaven?"

"That's right, I'm Byron." She was in a good mood, now that she was away from work and among friends, as well as a bit tipsy from drinking.

"How long are you staying?" she asked.

"Through tomorrow night."

The bartender placed the pitcher of beer on the counter. "Two dollars, Beth."

"Take it out of this, bartender," I interrupted, pushing a five-dollar bill across the counter.

"No, no," objected Beth politely, who appeared a bit surprised by my offer. Not knowing whose money to take, the bartender grew impatient and exhaled a deep breath.

"Take it and breathe easier," I said waving the bill in his face, which he abruptly snapped from my fingers. Then he placed the money in the cash register, withdrew my change, and slapped it on the counter in front of me.

"Thank you so much. You didn't have to do it," Beth said as she grabbed the pitcher.

She invited me to join her and her friends, whom I quickly found to be an insolent barrel of buffoons. Among them were the twins, Tim and Todd, who were as ragged a pair of urchins that you would find in a Dickens' novel. What misery their mother must have undergone to have the mishap of birth doubled. They were ugly creatures in both looks and manners. They resembled squirrels with their small narrow heads and converging eyes, and when Beth introduced me they merely grunted like Neanderthals. At the table too was Christy, a girl about seventeen who looked like a ferret, with dark, bulging eyes set more to the side of her face than in the front, giving her only lateral vision; she could probably see her ears. And her long brown hair clung in strands from lack of washing. I felt I was in the company of rodents.

The ferret asked me where I was from, so I told her.

"Lots of people visiting here from New York City," she rejoined. "I was there only once on a school trip when I was in the seventh grade. My classmates and I were watching the Thanksgiving Day parade on Fifth Avenue, and I was standing on a corner and next to me was a policeman mounted on a horse. The bad smell from the horse made me throw-up on a little boy standing in front of me. That was my only experience of the big city."

"Christy, you probably caused the horse to throw-up, too," interrupted Tim.

Everyone at this table, save myself, was not of legal drinking age, and later I learned this tavern was notorious for admitting under-age drinkers. Every so often the sheriff would come in and scatter the youngsters, and warn the tavern owner he would lose his liquor license if ever he served minors again. But the grog shop remained open and teens still frequented it. But in rural towns where there is little amusement, teenage drinking is a fact of life. And most parents including the sheriff agreed that as teenagers will always find a place to drink, better that they do it where parents know where they are than to drink covertly in a park, in the woods, or in a car.

Then there was Eric with glazed eyes and wearing a silly grin. The girls at the table were attracted to Eric's goofiness like bees to nectar. He flicked his tongue in and out like a reptile, made clacking sounds like a hen, and strummed his lips with his finger. He was completely incoherent and nauseating, but everyone at the table was captured by his lunacy. I was out of place, feeling I was among children in a sandbox. After taking a few sips of beer, I got up and left the tavern without anyone noticing my departure.

When I got into my car I remembered there was a pizzeria a few miles further up the road, where I had been with my family on previous vacations. The tiny restaurant was still there, as was the same Italian man who owned it. I ordered two slices of pizza, which the proprietor acknowledged by slowly closing his eyelids and opening them, like a lighthouse giving a lazy blink to a passing ship. He handed me the pizza on a plate; I paid him, and then he lowered his lids as if to say "grazie."

I sat at a table facing the window façade which, glossed to opaqueness by the ceiling lights, reflected the interior of the pizzeria like a mirror. From the reflection on the window pane, I observed the lonely pizza man with his arms folded and leaning against the counter staring vacantly into space. I had never seen him smile or heard him speak. He was sapped of emotion, reduced to a shell by his routine chores and lonely nights waiting for customers. When I finished eating I rose from the table, and facing his reflection in the window gestured "goodbye" with my hand. His reflected image responded with a nod.

It was ten thirty when I returned to Brookhaven. On the way to my room I passed the lounge and saw Mrs Van sitting on a barstool wearing a black evening gown. She was talking to Danny who, with face sunk in his hands and elbows planted on the counter, appeared in silent suffering as he listened to the drunkard. They were the only two in the lounge. It would be another night of lonely terror for the Irishman.

When I reached the cottage I sat on the porch. The air was fresh and the sky was salted with stars. Here I lingered for a few minutes before retiring to bed. Shortly after midnight I was awakened by a clamor from outside. I heard several voices and recognized Beth's among them. She and her friends had returned from town after another night of carousing. The loud voices moved across the grounds toward the swimming pool. Then I heard a shriek, followed by a splash in the water, and then a roar of laughter. Another shriek, another splash, and more laughter; and on it went several times as the gay party continued their debauched revelry in the swimming pool. I listened from my window; fun and laughter was an earshot away, while I was alone in this dark, monastic-quiet room. The raucous shouting gradually diminished. But I could not fall asleep, and I rolled back and forth in bed like a log in water. I was lonesome and depressed knowing that tomorrow I would be back in the sweltering heat of the city, where I would waste away the remaining weeks of summer.

III

At eight o'clock next morning I sprang up in bed, awakened by the loud ringing of the breakfast bell, and momentarily forgetting where I was. I showered, dressed, and went to the dining room, where the spinsters were already seated at their table. I smiled to them but they responded with suspicious looks, as if I had committed a perversion by being friendly.

A few minutes later Beth emerged from the kitchen with a pot of coffee and poured the old maids their cups. Next she came to my table. Her eyes were bloodshot, and she yawned "good morning" as she filled my cup. Then she returned to the kitchen, passing through one swinging door as Peggy came out the other holding a tray with bowls of steaming oatmeal. After serving the spinsters she set a bowl of the awful gruel on my table.

"Take this away," I said, pushing the oatmeal away.

"You don't want it?" she asked in a voice dehydrated from a night of boozing.

"Porridge is for orphans." No sooner had the words left my lips when I wanted to crawl under a rock, as I remembered that she and her sister were from a broken home. A pained expression crossed the girl's face.

"What's the main course?" I asked sheepishly.

"Eggs with sausage and toast," she mumbled.

A short time later Beth arrived with my plate of eggs with all the extras. "Would you like more coffee?"

"Please." As she poured the coffee I asked, "How many laps did you swim last night?"

"Did you hear us?" she asked nervously.

"I heard a little noise."

"I hope we weren't too loud." Then she whispered, "We were drunk." As she walked back to the kitchen, she looked over her shoulder and said, "Thanks for the beer."

The word "beer" caught the ears of the puritanical spinsters, who looked at each other with scandalized shock. This pair of chaste antiques would have delighted being at Salem witch burnings. I could see them holding burning faggots as a young woman condemned for revelry was tethered to a stake in the town square, and then tossing the faggots onto the kindling and watch the hapless girl go up in flames.

After breakfast I sat by the pool. An empty beer bottle was floating on the surface, a remnant of the previous night's gallivanting.

"Good morning, lad," I heard a familiar voice call from behind. It was Danny.

"Morning."

"Did you hear the ruckus last night?" he asked, as he sat on the concrete apron and dipped his bare feet into the pool.

"It woke me up."

"Sure they keep me up all night. I wish I could get another room, but Mrs Van refuses. Wants to keep all her chickens in the same coop." Then he spotted the floating object. "If the old lady sees that beer bottle, she'll shoot us." He stroked the surface with his foot to draw the bottle to the pool's edge. Then he picked it up, and threw it in a nearby trash can. "Did you go into town?" he asked as he resumed his place by the pool.

"Yes. And I met Beth and her friends at Pinewood Tavern."

"They go there every night. They hang around with this crazy kid named Eric. He's a real hell-raiser, and is strung out on drugs all the time."

"I met him. Wears glasses and has long, shaggy hair, yes?"

"Aye, that's him. Beth and her sister think he's the greatest thing since canned ham. Those who work in these resorts are a rowdy bunch. They're epicureans is what they are. Their only concern is to live for the day, and cram as much fun into twenty-four hours regardless of the consequences." Then the garrulous Irishman went into a lengthy discourse on the moral corruption of American youth. When he talked his tongue became a runaway train, but he was an interesting fellow and full of opinions. Danny talked about rampant drug use in the United States, and he speculated on how the next generation would turn out mentally enfeebled, sired by parents who were poisoning themselves with narcotics. "Smoke marijuana?" he asked.

"No."

"Nor do I. As I'm reading the law, I need to preserve my faculties. I hope to teach law at Trinity College someday and become a judge. I've even started to write a treatise on constitutional law, but I've set it aside. But I'll finish it eventually. To advance in the profession of jurisprudence one must establish himself as a scholar. My point is that if I were to screw my head up with drugs and drink like most youth is doing today, my brain would be sawdust in no time a'toll. Young people are frying their brains and turning themselves into zombies. America is a scary place; it's filled with landmines." Then he yawned, rose from the poolside, and stretched his length across a bench. "I didn't get a wink of sleep last night," he said as his voice trailed off. A moment later he was fast asleep.

I left the legal scholar to his dreams, and walked from the main grounds to a back road a short distance away that communicated with a one-lane trestle bridge traversing a stream. Crossing over to the opposite side I walked down a winding footpath that descended to the streambed. The water was limpid and glistening, and schools of minnows darted through the shallow water. Fifty yards ahead the stream descended into a hollow, where it flowed in sheets over terraced layers of slate before emptying into a deep gorge. The gorge was secluded, walled on one side by limestone; and on the opposite side lay a narrow swath of level ground paved with smooth river rock. Here, I sat languidly tossing stones into the water watching circles radiate on the surface.

Then I rolled my dungarees up to my knees and stepped into the stream. The water was cold, and I waded slowly to acclimate my body to the temperature. I returned to the bank, stripped my clothes completely, and waded back into the stream. Soon, I was frolicking in the water like a dolphin, enjoying the Eden-like freedom of nakedness and nature, when after ten minutes I began to chill and headed back to the bank. As I was about to emerge, civilization intruded in the form of a mother and her two young daughters wearing bathing suits. They had issued from the woods and planted themselves on the bank, not more than thirty feet from where my clothes lay.

Now consider my dilemma: I was freezing, and had to get out of the water but not without exposing myself to these ladies. The two sisters, who looked twelve and thirteen, came to the water's edge and gingerly dipped their toes into the water like a pair of fawns testing it before crossing a stream. They lingered by the bank, standing in the direct path between me and my clothes. I was waist-deep in water and my lower torso felt like an icicle. My lips were purple and my teeth chattered like a telegraph. I could not wait any longer. I waded slowly to the bank, the length of my body rising above the water line with every step, and just as I was ready to dash from the steam to retrieve my clothes, the mother called out: "It's time for lunch, girls. Now come with me to the car and help mom carry back the picnic basket." The girls scurried to their mother, and when they were out of sight I leapt out of the water and collected my clothes.

I retreated to the woods and found a patch of sunlight to warm myself. After thawing my body I followed the stream through a narrow and curving gorge which became an echo chamber, reverberating the slightest sound. After trekking a few hundred yards I scaled the wall of the gorge that rose some twenty feet above the stream to a ledge. The ledge was a flat slab of rock quarried by nature to a perfect square. From here unfolded a prospect of sky, stream, mountain, and vale—the essence of the Catskills. There was a spiritual aura to this site, and I wondered if it might have once been a sacred altar used by the Indians in their worship.

With the gurgling stream below and the clear sky above I felt a visceral attachment to this landscape, and I thought how at this time tomorrow I would be on my way home to New York. I superimposed the dreary cityscape on the beautiful setting around me; the stream had become the murky East River, and the walls of the gorge had turned into tenement facades. Then I heard a voice from within say, "you must stay in the Catskills."

Afterwards, I spent most of the day roaming along creeks and ravines. I did not return to Brookhaven until late afternoon, and after taking a short nap it was time for dinner. In the dining room that evening Beth was very friendly. She mentioned that she and her friends would be at Pinewood Tavern that night, hinting I was welcome to join them. After dinner I stopped at the Brookhaven lounge, where I found Danny hunched over the bar counter absorbed in Yeats.

"Ah, 'tis you lad," he said with a start when he saw me enter. "I thought it was Mr Van. The fat goon roars at me when he catches me reading," he added, as he set aside his book of poetry. "Will you have a drink?"

"A beer," I answered as I planted myself on a barstool.

"What did you do today?" he asked as he set a chilled glass of brew in front of me.

"I hiked through the countryside and the woodland spirits told me not to go back to New York. I intend to find work in the area." I took a gulp of beer.

"Good luck, lad."

"I can't remain in the city for the rest of the summer. As bored as you are here, I would trade places with you in a blink," I said as I wiped a foamy lather from my lips.

"Who knows? You might stumble upon something. But I warn you, the resort owners treat their help like slaves. On the other hand, you would be working with young people and have a rip-roaring social life."

"I'm joining Beth and her friends at Pinewood tonight. But I don't think I'll stay long, being her companions are nitwits."

"Aye, you like Beth?" he asked grinning ear to ear.

"I do."

"If I were you I'd try to take a shot at Beth tonight; being it's your last night here you have nothing to lose," he said with a wink of his eye. "By the way, I might go there tonight, too. The old lady is not feeling well, and if she doesn't come in I will close the bar early."

Mrs Van never showed up at the lounge that evening, and Danny closed shop at ten o'clock. We drove to town in my car, and Beth spotted us as we walked into the tavern, signaling us to join her at her table. She was cheerful and introduced me to her girlfriends, all of whom worked at local resorts. Much to my relief, none of her bosom buddies from the previous night were there.

No sooner had I pulled a chair up to the table when Danny said to Beth: "Byron told me that he wants to find work at one of the resorts."

"You want to stay here! Great!" said Beth excitedly.

Then Eric walked in. He stood in the frame of the door with a lost look and glanced around. Then he came to our table but spoke not a syllable to anyone. The creep stared at me with a crazed expression, and occasionally would break out with hideous shrieks causing Beth and her friends to laugh. Danny nudged me and whispered, "They aren't made any crazier than him."

A short time later Eric got to his feet and asked the girls, "Anyone in the mood?" as he placed a thumb and index finger to his lips to gesture smoking. In the cuff of his other hand he displayed a marijuana cigarette. Two of the girls looked at each other, shrugged their shoulders as if to say "why not," and followed him outside.

"Eric is so zany," remarked Beth affectionately.

"Eric's brain will be the size of a walnut by the end of the summer," retorted Danny.

"Danny, you're a prude," answered Beth.

"A prude!" exclaimed the Irishman in mock contempt. "Drugs diminish a man's libido, I'll have you know."

"Haven't noticed your being a flaming Casanova for lack of them," she replied.

"I'm the grandest coxcomb ever begotten by man and conceived by woman," he retorted.

"A what?" she asked, seeking a translation.

"A ladies man."

"Ridiculous," said Beth.

"Ridiculous nothing. Years from now Schoharie County will be filled with tykes bearing my spitting image. As my beloved grandfather used to say, 'If you have good seed, sow it,' thus corroborating the biblical injunction: 'Be fruitful and multiply.'"

"Let's get some beer," I suggested as I signaled a waitress.

The waitress returned with a pitcher of brew and five frosted mugs. Ten minutes later Eric and the two girls returned glassy-eyed and strung-out. Eric was muttering and was thoroughly unintelligible. I thought him an idiot and Danny despised him. He kept grabbing others' beer glasses and taking sips. As for the other two girls, they did not know what century they were in. Danny was tired and I was to leave in the morning, so after draining our mugs we bid goodnight to Beth and left.

IV

At breakfast next morning Beth startled me with welcome news: "After you left the pub last night I met a girl who works at The Timberhaus resort, and she told me they are in need of a dishwasher."

"Where is the place?"

"Several miles from here. It's a sprawling place on a couple of hundred acres with a pond, horses, and all the works. I know several people who work there."

Beth gave me directions to The Timberhaus, and after breakfast I drove there. It was an impressive resort with wide, rolling pasture cut by creeks, and configured with chalet-style cottages that resembled a Tyrolean village. I went to the office where I found a young lady tabulating a stack of receipts on an adding machine. I told her I was here to apply for the dishwasher position, and without saying a word she rose from her desk and knocked on the door of an inner office. A moment later, a thirtyish, wiry man wearing glasses came out. "He's here about the dishwasher job" she said to him, and then went back to her adding machine.

"What can I do for you?" he asked, apparently forgetting what the lady had just told him.

"Is the dishwasher job still available?"

"Oh yes, yes. I'm still looking for a dishwasher. Do you know anyone who's interested?"

The man baffled me. "Yes, I am," I replied awkwardly.

"Oh, I see," he answered scratching his forehead. "Can you start today?"

"Tomorrow. I'm driving home to the city today. I need only pack and I can be here tomorrow evening."

"What's your name?"

"Byron."

"How old are you?"

"Twenty."

"The pay is fifty-seven dollars a week, which includes room and board." Then he turned to the girl. "Heidi, give—what's your name?"

I told him again.

"Heidi, give Byron the papers to fill out."

"What time will you be here tomorrow evening?" he asked me.

"I don't know exactly. I'll be taking the bus."

"The last bus from the city arrives in town at 8:00 pm," said Heidi.

"Then I will be here at eight."

"I will meet you at the depot tomorrow night, and pick you up," said the man.

"Thank you, I would appreciate that."

Then he stared vacantly at me, and I was not sure if he had anything else to say. He scratched his head and looked at Heidi as if to say, "you take it from here." Then he stepped back into his office and closed the door after him.

I filled out a brief application and handed it to Heidi, who after scanning it said: "Welcome aboard, Byron, I'll see you tomorrow."

"Was he the owner I just spoke to?" I asked pointing to his office door.

"The owner's son. His name is Gunther."

"May I take one of these?" I held up a brochure that I had taken from a stack laying on her desk.

"Of course."

Happy as a tart, was I, as I walked out of the office. Only yesterday had I gotten the notion to remain in the Catskills and now I had a summer job. Not far from the office lay a pond where people were rowing, and in the distance horses were grazing. And there was a large, rustic lodge made of hewn timber where band music and dances were held nightly. In the brochure were pictures of chalets with fireplaces, double beds, and spotless bathrooms, where no doubt I would be quartered. I would be fed three hearty meals a day, and on my days off I might even build up the courage to ride a horse. Who was the fool, I wondered, who quit his dishwasher job leaving me this magnificent opportunity.

I hurried back to Brookhaven, and spotting Beth, Peggy, Stubby, and Danny at the pool I delivered them my good news.

"You'll have fun working at The Timberhaus. And you'll be working with *Eric,*" Beth said.

"Not the same guy who was with us last night?" I asked.

"Yes," she said exuberantly. "He is so much fun!"

Danny shook his head in disgust. "Aye, Eric should be strapped to a psychiatrist's couch."

"Danny, that's not nice," replied Beth as she tenderly slapped the bartender's shoulder.

I promised them that I would be a regular visitor, now that I would be working nearby. After hugs and handshakes I went to my room, packed quickly, and sped off in my car to New York.

I lunched at the same thruway restaurant where I had stopped on my drive up to the Catskills. The same waitress served me, and recalling her prophetic advice that I should look for work in the mountains, I told her I had found a job at a Catskill resort. I showed her the brochure depicting the resort's bucolic layout with its streams, meadows, and equestrian trails.

"You are very lucky," she remarked. "You'll be working in beautiful surroundings and breathing fresh air, while I'll have to put up with customers blowing cigarette smoke in my face all day."

"I am, I am lucky," I agreed, counting myself the happiest man in the world who ever earned fifty-seven dollars a week, however abysmally low a salary.

V

When I reached home that evening I burst into the living room, and broke the news to my family.

"Can you believe that! I had a premonition in my sleep last night that you found a job," my mother exclaimed. It was another in an endless line of mom's "premonitions." Once when my sister had a minor auto accident, mom claimed to have seen in a dream my sister riding a broken chariot; and one winter when I broke my wrist ice-skating, she said she had dreamt the night before of a donkey breaking its foreleg. And so it was whenever a friend or relative died, a baby was born, a couple divorced etc., my mother traced forebodings of these incidents—however remote or abstract—to a dream.

"Where will you be working?" she inquired.

"Where did your premonition tell you I'd be working?"

"Don't be smart with your mother," she snapped.

At dinner I talked excitedly about the adventure awaiting me in the Catskills. I did not touch a bit of food because every time I was about to put a morsel in my mouth, I thought of something else to say and my meat and vegetables turned cold on my plate. My parents admitted relief that I would not be moping around the house for the rest of the summer, and my brother was happy that he would have rule of our bedroom while I was away.

Later that evening I went through my bedroom drawers to select the clothes I would bring—light cottons to wear during warm days; heavy flannels for chilly nights; a vinyl pullover when it rained; a couple of sweaters and shorts and an extra pair of blue jeans; sundry items; and a book to sustain my faculties. But after collecting everything I needed the clothes would not fit into the suitcase, and so came the ordeal of subtraction. There is no way, I groaned, I can do without this shirt or these socks etc., but I eventually managed to eliminate some articles. Still the suitcase bulged from the indigestion of too many garments, and I could not fasten the metal buckles. So, I knelt with my full weight on the suitcase, and pushed down hard with my hands to compress the clothes like a policeman trying to overpower a criminal. Finally, I was able to subdue the rebellious luggage and the buckles snapped into place. Then I remembered I had not packed my toothbrush and shaving razor! I would soon have opened a grave, than re-open that damn suitcase! But open it I did, repeating the ordeal. When I finished, the swollen suitcase looked like it would explode from the slightest disturbance, so I girded it with a cord which I secured with a firm knot.

On the following morning before leaving, I joined my family at ten o'clock Sunday services. We have been long-time worshippers at our local church where Reverend Hazelton presides as pastor. From cradle to grave the good cleric has been part of our family life. He baptized me and my siblings, presided over the marriage of my cousin, and conducted the funeral services of my grandmother. I shall never forget when, as a boy of eight, I was deeply saddened by the death of my closest friend. I knocked on Hazelton's door, and when he answered I tearfully opened a shoebox containing the remains of Jupiter, my turtle. The good prelate blessed it, bid it godspeed to Heaven assuring me that in God's realm there is always room for all His creatures. When I buried the turtle in the backyard of our house, how joyful and relieved I was knowing that Jupiter was now a fine pet for a boy angel.

That afternoon my parents drove me into Manhattan where I reached the Port Authority bus terminal at 4:30. Before boarding the bus I kissed mom and hugged dad. I would next see them in two months on Labor Day weekend in September. A few hours later when the bus approached East Durham, I wondered if absent-minded Gunther would remember to meet me. But there he was waiting for me at the depot when the bus arrived on the dot of eight. My excitement rose as we drove to The Timberhaus, as scenes of an idyllic summer scrolled through my mind. But never was such disappointment to follow on the heels of such enthusiasm.

When we reached the resort twilight had descended, with filaments of ground fog streaking the landscape and a sharp chill cutting the air. Gunther drove a short distance past the guest cottages to where the gravel road terminated at an embankment.

"The bunkhouse is right below," Gunther said as he stopped the car.

I could see the vague impression of a cabin partially hidden by tree branches and obscured in the shadows of dusk. No sooner had I alighted from the car with my suitcase, when Gunther swung the car around and drove off. I descended to the bottom of the grade and came face-to-face with a ramshackle. The entry door was partially unhinged and tilted precariously; the glazing was gone from the window frames; and, the building appeared no more solid than cardboard. The side walls leaned and the metal roof was heavily rusted. Inside, the floorboards were decaying into bare earth. An electric light bulb dangled from a rafter, revealing in its dim glow a place not suitable for humans. One half of the bunkhouse was an open area containing a couple of badly-worn couches, a small gas oven that was coated with black grease hardened to a crust, and a sink littered with broken glass and rotting fruit with cockroaches scurrying in and out of the drainpipe. The other half of the shack was partitioned into stalls, where filthy, soiled mattresses lay on the ground, shirts and jackets were hung on nails, and dirty clothes lay in a heap.

My initial reaction was that I had walked into the wrong building. *This is a stable!* But did horses sleep on mattresses and wear clothes? I stepped outside. There was no building to the left or to the right, and to the rear of this junk house flowed a creek. There was no mistake. This den of horror is where I would be living!

No greater disenchantment does life hold for one, than to discover something to be the polar opposite of what he expected it to be. My shock was no less than that of biblical Isaac, who expecting to find lovely Rachel in his bed, lifts the bridal veil the morning after nuptials and finds he had married her cock-eyed sister. I expected to find a cozy and clean chalet with a fire burning in a stone hearth; instead, I find a ramshackle barely fit for barnyard animals. I almost burst into tears! I wanted to find Gunther and demand that he drive me to the depot forthwith, where I would wait until morning for the first bus back to the city. I stepped outside, sat on my suitcase, and began moaning my dilemma when I heard the approach of loud voices. A moment later four figures emerged.

"Is that you, Chris?" one shouted.

"That isn't Chris. Hey, who are you!" demanded another.

"I'm Byron, the new dishwasher," I replied nervously.

"You must be takin' Ben's place," said the first voice.

"Is this where the help lives?" I asked anxiously.

"This is home."

I followed them inside. Each was drinking from a bottle of beer.

"Have a swish," offered a gravel-voiced youth with shoulder length hair that was in need of washing. He had a mahogany complexion with an angular nose and square jaw that testified to American-Indian blood.

I wiped the lip of the bottle with my palm, took a quick sip, and handed the bottle back.

"My name is Tom," he said. We shook hands.

"Where will I be sleeping?" I asked hesitantly.

"I guess you'll sleep where Ben slept," he answered. "I'll show you."

I followed him to the rear of the bunkhouse; it was dark and I couldn't see anything. "The light is here somewhere. Ah, found it," said Tom. He pulled a chain turning on a light bulb that illuminated a narrow stall. On the bare ground lay a dirty mattress with busted coils and yellow stains.

"Hurry Tom, or we'll be late," a voice shouted impatiently from the front of the shack.

"I'm coming," Tom shouted back in his grating voice. "Good

luck, Rick. See you later," he said as he ran out of the bunkhouse. A few moments later the voices of the four men faded into the night. I was now alone in this despicable hovel.

In the corner of my stall were a pile of rags. I gingerly touched it with the toe of my shoe, on guard if a rat or other vermin might suddenly spring out. I had not eaten in several hours and was famished. I opened my suitcase, removing from it my few valuables and wallet. I heard music coming from the resort's recreation center a couple of hundred yards away, and I went there to see if I might get supper. Inside was a spacious dance hall, fashioned in Old West décor with pinewood walls and an open rafter ceiling from which electric lanterns hung. Deer and moose heads festooned the walls, and the wood floor pulsed beneath the weight of some two hundred adults and teens dancing to the rhythm of a three-man band.

At the far end of the hall was a refreshment station, where Heidi the office clerk was busy selling soda and pouring beer from a keg.

"Can I get anything to eat?" I asked.

"Only pretzels and chips," she replied. "Aren't you the new kitchen worker?"

"Yes, I just arrived and I haven't eaten supper."

"Why don't you go into town?"

"No car. Got here by bus, remember?"

She told me the kitchen had closed a couple of hours earlier, so I bought a few bags of potato chips and a soda and ate my "supper" outside on the front porch, where I munched on the salty chips and listened to the loud, throbbing music. I felt my world had imploded beneath the weight of collapsed dreams. I evaluated my dilemma and assessed my options. Tomorrow I would speak to the owner or to Gunther and demand better accommodations; surely they knew of the miserable condition of the bunkhouse. Meanwhile, I was in no hurry to return to the "stable." I lingered outside the dance hall until eleven p.m., by which time it had grown quite cold. Exhausted from hunger and my day's journey, I returned to the bunkhouse like a reluctant inmate to his cell. Inside, I found the place consumed with the lavender haze and acrid smell of marijuana. Half-a-dozen teenagers were sitting on the earthen floor drinking beer and passing around a reefer. They were laughing like loons and talking incoherently.

"Hello," I greeted them sheepishly.

A couple of heads turned. "Hey guy, join us," said one in the group.

"I'm starting work in the kitchen tomorrow," I said as I crouched to the ground. "What time do…?"

"Have a swallow my friend," interrupted a groggy-looking fellow to my left as he extended me a bottle of beer. He had a dimpled chin and a baby face bracketed by long curly locks like those worn by the Amish or an Hasidic Jew. He and the others looked no more than seventeen, and were the picture of dissipation.

"No thanks," I mumbled. "What time do the help rise for work?"

"Rise at any time," answered one with heavy eyes who looked on the verge of passing out.

"Get up when you feel like it," said another who laughed like a hyena.

"You'll hear the bell in the morning," rejoined the teen with the baby face.

"Jingle bells, jingle bells, I hear bells right now; always hear bells when I'm toking on weed," another said in a voice that descended to a murmur.

I left the debauched youngsters, and went to my stall. I stood the mattress upright against the wall and brushed the sides with my hand, trying to remove as much dirt as I could from the mildewed fabric. It was either sleeping on the cold ground or on this ragged cushion, so I opted for the latter. I kept my clothes on, adding a sweater for warmth, and slipped myself into a zippered cotton sleep-sheet to buffer myself from any insects or grub oozing from the mattress. And using my goose-down jacket as a pillow, I then spread myself onto the filthy mattress. I left the light on, fearing that if I turned it off vermin would scurry out from the darkness. I felt like I did as a child, when after watching a horror movie I would go to bed and suspect monsters hiding in the closet or lurking in dark corners. In a short time I was fast asleep.

But I was awakened a couple of hours later by the hoots and hollers of a horde of revelers who had just arrived in the bunkhouse. When the noise subsided I fell asleep, only to wake up following another raucous outburst. And so my first night was a memorable one of restless sleep and intermittent clamor.

VI

At seven I was awakened by the loud pierce of the wake-up whistle. My limbs contracted in a shiver of cold, and I could see the vapor of my breath. The yawns and groans of others in the bunkhouse arose like a ghoulish chorus, and the morning light revealed the utter dilapidation of this shack. The shower stall was scummy and putrid, a veritable incubator of viruses, and the toilet was a bowl of floating feces. There were a dozen or more young men living here. The fellow occupying the stall next to mine was a busboy, and I followed him and several others to the kitchen.

The kitchen was buzzing with young waitresses scurrying to and from the dining hall, carrying breakfast cups and plates, and a chef and two young cooks were working feverishly behind the counter. I hated the chef at first sight. He looked to be in his early sixties, with jet black hair and mustache which likened him to Hitler. He had a nasty, imperious look and was constantly shouting at his cooks and the waitresses: "Sloppy! Sloppy! Stir and dip! Stir and dip!" he snapped, as he showed one of the cooks how to properly use the ladle to stir the oatmeal and pour a serving into the bowl. Then he angrily stepped to the grill and snatched the spatula from the other cook's hand. "You burn the pancakes! Flip them! Flip them!" he thundered as he demonstrated flipping the pancakes on the grill. "Now pay attention!" he yelled as he thrust the spatula back into the cook's hand. And he constantly berated the waitresses for moving too slow in picking up their plates from the counter. "Move! Move!" he shouted to them like a drill sergeant.

As this raucous scene was unrolling, John, the other dishwasher, was showing me how to operate the automatic dishwasher. As the plates and cups came through the dishwashing machine on a conveyor belt, I plucked the plates from the rubber racks and set them in stacks on a counter. The plates were red hot to the touch and I had to juggle them on my fingertips to keep the ceramic from scalding me. Add to this the steam from the dishwasher that made the scullery hotter than Vulcan's crucible. Few of the plates and saucers came out completely clean, so I had to either wipe any smudge or speck off with a cloth, or rinse it in hot water.

As I was wiping the plates, a cry of anguish rose above the din. It came from a short, old man who had just entered the kitchen. He stood at the entrance with one hand flat on his forehead as if he had migraine, and pointed his finger at me with the other hand. Everyone in the kitchen—waitresses, cooks, and busboys—stopped in their tracks, with heads turned and eyes focused on me.

"No, no, no!" cried the old man in apoplectic rage.

What had I done to elicit such a fitful reaction from him? Suddenly an expression of relief crossed the old man's face; John had rushed over and turned off the hot water that I had left running in the sink. "Don't run the hot water, it drives Papa crazy," he whispered to me.

Papa was the owner, and that was the appellation by which he wanted to be called. He was a rotund, German man just a few inches over five feet, with no neck and a large belly that hung over his beltline. His trousers were supported with suspenders, and the legs of his pants sagged in crumpled folds over his worn oxfords. Having recovered himself, Papa surveyed the kitchen from where he stood, and content that everything else was in order exited through the swinging doors and into the dining room.

Five minutes later a hot plate slipped from my hands and crashed into smithereens on the concrete floor. Otto, the chef, stopped stirring the oatmeal and looked angrily at me. His lips tightened to a wire and his nostrils became distended. I expected any moment to see the ladle come flying out of Otto's hand and across the kitchen at me. Instead, he bellowed a guttural "ack!" and went back to stirring the gruel.

After the dishes and silverware were washed and stacked, John showed me the pig barrel. At the far end of the counter where busboys and waitresses dropped off dirty plates, an aperture, about 18 inches in diameter, was cut into the steel counter through which food scraps from the dirty plates were scraped into a twenty-gallon container set right below. After every meal, each of the dishwashers took his turn to haul the heavy barrel outside, and set it next to the smokehouse where Papa carted it away on his little tractor to the pigsty. The pig barrel was filled to the brim—a 200-pound slushy stew of egg shells, rinds, meat chunks, and liquids. I struggled to drag the heavy barrel as its putrid contents sloshed about spilling brown, oily liquid onto my apron, dungarees, and sneakers. After I completed this mucky detail it was 9:30, and I was ravished with hunger and ready to sit down to a hearty breakfast. "You missed breakfast," John told me. "The help eat between 7:15 and 7:30 in the mess room."

I would not eat until noon when lunch was served, making it almost a day since I had a solid meal in my stomach. I returned to the bunkhouse thoroughly deflated in spirit. My clothes were stained and greasy; I was wringing with sweat; and my hands were blotchy red from handling hot plates. I showered in the filthy shower stall, and changed into fresh clothes. A few of the workers were fast asleep in their stalls; others were lying exhausted on the bare floor and talking about the music concert they had attended the night before in Saratoga. It was from this "rock" concert that they had returned at two o'clock that morning, when they awakened me with their hullabaloo.

"Who was barfing outside last night?" asked one of them in a sleepy voice.

"It was probably Chris. He was drinking like a damn fool," answered another.

"It wasn't me who was puking," shouted a voice from inside one of the stalls.

"You can't hold your beer, Chris," retorted a gruff voice. "I know it was you."

"I drank a six pack and it's still inside me," said Chris, proudly patting his lean belly as he entered the room. He had no shirt on and his dungarees were barely clinging to his skinny hips. He had a head cold, and was snorting mucous back into his nostrils to keep his nose from dripping.

"Chris, why don't you blow your nose and stop making that disgusting noise," added the gruff voice. It came from a strongly-built fellow about my age who was laying flat on the floor and puffing a cigarette.

"What's it to you, Bruce?" Chris shot back as he snorted again.

The husky man got to his feet and grabbed Chris's arm. "If you make another snot sound I'm gonna ram this cigarette up your nostril! Now blow your nose!" he threatened as he held the burning tip of the cigarette in front of Chris's nose. He released his grip and Chris went meekly back to his stall. A moment later he was heard clearing his nose like a trumpet blast. Bruce flicked the cigarette out the front door and returned to the spot where he had been lying, folded his hands behind his head, and closed his eyes.

"That was a great concert last night, Bruce-man," said one of the workers sitting a few feet from him. It was Tom, the same person I met when I arrived at the bunkhouse the night before.

"Yeah, great concert," replied Bruce in a drifting voice. Then his jaw dropped and he began to snore.

"The guitarists could make their instruments sing. Unbelievable, Bruce-man?" said Tom as his fingers mimicked playing a guitar.

"Tom?" I asked.

"Who interrupts me when I'm playing my guitar?" he asked as he continued strumming his imaginary instrument.

"It's me, Byron."

"Ah, the new guy. How are you, my friend?"

"Is there any other place where the workers live?" I asked.

"Nope, this is it. Why? Don't you like it here?" he asked as he continued strumming.

"It's not what I expected."

"This place is a rat house," said one of the workers.

"Are there rats here?" I tried to suppress the alarm in my voice.

"This hole is too dirty even for rats. One look and they flee," said another.

"Several workers live in guest cottages," came a muffled voice from inside a sleeping bag where one youth had cocooned himself; only a mop of brown hair could be seen flowing from the opening of the bag.

"Guest cottages?" I asked excitedly.

"Tell Papa you want to share a guest cottage. The kind old man will let you," rejoined Tom.

"Really?" My face lit up like a Roman candle.

"Dress like a woman, though. Only the waitresses live in the cottages," said Chris who had just reappeared.

My face darkened like a snuffed flame.

"Sleep in your car," advised Tom.

"Don't have one," I said.

"Don't have a car, don't have a car, so I'll live in this rat hole! rat hole! rat hole!" sang Tom as he continued to pluck notes from the air with his fingers.

It was apparent to me that these ragamuffins were content to live in filth, and that this cesspool would be my home for as long as I worked here. I decided I would finish out the day and return to the city tomorrow on the morning bus.

The workers ate lunch from noon to 12:30. With plates in hand we queued up in the kitchen to receive our portions of sliced pork. I felt like a prisoner, lining up for his meager ration. As Otto carved, one of the cooks served the slices while the other poured gravy from a ladle. When the cook placed too large a serving on one plate, Otto flew into a rage and furiously plucked the extra slice of pork off the dish as if the fatty pig meat were gold bullion. "Pay attention, Alex," the distempered German snapped as he dangled the rescued slice before the cook's face. And then Otto slapped the slice onto the next plate. The kraut generated his own weather system when he was upset: Beads of sweat on his brow would vaporize from the heat of anger, producing whirling storm clouds around his head like the rings of Saturn.

After receiving my portion I went into the worker's mess room. It was a small, cramped room with a half-dozen wooden tables arranged two abreast, where about twenty workers were eating. Of this number half were waitresses, most of whom appeared to be college age, and none whom I considered good-looking except for one with long, braided flaxen hair.

"Got room for another body?" I asked as I squeezed myself onto the crowded bench next to Chris. The checkered table cloth was stained and layered with grease. On the center of the table lay a pitcher of milk and a stack of dark pumpernickel bread. The milk was cold but sour, and the bread was a bit stale.

"You better like the taste of pork while you work here," Chris warned me.

"Why?"

"Because you'll be eating this trash for lunch everyday, and oftentimes for dinner." He did not touch his meat; he was eating only the bread which he dipped into the black, lipid gravy.

My attention was drawn to a waitress who was breathless from rapid-fire talking. She sucked in air to reload her lungs, and then continued gabbing. Indeed, she spoke so fast that her tongue clicked like a castanet. She was talking about last night's concert, which from her account seemed to have been a crazy and reckless affair. I noticed another waitress who was very young, a mere girl, who I later learned was only fifteen, but masqueraded as a seventeen-year-old. She had oily, margarine-colored hair and a chronic, hacking cough. She was sitting next to one of the kitchen workers, an ugly youth with drooping, lifeless eyes. He was nasty to her, telling her to keep quiet whenever she opened her mouth, yet she seemed genuinely endeared to him as if his insults were intended as compliments. Then the thud of heeled boots and clank of spurs announced the arrival of the two wranglers, Bruce and Tom, who carried the smell of horses to the table.

"Make way for the cowboys," thundered Bruce as he entered the room with Tom in tow. Bruce eyed the room, looking for a place to sit. "Get up, you nerd!" he shouted at a puny kid wearing thick eyeglasses. The frightened boy said nothing; he quickly left the table with his plate, and leaned against the wall where he continued eating.

"Susan! You almost got us all killed last night, the way you drove!" boomed Tom in his scratchy voice. He was addressing a waitress at the opposite table. She had a plain face and black, wiry hair that resembled a scouring pad.

"I was so stoned I can't remember anything about last night," she answered massaging her temples.

"You damn near missed hitting a speeding train," barked Bruce. "And you smacked off the wooden arms at the railroad crossing when you blew past it."

"Oh, my God! That must be how my right headlight got smashed," she said with a burst of laughter.

"This milk is sour!" shouted Bruce smacking his lips with distaste. "Chris! Grab a quart of moo-juice from the kitchen."

"Otto will whip me if I take anything from the refrigerator."

"Let him whip you. Just bring back some fresh milk."

"I can't Bruce," replied Chris in an agitated voice.

"You're a good-for-nothing idiot," snapped Bruce.

"Sour milk is no harm; it's good for the stomach," another worker said.

Bruce issued him an icy look and said, "Mind your own business."

"I'm gonna pour boiling oil down that Nazi's throat!" thundered a new voice. Every head turned. Standing at the threshold of the mess room with a maniacal look in his eyes was Eric. "Otto won't serve me lunch!"

"You're complaining about not eating this rat meat?" hollered Tom.

"Otto said: 'You are late! No food!'" growled Eric kicking the toe of his boot against the wall. Then he grabbed a couple of slices of bread from one of the tables, and with a knife scooped a wad of butter which he slapped on the bread. "No place to sit?" he complained. Every table was full.

"Sit here Eric," squeaked Cindy (the fifteen-year-old) motioning him to sit on her lap.

But Eric ignored her and plopped himself on the edge of one of the benches, and sidled himself inward until he was fully seated.

"Herr Otto should be forced to eat his own food. You need dinosaur teeth to chew this," moaned Eric who struggled to free his teeth after biting into the hard pumpernickel.

Eric worked as a groundskeeper who went about his chores with little supervision. He emptied garbage cans, cleaned the pool, swept porches and walkways, and was supposed to clean the horse stable, but he seldom did. Papa, who worked his help to the bone, never figured out that Eric's tasks only consumed a few hours of work each day, thus leaving Eric much time to spend the afternoons and evenings getting narcotized on a pharmacopeia of drugs. The free-spirited clown was seldom sober, and lived in a twilight world that made his behavior spontaneous and unpredictable. Like many of the other workers he was from The Bronx, whose parents had a summer home in the Catskills. As I would later learn, he began experimenting with drugs when he was fifteen, and now at age seventeen with one year remaining in high school he was addicted to hallucinogens and was an habitual "pothead." Pleasure was his only aim, and he was destroying himself to that end.

"After lunch you better beeline to the stable and clean out those stalls," demanded Bruce.

"I just cleaned them," snarled Eric.

"When?"

"Couple of days ago," riposted Eric, thrusting his jaw defiantly at Bruce.

"Liar! You haven't been to the stables in over two weeks, and the stalls are knee-high in dung."

"Clean them yourself," answered Eric in a calm voice that belittled Bruce's anger.

I did not quit that day as I had promised myself, in part because of pride and the embarrassment of facing my family when I returned home. Oddly, within hours after firmly resolving not to spend another day here, I found myself challenged by the very obstacles of my situation. Sometimes the predicament which threatens to pull the rug out from under one's feet, is the one on which we stand firm out of sheer defiance. So, I decided to postpone my decision, confident I could survive one more day.

VII

Man is a creature that can get used to anything.
— Dostoyevsky

And I did survive another day, and another day after that, and so on until I completed my first week at The Timberhaus, which culminated with a day off from work. All week the weather had been beautiful, but as chance would have it heavy rain fell on my day of rest and I was very gloomy. There is no place more charming than the Catskills on a balmy day, and no place more dreary than when it rains. It is like women I have known who are so pretty when they smile, and so ugly when they frown. The countryside had all but vanished in mist and rain; and low, charcoal clouds enshrouded the hills compressing the daylight to a thin, horizontal layer above the soaked ground. I had planned to spend the day swimming and boating, and later hitch a ride into town to visit Danny. Instead I was holed up in a decrepit ramshackle, a prisoner of nature's mood, and surrounded by hedonistic youth who were bent on debauching themselves on booze and drugs.

One can accustom himself to almost any raucousness over the course of time. There are people who live for years in tenement apartments lying smack beside elevated subway tracks, to whom the thunderous rumble of trains becomes no more disturbing than the hourly chimes of a wall clock. Likewise, I was able to slowly acclimate myself to the clamor of the bunkhouse, where loud argument and boisterousness continued sometimes until dawn. Ironically, I was woken up at night not due to uproar but to its absence, as if my subconscious—adjusted to racket—becomes agitated by a calm lull.

New faces were appearing at the bunkhouse everyday. Friends

of workers would stay for a couple of days; then leave, and then return like stray dogs. Had these loafers any home or parents? One afternoon after finishing the lunch shift, I returned to my stall and found a stranger sleeping on my mattress. Despite my best effort I could not rouse him. I slapped his cheeks—no response; I shook his shoulders—no response; I tweaked his nose and pulled his toes—the same. Finally, overcome with frustration I tilted the mattress and the trespasser tumbled onto the hard ground. He groaned and muttered an epithet and fell fast asleep again. In the corner of the stall I found my blankets and sheet thrown in a heap. When I grabbed the blankets I felt a heavy object within. I released my grip and heard a thud, and pulling back the blankets found another person beneath! Alive or dead I could not tell, when suddenly the urchin's eyes opened and he looked at me with the silliest grin.

My patience was quickly ebbing. "Get up! Get up!" I demanded. He answered by pulling a blanket over his head, which I immediately yanked off him. He stared at me through dilated eyes, and I'm sure he had no idea where he was. I demanded again that he get to his feet, but he just stared at me with a ludicrous expression. So I grabbed his ankles and dragged him out of the stall to the front door where the fresh air might revive him. I returned to the stall and dragged the other fellow out as well, and set the pair of buffoons side-by-side lying flat on their backs. Returning to my stall, I shook out the sheets and blankets and folded them. I was furious; after all, a man's bed is his sanctum, but that means nothing to the riff-raff living here. As regards the two trespassers, I later discovered that they were friends of Eric who had been tossed out of their homes by their parents.

As regards my job I had begun alternating my dishwashing chores with bussing tables. On the first morning that I bussed tables I was very tense and awkward. When I passed through the swinging doors of the kitchen and into the dining room pushing my tray cart ahead of me, I was like an actor stricken with stage fright. I could feel the weight of critical eyes bearing down on this tall, bungling kid lumbering through the aisles. My face blushed so red hot I thought my hair would ignite. And the more I tried to calm myself, the more agitated I became and could not concentrate on what I should be doing. Clearing tables of dirty plates is such a brainless chore, that I felt so humiliated whenever I removed a plate before the guest had finished eating only to have him snap it from my hand and remark in a Brooklyn clip: "I ain't troo yet!" Or feel the tug on my apron when guests were impatiently waiting for their plates to be taken away so they could be served dessert.

And there was one razor-tongued waitress who found fault with everything I did. Sandra was a double-faced shrew, gracious and fawning to the guests, but once inside the kitchen she turned into a veritable witch, blasting me for being too slow in cleaning her tables, and screaming at the other dishwasher if the plates and glassware were less than spotless. She was a spiteful miss, and at most every meal apologized to the guests for "that lazy busboy" who impeded her service, and saying it within earshot of me. The other waitresses disliked her too, but dared not cross swords with this malicious virago. What's more she had an evil eye, much like the gypsy in fable whose glance could cast a curse.

My God, I felt I was at the end of my rope. And tokens of depression were becoming manifested in my being poorly fed, enduring Sisyphean labor, and living in a vermin-infested madhouse. What's more, I was lonely. Other than having a serial number branded on my forearm, The Timberhaus was a genuine concentration camp for its workers. And the bunkhouse was like a stalag. If the grounds were enclosed with barbed wire and secured with guard towers, I would not have felt any less at liberty. I would trade places with an owl to live inside of a tree, or with a rabbit to live in a warren. Were it not for the creatures of the night that slither and growl, I would have slept beneath the stars on the cold bare ground.

Such a wretched situation! But when I am weighed down by misery, I think of Dostoyevsky who endured plenty of it. He lived in 19th century Russia, and got on the wrong side of the Czar. At age twenty-eight he was convicted of political crimes in Russia and sentenced to death. He was taken out to be shot in a public square, and as he stood before a firing squad received a last minute reprieve. His sentence was commuted to hard labor in a Siberian military prison, where he spent the next four years in a living hell. He wrote

The House of the Dead based on his experiences there. He lived on a diet of roach-infested bread and cabbage soup, and slept on plank beds huddled with other prisoners to keep warm on nights that dropped to minus-thirty degrees. Any movement was accompanied by the clanking of ankle fetters, and the barracks were befouled with the stench of human excrement. Barbers shaved his head with coarse razors, and the sadistic warden would enter the barracks in the middle of the night and beat a prisoner for no reason. Later, he suffered from epilepsy and piled up huge gambling debts. But it never stopped him from writing some of the greatest novels in literature.

My situation, of course, was not near as severe. One year at The Timberhaus would not come close to equaling one day in a Siberian prison. I was not serving a sentence, and could leave at any time. So I tried to rally my spirits from the trough of despair by envisioning a chain of achievements after finishing college, that would propel me from the ordinary life into one of status and fortune. Ah, imagination! Without it I would be trapped within four windowless walls of reality.

VIII

Mad with rage, it filled the air with its triple barking.
— THE THREE-HEADED DOG,
FROM OVID'S "METAMORPHOSES"

There is a tomcat who until recently was a wily thief. He would sneak into the kitchen and make off with one of the salmon steaks that Otto was preparing for dinner, sending the chef into a frenzy who would hurl at the rogue the first thing he could put his hand on. But the cat was an artful dodger and escape unscathed with its trophy of fish.

One afternoon as I was hauling the kitchen garbage outside, I found the cat perched on the roof of the trash shed ready to fall upon the scraps and refuse. It struck me that Otto's headache would become my remedy for rodents. I returned to the kitchen and came out with two bowls of milk, and set one the ground. The rascal instantly leaped from the roof and began licking up the milk. A short time later the furry critter had polished the bowl clean. Then it raised itself on its hind legs and placed its forepaws against the other bowl I was holding, but instead of setting it before the hungry cat, I held it aloft like the proverbial grapes over the fox and led the cat to the bunkhouse where I placed the bowl beside my mattress. After gulping down the milk the cat stretched and yawned, laid on its side and, like Goldilocks after a heavy meal, fell asleep. I feed it every day now, and it has berthed itself permanently in my stall.

I am no lover of cats because they eat birds who fill the morning with song, but I hate mice and rats. Thus, "the enemy of an enemy is a friend." Appropriately, I have named the cat Churchill who, like the cat itself, had a bitter feud with another German. Churchill keeps vigilant watch, and I sleep better as a result. Since his arrival I have neither seen nor heard mice scurrying through the bunkhouse. His excellent police work was evident yesterday morning when I found the heads of two mice lying just inside the entrance.

This afternoon when I returned to the bunkhouse with a bowl of milk for Churchill, I experienced a tremendous fright. As I was passing through the narrow corridor to my stall I heard a thunderous growl. Then from the tail of my eye I saw a creature lunge at me from one of the stalls; it was all a blur it happened so fast. I thought it was a bear that had wandered in from the woods. My skeleton nearly jumped out of my skin, and the bowl of milk flew up in the air. Just as the animal was about to rip out my side, its progress was checked by the chain to which it was tethered. If the chain were a single chink longer, the beast would have locked its jaw into my torso. I froze momentarily with terror, and in that instant I discovered it was a mastiff chained to Bruce's stall. The dog was as ferocious as Cerberus, the three-headed canine who guarded the entrance to Hades. My initial fright had sent me into shock; I raced down the corridor and into my stall where I huddled in a corner, while my heart beat like an African bongo. For several minutes the bitch continued her savage barking, and was so determined to snap her bonds that the vertical post to which her chain was fastened shook so violently that I thought she would pull down the entire rat house, like Samson who, to free himself of his shackles, pulled down an entire building on himself.

The loud barking brought Hildegarde, the cleaning woman, to the scene who was cleaning one of the guest cottages nearby. With whisk broom raised high in one hand and dust pan in the other, she stormed into the bunkhouse like Brunhilde, Teutonic goddess of war. She fearlessly approached the angry dog and smacked it on the jaw with her broom. The fire in the eyes of the German Fraulein extinguished the ferocity of the rottweiler, who backed itself into a corner of the stall and became the most timid of creatures.

"Where you come from!" she shouted at the dog, as if expecting the cur to reply. "Who brought you here!" Hildegarde was an ugly woman with Rabelaisian looks—a witch's nose with warts, and strands of gray hair hanging from her chin.

The commotion had roused a laggard out of one of the stalls, where he had been sleeping off a hangover. "What's going on?" he groaned as he rubbed his eyeballs.

"Is this your dog?" she demanded.

"It's Bruce's mutt," he replied drowsily.

When the dog saw the youth it resumed its ferocious barking, but was quickly muted by a trenchant look from Hildegarde.

"When Papa hear of this, he will throw the woof-woof out und Bruce with it." Then the scrub woman screwed up her eye and looked intensely at the boy. "Und who are you? I never see you before?"

"I work here," the lad meekly replied.

"Doing what?"

"I'm one of the groundskeepers."

"You don't work here! You're probably a friend of that lazy, good-for-nothing Eric. Ja?"

"Ja," imitating her accent.

"You better clear out of here, right now, or I call police!" the feisty woman threatened, while holding the broom like a battleaxe.

The youth tossed a few clothes in a knapsack and walked out of the bunkhouse with Hildegarde's eye trailing him as he left.

"I catch you here again, und I break this broom over your head," she hollered. "Ack! Milk all over the floor, und a broken bowl. So woof-woof, you smash your bowl of milk, eh?" she said sternly to the beast.

"I spilt the milk," I answered hesitantly.

"Ah-hah. You been feeding dog!"

"The cat."

"Cat…hmm. A dog, a cat, maybe I find a pig und goat here, too. Does Papa know that you feed cat with Papa's milk? I will tell Papa!"

I told Hildegarde how the milk was spilt, and how helpful Churchill had been in driving rodents from the bunkhouse.

"Well, I suppose a cat is no harm," she said, but added in a rising voice: "But Bruce's wolf-dog must go! Today!" And then she stomped away with heavy steps that caused the floorboards to creak.

Meanwhile, Churchill was nowhere to be seen. He always waited faithfully every afternoon in the stall for his bowl of milk, but had obviously fled when the dog was brought into the bunkhouse.

"Churchill! Churchill!" I called out. But the only answer I received was the barking refrain of the mongrel, who after Hildegarde's departure had resumed its viciousness. As I approached the stall where the creature was tied, it let out low growls and bared its canines; I hesitated, and then dashed past it. Outside, I searched for Churchill, walking around calling his name and meowing, but with no luck. I went to the trash bin outside the kitchen expecting to find him rummaging through the garbage. But he was not there. A short time later I spotted Papa and Hildegarde heading toward the bunkhouse at an urgent pace.

At suppertime Bruce was a raging bull, cursing Papa who had told him that he must get rid of the dog before nightfall, or else he would call the sheriff and have the beast put in a pound.

"It's Hildegarde's fault. I'd like to send that ugly hag into the bowels of hell," he growled. He clenched his knife and fork as if they were weapons, and talked with his mouth full of food, with morsels flying like sparks off his lips.

Bruce's grandmother had been caring for the mastiff, but she could no longer cope with the satanic animal. Bruce had been raised by his grandmother; he never knew his parents. Meanwhile, Eric in his devil-may-care attitude fueled Bruce's ire when he suggested that shooting the dog would solve the problem.

"I'll blast the mutt with a shotgun and your worries will be over," said Eric nonchalantly.

Bruce's face colored crimson with rage; his neck muscles bulged and his eyes looked ready to pop from their sockets. He hurled a butter knife at Eric that sailed across the room, missing Eric's head by an inch, which then ricocheted off the wall and onto a table where it shattered a water glass. Bruce rose from his table, overturning it in the process, and attempted to grab Eric who quickly ducked beneath another table, and by crawling beneath one table to the next managed to reach the door and fled.

Chris was a lover of animals and found a ripe opportunity to curry Bruce's favor by offering to keep the dog at his parent's house for the remainder of the summer. Chris's proposal to bring the distempered beast into his household was ludicrous. Along with his six brothers and sisters, Chris lived in his parent's summer cottage together with three dogs, two cats and a Noah's Ark of other animals. Chris had not even seen the mastiff, yet had no reservations about sheltering the dog until he came face-to-face with the monster. Back at the bunkhouse the dog charged at Chris, exposing its canines with gooey saliva dripping from its blood-red gums.

"She's a lamb when she gets to know you," snickered Bruce as he un-tethered the chain that bound the dog to the wood post. The wrangler gripped the chain at the dog's neck to prevent it from surging forward and biting, but the rebellious demon tried to break free from its master as it rose on its hind legs and flailed its paws, pulling its owner forward in momentum.

Bruce secured the dog in the rear bed of his small truck—a pathetic jalopy about twenty years old—and he and Chris drove off, with the cacophony of loud barking rolling across the meadow and resounding through the hills. Chris was a bumpkin who only respected people who bullied him. Bruce was not one to reciprocate a favor, so Chris gained no merit by being obsequious to that arrogant brute, other than to check himself from sliding further into Bruce's displeasure. Bruce respected only his horse and his dog, and any favor done him only reinforced his belief in the power of intimidation.

Bruce and Chris returned to the bunkhouse an hour later. From the pieces of conversation that I heard, Chris's parents were not home when they delivered the beast to the property. Bruce was concerned how Mr & Mrs Grant would react when they discovered the dog, which he shackled in their barn.

"Don't worry, my folks won't mind having your dog at all," assured Chris who was trailing Bruce like a shadow through the bunkhouse.

"They better not mind," Bruce shot back.

"They won't mind one bit, Not one—"

"Shut up Chris! Just make sure the dog gets fed."

That night I was awakened by a soft patter on the floor. I shone my flashlight in the direction of the sound, expecting to see a pack of field mice invading my stall. Instead, a pair of eyes low to the ground shone back at me. "Churchill," I cried. Immediately the cat sprang onto the mattress. "That terrible dog is gone, Churchill," I assured him as I stroked his coat of fur while he purred. Then he alighted to the ground, sniffed the corners of the stall, and lay himself at my feet like a faithful sentry.

IX

At the turn of the century and through the 1970s the Irish, Italians, and Jews were New York City's major ethnic groups, and in summer the Catskills became their vacationland. Just as each ethnicity had carved out its own neighborhoods in the city, each group staked claim to certain areas in the Catskills, with resorts catering almost exclusively to one of these nationalities. It is where immigrants and the children of immigrants could escape the New York polyglot, and socialize with people of their own stripe for a week or two.

The Timberhaus was Roman colony and its vacationing families hailed from Italian neighborhoods in Brooklyn, the Bronx, Staten Island, and south Queens. Many families returned here each summer at the same time, and developed close relationships. First generation Italian-Americans are a folk who revel in the companionship of their own clan, so much so that they are reluctant in having fraternity with other nationalities. I have heard a few theories which attempt to explain the reasons for the Italians' restricted society: One is that when emigrating to this country in heavy doses during this century few Italians knew English, and being unwilling to part with their mother tongue had limited intercourse with other ethnic groups. But Italians have been the victims of a cruel misconception, which is that any culture that is fiercely protective of its birthright would naturally disdain other cultures and be labeled xenophobic. However, Italy, at one time the seat of the Roman Empire, lay at the crossroads of eastern and western Europe and was the nexus of trade routes spanning from the Iberian peninsula to the far East and across North Africa. The influx of foreign cultures, whether from trade or hostile incursions, encroached upon Italy throughout her history, and though augmenting Italian culture to some extent also threatened to dilute the richness of her language and customs, for no culture can absorb new ideals without sacrificing part of its native ones. Whenever the ethos of a nation is threatened, its people cling tightly to their heritage as the Italians have, lest their culture be swept away in the tide of ethnic assimilation.

The camaraderie among the guests at The Timberhaus was strong, and the dinner table was the focal point of their fraternal atmosphere. Italians revere good food like a sacrament, and dinner echoes a celebration found at a wedding reception where the men eat themselves into ecstasy. After finishing dinner families lingered at their tables drinking strong coffee and smoking cigarettes; Italian was interspersed with English as the men talked baseball and the women compared recipes. When they adjourned from their tables the men ambled slowly from the dining room, their legs slightly bowed under the weight of fettuccine, chicken cacciatore, rolls, and spumoni. They patted their inflated stomachs with the pride of having eaten well, while the women fretted that they may not fit into their swimsuits. Families also used their summer vacation with an eye on the future; seeking to pair-off their teenage children with a suitable Tony or Donna in hopes that at some point the waters of the Tiber will flow pure into the veins of the next generation.

I am reminded of a girl born of Italian parentage who I met in high school. On our first date when I called on Celeste at her house, her mother answered the door and gave me a look with eyes that were two gun barrels leveled at me. For ten minutes I sat in the living room with Mrs Ricci while waiting for her daughter. She spoke not a word, but sat in an armchair crocheting a black shawl and watching me from the corner of her eye, as if I were a thief waiting for the chance to snatch a candlestick. A week later when I went to Celeste's home, Mrs Ricci came to the door again, but this time her bellicose expression had mellowed to a sour look. Again, not a word was exchanged between us. But the following week when I came for Celeste, her mother was quite civil to me and we had a cordial conversation. And as I was leaving the house with her daughter Mama

Ricci took me aside, warmly clasped my hands and said: "Celeste tells me good things about you, Byron. You're nice boy, not Italian, but still nice boy." Alas, just when I the barbarian was winning Mrs Ricci's confidence her daughter was moving in the opposite direction. A short time later she gave me the boot, dropping me for a guy who drove a fancy sports car.

Occasionally, I would walk beyond the stables and watch the horses canter across the meadow. A playful colt would gambol in circles around its mare, as stallions sauntered and chewed dry grass. A powerful and honest creature, the horse has been man's loyal partner in the shaping of civilization. Before railroads and automobiles this trustworthy equine transported the masses on its back, aiding man's dispersal to new frontiers. Ever since Alexander the Great rode his beloved Bucephalus, the horse has carried cavalries into battle and has been as heroic as any field commander who received laurels and accolades, while the beast who earned the victory got oats. And because of his cooperative nature the horse has been falsely branded a dumb creature, because he bears a noble trait that humans disdain—unselfishness.

I recall the tale of *Gulliver's Travels* which I read as a youth. In his final journey Lemuel Gulliver visits the Land of the Houyhnhnms, where horses rule and humans or "yahoos" have reduced themselves to beasts. Gulliver learns the language of the Houyhnhnms and is impressed with the civility of their society which has no lawyers, politicians, murderers, or back-biters. Conversely, the Houyhnhnms are horrified when Gulliver relates to them the horrors of human society filled with its wars, greed, poverty, and corrupt judges. Ah, judges—the geniuses who have turned the legal system into a labyrinth of nonsense! Imagine this nation without a convoluted legal system. Imagine a judiciary where judges did not turn into demigods once they entered the courtroom, and judgments handed down by a court would immediately take effect and not travel through a chain of appeals before it was either overturned or stripped of its substance. Such has the American legal system strangled itself with conflict and indecision, that it would be better exemplified if Lady Justice removed her blindfold and fashioned it into a noose. Consider that if the Hebrews had American jurisprudence the Ten Commandments would still be under judicial review. Gone are the scepter and crown after America won its independence from England, only to be eventually replaced by black-robed despots who manipulate the scales of justice. Nature loves democracy, but autocrats manage to emerge like weeds among the best-tended garden.

How odd that courthouses, with wise epigrams inscribed on its walls and busts of legal scholars filling the niches of its hallways, should turn out decisions with as much wisdom as if they came out of a kindergarten class. And what other discipline produces volumes of statutes written with the foreknowledge that much of it will be ignored, unenforceable, and eventually overruled. When Gulliver voyaged to the island of Laputa, he observed a physician pumping wind into the carcass of a dead dog by shoving the nozzle of a bellows into its derriere in order to bring it back to life—the same procedure he used to kill it. And so judges act as wayward physicians when the absurdity of their court decisions wind up destroying justice by their attempt to invigorate it. And so on this balmy afternoon as I was sitting atop the corral fence, I thought it interesting how idling on a simple topic like horses should spark a profound reflection on jurisprudence. Ironically, when the brain is relaxed it is then that spontaneous ideas come to light. Consider that Newton was resting under a tree when a fallen apple triggered his Law of Gravity, and Archimedes founded a geometrical principle while he was daydreaming.

I was coaxing the stallions with a handful of crisp, flaxen straw, who cautiously approached and chewed on the straw while I patted and stroked their strong, muscular necks. I envied the horses who, gifted with simple-mindedness and a tranquil nature, live in peace unencumbered by philosophy or laws. Then came a voice from behind.

"Hey, I'd like to try dat."

It was one of the guests; a husky, middle-aged man of medium height. I handed him a bouquet of straw, but when he extended it to the mare she turned on her hindquarters and galloped away.

"You stupid…" he shouted at the frightened animal, finishing his sentence with an epithet. "Hawses are dumb asses," he added disgustedly as he tossed the bundle of straw to the ground.

"You must gain their trust," I said.

"Ah, it's a beautiful day, ain't it?" he said, suddenly changing his tune as he inflated his chest by deeply inhaling the rural air through his swelling nostrils. "It feels great to be in the country."

"Where are you from?" I asked.

"Maspeth, in Queens," he said as he picked up a blade of straw from the ground, which he wiped by sliding through his fingertips before placing it in his mouth. "I bring the wife and kids here every August for a week."

"I'm from Flushing."

"My sister lives in Whitestone," he replied with the straw clinging to his lip.

Whitestone is a middle-class Italian enclave that lies next to Flushing and stretches north to the Long Island Sound. The houses are immaculate, reflecting Italian devotion to the home. The front lawns are manicured, many of them set with garden statues of Francis of Assisi, St Joseph, or the Blessed Mother. And at Christmastime, homes are elevated to fine artistry with lights and decorations.

"You work here?" he asked.

"Yes. I'm in the kitchen."

"You in high school?"

"University. I'll be a senior this fall."

"University! My God Almighty! You look like you still in high school!"

"I'm aging gracefully."

He belted out a hearty laugh, which caused several of the horses to whiney. "See dat. Even da hawses is laughing!" He drew the straw from his mouth, flicked it in the air, and hoisted himself onto the railing of the fence. Then he asked: "So what you gonna do when you graduate?"

"I'm considering a number of paths, maybe the advertising profession."

"So you wanna be a big shot ad man, huh?"

"And retire a millionaire by age thirty," I added.

"I'm makin' sure my kids go to college. I want my girls to be teachers or nurses." Then he added with a sigh, "I never went to college."

"Really? I would have taken you for a lawyer or banker."

His face beamed with pride, not picking up my veiled sarcasm. "Actually, I drive a truck for the New York City Department of Sanitation." He was a garbage man.

"What part of the city do you work?"

"In the Bedford-Sty section of Brooklyn."

"Dangerous area. How long have you been driving the picnic wagon?"

"Twenty-two years. It was my first job after I got outta the army. I enjoy outdoor work; I get lotsa exercise. And I got lotsa relatives in the department."

The city's sanitation department is almost the exclusive domain of Italians. New York's bureaucracy is such that different ethnic groups have hegemony over certain municipal jobs. For example, the Jews have public education sown up, and the Irish have the police department under lock and key.

"What's your name?" I asked.

"Rocco."

"I'm Byron." We shook hands.

Rocco looked at me askance, and in a curious voice asked, "Are you Irish?"

"Welsh."

"Welsh? I never met anyone who was Welsh. Wales is part of England, ain't it?"

"Part of Great Britain, but a separate country."

"Strange name for a country. Are there a lotta whales off its coast, is that how it got its name?"

"I'm not sure how its name was derived. Anyway, the country and 'fish' are spelled differently."

"I don't know much about the Welsh. What are they known for?" he asked.

"Dylan Thomas and coalminers. Anywhere you scratch the

ground in Wales you'll find coal. Many Welsh settled in the coal mining regions of Pennsylvania and West Virginia."

"So New York City don't have many Welsh because it ain't got coal mines, right?"

"I suppose. Why did you ask if I were Irish?"

Rocco looked around to see if anyone was within earshot of his voice. Then as if the horses might overhear him, he cupped the side of his mouth with his hand and said in a low but firm voice, "I don't like the Irish."

"Really?"

"For ten years I worked with an Irishman named Callahan. How he ever snuck into the department was a mystery. He retired several years ago, thank God. Callahan drove me crazy. Let me explain. Three men work to a truck—one driver and two collectors, with each man rotating as driver on certain days. On the days that Callahan drove, he would purposely move the truck forward just as I was emptying garbage into the rear bin, and trash would spill onto the street. Now the driver ain't supposed to budge the truck until the collector signals with a whistle. 'You dumb son of a—' I would yell at him, but he would just shrug his shoulders and smirk. And what a braggadocio! He never shut up about his two boys who were studying at Fordham University. And he always talked about the *Kennedys* as if they were American royalty.

"On St Patrick's Day one year Callahan comes to work wearing a green derby, and he starts in about how grand it is to be Irish. 'Enough of your nonsense,' I tell him as I slap the silly derby off his head. 'Now listen to me: You Irish ain't got nothing to be proud of,' I tell him. 'Show me your Michelangelos and da Vincis; name me your operas. Can the Irish produce a voice like the great Caruso? Can your women match the beauty of our signorinas with eyes like jewels and ample breasts? Did a Mickey discover America? Was a Padddy ever a Pope? And who invented the radio? Marconi!'"

"Marconi?" I repeated.

"Yeah, the great inventor."

"I had heard he was half-Irish."

"What! Marconi, part Irish!" he thundered. "He was as Italian as Caesar!"

"I had read that he was born of an Irish mother."

Rocco looked at me in disbelief, as if I had accused him of being part Irish. "Where did you read that nonsense?" he sneered.

"In high school, in an encyclopedia. I had to write a paper on 19th century inventors, and I read that Marconi's mother was of an aristocratic Irish family from Wexford, Ireland. That fact always stuck with me because who would ever think that a chap with the name Guglielmo Marconi could be Irish!"

"High school, eh? Well you read it wrong." Looking at me firmly he said, "Listen to me. The name of the man who invented the radio was Marconi. Not O'Marconi, not McMarconi, but Marconi!"

"But I read that…"

Rocco took a gulp to regain his composure, and then shot back with both hands raised like exclamation marks: "Next you'll tell me Columbus was born in Dublin!"

I broke out laughing because this proud Italian was becoming excited over a trivial fact, and fortunately Rocco quickly discovered humor in the situation, too.

"You Welshmen are practical jokers is what I think," he said good-naturedly.

So we changed the subject and talked about baseball for the next fifteen minutes. Rocco spoke no more of the Italians and Irish, fearing perhaps that he might learn from me that another of his famous Romans might be tainted with Gaelic blood.

X

If you would be wealthy, think of saving as well as getting.

— Benjamin Franklin

Saving money was riveted into my brain at a very young age by my mother, who considered it among the highest virtues. Each week she would take me to the bank and deposit a portion of my father's paycheck, explaining to me that money must always be set aside for an emergency. And if everyone followed the example of squirrels who collect and store acorns so that they will have food during the winter, society would never be in want. So, after accumulating two weeks of wages at The Timberhaus, I felt it my duty to squirrel away part of my earnings by opening a savings account in the local bank.

Durham Savings Bank was housed in a quaint Colonial building with gabled roof and dormers, reflecting the traditional and commonsense nature of its Yankee townsfolk. Founded in 1897, the town's only bank that was started by the late Thomas Ellsworth was a trusted depository for East Durham residents for three-quarters of a century. Even during the Great Depression, when most of the nation's banks failed and people lost their life savings, Durham upstaged the economic crises and kept its doors open, never missing a dividend payment to its customers.

Inside, its cedar wood floors were polished to a luster; its walls decorated with historical prints; and, hung above the fireplace mantle was a framed oil painting of the bank's founder whose dark eyes appeared to follow everyone in the bank. On the far wall facing the entrance were three mahogany teller booths etched with decorative moldings, and situated across from the teller booths were a pair of desks where two lady clerks sat chatting with customers, for the bank was as much a clearinghouse for town gossip as it was for transacting business. Adjacent to where the clerks worked was a separate enclosure partitioned by a three-foot high walnut hand rail. This was the executive quarter of Thomas Ellsworth III, manager of the bank and grandson of its founder, who not only bore his grandfather's name but his likeness as well, with matching coiffure and mustache, and attired in a waistcoat and bowtie.

When I entered the bank Mr Ellsworth was pouring over papers at his cherry wood desk, fashionably designed in rococo with scrolled paneling. As I walked toward the teller booths he scurried from his desk, passed through the partition's low swing-gate which flapped back and forth in the wake of his urgent exit, and intercepted me with a cheerful greeting: "Thomas Ellsworth! How are you sir?"

"Fine, thank you."

"Here to open an account?"

"Yes."

"Let me assist you. Come with me, please." I followed him to his desk.

"Have a seat," he said, moving an armchair closer to his desk. "And you are...?"

"Byron Rutledge." We shook hands.

"Is it a savings account you wish to open?" he asked as he sank into his Spanish leather chair.

"Yes."

He cleared a stack of papers from his desk, and drew an application from a drawer.

"Spell your last name, Byron." And when I did he asked, "Are you working in the area for the summer?"

"At The Timberhaus."

"Is that the address you want on your account?"

"Yes." And just as I started to give him the address he broke in, "Know the address well. I've known the Rudiger family for years. What do you do there?"

"Wash dishes and mop floors." I was about to add that I hated the place but he was, after all, a friend of Papa.

"You were about to say something?" he asked, anticipating my unspoken thought.

"No sir."

"And your date of birth?" he asked, when he came to that line in the application.

"Twenty."

"Attending college, Byron?"

I told him I was entering my final year at Pacton University.

"What are you majoring in?"

"Humanities."

"Planning to teach?"

"No, I'll probably go where the money is—the business world."

"When I graduated Yale I worked for an investment firm on Wall Street for five years and did quite well. But money wasn't giving me satisfaction. So, I decided to return to the family business and have never regretted doing so. Most of my classmates have grown quite rich, and they still think me crazy for having returned to work in this small bank. But the bank gives me a gratification that could never be matched working in one of those haughty, big-city banks. Durham Savings will never be a large bank, but it will be around for as long as the town, itself.

"A couple of months ago a fellow came visiting from a big New York bank—darn, I can't remember his name—and offered to purchase my shop at twice its asset value. Twice value! Can you imagine that! I gave him a firm *no*, and told him that selling this bank would be auctioning my birthright, and that I was no Esau. My axiom is that banking's primary purpose is to serve people properly and fairly, and profits will follow. But nowadays banks have reversed that order. Their goal is to make money, money, and more money, and serving the customer has become a distant second. And how are they earning money? By buying out other banks, and closing branches and throwing employees out of work. It's called 'streamlining' and supposedly has the noble purpose of enhancing profits. But the real motive is greed. However, greed has its comeuppance, and the banks which are gobbling up other banks will one day be devoured by a bigger fish. I call it 'food chain' economics. Now where was I? Ah yes, how much will you deposit today?"

"Forty dollars." I drew several bills from my wallet and counted the money in front of him.

"I'll be right back with your receipt." Ellsworth scooped the cash into his hand, went into the teller cage, and returned with my receipt.

"Sally is drawing up your savings book and will be finished shortly. Enjoy a lollipop while you wait." He took a raspberry sucker out of a glass jar lying next to his penholder and handed it to me.

"Thank you." The lollipop tasted like bad Halloween candy. I quickly took it out and rubbed my tongue against the roof of my mouth to kill the bitter taste.

"The university you're attending is...?"

"Pacton."

"Yes, of course. Second time I asked. Think your academic curricula and years of study will provide you the foundation for success?"

"I'm confident they'll unlock a few doors."

Then he leaned forward in his chair and scrutinized me like one examining a rare antique. "I think you'll fail," he said calmly.

Was he joking? Did he think his Yale pedigree gave him license to insult me? "Why do you think I'll be unsuccessful?" I responded testily.

"You won't be," he replied matter-of-factly.

"You just said..." But he raised his hand to prevent further remonstrance.

He leaned back in his chair, folded his hands behind his head, and smiled as if to ridicule my indignation. "Anyone who reaches the pinnacle of his success will have failed many times. It's inevitable. Failure tests one's character. It's an elimination process. After graduation many young men flop in their first job. Some are overwhelmed by their initial disappointment and never rise to the level they were capable of achieving. Others see it as a test of their mettle; they learn to navigate rough seas and tack course to keep their goals afloat. University professors teach students about success, but seldom how to plan for failure. They fear that if they give their students the impression that they could fail, it would detract from their own qualifications as educators."

"Is he an ancestor?" I asked changing the subject. I was referring to a daguerreotype set in a silver frame on his desk. It was the likeness of a fortyish man dressed in a tweed suit with a walrus mustache.

"William Dean Howells."

"The writer?"

"Correct. Wrote *The Rise of Silas Lapham*. My grandfather knew him."

"I started reading it in high school, but never finished it."

"It's the most successful book on failure ever written. Silas is a New England businessman who put ethics before profit and lost everything as a consequence."

"Unfortunately, decent people make lousy businessmen," I replied as I gazed at my fingernails.

"Read the book again, and finish it. Without spoiling the story for you, Silas Lapham is the co-owner of a New England paint company which he worked all his life to build, and it is about to go belly-up and his personal fortune along with it. But he has one last chance to rescue himself from financial disaster, when three English businessmen offer to buy one of his factories. But there is a glitch; the railroad connecting the factory to its distribution points is planning to rip-up its tracks in another year rendering the factory worthless. But the Englishmen haven't a clue about all of this."

"Yes, I recall bits of the story now. Doesn't Silas decide not to sell his factory to the Englishmen?"

"Exactly. He refuses to sell the factory to the unsuspecting investors, who despite their wealth could absorb the loss, and ignores pleas to do otherwise from his desperate partner who also faces ruin. And to spare Silas's conscience of wrongdoing, the partner offers to buy him out, and in turn sell the factory to the Brits himself. But Silas remains firm and refuses to do what most people in his predicament would. As a result he goes bankrupt; he is forced to sell his home in a prestigious Boston neighborhood, and winds up on his boyhood farm in Vermont milking cows. And that's the crux of the story; through his downfall in business, Silas Lapham rose as a man."

Just then Sally returned with my savings book and handed it to Ellsworth. I used this distraction to flick the lollipop into a trash can a few feet away.

"Your account is officially open, Byron," the banker proudly announced. He leaned across his desk, and using the tip of his pen pointed to my name and account number typed in boldface on the inside cover of my savings book, and then pointed to a column on the facing page where the amount of my deposit was entered.

"Everything looks in order," I remarked.

"Good. If you ever have questions about your account, please call or drop in." He handed me my savings book, and then gave me a surprised look. "My goodness! Have you finished your lollipop already? Here, have another." And he reached into the jar and drew out a purple one.

"Thank you," I said forcing a weak smile.

"You gobbled the first one so quickly; you must love the stuff. Have a few more to take with you," he said reaching into the glass jar again.

"No, no. Candy can be addictive and Lord knows I can't afford another vice."

"Indeed, indeed. And we don't want our teeth falling out of our mouths." Then he chomped his teeth for comic effect.

I rose from the chair, shook hands with the banker, and left. As I pedaled back to the resort I reflected on Ellsworth's philosophy, and thought him a refreshing counterweight to the growing avarice in the business world. My forty dollars was as much valued by him as a four thousand dollar account. In a nutshell, he was a decent man.

When I reached The Timberhaus I stopped at the office to check for mail, and found a letter from my brother:

Dear Byron,

If you find yourself reading this letter at a quick pace, it's because I have written it with a swift pen, as I believe the faster words are written the more quickly they will be read.

You've been away only a couple of weeks, but I miss you. How much, you ask? More than you miss me which is probably saying little. The house is bare without you. As I ramble from room to room during the course of the day, your absence is striking. When I am in the kitchen you are not there sipping on your fourth cup of coffee, while strumming the table top with your fingers to the beat of "what will I do today?" In the evening when I am in the living room, I can now enjoy watching television from the couch where you used to spread long and stiff like an ironing board, from the time the family finished dinner until the cuckoo clock on the wall chirped midnight. And when I pass your room and see your vacant bed, I think how odd not to see you there continuing your nocturnal slumber well into midday.

Honestly, I miss you brother, and your absence was keenly felt when the evenings were no longer filled with the music that you loved to listen to. So, to fill that void I have started playing your music records everyday. Yes, the same records which you swore if I ever touched, you would sever every finger from my hands! Ah, but when I listen to those forbidden melodies, it seems as though you never left home.

The other day Mom remarked how fast I was growing, and how well your shirts look on me. And I nearly have the same shoe size as yourself, give or take a couple of inches. Last week I took the liberty of wearing your leather suede shoes to church, as my Sunday shoes were still in the cobbler shop. How well your shoes absorbed the water from the pouring rain that day! And last Tuesday I had a baseball game to play, but I couldn't find my fielder's glove so I used yours. A friend remarked how nice the mitt was, and asked if he could borrow it for a week to take with him on family vacation to the country. So, I loaned it to him.

By the way, a lady telephoned a few days ago and asked for you. I told her you were not in, and when I prompted her for her name she only replied that she was a classmate of yours. When she asked when you would return, I was about to tell her where you had gone for the summer, but I thought why should I give any information to a stranger who refused to say who she was or why she was calling. But she persisted in her inquiry, so I told her you were on an expedition in South America to study endangered species and would not return until fall. Wouldn't you agree that sounded much better than scrubbing dishes in the Catskills? Whoever she was sounded very disappointed when she learned you were away. She sighed, mumbled "good-bye," and then hung-up. Who could

> *that mystery woman be? A secret love? A bashful admirer who has a crush on you? You may be more popular than you think, Byron. Adieu, mon frère.*

Who was it that called? And why didn't she leave her name? I thought of several girls from the University who were good friends, among them one lady whom I was quite fond of, and wondered if it might be she. What a lift to my self-esteem if it was she who had called! Hapless me, I would never know. For who would ever admit to being an anonymous caller? Most likely it was a girl I had known from high school who decided to give me a "curiosity call." Then again, my imaginative brother could have concocted the story. As for the other information in the letter, if it be true, I promise to deliver a few hard smacks to him when I get home.

XI

Some scenes are better expressed on canvas than in words to capture the beauty of nature as it appeared on this beautiful mid-summer morning, but lacking a painter's talent my words must be my palette. Tiered, stratus clouds rose like an ivory stairway into a vaulted sky of powder blue. Below, gentle hills of Lincoln green rippled the countryside, and in a mild breeze Creation whispered: "The world is just right."

I went to the pond and sat on the wood dock, rolled up my trousers, and immersed my legs up to my knees. I opened the morning newspaper, which sadly reminded me that the world is not right after all. Newspapers are the daily ledger of human activity: There are births and deaths, destruction and renewal, poverty and wealth, absurdity and sanity. Not a day nor an hour passes without these episodes occurring. It's as if these events are destined, a "fait accompli," with only new names and faces inserted into the same old picture. The headline on the front page read: "Family Killed in Car Accident"

> A family of three including an eight-month-old infant was killed Thursday night when their car was struck head-on by a drunk driver. The collision occurred around eleven p.m. on Route 112, three miles east of Evergreen. The driver, John Samson, 27, and his son William were pronounced dead at the scene. Samson's wife Edie, 26, died a couple of hours later in surgery at an area hospital.
>
> The driver of the other vehicle, thirty-one-year-old Ernest

> Duran, suffered only minor rib injuries. Duran was intoxicated at the time of the accident, and will be charged with dual misdemeanors of driving without a license and drunk driving, penalties which only carry a six-month jail sentence. Drunk driving, even if resulting in death, is not a felony in New York State as long as the driver does not flee the scene of the accident.

How disgusting, I thought. Only when a politician has his family wiped out by a drunk driver will laws change to put road murderers in prison.

Page 3 carried a photo of a burning US army truck, and in the foreground was a Vietnamese farmer carrying a pair of water buckets suspended from a shoulder yoke, completely oblivious to the destruction around him.

The news was becoming more depressing. On the next page was a large photograph depicting a crowd of mourners standing beneath umbrellas in a Catholic cemetery in Belfast, gathered around a casket draped in a green, white, and gold flag. A story followed:

> Amidst rainy skies family members and hundreds of mourners laid to rest twenty-year-old John Kirkpatrick Wednesday morning, who succumbed to wounds several months after the Bogside Massacre in Derry, northern Ireland. He was the last to die among the thirteen other unarmed, political demonstrators who were killed by British soldiers on Jan 30th of this year. In all, twenty-six protestors were shot on that infamous day, now referred to as Bloody Sunday. This worst attack against civilians since the 1918 Uprising has provoked riots throughout Catholic neighborhoods in Belfast, as well as widespread protest throughout Ireland and in the United States, where Irish-Americans are demanding that the President institute strong sanctions against England. The killings climaxed weeks of tension brewing between Irish Catholics and Protestants, whose rivalries date to the 17th century during Oliver Cromwell's reign of terror against Catholics.

But as I thumbed through the pages the news became more amusing as with this eye-bulging headline: "High School Teacher Claims He Slept With Female Students To Improve His Sleep"

> Benjamin Dart, mathematics instructor at Lexington High School in Denver, Colorado was arrested last Friday for sexual misconduct with a dozen female students. At his arraignment Mr Dart vigorously defended his action, insisting he had slept with the girls so he could sleep better. The teacher claimed he was repeatedly awakened by knocks on his door in the middle of the night by female students claiming they needed help in geometry. The visits occurred well after midnight on Fridays and Saturdays, each time by a different student, and continued for several weeks causing him sleep deprivation and stress. Realizing his efforts to deter the girls were useless, Dart contended his only option was to invite the girls into his house and offer them tutoring, only to discover they made a beeline to his bedroom. "I gave each girl a half-hour's gratification, provided she would leave when it was over and allow me to resume my sleep."
>
> The students, all of whom were doing poorly in geometry, had a different story, claiming Dart warned them that they were in danger of failing if they did not come to him for nighttime "lessons." Upon hearing how their children were victimized, the parents were furious as they were under the impression that their daughters had been invited to stay overnight at a girlfriend's house.
>
> Dart stands to catch up on his sleep for many years in a prison bed. Prosecuting attorney Paul Wist said Dart faces fifteen years in prison if convicted.

And sharing the same page was this story from California: "Berkeley School District Bans Cinderella from Classrooms"

> Following a unanimous vote by its seven members, the Berkeley City School Board has barred the reading of "Cinderella" from its classrooms. Citing that Cinderella

> does not promote a positive image for women, school board chairlady Verna Watts claims the scrub woman prostituted herself to win a wealthy man. "She's nothing more than a slut who seduced Prince Charming. Leaving behind her slipper as she fled the ballroom is a metaphor for losing her virginity to the rakish prince," contends Watts. Board members claim the fairytale gives young girls the impression that intellect and talent are subordinate to using their bodies to achieve success.
>
> But the Fairytale Inquisition does not end with "Cinderella." The school board is also targeting Mother Goose nursery rhymes, particularly "The Old Lady Who Lived in a Shoe," which depicts a woman who could not keep count of all her children. "This is a classic example that women are meant to say at home and raise babies. All fairytales convey a subliminal message that females are inferior, which perpetuates a condescending portrait of all women," added another board member.
>
> How this attack on traditional folklore will play out with parents of schoolchildren will determine if the board's decision will have a fairytale ending.

Can it get any more ridiculous? Then my eyes gravitated to a headline on the opposite page. More news from California: "Unidentified Man Leaps to Death from Golden Gate Bridge" Hmm...he was probably upset over Cinderella.

The sports page bore happier tidings picturing a dozen smiling Little Leaguers posing with their baseball coach. The caption read: "East Durham Bobcats Win 9 in a Row"

On the same page was pictured a beaming fifteen-year-old accepting a first-place medal around her neck for winning the Catskill Girls Swim Competition. And at the bottom of the page was a photo of the East Durham Bowling Team—five cheerful, grossly fat men in their fifties posing in front of a bowling lane.

I turned the pages, browsing the headlines until I came to the obituaries, where I paused to read a post-mortem:

> A funeral was held August 16th at Mountain Congregational Church for Thomas Dunne, dairy farmer, who died August 14th at his home from natural causes. He was 79. A native of Schoharie County, Mr Dunne served as a sergeant in the US Army during World War I, where he was wounded in Belgium…married Betty Hart, an army nurse in 1920…active in local charities…hosted the Halloween Pumpkin Festival each year on his farm…

I scanned other obituaries, and then reflected on these brief stories of the deceased. Obituaries, I decided, are not about the dead; they are intended for the living. All that surrounds us—literature, architecture, science, government—is an obituary, a reminder of the achievements of those who have preceded us. Time will efface the inscriptions on gravestones, but those who have enriched society, from the humble housewife and mother to the great inventor, will leave an indelible footprint of their contributions from which generations will benefit.

Finished with the newspaper, I left the pond and went to the office where I borrowed a bicycle and headed into town. There, I stopped at a diner and ordered a sandwich of melted cheese and tomato with crispy bacon on two thick slices of pumpernickel, and with it a pickle the size of squash. Afterwards, I pedaled some distance through a back-road where, stopping at an apple orchard, I plucked a pippin from a branch and devoured it to its core. Onward I cycled until I came to a pasture where billy goats were eating grass, leaving bald patches on the landscape. I stopped and watched them through a wood fence, when one of the bearded goats sprinted towards me and butted its head against the wood slats in front of where I stood, indicating his displeasure at my visit. This encouraged me all the more to spite him. I took a fallen branch off the ground and dangled it over the fence while mimicking the neigh of a goat, whereupon the grumpy goat charged the fence again with a full head butt. I repeated this tease a few times, each time the goat striking the wood fence, and then left satisfied I had given the nasty creature a royal migraine.

Ten minutes later as I was speeding along the road I spotted a cottage where on the front yard sketches and oil paintings were displayed for sale, guarded by a hound who was fast asleep. I hit the brakes hard, causing the rear wheel to fish-tail and was nearly thrown off the bike. The artist was a gracious woman in her forties, with a full head of gray hair tied in a bun who invited me to browse. The paintings were of florals and landscapes, all of them quite good. I complimented the artist, Emily, on her work, and asked her what makes a good artist.

"Patience, patience. Isn't that right, Snowball," she said to the sleeping dog as she nudged him with her toe.

"And what makes a painter a genius?" I asked.

"Michelangelo said 'genius is eternal patience.'"

Patience! Was it not the Creator's patience over billions of years, not seven days, that begat the world with its wondrous formations: Where cracks on the crust became beautiful canyons; where antediluvian floods slowly retreated to become lakes and inland seas; where a single amoeba became the parent of the human race! Too often, an impatient person feels that if he doesn't grasp a discipline—art, mathematics, whatever—then he lacks aptitude for it and abandons pursuit. A fool retires early, but a genius keeps the lamp oil burning.

The day that started with a cool morning was now turning hot, so I decided not to venture any further. I thanked Emily for allowing me to visit, got on my bicycle, and headed back. Whereas the road had a slight descent leaving town allowing the bicycle to coast, I now had to pedal against an incline. My body sweated in the humidity as I cycled, and there was not a breath of breeze to offer relief. Half-an-hour later, just before reaching East Durham I stopped at a roadside pub. The tavern was empty save for the bartender and one ragged soul who was sitting at a table sipping from a beer mug. The tramp's clothes were tattered and filthy, his long hair caked with dirt, and what little face could be seen beneath his wooly, dirty beard was charcoaled by the sun. The bartender was sitting on a bar stool with his back turned, but looking at me from the wall mirror behind the bar as I entered.

"What can I get you?" he asked addressing the mirror.

"A seltzer water, please."

Without getting up he leaned over the counter for a glass, scooped in ice, and then poured the tonic from a soda gun. "Fifteen cents," he said handing me the glass. Then he looked at the wall clock. "Three thirty; an hour and a half left," he sighed, sounding like five o'clock was light-years away.

"Watching the clock makes the minutes drag," I replied, as I pulled a quarter from my pocket and placed it on the counter.

I sat myself at a table in the center of the tavern floor. The ceiling fan gyrated slowly, as if it too were wearied by the midday heat. The tramp was rambling to himself, and as he drank from the mug beer dripped from his lip and down his beard in a foamy trickle. With eyebrows knitted and eyes squinted he spoke to the invisible companion sitting at his table. At times he conversed in a whisper, muttering cryptic phrases like a deranged oracle. Then, shaking his head to rouse himself, his voice spiraled upward to a schizophrenic crescendo: "Copernicus is now in a Miami prison, which is not to say the dinosaur was promiscuous…I too, can recite the Greek alphabet, but does that make me a Chinaman?…I will pay for the beer…But the greater issue at hand rests with…I said I will pay for the beer… The greater issue is twofold…Last time you put hemlock in my beer, for it was you who poisoned Socrates…"

The crazed man was pathetically amusing, and I wondered if he should be envied or pitied. He was creator of his own world, from which he could conjure friends, rule as king, and proclaim himself the wisest on earth; yet he was also a prisoner of private demons that locked him in paranoia and fear.

"He's been coming here for years. He crisscrosses the region on foot, and drops in when he passes through town. He looks no older or ragged when I first saw him ten years ago," the bartender told me when I went to get another glass of seltzer.

"I wonder if he ever had a good job, or came from a prominent family," I said.

"Once I tried to get information from him on his past, but he only talks to his spirits."

Minutes later I experienced an unusual sight, when a slightly-built Hindu wearing a black suit that was shiny from wear entered the pub. It was surreal; he dropped in from nowhere, and seeing him here was as rare as finding a Yankee in a Vishnu temple. He paused at the entrance, set down his battered valise, and dabbed the beads of sweat on his brow with a handkerchief. He blinked his eyes a few times as he adjusted his vision to the dark tavern, and then made his way inside where he sat at a table next to mine.

"A very jolly afternoon to you, sir," he said with a broad smile, that revealed rows of pearly teeth set off by his bituminous complexion.

I mumbled "hello" and avoided looking at him. He was obviously wanting to sell something and I wished he would vanish.

"For me it has been a most exhausting day, belabored by long hours of driving. Fortunately, I spotted this inn and shall recompense myself with a bit of rest and beverage, and take shelter from the heat of the oppressing sun." Then he set his valise atop the table and said, "Excuse me, I must needs refresh myself." He went to the bathroom, from where he emerged a minute later and then went to the bar. The bartender was absorbed in his crossword puzzle, and never noticed the Hindu was in the tavern. When he looked up and saw the dark figure, he started in surprise as if the stranger had just materialized from a genie's bottle. The Hindu returned to his table with a lemon tonic, opened his valise, and began rearranging its contents.

"Forgive my familiarity, my name is Alpesh. And may I know yours?"

"Byron," hesitating my reply.

"Byron? Ah, my best friend shares the same name." Then he turned his open briefcase to face me. Inside were combs, brushes, and lotions.

"May I interest you in articles of personal groom and hygiene?" he asked.

"No thank you."

But the Oriental was undeterred. "Byron, this fragrance is most appealing to women," he said, displaying a bottle of musk. He uncapped the bottle, sniffed it, and rolled his eyes. "It's aroma is most bewitching. This was an especial favorite of my wife, who blessed me with sons and daughters in abundance. For seven years I was married to a most virtuous woman, who of late has departed this life, but not before generating as many children as were the years of our marriage."

"I'm not interested in what you're selling," I answered smugly.

"Oh, not selling Byron, but as a gift to you," he said placing the small bottle beside my glass.

"Keep your gift," I replied tersely pushing the bottle away.

He smiled obsequiously, took a gulp of tonic water, and then withdrew a deck of playing cards from inside his jacket.

"Do you play poker, Byron?"

I nodded.

"Then you will want this fascinating deck of playing cards." He spread the cards in a semicircle across my table with the suits facing up, then flipped one of the end cards over which triggered the other cards to turn over in chain reaction, revealing nude women on the reverse sides. "Your poker games will never be dull. And watch this!" He scooped the cards into a stack, and then fanned the cards setting in motion a sequence of images showing women performing lewd acts. "This entertaining card deck is free with the purchase of this hair brush."

"How much is the brush?" It was a fine-looking brush with a carved wood handle.

"Merely twenty dollars," he answered.

"Too expensive," I replied.

"Then twenty dollars less five. Yes?"

"No."

"Then half-twenty; I cannot descend the price further, even for you, a friend."

I shook my head.

"Nevertheless, for the token sum of fifty cents, you may have the playing cards."

Just then the crazy hobo who had been mute for some time erupted into another psychotic monologue. "You despicable harlot! You're a temple prostitute whom I rescued from Babylon! I pulled you from the gutter and made you an heiress. But to the streets you shall return, where dogs will lick your sores and scraps shall be you sustenance."

"Ask that chap if he will buy your brush. He can certainly use one," I said.

"Would that he should be groomed with a horse brush, but such item I do not sell," he replied hastily.

The Hindu placed the deck of cards and brush into his valise, and was about to pull out another item when the bartender approached him from behind and tapped his shoulder. "Excuse me bud, soliciting is not allowed here," he said firmly.

"I am most sorry, sir. I will depart forthwith." He shut his briefcase, and with hasty gulps drained the tonic from his glass. Rising from his chair, the Hindu tipped his head in deference and said meekly, "Good afternoon, sirs." With swift but light steps, he walked to the front door and was gone.

"Ever see him before?" I asked the bartender as he was wiping the table tops.

"Nope. But if he comes here again to peddle his wares, he'll make his exit through the roof."

I felt a tinge of pity for the Hindu who, though a nuisance, was trying to earn a living. The bartender returned to his crossword puzzle, and the crazy man continued ranting to himself in a desperate voice that rose and fell in eerie cadence.

A few minutes later I left the tavern. As I mounted my bicycle I discovered the front tire was flat, punctured by a small nail. So, I wheeled my wounded bicycle to a gas station down the block to have the flat repaired. As the service attendant was about to seal the puncture, a car drove up to the fuel pump and the attendant left to greet the customer. It was the Hindu.

"Five dollars of gas, plees," he told the serviceman as he got out of the car. Then he headed to the restroom. "Oh, we meet again," he said cheerfully as he passed me.

When he returned to the pump he reached into his rear pocket. "I must have left my wallet in the car," I heard him say to the attendant. He looked on the seat, and searched the floor of the vehicle; then he opened the rear door and inspected the back seat and floor. The Indian had a desperate look. "Sir, my wallet is lost! And with it fifty dollars that I had earned today."

"The gas will still cost you five dollars," the attendant answered impatiently.

"Good sir, I have no money."

"You better find your wallet fast, or I'll call the police."

"The police! Surely you will not further the woes of an honest salesman whose entire day's earnings have been erased by misfortune!"

The attendant responded with a hard look.

Then the Hindu fumbled through his pockets and pulled out a couple of bills. "Alas! I have found some money," he said with elation. "Here is three dollars," he said as he offered it to the attendant.

The man folded his arms across his chest. "The gas is five dollars," he answered sternly.

"Would that I were in possession of such sum I would gladly pay you. But what I hold in my hand is all that I show for a hard day's labor. Please to accept it."

The attendant snapped the money from the salesman's outstretched hand.

"Thank you, sir. You have been most considerate," he said obsequiously as he back-stepped toward his car, entered it, and drove away.

The serviceman returned to my bicycle and began to patch the tire. I told him about my meeting the Indian only minutes earlier in the tavern. The attendant was very frustrated, saying he would have to make good on the two-dollar shortage to the station's owner. The tire was mended in no time at all. I paid him fifty cents, and pedaled back to The Timberhaus.

XII

The world is a republic of mediocrities.
— Thomas Carlyle

The following afternoon as I was wandering about the resort, I noticed a young lady practicing her serves in the tennis court, located just before the stables. The court was as neglected as an ancient ruin and seldom used. It was overrun with weeds and the metal fence enclosure was heavily rusted. From a short distance I watched as she tossed a ball above her head, reared her arm back, and struck the ball which went sailing over the net. She drew another ball from her pocket, and began her motion to serve when she spotted me.

"Do you need to use the court?" she asked as she let the ball drop to the ground.

"No. I'm just passing through, and I apologize for distracting you. You're the first person I've seen on the court."

"And from its appearance, perhaps the only person who's used it in a long time," she replied as she scooped the bouncing ball into the webbing of her racket. "Do you play tennis?"

"Tried it a couple of times."

"I have an extra racket, if you'd like to rally."

"Rally?"

"Hitting the ball back and forth to each other."

I stepped inside the court and she handed me a racket that she removed from a vinyl athletic bag.

"And my name is Stephanie," she responded after I introduced myself. I told her I was working at the resort for the summer, and she told me she had arrived that morning for a three-day stay.

"Hold the handle of the racket as if grasping a hammer, but don't squeeze. When you're about to return my serve, keep the racket in back of you and then swing forward, meeting the ball just as it bounces in front of you," she explained as she illustrated the movement in slow motion. "It's called the forehand stroke."

"It looks simple," I replied confidently. After I walloped the first ball and then the second ball out of the court, she cautioned me to hit the ball firmly but gently. The next ball she served bounced softly and seemed easy to return, but I swung and missed the ball as if my racket had a hole in it. The next several balls I hit flew everywhere, like pigeons let out of a cage. Some ricocheted off the top of the fence; others sailed over it. I am an athletic person and consider myself well-coordinated. I can slam hockey pucks and whack baseballs, but I was dumbfounded by being unable to lob a small rubber ball over the net and onto the baseline of the court.

"I'm sure you can appreciate the subtleties of tennis," she said as she walked to my side of the court.

"I'm embarrassing myself," I said with frustration.

"It's to be expected for a novice. Now I'll let you serve the ball."

The first ball I served flew sideways. And I pounded the next ball to the ground, as if I hit it with a frying pan.

"I'm hopeless," I sighed.

"It takes practice. Hit some more."

I hit several more balls, which went in every direction like a broken compass.

Then Stephanie came over and gave me tips on the mechanics of serving. She grasped my wrist and extended my arm above my shoulder, tilting it just right of center. "This is where you want your racket to meet the ball," she said using the handle of her racket as a pointer. "And then follow through with a downward swing. You could be a good tennis player if you work at it," she said reassuringly. "Your height and long arms give you an advantage in reach."

This time I managed to deliver the balls over the net, which Stephanie returned with fluid strokes, making it appear so easy that which I found near impossible. I found Stephanie to be a distinctly attractive woman, yet none of her features were striking or dominant. Some women are known for their beautiful eyes, or curved breasts, or flowing hair, but she possessed none of these attributes. Hers was a discreet beauty with well-formed and proportionate features, that added up to a singular, unique comeliness.

After finishing the rally, we lingered at the net and chatted. Stephanie had an easy personality, and talking to her was like talking to someone I had known for years. I reckoned her age to be in the mid-twenties. She told me her visiting The Timberhaus was a spur-of-the-moment decision to take a few days off from the aerospace firm where she worked on Long Island. Of having a boyfriend or maybe a husband she said nothing. Then it was time to get ready for the dinner shift. I thanked Stephanie for her tennis tips, and told her I hoped to see her before she left.

Around mid-afternoon the following day, I was occupying myself perched atop the wood fence at the entrance to The Timberhaus, with my attention focused on a deer meandering through the verdant grassland. Suddenly the beep of a car horn startled the animal who quickly darted across the road disappearing into a thicket. I turned and saw Stephanie waving to me from inside her sedan as she slowed to a stop.

"I'm going into town. Would you like to come?" she asked, her head protruding from the open window.

Without saying a word I hopped off the fence, entered her car, and a few minutes later we were in East Durham where we stopped at a pastry shop for donuts and coffee. As we snacked Stephanie told me how peaceful and relaxed she was being in the mountains, and had a notion to buy a cabin here to spend her weekends as a respite from her job which she thoroughly hated. "Seven hours a day my fingers dance over a calculator adding numbers in columns. Then I make copies of the ledgers I have totaled and place them in a box, where a clerk picks them up and drops off a fresh batch of ledgers for me to reconcile. But when I make a simple error, my administrator acts as though I miscalculated the federal budget. He storms over slapping the ledger on my desk, and warns me to stop rushing and make fewer mistakes. But when I slow down he tells me I'm working too slow and need to speed up."

I told her that graduation couldn't come soon enough for me, as I was so anxious to start a real job.

"Six months after you graduate, you'll wish you were a student again," she countered. "The novelty of starting a career doesn't last long before the routine of work tarnishes its luster, and a university degree becomes merely status quo within a professional environment. And don't presume that you'll be able to apply everything you have learned. A chimpanzee from the wild could be trained to do my job. It's a frustrating paradox: Academia provides you with a range of skills, in order to find a job where you'll apply only a fraction of what you've learned. But you'll discover that in time."

"It will be different for…"

"No it won't. It will not be different for you," she interrupted. Then she reached across the table, and placed her hand gently on mine. "Pardon my abruptness. I'm turning into a veritable grouch. That's what happens when life becomes mechanical. Many ladies my age have their 'best times' ahead of them, but a gypsy would fall asleep if she looked into my crystal ball."

"Find another job," I suggested.

"I've changed jobs a few times, but there is no escape from drudgery. I'd rather be in the kitchen. Ah! I never thought I would hear myself utter that, but as I'm getting older I find more truth in it. My mother received more fulfillment baking cakes and knitting sweaters for us kids. Nowadays, young women believe they must be liberated from the apron strings, and not be like their mothers who were anchored to the house rearing kids and doing laundry. Instead, they find themselves stuck in an office all day doing monotonous tasks, and realize that the corporate world is not their happy bailiwick after all. Then, after several years they regret the time they forfeited with their husbands and children by having put career ahead of their family. Balancing a profession and home life can be as precarious as balancing a hand grenade on the tip of your nose.

"You see, a husband and wife should not compete with each other, but complement one another. When a husband is in his office all day pouring over financial statements, or blueprints, or medical charts, do you think when he comes home in the evening he wants to hear his accountant-wife rattle about tax write-offs, depreciation schedules, and capital gains? However much a man admires his wife's brain, he is equally gratified by the passion of her body. There is no getting around our genetics: man is diurnal; working from morning 'til evening, at which time a woman begins the nocturnal shift making dinner, and continuing her duties into the night in bed. Of course, if a woman feels it is an indignity to shift gears and become a harlot, then she can divorce and enjoy the freedom of being a well-educated professional in the solitude of an empty apartment.

"Some years ago I was a college student like yourself, devoting my nights and weekends to writing term papers and studying for exams, while holding part-time jobs to pay tuition. A year after graduating I met a man whom I fell in love with and we became engaged. What an exhilarating time that was. The reward for my toil and sacrifice had arrived, and I believed I would live happily forever. Everything had fallen into place." Then her expression dampened as if a dark cloud carrying a sour memory passed through her mind. "But happiness is fleeting. My fiancé and I broke up, and my dreams of Camelot were dashed."

A brief but awkward silence followed when neither of us knew what to say next. Then the waitress came to our table holding a carafe of coffee. "No more, thank you," Stephanie said.

"And you, sir?" the waitress asked me.

"I'm finished."

As Stephanie drained the remaining drops from her cup, she grabbed the bill which the waitress had left on the table that I was about to reach for. "I'll pay," she said, drawing two dollars from her purse. "Let's go for a stroll," she suggested.

We walked along the three-block stretch of town, pausing at shop windows until we came to Reilly's Pub, when Stephanie suddenly felt an urge for beer. There is a regional beer found in the Catskills that is one of the finest in North America. It is a favorite among visitors to this area because it is brewed from the Catskill steams, the purest drinking water found anywhere. New Amsterdam is a terrific lager which would turn an adamant tea-totaler into an ardent drinker.

We stepped inside and asked the bartender to bring us a pitcher of it. Meanwhile, my curiosity was piqued when Stephanie alluded earlier to her broken marriage engagement. I wanted to know more about this woman. What caused her to break up with a man whom she loved? Was there another man in her life at present?

"Pardon my asking Stephanie, but are you dating anyone?"

"I am not. At one time I was content dating most two-legged males who walked upright. But I use more discretion now."

"What caused the break-up?" I asked sheepishly.

She forced a smile as she shook her head in dismay. "During our engagement we were living together, but I kept putting off a wedding date. I wanted to marry and have children, but I also wanted to further my career. And there was an accumulation of conflicts that erupted into a seismic argument one evening. We each said things which neither of us could ever forgive the other for saying. A storm of words lasting twenty minutes ended a two-year affair. But that's over; the curtain has closed on that drama in my life. Still, it hasn't been easy finding a meaningful relationship." Then a broad smile widened her face and she said, "I'd like to settle down and raise a family, but it's not easy—especially after dating an astronaut, a spy, and an international arms dealer to name a few."

"How did you meet these men?" I asked in astonishment.

"At social gatherings. But none were whom they claimed to be. I met one man at a girlfriend's wedding who was handsome and rather intelligent. Unfortunately, he had low esteem and craved to be someone other than himself. We had been dating a few weeks when he told me—'in strict confidence and never to be told to anyone'—that he was a professional assassin. He boasted of making several killings a year, mostly of South American politicians, that earned him twenty grand a hit. Another short-lived flame claimed he was a bodyguard for the President, and had slept with the Chief Executive's two daughters. I would be thrilled if I met a normal man. Men are such charlatans. But women are to blame, too. When a woman is smitten, she excuses a man for his vices: If he doesn't have a job, he's an idealist; if he's a glutton for food, he has gourmet tastes; if he is lazy and never leaves the couch, he is meditative; if he hates religion, he is spiritual; if he is moody, she considers him introspective; should he have a nasty temper, he's to be admired for his honest emotions; if he has no friends, he's a shrewd judge of character; if he's forgetful, he's intuitive; if he's cheap, she thinks him a wise steward of his money; if he takes humor in imitating the handicapped, he's an artist of pantomime. But when she comes to her senses she finds that the man she loves is nothing more than a stingy, lazy, distempered, misogynous pig. Someday, I hope to find the right man. But I will never rush into marriage."

"You're still a young lady, Stephanie."

"I'm twenty-eight. Do you think that old?"

"Not when I reach your age. Actually, I took you for being younger. Now, you've shared your personal qualm with me, so I'll tell you my greatest apprehension."

"Which is?"

"Living a life of mediocrity. I don't think I could ever reconcile myself to being like everyone else. I feel that if I don't accomplish some noble achievement, then it's not worthwhile laboring for lesser goals."

"If you detach yourself from mediocrity, you remove yourself from society wherein mediocrity thrives. You'll be a lonely man, befriended only by your noble achievement. And what great accomplishment have you in mind anyway?"

"Everyday it is something else. If I told you I would sound like those crackpots you dated."

"Byron, you have the agonizing restlessness of youth, with an incurable itch to conquer the world; and where so many things are possible. If everyone carried that throughout their lives, we would never grow old; of course, we would never grow up either. But a point arrives, a time of reckoning, when each person must adjust his scopes and focus on a specific goal. And that can be arduous. Dreaming is fun, but achieving is hard work."

"I'll work hard to be successful, once I figure out what I want to be successful in."

"Success is paradoxical. A person labors long and hard to achieve success, only to find there remains in this fleeting life but a brief time to enjoy the fruit of his work. He will forgo the pleasure of friendships, the intimacy of relationships, and other amenities in order to realize his ambitions. For example, scientists cocoon themselves in laboratories, and writers cloister themselves in attics. They endure the suffering of creative labor, and scorn pleasure as a costly Epicurean distraction from achieving their goals. And to those who earned but never received acclaim in their lives, we bestow them with 'posthumous recognition'; as if the dead can be consoled with honors from an expired realm. Now, should great success be envied given the sacrifice it entails? Why reach for it?"

"The answer is simple: When weighed against its alternative, the purgatory of sacrifice is better than the hell of mediocrity. Furthermore, mediocrity won't attract a good woman."

Looking at me with intent eyes Stephanie replied: "Let me offer you a bit of sage advice. Live the simple life, and you'll be a happy man even if you only attract a simpleton for a wife."

"But your antidote only creates a new dilemma. How can the average life appeal to a man of talent, when his gifts will naturally gravitate him toward higher aspirations?"

"Obsession with mediocrity can destroy your life. You're falling into the same trap that snared me some years ago, when I felt that all my accomplishments were no more than second rate. No matter what I accomplished, gratification was always one goal away. There was always the 'something else' that had to be fulfilled. The gap never narrowed. So, success remained elusive like Tantalus trying to catch the ever-receding wave. But what special talent or aptitude can you boast of that should concern you with this problem?"

"At this point, none."

"Then why this discussion?" she said raising her hands in annoyance.

"Though I have no exceptional gifts does not mean I cannot cultivate talent. A person should not define himself by his limitations but by his potential; otherwise, he allows no room for growth. For example, there are some people whom we call 'naturally gifted' because their excellent faculties never require further enhancement, while most others must probe their minds with great effort to draw forth latent talents. Just as some regions of earth are rich with abundant streams and fertile soil, other regions are barren wastelands whose riches lie deep beneath the surface waiting to be tapped." Then I leaned back in my chair and folded my arms behind my head, with a look that read: "Try to top that, lady."

"My God, Byron, you need not sound so brainy! It's only ordinary Stephanie you're talking to. Save your metaphors for a doctoral thesis. After all we're in a bar, not a lyceum. Just remember this, buster: If you want to impress this lady, tell her a good, dirty joke. Now drink your beer and relax."

With that single stroke of condescension, she whittled my clever remark to mere prattle.

XIII

I who once wrote songs with keen delight am now by sorrow driven to take up melancholy measures.
— Boethius

We passed a couple of silent minutes sipping on our beers, when I picked up the threads of our conversation and asked Stephanie what was the one thing that had eluded her. She set down her glass, and leaned her cheek against her hand while considering my question. Then she replied: "Finding who the real Stephanie is. I went out of my way to impress men, when I only needed to be myself. I doted on my personal appearance and used the choicest words when I talked. I was the height of ostentation. I even began studying French for added polish. I convinced myself that without the trappings of education and a good-paying job, I would never hook a good husband. But I was masquerading; I was as artificial as those clownish men whom I spoke of earlier. No doubt that contributed to the break-up of my engagement. My fiancée had seen the veneer peeling from the surface and saw an impostor." She lowered her head, placing her palms to the sides of her face to frame her disgust. Then she raised her head and continued:

"Listen…listen. As you're entering your senior year in college, I've a story that might interest you which happened when I was around your age and finishing up my final year at the university. I met a student, the same age as myself. He was so handsome, and had an appealing awkwardness and shyness about him. We sat arms-length from each other in class, but never exchanged a word until the last week of the semester when, by happenstance, I was walking across campus and ran into him. He was with Cecil, an acquaintance of mine, who in turn introduced me to him—Roger was his name. The three of us strolled to the cafeteria where we chit-chatted for half-an-hour. That casual meeting broke the ice between me and Roger, and during that chat our mutual friend Cecil invited me to a graduation party that he was hosting the following weekend.

"The next day in class the topic of Cecil's party came up between me and Roger. I told him I had no means of getting to the party without a car, but Roger readily offered to pick me up. So, the following Saturday night I was at the party with this tall, gangling twenty-one-year-old, whom I had first spoken to only a few days earlier. But the party, in fact, was only a small gathering of several people, which made for a more intimate setting. But Roger was reserved throughout the evening, adhering to protocol by not presuming I was his date, and sticking to his role as my driver. As he was driving me home after the party, we talked about graduation day two weeks hence, and how glad we were to be rid of books and classes and term papers, but he never hinted of our getting together again. I didn't speak to him again until graduation day, when right after the ceremony he came over to congratulate me and introduce himself to my parents. When I told him to keep in touch, his expression brightened and said 'of course!' Then he turned and disappeared into the crowd of graduates and family members.

"A few days later he telephoned me, and asked if I would like to see a baseball game with him. After that we dated regularly. That bashful young man quickly turned into a prince, and I was absolutely head-over-heels with him. Meanwhile, we had both started jobs. He worked for a chemical company, and I had joined an accounting firm as an apprentice auditor that required out-of-town travel every month. But while on business trips I met other men, and soon realized that the world was filled with 'good catches.' Six months into dating Roger, our relationship soured. My prince had turned into a frog. Roger was just an ordinary man with an ordinary job. And I deserved a special, extraordinary man. One evening just before he was about to leave my apartment I told Roger I would not see him on New Year's eve. His face blanched and his eyes misted. He knew that our relationship was over. He began mumbling, taken off guard by the news, but quickly regained his composure. Then he gently placed my hand in his, softly kissed my cheek, and wished me the best. He walked toward the door, and as he placed his hand on the knob he turned and said a few simple words which I will never forget. But over the next several years…"

"Stephanie, what did he say?"

She took a deep breath before exhaling her reply. "He said, 'Stephanie, you will never marry.' His tone was not malicious; it merely sounded like an impartial observation and I took no offense. But as I'm getting older those words are carrying the weight of a curse."

My question had reopened a bitter wound. To stanch the flow of her painful memory I switched our conversation. "You started to say something before I interrupted."

"Oh yes, yes," she said rubbing her forehead to recall her thought. "Over the next several years I dated nice men with good incomes, but nothing blossomed from these relationships, except for that ill-fated engagement I mentioned before. When would I find that one special man? I often mused. One evening as I lamented my misfortune like a prisoner in a cell, I thought of Roger. I realized he was the only man who had cared about me, and that he had been a special person. He was natural, stripped of pretense, unlike other men who pass themselves off as Rembrandts but are nothing more than cheap imitations. Alas, he was my first love too, and women are cautioned against marrying their first love, but only to use the man to get their feet wet to explore other relationships. But he was the man whom I would have been most happy with," she said with a wistfulness about a time that she wished she could have back again.

Stephanie and I continued talking, but shifted to more cheerful topics as the beer oiled our tongues, making us more garrulous and Stephanie less maudlin. After draining the pitcher of delicious beer, we left the tavern and returned to her car. The sedan was parked on a side street, from which unfolded a vista of blue-green hills ascending to a cloud-puffed sky. As Stephanie was about to start the motor she remarked on the beauty of the landscape, and asked if I would not mind relaxing with her a bit to observe this reposing scene framed within the car's windshield. So, the two of us sat in the car, feeling as much composed by the tranquility of nature as by the beer we had drunk, which had made each of us a bit tipsy.

"Ah, the Zen of watching mountains grow," Stephanie said. Then she burst into laughter, and slapped my knee. "I hope you don't think I'm serious. I'm not at all into Eastern philosophy, or anything Eastern for that matter. I won't even eat Chinese food!"

She slouched in the seat, folded her hands behind her head, and resumed staring through the windshield as if she were watching a drive-in movie. We sat quietly for a couple of minutes absorbing nature, when from the tail of my eye I noticed her staring at the southern province of my body.

"My goodness. You do have a large one," she remarked suggestively.

I blushed.

Pointing to the member of my anatomy she had been fondly observing Stephanie said, "It figures a tall lad like yourself would have one so big and long."

"Yes," I answered proudly, feeling more at ease.

"Slip it out," she cooed.

"Here? Now?"

She nodded impishly, with the tip of her tongue curled upward to the roof of her mouth.

In no time I laid it bare and fully exposed before Stephanie's eager eyes. Maneuvering myself sideways in the seat to give her better access to it, she took my article gently in her hands. She stroked it and caressed it reverently, and bringing the tip of it to her lips she glided her tongue across the hard flesh as I sighed approvingly. The hungry woman continued her oral massage on my member with a delightful sequence of licks, sucks, and kisses. Then she paused and asked, "Ever had it before?"

"First time," I confessed.

"You should have this little wart removed," she remarked as she scrutinized my unit.

"I had it incised, but it grew back like a weed."

"And I notice it's bent and swollen right here," she said as she continued her examination.

"That's from a hard whack I received as a kid."

She cringed. "Ooh, how painful that must have been."

"Excruciating."

Then she resumed her play for several minutes, until her desire was satisfied and she stopped.

"You must have thought me bold in asking you at first, but I'm glad you enjoyed it," Stephanie said.

"I loved it. Do the other if you like?" I offered.

"I've had enough. Oh, let me do that," she said as she snatched the sock from my hand. Once again she took into her hands that which had been the object of her affection—the toes of my right foot—and slipped the cotton sock back on it.

"And do have a doctor look at that toe which you banged. Perhaps, he can align it."

Then Stephanie started the car and sped back to The Timberhaus, where I had only ten minutes remaining to get ready for dinner. Arriving at the entrance to the resort, she stopped the car, leaned toward me and, cupping her hand around the back of my head, drew my face to hers and imprinted a quick kiss on my lips. "Now get out, dear boy; you'll be late for work," she admonished gently as she edged away.

I was stunned. Her kiss was a lightning bolt sending a surge of rapture through my body.

"Please, Byron. You must go."

When I alighted from the car I stood on feeble legs as I watched her drive away. I hobbled to the bunkhouse; my knees were rubbery and my palms sweated. I was dazed and confused. I felt nauseous and my stomach was knotted. What an upsetting feeling! What a wonderful feeling! I was in love! Like the fairytale where the princess' kiss turned the toad into a prince, I was transformed when her lips met mine, and she had become to me the most perfect creature on earth. After I freshened myself, my queasiness gave way to euphoria. There was a bounce in my step as I walked to the dining hall to begin the dinner shift. It was stifling in the kitchen, but I could be working in a tar pit and not have minded. I asked Chloe, the waitress who was serving the section where Stephanie sat, if she had seen her, but she said she had not and her table was vacant.

XIV

For all sad words of tongue and pen,
The saddest of these,
'It might have been.'
— John Greenleaf Whittier

That evening I went to call on Stephanie at her cabin, but she was not in. An hour later I returned but with the same result. As I was walking from her cabin, I spotted a pair of car headlights approaching from the distance. The parallel shafts of headlight beam swung ninety degrees, as the car turned into the row of chalets and stopped at the end of the dirt lane. Stephanie got out of her car and entered her room. I was tempted to knock on her door, but my courage failed. Again, I felt my legs weakening and my palms moistening.

I walked to the side of her cabin and tiptoed to the window where the shade was half-drawn, staying clear of the sheet of light that shone through the casement. I bent down and peeped just above the window sill. Stephanie was lying on the bed propped on one elbow, as she flipped through one of several magazines strewn across the mattress. She tossed the magazine aside, took another and fanned through its pages, and then flung that one aside. Next, she rolled on her back with hands folded atop her head, and gazed at the ceiling for a couple of minutes. Afterwards, she turned on her side facing the window, and stared listlessly. She appeared lonely and bored, reminding me of my lethargy during the early days of the summer when I languished in my bedroom with nothing to do. If at that moment I climbed through the window and stood in front of her, I am certain she would not have seen me, for from her somber aspect I could read that she was absorbed replaying scenes of the past in her mind's eye. Was she recalling joyous times which would never return? Or retrieving memories of lost love? If only I could antennae her thoughts.

Her expression grew more dismal and painful, and she wiped a tear from the corner of her eye. Moving to the edge of the bed, she sat up and dropped her face into her hands. Then raising her head, she slung her streaming hair over her shoulders and moaned, "What's the use." She fell back on the bed with eyes fastened on the ceiling light, around which whirled a moth in erratic flight. Then reaching back on the wall, she flicked off the light switch.

I observed the dark outline of her supine, motionless body, and was overwhelmed with an urge to be with her. I wanted to knock on the door, and imagined how thrilled she would be to see me. She would wrap her arms around me and for the rest of the night we would make sweet love. No sooner had that fantasy played out in my mind, when it was tempered by the prospect of her becoming angry at my sudden intrusion and slamming the door shut in my face. Whatever her private anguish was it would have to run its course, and she would have to resolve it alone.

I thought of the moth that had whizzed around the ceiling, and how it was privy to seeing the unknown side of Stephanie. When a woman or a man closes himself in a room, he sheds his mask like an actor returning to his dressing room, leaving behind the character he portrays on the stage. Within the confines of four walls, Stephanie released her emotions; her privacy breached only by a tiny moth, and a lonely admirer who stood barely several feet from where she lay in personal distress.

To linger at the window any longer would be wrong, and I felt guilty for having observed the private moments of another. I withdrew from the window and retreated through a wooded area backing to the rear of the cabin, and then headed to the recreation hall.

"She's gone?" I asked incredulously.

"She checked out this morning," Heidi answered as she folded a letter and inserted it in an envelope.

"But she told me she was staying through Sunday."

"Yes, she did reserve a chalet through the weekend." Then she licked the corners of the envelope and sealed it. "But what's it to you? Do you know the woman?" Heidi asked.

"Not as well as I thought," I muttered, as I glumly headed to the door.

"Wait, drop this in the mail box outside, sweetie," Heidi said as she stretched across the desk waving the envelope.

I snapped it from her hand, left the office, and headed to the pond to try to collect myself and relieve my frustration.

I had a crush on Stephanie. Following our afternoon excursion, I imagined a wonderful romance with this single and unattached woman. And now I was embarrassed by my puerile fantasies, and rebuked myself for having carved love castles in the clouds for a person I hardly knew. Indeed, my youthful romanticism carried me to great heights, only to send me plummeting back to reality.

From eavesdropping the night before, I knew she was troubled about something. In my mind I scrolled through the entirety of yesterday's outing, trying to recall if I had said anything to upset her. Perhaps, I was too inquisitive about her personal life? Perhaps, she felt awkward being a lone guest in a family atmosphere and bolted? Perhaps this, perhaps that; back and forth I went, cross-examining myself until my mind was dull. As I probed for answers I only compounded my confusion. What torture it is when one's thoughts are so scrambled, that nothing makes sense and reason has flown away.

So distracted was I that in the scullery that evening I broke more dishes than I had in all my previous shifts. Otto was furious: "If you break another dish, you pay for it!" he thundered. Even Nick scowled at me: "Put aside whatever is bothering you. You're making a mess!"

So I focused on my task, and pursued the menial and repetitive chore of dishwashing with diligence. When the last plate was cleaned, I wiped down the dishwasher, and next I mopped the kitchen floor until it sparkled. When everything was finished, I was soaked with sweat and slick with grime. But in the course of my physical toil I had expelled my mental anguish, as hard work is the remedy for every worry and problem. My mind was rinsed, and I was mentally fresh.

I went to the bunkhouse to shower, and afterwards to the dance hall where I relaxed drinking a couple of beers until ten o'clock, before retiring for the night.

But Stephanie was my first thought when I woke up next morning, and I was downcast the entire day. The following day I felt the same. But on the third day I received a letter postmarked from Long Island with no return address.

Dear Byron,

How rude you must think I am to have taken flight without extending you the courtesy of a goodbye. But you would not think my hasty departure imprudent were you to know the reasons necessitating it, which I must forebear from disclosing.

How odd that I found myself revealing my personal affairs to you, as if I were a penitent and you were my confessor. Perhaps, because you were an impartial listener, a neutral party, I found it easier to be candid than I would with long-time acquaintances.

As stingy as life is in apportioning her fortunes, may you be allotted more than she grants others. And throw off the cloak of mediocrity that you wear like a yoke. This world is too complex to allow mediocrity. Regardless of his station each human is visited with anxiety, fear, privation, and drudgery in the span of a single day, and meeting those challenges require heroic stamina. No, mediocrity doesn't exist!

I truly enjoyed meeting you, Byron. And now I rest my pen and my thoughts. By now you have guessed that this letter is sent from your friend,
Stephanie

I was relieved when I read her letter. It put into context the meaning of our brief friendship, which was simply an honest exchange of each other's gripes and troubles. The reasons she wouldn't disclose for her "hasty departure" were apparent to me. What I had observed from her cabin window that night spoke of an unresolved turmoil, which even her Catskill holiday afforded no respite.

I slipped the letter into my pocket and walked a short distance beyond the bunkhouse to a brook that courses down the hills, and makes its way along the outskirts of the resort. There I sat on a rock, carved comfortably flat by nature, and read the letter once more. Then I folded it and held it between two fingers, as I debated whether to keep it or discard it. Keeping the letter would be a meaningless nostalgia, a reminder of a woman who would never enter my life again. But to crumple it into a ball and trash it would be disrespectful, for Stephanie's kind words gave the paper an air of reverence. Parting with the letter was parting with a friend. It is said that South Pacific islanders place the remains of a departed one into a canoe, and let it drift into the ocean as a final resting place. So I set the letter, moistened by a fallen teardrop, gently on the water where it floated downstream, and disappeared from sight. And with that symbolic act I bid goodbye to a woman of fleeting acquaintance, whose impression would remain with me for a considerable time.

XV

Fred was twenty years old, of flimsy construction, and had a sallow complexion that gave him an antique appearance; indeed, his skin was like parchment that thinly covered his bony features. He was medium height and very skinny, with long thin arms like the branches of a sapling. His hair was cut to a stubble, revealing a very irregular and dented head with one ear hung lower than the other. And he had small dead-looking eyes like a pair of black marbles, that peered through rimless glasses which rested on a hideous nose resembling an onion bulb. He had a hyper-extended jaw, and a protruding, thick lower lip which he had the habit of curling into his gums. Add to this his nervous practice of scratching his forehead and chin like a chimp, one could argue that an evolutionary reversion had resurrected the traits of a simian ancestor. At first glance one would say of Fred, "What a pitiful creature." And any mother would sigh, "Thank God he's not mine."

When I first spotted Fred at The Timberhaus I thought, "It can't be him! Please God, it can't be him!" As soon as he recognized me he ran over to greet me.

"Byron, what a surprise meeting you here! Are you vacationing?"

I told him I worked at the resort.

"So do I! I just got hired!"

"You're working here!" I exclaimed.

"I arrived this morning!"

I had last seen Fred seven years ago when we graduated from grammar school. Fred looked no different now than when I met him in the first grade. Even at the tender age of five, I recall his being the feeblest-looking person I had seen, and remember telling my mother about this pathetic boy who sat next to me in class. Throughout elementary school Fred was a pariah. Ugly, witless, and a weakling, he was the target of pranks and bullies. In winter, before the start of class in the morning, a student would swipe the wool cap off his head and toss it to another student who dangled it before Fred; just as Fred would reach for it, the boy would toss it to another student. Fred scurried to and fro among several classmates trying to retrieve his cap, until one of them would throw the cap into the air where it might end in a mud puddle, a roof gutter, or once on the head of the eight-foot statue of the school's founder.

It was a common ruse among bigger boys to challenge Fred to a schoolyard fight. A student would allow Fred to punch him with his puny fist, whereupon the boy would fake injury and fall to the ground. Pretending to writhe in pain the boy would wobble to his feet, pleading with Fred not to hurt him, while a dozen others would counter with: "Slug him Fred, slug him!" Rearing back his skinny arm, Fred would strike the boy with the force of a three-year-old, and beam with pride as his larger opponent sank to his knees. But victory was short-lived as Mary Jo, a nasty butch-to-be and as vicious as a junkyard dog, would burst upon the scene grabbing Fred by the seat of his pants and hurl him like a missile into thorn bushes, causing the entire schoolyard to erupt into laughter.

Fred desperately wanted me as his friend. But I would have nothing to do with him. It was embarrassing just to be in his company. During his first week at The Timberhaus he followed me like a shadow. When I relaxed at poolside he would pull up a chair and strike up an asinine conversation, which so irked me that I would have shoved him into the pool had he been able to swim. Hard to elude, he followed me to the pond, and tailed me as I left the kitchen after every shift. He truly nauseated me.

Fred's mental and physical characteristics complemented each other for he was as dumb as he looked. If you asked Fred to name the President, he would pause to think. Spanish on his father's side and English on his mother's, I once asked him where in England his maternal grandparents were from. "Madrid," he answered. Cretin that he was, Fred nonetheless had a remarkable faculty for sports memorabilia. He could quote you the statistics of any professional athlete like an idiot savant. His goal, he once told me, was to be a professional athlete. His goal, of course, was ridiculous. His lithe body did afford him fleetness of foot, but I heard he was thrown off his high school track team in sophomore year for passing the baton to opposing runners in track relays. The workers were also rude to Fred, believing he lacked the aptitude to comprehend insult and humiliation. I agreed. If he were a dog, you would kick him; a horse, you would whip him and not feel any compunction.

The only time Fred ate his meals in the mess room was when it rained. He huddled himself in a corner, toying with his knife and fork like one who knew not for what purpose they were intended. Otherwise, he preferred taking his plate of food outside to avoid the taunts of others. Nor was Fred immune to ridicule from the guests. Fred walked bolt upright with a hurried step like one rushing to a lavatory. Children mimicked his gait as he passed them, and grown-ups witnessing this parody burst out laughing. After I shunned Fred for two weeks, it sank into his vacuous skull that I did not want to be his friend. He stopped speaking to me. This relieved me very much.

XVI

A lake...is earth's eye.
— Thoreau

Inlaid like turquoise within quiescent, scalloped hills, Jewel Lake lay sequestered a half-mile in from the main road. The winding dirt lane leading to it gave no hint of its presence, until after rounding a bend the lake surprised my eye with its sudden appearance. It was Wednesday, my day-off, and I arrived here after bicycling five miles. The path terminated at a rickety cabin at the water's edge, where scattered outside were a half-dozen aluminum canoes. Above its entrance hung a dilapidated sign with peeling paint that read: "Boat Rentals."

"I'd like to rent a canoe," I announced to the man inside who was leaning against the counter and thumbing through a newspaper. He appeared a bit agitated that I had interrupted his reading, and pitched the paper aside.

"Four dollars plus five-dollar deposit for the canoe," he answered glumly.

"Your sign says three dollars."

"It's an old sign. Price has increased."

I paid him with a ten-dollar bill which he placed in the cash register.

"Sign here, please," pointing to a registry on the counter.

"You owe me a dollar in change. Or has the price just increased in the last thirty seconds?"

He drew a dollar bill from the register and handed it to me.

"Why do I have to sign the registry?"

"In case you drown, I'll know whose body I have to fish out of the water."

Then the proprietor took an oar from the dozen or so set against the wall and handed it to me. "Know how to paddle?"

"I sure do."

Next he reached below the counter and pulled out a life jacket. "Wear this while you're on the lake," he said tossing it to me.

The canvas life jacket was badly tattered, and if it had a tongue would say: "I hope you can swim." Then we stepped outside and I selected a canoe. The proprietor slung a rope over his shoulder that was knotted to the nose ring of the canoe, and then dragged the craft a short distance to the grassy bank. Then he flung the rope into the canoe and nudged it halfway into the water. I put on the life jacket, slid the oar inside the canoe, hopped in, and cast off.

The small vessel sliced across the water, its emerald green hue born of mineral springs within its depths. The lake was so quiet and placid, that I wondered if it be improper to disturb its tranquil surface with the plash of my oar. I had paddled some six hundred yards when I spotted a narrow channel along the western lip of the lake. I shifted course in that direction, and as I entered the strait the water turned to marsh with a depth no more than three feet, with thick shoots of reed rising from the shallow bottom. I expected I was nearing a dead end and was set to turn around, when the thicket cleared and before me loomed a continuation of the lake, as vast as the body of water I was exiting.

I paddled toward a solitary islet reposing in the center of the lake, and there I went ashore on this tiny mound of grass spiked by a willow tree. This islet was no more than fifty feet in diameter, but was so peaceful and cozy that I would not have traded this patch of earth for a continent. Not a soul was in sight. I was Robinson Crusoe, and could remain here forever never caring to see another human being. I fingered a small hole in the grassy ground where I planted a coin to establish title, and proclaimed this morsel of land as "Byron's Island."

I took off my sneakers and removed my tee shirt which I rolled into a pillow, and spread my bones on the soft ground. As I chewed on a blade of grass and stared at my toes, I thought that doubtless many an Iroquois squaw of yesteryear had lost her flower to her warrior-lover on this secluded sanctuary. I felt delightfully lazy and grew drowsy; soon I was fast asleep.

After dozing about an hour, I was rested and energized and ready to hop in the canoe to continue my navigation. But where was it? "I'm sure I docked it right here," I said to myself, looking at the spot where I had come aground. With rising apprehension I scurried through the drooping branches of the willow to the opposite side of the islet, but saw no canoe. I was certain I had pulled the canoe well in from the water, but it had somehow drifted away. Shielding my eyes from the sun with my hand, I spied the lake and spotted a glare on the water about one hundred yards away, where the sunlight reflected off the aluminum craft. I shed my trousers and waded slowly into the cold water, and when my body adjusted to the lake's temperature I plunged in head first and swam toward the mutinous vessel.

After swimming fifty yards I discovered that rather than halving the distance between myself and the canoe, it had drifted further away. I increased my strokes to narrow the gap, only to find the canoe was escaping at a distance commensurate with my pursuit. I was growing tired so I floated on my back to conserve my strength, facing directly into the blinding sun that even with eyes shut I could feel its fierce penetration against my lids.

So I abandoned my attempt at recovery and started to swim back to the islet. But I had swum too far and too fast, and now I felt the consequences of my recklessness. My arms now grew heavy with every stroke, and in my exhausted state the islet seemed miles away. I plumbed the depths with my feet, but could find no bottom to stand. My arms became leaden, and I felt I was towing a ship.

With increasing frequency I floated on my back to recapture my stamina, yet even this was an effort as my weary arms and legs could not provide the equilibrium to keep my face and mouth above the water line. No longer able to float, I allowed myself to sink below the surface and then pop up to grasp air, repeating this several times in order to rest my muscles before resuming strokes. Coming within twenty yards of the islet, I summoned what little energy remained and made a final dash to safety. When I reached the shallow, muddy water I crawled on hands and knees to the rim of the islet, and clawed my way onto the grassy mound. As I lay face down gasping for air, extreme nausea overcame me and I vomited. Weak from purging my system and with every ounce of my energy spent, I collapsed and lost consciousness.

When I awoke I dug my hands into the soil to assure myself I was safely on land and alive. This tiny island was now the most precious chunk of earth, safe haven that it had become. How one misfortune quickly supplants another! When I discovered my canoe missing a thousand alarms sounded, and I thought all was lost only to have that misfortune replaced by nearly drowning. But it was not long before my celebration of deliverance yielded to the grim reality that I was marooned, and how long would I wait before help arrived? Surely the boatmaster would search for me when I failed to return. I'll bet that lazy buffoon was waiting for this day when a touch of excitement would be added to his boring life by possibly having to "fish a body out of the water." When I didn't return and he discovered the empty canoe, he'd envision finding my drowned body bobbing on the surface like a corked bottle and chortle, "I get to keep his five-dollar deposit," as he hooked a rope to my legs and towed me to shore. Then he would see himself on the wharf standing before newspaper photographers next to my bloated body with lifeless eyes and drooping tongue, suspended upside down by cables, like a fisherman posing beside a prize marlin. But I will disappoint the nasty weasel. Nothing to worry about, I assured myself. I will be rescued by dusk.

I put on my shirt and dungarees and sat on the roots of the willow with my back against its trunk. It was about five o'clock, and an evening band of shadow collared the ridge of the surrounding hills. At the far end of the lake a squadron of Canadian geese, flying in V-formation with wings flapping in synchrony, descended on the water. For the next couple of hours as evening inched down the hills and the greenish-blue waters darkened to violet, I kept an alert eye to flag down any boat that should appear. By eight o'clock dusk had settled and I had not seen a single soul. I was growing anxious. Where was the boatmaster? The canoe rental was already two hours overdue.

The geese who had earlier settled on the lake now came aground on the islet. Envying the freedom of winged creatures whom water or walls could not imprison, I recalled the words of the Psalmist, "Oh that I could have wings like a dove and flee..." They wobbled about and started their boisterous honking, and then began littering my little colony with their duck goo, such that I had to tiptoe like a ballerina to avoid stepping on their droppings. A couple of rascals even charged me with wings outstretched in belligerent display and pecked at me, chasing me from where I had been sitting. The islet was their nesting ground, and I was as much an intruder to the geese as they were to me. But I quickly reestablished dominion over my parcel by hurling a few stones at their feathery rumps, causing them to retreat in a group to the rim of the islet. Then I plucked sheaves of tall rye grass and carpeted it around the trunk of the willow where I sat and waited. And waited.

It was now nightfall. The indigo sky was sprouting stars, and the night was melding lake and hills into seamless darkness. The islet was all but invisible to the naked eye, and my chances of being found were rapidly waning. I began to fear the boatmaster had forgotten me and went home. I rounded the circumference of the islet screaming, "Help! Help!" But every time I shouted the awful geese drowned out my desperate cries with their loud honks.

"Shut up!" I pelted them with stones and they quieted, only to resume their riot of honks each time I cried out in distress.

The night air had descended like a cold veil and chilled me to the bone. I had not eaten in hours and was extremely weak, and I was concerned about falling victim to exposure. I thought of snakes and rats and bats; every noise played on my fears. I reassured myself that help would arrive, expecting at any moment to see searchlights streaking across the water coming from the sheriff and his rescue party. I prayed that the geese, heretofore such a bloody nuisance, would not dessert me. I coaxed a couple of them toward me, and then snuggled beside them to keep warm. Soon, I no longer felt the cold or feared the night, as blessed slumber came upon me like a savior.

I don't know how long I had been asleep, when I was awakened by the plash of oars on the water. I sprang up, startling my feathery bedmates who scurried away to join their flock. I made out the prow of a skiff emerging from the darkness as it floated toward the islet. I jumped to my feet and shouted jubilantly, "I'm here! I'm here!" Rescue had arrived!

A man alighted from the rowboat into the knee-deep water and pushed the craft aground.

"Thank God you found me!" I cried. "You've probably been searching all night. My canoe drifted away, and I nearly drowned trying to retrieve it. You didn't come any too soon; I'm freezing. Had to snuggle with those smelly geese, or I would have died of hypothermia. Would you have a blanket or a jacket I could wear?" I asked in a shivering voice.

The man stood in silhouette against the black water and said nothing. Then he shone a flashlight on me. I turned my head sideways to avoid the direct beam of light and addressed him: "My name is Byron. You *are* the man who rented me the canoe, aren't you?" He made no reply so I continued: "I'm dreadfully sorry for losing the canoe. You must think me an ass."

"Who dares step foot on Captain Klugg's island?" replied an imperious voice.

"Who are you?" I asked in a low, guarded tone.

"Are you deaf, lad! I'm Captain Klugg!" he roared, sending the frightened geese scrambling into the water.

Then he walked towards me, as I backed-stepped before bumping into the tree that arrested my retreat.

"You're not afraid, are you?" he asked sarcastically. He now stood a few feet from me.

"What do you want?" I asked in a shaking voice. No sooner had the words left my lips when the stranger whipped out a sword from a scabbard hanging from his belt.

"I want you off my island, you son of a sea witch!"

The tip of his sword was now pressed against my crotch.

"Leave or I'll slit you in two up the middle," he said angrily as he jerked the sword slightly upward, so that I had to raise myself on my toes to avoid defilement. For thirty dreadful seconds I stood on the tips of my toes, pinned against the trunk of the tree sucking in deep draughts of air; then, he mercifully lowered his weapon and I descended to the heels of my feet.

"I didn't know this was your island," I answered gasping for breath.

"Many a man didn't; many a man perished," he trumpeted.

"I have no boat; I'm unable to swim these waters!" I said desperately.

"Ask the duckies to help you," he snickered, pointing his sword to the flock of geese floating about the margin of the islet.

"Listen to me," I pleaded. "I came here this afternoon only to relax a bit, but my canoe drifted off and I was stranded!"

"I have no berth for stupidity," he replied casually, as he drew the blade of his sword between his thumb and index finger like a bow across a cello. Then suddenly stepping back he flourished his sword in the air and shrieked: "For the high crime of wanton trespass and invasion, and criminal intention to depose Captain Klugg as the island's head of state, I declare you a prisoner of the aforementioned Klugg, who by the authority of Divine Right and Papal edict is sovereign of this island and protector of the waters that wash its shores!"

This man was insane. He was in his fifties, and very slightly built whom I could easily lay flat with a firm slap. But he was nimble with his sword and I was consumed with exhaustion, and to dismiss him as anything less than a serious threat might be a grave mistake.

"How long will I be detained?" I asked in a rapid breath.

"Until morning."

I drew a relieved sigh. "Then we cast off tomorrow, right?"

"When the sun rises you will be executed," he replied calmly.

I was completely benumbed. With my back to the tree, I slid down the trunk and slumped to the ground like a puppet whose strings had been cut. In a fleeting moment all of my life's misfortunes streaked before my eyes, and it occurred to me perhaps it better I were dead. I stared dazedly out on the tenebrous waters, devoid of all emotion as if I had been turned to stone. Meanwhile, my captor was slicing the air madly with his sword, as if an armada of invaders had landed and he were the only one to defend the islet. At times he maneuvered into a defensive posture fending off fantasy assaults, before recoiling and attacking his imaginary enemies with gallant strokes of his blade.

"Have you any food?" I groaned.

He stopped with his sword suspended in mid-air, and glared at me through the whites of his eyes. "Food! I didn't come here as a missionary!"

"A condemned man has a right to a last meal, yes?"

He stroked his chin, raised an eyebrow and asked, "When did you last eat?"

"Half-a-day ago," I answered frailly.

"And what did you have?"

"Frankfurters and sauerkraut."

"Hah! Then consider that your last meal!" whereupon he resumed his duel. "Take that! And that!" he shouted, gutting every phantom foe with thrusts of his sword. Had it been actual combat, the islet would be sinking beneath the weight of disemboweled bodies and severed heads.

Devoured by fatigue I summoned myself to stay awake, lest this lunatic kill me in my sleep. I had to risk an escape, because my hour of execution was but a few hours away. Yet I barely had strength to stand, so fragile was I from hunger. However, I noticed that the illusionary combat was taking its toll on the old pirate; he was exhausting himself and appeared on the verge of collapsing. Now might be the opportunity to rush to the boat and flee. As I was weighing this decision, Captain Klugg planted the tip of his sword on the ground and leaned on its handle while he captured his breath. It was then I saw something unusual that revived my courage. I noticed the blade began to bow considerably beneath his weight, much more than a real sword of steel could. Then to my amazement it appeared that a layer of steel was peeling from the blade. Indeed, the sword was only made of plastic veneered with aluminum foil! The relief that my fear was for naught sent a rush of adrenalin through my body, rocketing my spirit and energy. I raised myself on my knees and looked amusingly at the toy that had terrified me.

"Are you practicing the smirk that you'll wear when it comes time to lop your head off?" sneered Klugg.

I broke into laughter. "You will need more than a child's toy to carry my head off as a trophy."

The crazy man glanced at his sword, and jolted momentarily when he saw it coming apart; then he quickly placed it behind his back like a toddler hiding candy from his mother.

"What are you doing?" he yelled as I placed a foot inside the boat.

"I'm leaving."

"I command you to stay! Get out of my vessel!" he shouted in an agitated voice.

"Your game is over, old man. I'm taking the navy, but leaving you the kingdom."

He charged me with his plastic sword, but I easily disarmed him and flung him to the ground.

"You would have me freeze to death," I hollered as he lay sprawled on the cold earth. "You can rot here. And if you stop me from leaving, I'll split your head open." Then I got into the boat and pushed off with an oar.

"Don't leave! Don't leave! The flowers! The flowers! Leave me the flowers!" he cried hysterically as he rose to his feet.

I spotted a floral bouquet lying inside the stern. I picked it up and hurled it at the madman.

"You have desecrated my island!" Klugg shouted as I paddled off. Then he waded waist-deep into the cold water, and fired off a volley of epithets while waving his little fists at me.

As I observed his tantrum, I wasn't sure if I should abandon this nut to himself. I thought he might give himself a heart attack at any moment. Also, I was leaving in his boat, and should anything happen to him I would be held culpable. When he exhausted himself from yelling, he waded ashore and picked up the bouquet and gathered a few of the stems that had scattered. He cradled the flowers in his arms, and then slumped to his knees and began sobbing uncontrollably. It was a sad sight. He whom I had feared a short time earlier, had turned into a harmless, pitiful creature. He whom I had loathed, I now wanted to help.

I strained my faculties to make sense of what was happening. Klugg had come to this islet in the middle of the night, bringing with him flowers. When he found me here, he became incensed. Had my presence spoiled his rendezvous with a lover as mad as himself? Had he come to perform a warped ritual to a deity of insanity? What was his intention?

I returned ashore and walked to within ten feet of the captain, who was kneeling with his head buried in the bouquet. Suddenly, a flash of light illuminated the islet momentarily, what at first I thought was lightning. I turned and saw a beam of light sweeping the water's surface, accompanied by the whine of a motorboat engine. I shouted and waved my hands frantically, and less than a minute later a deputy sheriff alighted from his boat and came ashore.

"Are you Byron?" he asked.

"Yes! Yes! Thank God you're here! Have you a jacket or something warm I can put on? I'm an icicle," I said in staccato voice as my teeth chattered. The deputy retrieved a heavy wool blanket from the boat and gave it to me.

"How did you lose your canoe?" he asked.

"It floated away. I came here to rest, and when I looked again it had drifted half-way across the lake. Later, this man arrived, held me hostage, and threatened to kill me for trespassing. It's been a nightmare, sir."

"It's been a nightmare for me," the lawman answered testily. "Because of your carelessness, I've spent hours searching for you." Then he shone the flashlight on Klugg, who all this time had been silently weeping.

"Carter, are you alright?" the deputy asked sympathetically, as he stooped beside the kneeling figure. The two men talked in a low voice, barely higher than a murmur. I heard bits of what the officer was saying: "He didn't mean any harm…he was lost…" Then the deputy helped him to his feet, placed his arms around his shoulders, and continued talking to him in a conciliatory manner, until Klugg or Carter—whatever his name—had regained his composure.

"I'll be fine, Larry," I heard him tell the officer. He sounded normal and relaxed, like someone who had just snapped out of psychosis. The lawman patted his back and said, "Take care of yourself, my friend."

"Let's go sonny. Get in the boat," the deputy said to me with an authoritative tone.

"You're not taking me to jail, are you?"

"I'm taking you back to the boathouse. Now get in the boat. I'm tired and I want to go home, too."

As the motorboat cut across the open lake night was yielding to morning. And the biting pre-dawn air, fanned to a stinging wind by the speeding boat, chilled my damp and cold body to the marrow, despite the heavy blanket wrapped around me. When we reached the boathouse I asked the deputy who that man was. He appeared uncomfortable with my question and replied, "It's a long story, Byron. Go home."

"But I haven't a car. I'm staying at The Timberhaus where I work; it's several miles away. And I think I've caught pneumonia. Please drive me back," I asked weakly. I was as cold as a corpse and ready to collapse.

"How did you get here?"

"I bicycled."

"Grab your bike and stick it in here," he said as he opened the trunk of his police car. As we drove off, I again asked the deputy what he knew of the man he called Carter. Then he began to tell, albeit reluctantly, the depressing story of that wretched man:

"Carter Klugg was a thriving farmer and merchant once upon a time. He's one of the Old Dutch whose ancestors settled here three hundred years ago. Over the generations his family has operated textile mills and dairy farms, and at one time owned most of what is now Schoharie County. Klugg has a good education, too. He was married to a very fine lady. Charlene was a wonderful woman. The two were wed but a few years when an accident happened." The officer paused and shook his head sadly; then he continued: "She drowned twenty-five years ago. She drowned in Jewel Lake. Klugg has never recovered from his wife's death. He blames himself for it. He turned to alcohol, and now and then has bouts of delirium. But the old man is harmless."

"He's very possessive of that clot of land. Claims to be its sovereign, and accused me of invading his island and other such nonsense," I replied.

"Klugg saw you as an intruder. It was a solemn occasion that brought him there last night. He and Charlene often went to the islet. It was their personal getaway. And it was at that spot where she drowned. He often goes there and leaves flowers."

I felt miserable upon hearing this. Replaying in my mind was the sorry sight of the man on his knees crying and clinging to a bouquet of roses, and the echo of the harsh words I shouted at him. I said nothing more until we reached The Timberhaus, when I asked the deputy if he would convey my apology to Klugg for the pain I had caused him.

"Don't blame yourself, young man. Get some sleep, and stay warm," he replied with a yawn.

It was now five a.m. I went to the bunkhouse, got out of my wet clothes, and insulated myself in dry layers of clothing. Then I heated water to a boil, and sipped on it to thaw my body that was rigid with cold. Next, I wrapped myself in a musty blanket and fell asleep on the mattress. I slept straight until noon, despite efforts by others to rouse me throughout the morning. I got an earful from Papa for missing the breakfast shift, who would not listen to my explanation and accused me of having gotten drunk. And as punishment I was not given lunch. But one of the waitresses managed to sneak a couple of sandwiches to me, which was my first meal in twenty-four hours.

I thought about all that had occurred in the last day. It seemed impossible that so much could have happened within the span of two sunrises. At times I doubted it had happened at all—that it must be a dream in which, like De Quincey, I had lived one hundred years in a single night.

XVII

Whom the gods would destroy, they first make mad.
— Euripides

The closing years of the Sixties were a period of social upheaval, when morals were challenged and traditions mocked by many American youth. And it was a time when young people, bewildered by the rapid and astounding changes wrought by industry and technology, wanted to return to rural life. They turned to Thoreau as their archetype, and studied his 19th century essays on civil disobedience and nature to legitimize their beliefs and lifestyles. It was also during this time that the mystical message of drug gurus appealed to the malleable and restless minds of youth, eager to escape the ennui of everyday routine. The gurus deceived their followers by "intellectualizing" drugs. They lauded the potential of hallucinogens like LSD and mescaline, which they claimed could enlighten the mind and allow the individual to tap a higher consciousness that would elevate him to a Nietzsche-like "Overman," where man, not God, becomes creator and gives meaning to life. Drugs offered passage to a new realm removed from the perplexity of earthly existence. But within a few years the drug cult collapsed from its own excesses. Instead of bringing an earthly Nirvana to its followers it left in its wake destroyed lives, and in the case of Johannes, a schizophrenic mind.

Johannes was very tall, about four inches over six feet, and slender as a reed. He dressed in faded overalls and leather sandals, and had long, blond, disheveled hair and a beard like an Old Testament prophet. At age twenty four he was older than the rest of us, and lived as a semi-recluse in the wilderness. During the late Sixties he had attended Columbia University, when that campus was the epicenter of anti-war and social protests. Johannes had become active in student demonstrations, and was part of the avant-garde lifestyle popular at the time. He left Columbia after two years, and then immersed himself in the drug culture.

Johannes cultivated marijuana on a small plot tucked in the Catskill woodlands where he lived in a shack. There he also kept a drug lab where he concocted his pharmacopeia, which he sold to locals including Eric. He did not sell drugs to become wealthy; rather, he was on an apostolic mission to transform and illuminate people by manufacturing that which would poison them. He claimed to be a mystic, and had the transfixed look of a Delphic Oracle, not owing to any divine aura, but because his brain was toasted from hallucinogens. Yet he still retained remnants of the brilliance that had earned him entrance into a prestigious university. Even when his conversation turned random and senseless, he still spoke with an amazing flourish of imagery and conviction that captured the listener's ear.

Johannes came to The Timberhaus once a week to peddle his narcotics. On this rainy evening he was sitting on the bunkhouse floor, his long legs crisscrossed as he traded puffs on a marijuana cigarette with Eric, Bruce, Tom, and Nick, who were all gathered in a circle enshrouded in a fog of pungent smoke. I had just come in from the downpour and caught their conversation.

"The world will end before the close of this decade," said Johannes prophetically.

"Says who?" asked Tom.

"The Sanskrit texts of India. These ancient Hindu writings describe cataclysmic events that foretell the destruction of the world. These events are now occurring—war, pestilence, plague, drought, the atomic bomb…"

"How would those turban heads have known about the atomic bomb in ancient times," interrupted Tom.

"They didn't," replied Johannes.

"You just said they did!"

"Shut up you imbecile!" his voice bristling. "As I was saying," resumed Johannes in a calm tone, "our fate is unalterable; mankind is doomed."

"Who cares," slurred Bruce.

"I think it will be fascinating to witness our own destruction. To be here when the last chapter of man is written," said Nick.

"Wonderful, wonderful. I hope I live to see it," added Eric groggily.

Johannes proceeded with his discourse: "The earth will explode into billions of fragments which will disperse through the universe, and seed the barren moons and planets of other galaxies with life-building nutrients and carbon. Evolution will begin anew and mankind will be resurrected on different worlds. It was through this exact same process that we became the offspring of inter-stellar civilizations destroyed by similar cataclysms, which blasted minute organisms throughout the cosmos—like wind scattering seeds—fertilizing Earth, and procreating plants and beasts and man. Just as we are the children of extinct worlds, so are we the parents of future civilizations waiting to be born in distant galaxies."

"They won't have too long a wait since we'll all be blown to smithereens in a few years," remarked Eric.

Suddenly, the tenor of Johannes's talk shifted to an enigmatic and frightening soliloquy; it was as if a medium had taken hold of him and recited a warped version of Revelations: "I visited God in His empyrean palace. He wore a crown encrusted with stars plucked from the constellations, and from a ray of light he fashioned a sword and with it knighted me an archangel, while all the Hosts of Heaven broke into thunderous chorus that quaked the universe. Then, I reached into the abyss and snatched Lucifer from his evil warren and hurled him across the galaxies, and in his wake streaked a red comet a billion miles long. I have trekked the universe to the outermost nebulae, and with my own hands have molded stars from whirling gases. I have traveled twice the speed of light and smashed the prism of time, moving between past and future at will. I was inside that tiny ball of dense matter at the moment it exploded and whelped the universe, and I was there at the End as I watched the universe implode and return to that minute ball from which it was conceived."

Then he grew stone silent, as if the crazed spirit who had spoken through his body had now departed. Johannes was insane, and downright frightening. Not wanting to hear anymore of his lunacy, I went outside into the pouring rain and headed to the recreation hall.

XVIII

A horse, a horse! My kingdom for a horse!
— Shakespeare, "Richard the Third"

Guests typically arrived and departed on Saturday, and on this day at lunchtime new faces appeared at the dining tables. One Saturday four fresh faces were occupying a table in the corner of the dining room; four ladies in their mid-to-late teens. I thought it odd that they should come to The Timberhaus which caters mostly to young families, and not choose a getaway like the Jersey Shore or the Hamptons which are celebrated stomping grounds for girls their age.

The quartet of ladies was comprised of two pairs of sisters, evident by their resemblance. One pair had flame-red tresses and milk-white skin with freckles. The other pair had Mediterranean complexions and flowing, chestnut hair. The first time I serviced their table I felt very awkward. They stared at me as if I were a hydra-headed creature; I said nothing to them, and they spoke not a word to me. Over the next two days whenever I approached their table, the four damsels would stop talking and their faces grew solemn, as if I were a stern schoolmaster who had just caught them talking in class. I decided they were a sour lot, and I disliked them more every time I saw them.

The following Tuesday at mid-morning I was in the swimming pool, and after taking several vertical dives off the springboard I swam to the side of the pool to catch my breath, when I heard a voice say, "You're a good diver."

Using my hand to shade my eyes from the glare of the pool, I saw standing a few feet away the four young ladies whose table I had been tending in recent days; but whereas before they were distant and glum, their expressions were now friendly and sweet. "Thank you," I replied as I folded my arms across the rim of the pool. "Where are you visiting from?"

"We're Brooklyn girls," piped one of the red-haired ladies.

"Are you from this area?" It was the younger of the two olive-skinned girls who asked.

"I'm from Queens. Working here for the summer. How long are you gals staying?"

"Three weeks," they answered in unison.

I hoisted myself out of the water and sat on the apron of the pool. "Are you enjoying your stay?"

"We've been riding horses everyday," the elder redhead quipped.

"Twice a day," added her sister.

"I've been on a horse only once," I said as I stroked my foot through the water.

"Only once!" the girls exclaimed. They sounded as shocked as if I said I had never been kissed.

"I'm afraid of horses," I admitted.

"What is there to be afraid of?" asked the older red-haired girl, as she stepped to the edge of the pool and swished the surface with her toe.

"Horses are rambunctious. Like the one I rode a few years ago. When I wanted it to trot, it galloped. It lurched and kicked, and I'm certain it wanted to kill me. I was so traumatized that to this day I won't even ride on a merry-go-round."

"Busboy who is afraid of horses, what's your name?" asked the younger of the other sisters.

"Byron."

"I'm Carmen and this is my sister Monica," she replied. "And these are the Rogan girls, Diane and her kid-sister Tara."

Carmen was quite attractive. She was short with a pleasing form that boasted well-developed and shapely breasts. She was that category of female who physically matures from child to woman without pausing for adolescence. Monica was taller and had a very pretty face, highlighted with fine eyebrows and framed with long, silky hair. She impressed me as one having a serious nature, but with a reticence that was provocative and a subtlety that was striking. Sitting on a pool chair, she leaned forward with elbow planted on one knee and chin resting on her palm, staring at me through the windows of large oval eyes that never blinked.

The Rogan girls were not as good-looking as the other two. Tara looked like a cartoon character with her mop of curly hair and a pug nose, and a face so cluttered with freckles as to provide natural camouflage. Diane was a few inches taller, was less be-freckled, and had long and wavy hair.

The foursome told me they grew up and lived on the same block in the Bay Ridge section of Brooklyn. Carmen and Tara were both sixteen; Monica was twenty and in college; and nineteen-year-old Diane worked as a clerk for a Wall Street stock brokerage. The girls could not linger to talk further as they had to leave for their afternoon trail ride, but suggested I join them for a midnight ride that evening.

"Who would ride horses at midnight?" I asked, thinking they were joking.

"Barson Ranch has a trail ride tonight that starts at nine and returns at midnight," said Carmen.

"And it's only held during a full moon," rejoined Diane.

"It's great fun. And there is a bonfire," added Tara.

"Hmm, I don't think so."

"We'll cure your fear of horses," said Monica in a low, convincing voice.

As the girls walked from the pool area Diane shouted, "You'll miss a wonderful time, Byron."

I later thought about their invitation, and realized how foolish I was in declining it. Four young ladies had invited me on an outing, and I turned them down. I had exaggerated my fear of horses to them, though riding was a bit scary to me; but here was an opportunity for much needed fun and diversion. At dinner I told the girls I had reconsidered their offer, and would join them on their nocturnal excursion. They welcomed my change of mind, and at 8:30 we left for Barson Ranch in the car of another family who was also going on the trail ride.

Twenty people had turned out at Barson Ranch. It was a magical night with a full moon rising toward its zenith, bleaching the hills an oyster white. One of the wranglers spotted the rubber-sole shoes I was wearing and remarked, "You should be wearing boots. The horse won't feel your heel in its flanks. It will be like trying to drive a rubber nail with a hammer."

I told the wrangler I was inexperienced, and that I would like a horse that was not fast.

"Jethro," he called to the other wrangler, "bring out that three-legged stallion; this fella wants a slow horse."

I was mounted on a palfrey, a "ladies horse," which the wrangler assured me was manageable and had a good disposition. Diane gave me tips on using the reins, and warned me to stand in the stirrups when the horse galloped, or I would have sore buttocks for a week. When every rider was mounted awaiting commencement of the ride, one of the horses came alongside and pressed its hindquarter against the side of my palfrey, catching my left leg in a vise-like squeeze of horseflesh. I tugged the reins but my nag would not budge, and the rider of the other horse, who like myself was a novice, could not get her stallion unglued from mine. With my leg trapped I shouted for help, and the wrangler quickly moved in and grabbed my horse by its bridle, separating it from the other stallion. The rescue came not a moment too soon, for my leg was on the verge of being crushed.

"How's your leg, pardner?" the wrangler asked with surprising lack of emotion in his voice.

"Everything is numb below the knee," I answered, as I rubbed my leg to revive the circulation.

"Walk around a bit and test it."

I dismounted and took several paces. I felt like I had a wooden leg, but feeling quickly returned and I had no pain.

"Doesn't look like we'll have to amputate after all, pardner."

"I'm fine." And then I re-mounted.

Just before we exited the corral our guide Adam, a tall, bony man, told us to follow his lead and never let our horses get ahead of his. He assured us that the horses knew the trail by heart, and could negotiate their way blindfolded. "We'll ride for an hour, and then relax at a bonfire before returning here at midnight. And if we're late getting back we'll all turn into pumpkins," whereupon he belted out a loud laugh that caused several of the horses to whinny. "Let's head out!" he hollered.

The horses filed out of the corral, and sauntered along open ground for ten minutes. Diane rode behind me and the other girls in front of me, keeping close in case I ran into trouble. The trail turned into a grove of birches, swallowing each rider one by one into the darkness of the woods. After emerging from the thicket, the trail descended to a shallow stream where we paused to allow the horses to drink. Then we sauntered along the gravel margin of the stream, pebbles crunching beneath the weight of hooves, where the shower of moonlight turned the water into a milky iridescence. The horses proceeded onward at a solemn trot as if the pearly disk in the sky exerted over them a mysterious sway, that would make one pause to ask, "Could these beasts have intuition of a higher power?"

A half-mile ahead the stream fragmented into rivulets, where our guide led us up a low but steep embankment that connected to another trail. One by one each horse slowly approached the embankment, and then with a quick and powerful burst of energy surmounted the rampart with a near vertical leap. When my palfrey went atop I was thrust backward in my saddle losing grasp of the reins, and would have been thrown had I not grabbed the horn of the saddle with both hands. Sensing I had lost control, the horse asserted itself and broke into a gallop and raced ahead of the pack. But the horse had not carried me far when Diane galloped astride of me, grasped the dangling reins, and brought the insurgent horse to a halt.

Our party then entered a winding trail that led to a broad meadow. It was a magnificent and enchanting scene, for at the northern limits of the meadow lay a table-shaped mountain looming like a giant tabernacle, and above it hung the moon like a sacramental wafer that seemed to consecrate the meadow into hallowed ground. We headed in a northwesterly direction across the meadow, piercing a pine forest where the air was scented with menthol, and dappled moonlight carpeted the woodland floor. I felt as distant from civilization as one could get, until we passed from the forest curtain and came suddenly upon a two-lane highway.

Adam instructed all the riders to line their horses in single-file hugging the edge of the road. Then as he dug his spurs into the flanks of his stallion he raised a loud "yah," and his horse burst into a gallop with the other horses following suit. I was terrified during the first minutes of the gallop, having to throw complete confidence into the palfrey. But the horse negotiated the darkness as if it were daylight, and as it leaned in and out of curves with fluid agility my doubt yielded to trust, my adrenalin flowed, and excitement overtook fear.

Hedged by rising hills on one side and forest on the other which screened the moonlight, we galloped in pitch blackness along the road, with each horse barely clearing the overhanging boughs. I raised myself in my stirrups and tucked my head behind the neck of the horse, its mane whipping against my cheeks as it raced into a cold wind that caused my eyes to stream tears and numbed my knuckles. I felt the power of the horse as its hind muscles pumped like engine pistons, and its veins bulged from its muscular neck. I felt that the horse was not carrying me as a vehicle carries a passenger, but that I were a visceral part in generating the speed of the horse as if my limbs and the horse's were one. Further ahead the road was streaked with moonlight, and as the horses galloped through these alternating shafts of darkness and light they appeared to move in slow motion, similar to the effect created by a strobe light when its flickering stutters the sequence of movement.

After five minutes of steady gallop we slowed to a trot, allowing the steeds to replenish their lungs and I my nerves. We resumed galloping for several minutes, and then left the highway and entered a dirt trail that led into a grove, where a blazing bonfire was waiting for us. We tethered our horses to the trees and collected around the warm fire, with each face catching the red glow of the blaze. The flames cast distorted shadows across the ground, and the undulating firelight seemed to give sway to the trees.

The ranch owner, Ollie Barson, and his wife distributed bags of marshmallows among us, which we speared with twigs and roasted over the flames.

"Have you conquered your fear of horses?" It was Diane who spoke, as she knelt beside me and dipped her marshmallow into the fire.

"Somewhat. Now I just have to overcome my fear of the dark."

"Are you afraid of ghosts?" she asked, as she drew her marshmallow from the fire. It had ignited and was quickly turning into a black crust before she blew the flame out.

"I fear my nag will stumble in the dark and make a ghost of me before the night is over."

"In which case your horse will become a ghost too, and both of you will spook the night highways. You'll become as big a Catskill legend as the Headless Horseman."

"Quite so."

Just then Tara squeezed between me and Diane, as she awkwardly stuck her marshmallow-tipped stick into the flames. "Excuse me, Byron," she said impishly.

"Give it to me," said Diane brusquely as she snapped the stick from her sister's hand and fed the doomed marshmallow into the fire. Freckle-faced Tara gave me the mischievous look of a younger sister who had just upstaged her elder sibling. "Take it," said Diane, as she handed the stick of charred marshmallow to her intruding sister.

The Catskill nights are chilly, and the fluttering flames provided a cloak of warmth. Cold nights and a warm fire inspire ghoulish tales, and I entertained the four ladies with ludicrous ghost stories made up from the top of my head. There was neither rhyme nor reason to the tales, but the girls enjoyed them and as soon as I finished one story they begged to hear another.

I fashioned my characters after my listeners. One story was about an evil griffin, who flew above Brooklyn at night searching for teenage, red haired girls as well as those with long, brown hair. He would swoop down on them from the sky like a vulture, and carry them in his huge talons to his nest atop the Brooklyn Bridge where he would bite their backsides—at this part I pinched Carmen on the buttocks causing her to shriek—turning them into gargoyles. Then the terrible griffin deposited his victims on the roof pediments of public buildings throughout New York. But one day a handsome university student slew the griffin, which reversed the spell returning the gargoyles back into Brooklyn beauties, who rewarded their charming hero with hugs and kisses, and promised to iron his shirts and launder his clothes for the rest of his life.

Another tale I spun was about Papa, the evil Hermit of Deutschland, who sent Hilda the witch, a cleaning lady by day and sorceress at night, across the moonlit sky looking for boys and girls to steal and take to Papa's mountain cave, where they would be slaughtered and sold as pork sausages to Bavarian restaurants.

I was weaving another tale of nonsense when the wrangler cried: "Saddle up!"

"Well ladies, I'll continue this yarn on another night," I said.

We mounted our horses and sauntered from the grove to begin our ride back along the same route. Jets of vapor blew from the horses' nostrils as the temperature had fallen in the last hour, with the frosty air quickly snuffing our bodies of the insulating warmth of the bonfire. We galloped along the highway taking us back to the pine forest, where we threaded its narrow trails that took us to the meadow, and from there to the stream which now lay in darkness as the orbiting moon had dipped below the mountain ridges. The scene resembled Remington's *Night Ride* painting, whose images emerge from the darkness and remain partly obscured in shadow, as did our riding party as we trotted along the meandering waters.

We returned to the corral at the witching hour. The ride had jogged every bone in my body. I was sore all over and my legs were wish-boned from the saddle, and I ambled like a chimpanzee when I dismounted. On the car drive back to The Timberhaus, the Brooklyn girls pleaded with me to finish the story I started telling at the bonfire. I told them I was too tired, but promised that at another time I would spin a tale that would make their hair bristle.

"How pretty the moon is," remarked Diane who was sitting beside me. The full moon hovered low in the heavens directly ahead. It looked like a portal in the sky, to where the road we were driving on would give us passage to eternity.

"It makes me want to howl like a baying hound," I said in a voice affecting derangement.

"I just saw Hilda fly across the face of the moon on her broom," exclaimed Tara.

"She's after you," I warned.

When we got back to The Timberhaus the girls and I went to the recreation hall to wind down the evening with a round of sodas. I told them how I envied their having a bed to sleep in, and not having to rise early for work. I described the state of the bunkhouse, and they were shocked that such abominable conditions existed. We left the hall at one thirty. I was exhausted from work and riding, and as soon as I laid on my mattress I fell fast asleep, the only night I had ever slept soundly in the rat shack.

XIX

Spend your nights under the stars—
better to stare at constellations than a ceiling.
— R. Mangan

On the following night there was an uproar in the bunkhouse; Bruce and Tom had invited several rowdies over, and a drunken brawl broke out. Beer bottles were smashed, and from the clamor it sounded like everyone was trying to murder each other. Churchill, poor cat, was terrified and disoriented from the ruckus, and ran in circles before fleeing outside. Following this outburst I resolved never to return to that madhouse. But where would I go?

During my afternoon break the next day I went row-boating on the pond. I was locked in great anxiety and despair as I dwelt on my despicable living and working conditions. As the boat drifted I looked at my reflection on the water's surface, hoping it would call out an answer to my dilemma. My impression of the Catskills had forever changed; my fond childhood memories of this region had been erased by this horrible summer. The landscape, heretofore engaging and benevolent, was now a metaphor for imprisonment. The surrounding mountains were a fortress, its ridges were battlements, and the tall pines were sentry guards. Why was I remaining here? I was my own turnkey, and I could unlock myself and leave anytime. Was it warped pride that kept me shackled here, as if my loathsome situation was a worthy challenge? Was I performing an exercise in stupidity? What merit was there in remaining? What disgrace was there in fleeing? My mind was a maelstrom of confusion.

Common sense exhorted me to leave, but an inner voice counseled me to stay. In later years I would recall situations where that unknown voice would tell me not to abandon an effort, when it appeared acting to the contrary would be the more sensible thing to do. And in almost every case having stuck with my original plan and not tacking course turned out to be the wiser decision. And so, I decided to rely on my intuition—that subconscious seer—which sees things the eye does not, and discerns phenomena which the conscious mind can not.

I worked out my frustration and confusion by rowing vigorously across the pond several times until I was exhausted. Then I pulled in the oars and slumped in the boat to rest. Suddenly, as if Triton had rose above the water's surface and clunked me on the head with his conch shell, it dawned on me that this boat could be a bed—a "lit bateau"; for just as Napoleon slept in a bed designed as a boat, I could sleep in a boat fashioned as a bed. Eureka! I had been sitting on my answer all the time!

That evening when I got off work my four lady friends and I went to the recreation center, where a rock 'n roll band was playing. The dance hall was packed, and the mood was lively. We parked ourselves at a table in the corner, and kicked off the evening drinking sodas and Scotch whisky which made us giddy and loud, as none of us were used to drinking hard liquor. I had brought a bottle of Scotch, one of three bottles given to me by a guest a couple of weeks earlier who was a liquor wholesaler. They were a gratuity, as it is customary for guests on the final day of their stay to tip the busboys, and I intended to give the bottles to my father when I returned home. But Scotch is tempting and I quickly learned to tune my palate to its biting flavor. By summer's end only one bottle would survive for dad. As the pinewood floor vibrated from over two hundred dancers, and loud music was raising the rafters, the girls told me about their day, which was spent mostly with their backsides fastened to a saddle. And then I told them about my new sleeping quarters.

"What if you fall out of the rowboat and drown in your sleep?" asked Diane.

"I will pull it ashore each night."

"But will you be comfortable?" asked Monica.

"I will pad it."

"You will be cold," said Carmen.

"I will wear sweaters and a jacket."

"Have you a blanket?" asked Diane sympathetically.

"Just a threadbare rag from the bunkhouse."

"I have one you can borrow," she offered.

After knocking off a few drinks I danced with Diane and Monica; earlier Tara and Carmen had wandered off with friends. In the three days since I made acquaintance with these ladies we had developed a fast friendship, and I felt I had known them since boyhood. Diane was bubbly and talkative and scrambled her words when talking fast. For example, "I'm having a good time tonight" would come out as "I'm having a time good night." Other times she would finish her thought by saying, "Well, you know what I mean," which most times I did not. But Monica was quiet and mysterious. There was a secrecy about her that beckoned inquiry. Monica seldom laughed and was not outgoing, yet she was neither melancholy nor unfriendly. She had a pleasing physiognomy better suited for a serious pose than a smile.

"Byron, you're an entirely different person from whom we imagined you were," said Monica.

"What do you mean?"

"When you came to our table for the first time you looked like you were angry at the world," she replied.

"That's right, Byron," added Diane. "We were afraid to say a word to you. I said to Monica, 'what is it with this guy?'"

"You're kidding me!"

"Absolutely not," said Monica.

"I guess my expression was reflecting my lousy attitude, given hard work and terrible conditions. I wonder how many other guests I've alienated."

"Don't worry about it. Just put a smile on your face, and as you push your cart through the dining hall, think of it being filled with diamonds and not greasy plates," said Diane.

At nine o'clock I left the dance hall with the two ladies, and followed them to their cottage to get the blanket.

"This is not a guesthouse blanket," I said taken aback. It was a heavy Afghan knit of fine quality.

"I brought it from home," replied Diane.

"It's too fine a blanket; it will get spoiled if left out in the night." When I tried handing it back to her, she shoved it back in my arms.

"Take it. It will keep you warm," she insisted with a velvet voice that added affection to her gift.

"I'll take good care of it," I promised as I headed to the door.

"You forgot your whiskey," said Monica. I had left the bottle of Scotch, of which only a bit remained, on the bureau.

"Keep it. I've got more. And don't tell anyone where I will be sleeping. It's our secret, OK?" The ladies answered by placing a forefinger to their lips.

As I opened the door to step outside, Carmen and Tara sailed right past me and into the room.

"Where have you two juveniles been?" demanded Monica.

"Picking up men," answered Carmen, as she plopped on the bed and rolled on the mattress while hugging a pillow.

"I'll see you at breakfast," I said to the ladies through the screen door.

I returned to the bunkhouse and gathered some warm clothing, while Churchill lay on my mattress scrutinizing my every move as if sensing a change of sorts. "C'mon boy." I gestured to the cat to follow me, but as soon as we were outside he wandered into the darkness. I went to the pool and removed a six-foot long foam pad from a reclining chair, and headed to the pond. I untied the rowboat from its mooring, hauled it ashore, and then readied it for sleeping. Next, I lifted out the two slat-board seats which were loosely fastened and then cushioned the hull with the foam. It was not an uncomfortable bed, and the Afghan kept me warm.

The night pulsed with the chorus of crickets to the refrain of croaking frogs. I wondered if the cadence of these night sounds might have inspired our primitive forebears to develop the musical rhythm and harmony of what would become our diatonic scale. Could the origins of our great symphonies lie in the simple chants of earth's basic creatures? I had other creatures on my mind, too. Would I awaken in the night and find a copperhead snake coiled in the boat? Would bats swoop down and bite me? Would I find myself looking into the eyes of a bear? As I was preoccupied with these unsettling thoughts, something pounced on my chest. I screamed, causing the animal to screech and leap straight in the air, with its back arched and four legs stiff and vertical.

"Churchill!" I cried, as the frightened cat landed all fours on my chest, and then sprang out of the boat. "Come here, fella. Don't be afraid," I coaxed. He hopped in the boat and sprawled himself across my stomach. I stroked his coat affectionately, which still bristled from the fright he had received. With Churchill beside me I felt more secure and relaxed, and the heavy mountain air was having the effect of an elixir that quickly brought on drowsiness. Within a few minutes I was fast asleep.

I awoke at dawn just as the yellow rays of gentle sunlight spilled over the eastern peaks putting darkness to flight. My face was moist, and dewdrops on the grassy ground glistened in the morning light. The sparrows had begun their song, and were swooping down from branches in low-flying squadrons plucking worms from the ground. My first night in the terraqueous surroundings of land and water went well. I had slept only six hours, but I was refreshed and energized. I walked around the pond tossing pebbles into the water like a carefree boy, and then I collected my belongings from the boat including the foam padding, which I returned to the pool-side chair from where I had taken it. Next I headed to the bunkhouse to shower and change clothes. Afterwards, I returned to the pond and moored the boat, leaving no hint that I had ever slept in it. It was now approaching seven, and I went to the kitchen for breakfast.

XX

Till a garden with two hands; till a pond with two oars.

— R. Mangan

Debra was a young lady, no more than twenty, who helped Hildegarde with her cleaning. She was dim-witted and went about her day oblivious to others, rarely speaking to anyone. Debra did not board at The Timberhaus, but lived in the area year-round with her mother, who every morning drove her to the resort and later picked her up in the afternoon. Fennimore Cooper wrote that the Iroquois gave special status to those with dementia, believing they possessed clairvoyant gifts. Such was the impression Debra gave me: She had bright, royal-blue eyes, and a transfixed look as if she were gazing into a world not visible to mortal man. The left side of her face was slightly distorted bearing the signs of a paralysis. And were it not for that one tragic moment gone wrong at childbirth that would forever impair her features and faculties, Debra would be a woman of fine looks and intelligence. Some days she enjoyed reasonable clarity, and would flash a crooked grin and say hello to me; other days she did not know me.

After finishing the lunch shift I often went to the recreation hall to relax for a bit, where it was cool and at that time of the day empty. On this one afternoon Debra was inside dutifully sweeping the aisles with a whisk broom. When she came to where I was sitting, she set her broom aside and sat on a bench across from me.

"Rest time," she said, exhaling an upward puff of air that ruffled her forelocks. A smile lit the right side of her face, which her palsy reduced to a wry expression on her left side. She looked at me with her piercing eyes, and then her gaze drifted to a distant point in the room.

"You have a lot work to do," I said.

As if awakened from a reverie, she quickly shifted her focus back to me. "Yes, lots of work," she said proudly.

"Your name is Debra, isn't it?"

"Yes, yes, Debra is my name," she replied bashfully as she drooped her head.

"It's nice to meet you, Debra. My name is Byron."

She looked up and stared at me. Her smile disappeared, and her eyes wandered for a few seconds. Then her attention snapped into place, and her distorted smile reappeared. "Uh, oh. Time to go back to work." Then she grabbed her broom and resumed sweeping.

"Goodbye, Debra."

"Goodbye," she answered, barely above a whisper.

Just then Fred entered the hall and went to the vending machine for a soda. As he was drinking from the can he walked in the direction of where I was sitting, but when he recognized me he froze in his tracks. He looked awkwardly around, and then turned and left the building. Good riddance, Fred.

That afternoon I went rowing. It is excellent therapy for psyche and soma, for plowing the water with oars not only strengthens the muscles, but the repetitive stroking acts as a mantra and relaxes the mind. "Mens sana in corpore sano"—a healthy mind in a healthy body. My rowing technique was rapidly improving, too. When I first put oar to water during my first week at The Timberhaus, I could not pilot the vessel at all. When I wanted to steer it right, it veered left; and when I wanted to turn left it moved right. Other times, I found myself zigzagging like an out-of-control kite. The boat was like a stubborn child doing the exact opposite of what it was told. So, I figured that the trick to get the moody craft to move in the desired direction was to steer it in the opposite direction.

I rowed vigorously for twenty minutes, and then I brought the boat to rest in the shade beneath the sagging boughs of a weeping willow where I opened a book. I had been reading a short time when I heard the tread of feet behind me. Turning my head, I saw

Debra passing through the chartreuse veil of drooping branches. She approached the rowboat and looked at me with wide, bright eyes.

"Hi," she said timidly. Then she knelt at the water's edge and gazed across the pond.

I set aside my book, and turned around in the boat to face her. "How are you Debra?"

"I saw you rowing," she answered.

"It's good exercise."

"Yes, good exercise." Then she added in a delicate voice: "I like boats. My father used to take me rowing."

"And does he still?"

A crestfallen expression swept across her face. "Daddy's in Heaven," she answered in fading words.

My question had upset her, so to offer amends I asked: "Would you like to cruise around the pond?"

"Yes," she replied eagerly, instantly forgetting her grief.

I maneuvered the boat flush to the rim of the pond, and stabilized it by planting an oar into the water's shallow bottom. "Be careful getting in," I cautioned. As she stepped into the boat she lost her footing and pitched backward, but I grabbed her arm and she recovered her balance.

"Wow, that was close," she said excitedly as she sat down on the cross plank.

I pushed off on an oar, and in a moment we were gliding across the pond.

"It's a pretty day," she remarked.

"Yes, but very warm and humid," I said as I plied the oars to the water.

"Yes, very warm," she repeated.

Debra amused herself like a little girl, scooping water from the surface and tossing it into the air, each time shouting "Splash, splash!" But when she accidentally doused my face with water, she became very disconcerted and her eyes welled.

"I'm sorry! I'm sorry!" she pleaded apologetically.

"I'm all right, splash all you want Debra."

"No, better not splash anymore," she said contritely. Then she drifted into her private world, and began singing "la-de-la, la-de-do."

"Look!" she cried. She spotted something in the water. It was a frog swimming at a rapid clip beneath the surface keeping pace with the boat.

"Do you like frogs?"

"They're ugly," she grimaced, wrapping her arms around her shoulders in revulsion.

After circling the pond I steered the boat back to dry land, when a dolorous look came over Debra. "All over?" she pouted.

"Do you want to go 'round again?"

"Yes! 'Round again! 'Round again!"

So we circumnavigated the pond a second time which made her happy and me tired, because I had been rowing earlier and my arms were a lead weight.

"Did you enjoy the voyage, Debra?" I asked, as the boat drifted to a stop.

"Yes, yes. I had fun!" she answered sprightly. I expected her to alight, but she made no attempt to leave the boat. Her expression grew serious once again, and she stared at me with frightened eyes.

"Is something the matter?" I asked gently.

"I must go," she replied as her voice trailed off. Stepping out of the boat, she walked several paces when she turned around, and shifting abruptly from her blues said cheerfully, "Thank you, Byron." Her eyes shone bright, and a smile was etched across her crooked visage. Then she darted through the hanging willows and raced up the knoll, disappearing over the other side.

I dwelt on Debra for the rest of the afternoon. When we rowed on the pond, I sensed in the girl's distant look her recalling memories when she and her father had enjoyed afternoons of rowing and singing. She had escaped to happier times, but when our short cruise ended she awakened to the melancholy of the present. Her mild retardation was probably a greater misfortune to her than if her malady were more severe, because she suffered the anguish of straddling the realms of disorientation and normalcy. When she snapped out of her dream world, her dull eyes would sharpen to electric blue and her stare would gain a focused look. But normality was fleeting; her cognition would soon dissemble, and I could see her sadness and frustration as she struggled to keep from slipping into the hinterlands of mentality. Debra held a mirror to any one of us who would take for granted the priceless value of his basic gifts and talents. I thought of Johannes spiraling downward into insanity by poisoning his great intellect. Why, I wondered, would wise Providence bestow brilliance on one who squanders it, while denying it to another who would make use of it?

XXI

Many think much is new, because they never knew what is old.
— Fulton Sheen

The stream that wends along the southern fringe of The Timberhaus is a shallow brook having its source in the western hills, where it weaves through sloping woodlands that are sheltered in shade, leaving the ground moist and spongy with lush vegetation.

The stream is an enchanting watercourse, with surroundings that fashion a natural cathedral lending it a monastic tranquility. Columns of robust maples flank the creek, and their interlocking canopies form a vaulted roof arching above a streambed of smooth, colored stones like a terrazzo floor in a church. A gentle breeze becomes the sigh of an organ, and the filtered sunlight of midday imbues this scene with a lemon radiance, instilling an ethereal aspect to the woods. It was Wednesday, the day following my chat with Debra and my Sabbath from work, when driven by a spirit of curiosity I hiked upstream deep into the foothills.

After walking for some twenty minutes in ankle-deep water, the stream appeared not to lead anywhere and I was ready to turn back. But curious to see what lay beyond a bend just ahead, I followed the curvature which broke into a colorful meadow. I felt like a knight errant of medieval legend, who stumbled upon a land of enchantment. The meadow was a patchwork of wildflowers quilted with crocuses of orange and Tyrian purple, with the finely scented air woven into its skein. The high humidity emitted a haziness giving the surroundings a grainy effect like a photogravure picture, whose aesthetics are enhanced by its very lack of crispness. As I wandered further into the meadow, I spotted a cottage partially hidden within a copse of poplars. It was brightly painted with fruity colors of tangerine and lime, set off by a chocolate-brown trim that reminded me of a cookie house one sees in bakery windows.

I walked toward this curious-looking house, and was within one hundred yards of it when a Doberman pinscher rushed from the rear of the cottage, and raced toward me with the ferocity of a lion. I was so frightened that my heart pumped like a piston. I was in open space and had no escape from the beast. I ran like a man with four legs, but the dog ran like it had eight and closed in on me rapidly. My only chance of eluding it was to reach the woods where I might lose him, but would I get there before he tore me to shreds? I felt like a swimmer trying to out-swim a pursuing shark. He was now within a few lengths of me, and from over my shoulder I saw his large, gaping jaw dripping with saliva. Suddenly, a loud whistle cut the air; the dog stopped in its tracks, turned on its hind legs, and raced back to the house as if pulled by invisible strings.

I was ready to collapse. Though I had not run far, I had raced at top speed, which coupled with the terror of being ripped apart left me completely exhausted. Had I been chased by a grizzly bear I would have been no less terrified. My chest heaved as I gasped for breath, and my knees had turned to rubber.

Then I heard a man's voice cry: "Antigonous! Antigonous!" A man in denim overalls was standing at the front door of the cottage calling the dog. The Doberman came to rest at the feet of the man who knelt on one knee and patted it. "What's got into you Antigonous?" I heard him say. "That's no way to treat a visitor."

I wondered how could he pat such an animal; I would sooner caress an alligator. The man rose to his feet and called out to me: "Halloo! I'm very sorry about all of this." I did not have the breath to reply. But reassured by the man's apparent mastery over the dog, I walked slowly toward the house. The cottage had a storybook aura, and I was curious who he was that lived here, shut off from the world in a meadow that was hemmed by mountain forest and no road leading to it.

"Was I trespassing?" I asked, as I reached the foot of the porch. The Doberman was beside its master squatted on its haunches panting, with its long tongue unscrolled from its cavernous jaw.

"Not at all. Very sorry about the welcome you received. You need not have fled; Antigonous would not have hurt you, would you brave warrior," he said as he stroked the canine's head. "But he does scare strangers."

I noticed that the dog's left socket was missing an eye. "A one-eyed dog," I said thinking aloud.

"Yes, hence its name. Antigonous of Macedonia was a one-eyed general. By the way my name is Horace," he said extending his hand. I told him mine as we exchanged a firm handshake.

"I like your house," I said as I swept an admiring look across its colorful façade. "I was surprised to stumble upon this meadow, much less find a house on it."

"Bought the house from the Hun two years ago."

"The Hun?"

"Yes, Herr Papa, the little German who owns The Timberhaus."

"I work there."

"It was a rundown shack when I bought it, but I spruced it up inside and out."

"It's gingerbread," I replied.

"Did you say you work at The Timberhaus? Mein Gott! I hear the old man is a slave master."

"We work hard," I replied in a tone of understatement.

I reckoned Horace was in his forties, though his age was hard to pin because most of his face was curtained beneath a mop of chestnut hair and a bushy beard and mustache. But through his shaggy covering there shone intelligent eyes, and his reference to the Macedonian commander hinted of an educated mind.

"By the way, I had poured a cold beer for myself just before Antigonous ran out to welcome you, and its waiting for me in the kitchen. You look like you could use one, too."

I readily accepted and followed him inside. With Horace merely clicking his fingers, the pinscher immediately left the porch and returned to the rear of the house. "You have an obedient dog," I remarked.

"I've trained the General well," he replied.

Upon entering the house we stepped into a living room lined

with books from floor to ceiling, and where a mahogany desk stacked with papers was tucked in an alcove that looked out on the meadow through a bay window. In the kitchen Horace took a gulp from the mug of beer that lay on the table. "Ah, still cold," he said as he licked the froth from the edges of his mustache. Then he took a beer from the refrigerator, uncapped the bottle, and handed it to me. On the table was a worn paperback of Hazlitt's essays turned face-down on the page where the reader left off.

"I'm not interrupting your reading, am I?" I inquired nodding at the book.

"Not at all. I was just paging through my old friend William."

"You have an impressive library," I said as we stepped into the living room. Indeed, the entire house was a library. Even the kitchen was rimmed with a wall shelf snug with volumes. And the hallway leading to the rear of the house was dressed with bookshelves, punctuated here and there by wall frames of historical prints. There was the famous photograph of Roosevelt and Churchill meeting at Yalta, and Matthew Brady photos of Civil War battlefields.

"This little house is the seat of culture for the entire county," Horace joked.

"If not all the Catskills," I rejoined.

"Have a look around," he said with a proud flourish of his hand.

I have always enjoyed being around books, not only to read, but to admire as objects of art in themselves. Open a book and smell its pages: The ink of a newly minted volume may recall that first storybook given you as a child for Christmas. Or the musty aroma of an old leather-bound tome suddenly dissolves the present and revives the past, when you rummaged through boxes in the attic and discovered one of your parents' schoolbooks. Just as some people wander the halls of museums admiring paintings and sculptures, I have often amused myself exploring the aisles of Manhattan's bookstores, where time is suspended as the mind is pleasantly distracted by pictorials, verses of poetry, medieval histories, etc.

Every prominent writer of every literary genre over the last two-and-a-half millennia was represented on Horace's shelves: The epics of Homer, the myths of Ovid, the tragedies of Sophocles, the essays of Pascal, the biographies of Plutarch, Norse sagas, French romances, tracts of Aquinas, treatises of Hume, the novels of Defoe and Hardy; Zola and Flaubert; Conrad and Kipling.

"Literature is our dialogue to the past," commented my host as I passed along the shelves scanning the titles on the spines of the books.

"What do you mean?" I asked, a bit distracted as my eye lingered on a title.

"Novelists are as much a medium of history as historians. You can learn much of class struggle by reading Dickens, and experience the revolutions that wracked 19th century France in the novels of Hugo and Balzac. As regards history, school children today are taught it from an anachronistic view."

"How so?"

"Our present history books are scripted by historians using mirrors, who look back and interpret the past. But when we read history written by those who never witnessed it, it's like learning history through a prism where fact is broken up and refracted. Furthermore, Byron, historical accuracy becomes diluted with personal opinion as it is channeled from one generation to the next. The key to understanding history is by reading first-hand accounts, that allow us to grasp the psyche of the recorded era.

"That book that you are holding, for example. (It was *The Histories* by Tacitus.) In the first century Tacitus wrote an accurate and inspiring account of the bitter turbulence within the Roman Empire, marked by three civil wars and four emperors who died violently. He lived during that period, and wrote as one who was familiar with the nature of the Roman people, and knew how the ancient mind worked. The past is best understood by reading the works of those who were part of the events they wrote about, such as Xenophon and his Greek military campaigns and Joinville's narrative of the Third Crusade. They are the windows to the past. It is one thing to read about Julius Caesar written two thousand years after his reign, but to appreciate the man and his time you must read his *Commentaries*, and journey with him in *The Conquest of Gaul*." Horace paused, dropped his eyes on the floor as if to gather new thoughts, and then raised his head. "The sign of a good historian is one who informs people that much of what they think is novelty is actually quite old."

"In other words, there's nothing new under the sun."

"Exactly. And too often, historians point out the 'wrongs' of past civilizations, without putting those times into proper context. As an example, let's return to the Crusades, which have been portrayed as an attempt by Christians to ruthlessly crush Islam. When Pope Urban II issued a call to arms against the followers of Mohammed in 1095, it was not a knee-jerk reaction to the Muslims conquering Jerusalem and taking over Christian holy sites. Rather, it was to check the resurgence of Islamic militancy that could spread to Europe. And such a fear was not unfounded. In the eighth century Arabs and Berbers from North Africa invaded Spain, bringing most of the Iberian peninsula and portions of France under Muslim rule.

"It's easy to look at the atrocities of past centuries and say people were evil. We judge the past unfairly by measuring it against present day standards; we have to judge the past by the ideals and mores that were in place at that time. We ask ourselves: How could a society have ever tolerated slavery as recently as the 19th century? But as late as the 19th century an Englishman could be plucked from the streets of London and impressed into the Royal Navy, and children in Great Britain were legally hung for picking pockets. And through the 20th century Hindu society had a caste system where a class of people were deemed lower than cattle. Indeed, less than a hundred years ago Americans worked eighty-hour weeks with one day off a month. From our present perspective of a forty-hour work week, with paid vacations and retirement benefits, it's incomprehensible that such human servitude could have ever existed. Charles Dickens and Jack London experienced those hellish times and wrote about them. When even a free man lived as a peon, there was a thin line separating so-called 'freedom' from slavery. But to marginalize the contributions of earlier epochs on the sole basis of its denying liberties to a segment of its people is to manipulate history into a propaganda tool. Indeed, I hear more of George Washington being referred to as a Virginia slave owner rather than our greatest hero.

"In a way history writes itself. Scholars merely chronicle events to explain cause and effect, which raises the question: Does man forge history, or does history use man to carry out its design? I am not in complete agreement when Voltaire said that man can shape history and not be dictated by it. But it seems history has the ultimate say in the outcome of events, evidenced by the apparently little leverage man has had in sculpting it. Is it on his own initiative that man invents, builds, destroys with war, and resurrects through peace? Or, is he induced by the same Unseen Mechanism that steers the comets through the heavens, and guides the planets in their course; and which orchestrates the rhythm of ocean waves, and fashions other events that are interpreted to us through history. Perhaps I'm sounding biblical, but history appoints the time when kingdoms shall rise and fall; when men shall wear shackles, and when men shall be free; when plague will strike, and when prosperity will reign. And in its own inexplicable way it can turn tragedy into good."

I paused a few moments to reflect on the brilliant commentary I had just heard, before confessing: "I find myself confronted by a polemical issue for which my modest faculties are not equipped to argue." Then I asked: "Have you read all these books?" Using dead reckoning I guessed 2,000 volumes were in his house.

"Of course, do you think they are here to insulate the walls?" He sounded offended by my question.

"What is your occupation?" I inquired.

"Formerly a professor of Latin and classics, and now a struggling writer."

"Where did you teach?"

"At the University of Rochester. I taught there fifteen years. They were the grandest years of my life." Then in a sunken voice he added: "I lost my post five years ago. It's been five years since I lectured on Virgil and Juvenal; five years since I've been called 'professor,' and as many years trying to get settled as a writer. I was a victim of a growing intellectual apathy that is pandemic in academia. Each year fewer students were studying humanities. They could not give a jot for the language and literature of Rome and Greece; it has reached the point where few students can even read Roman numerals on a sundial. Society will regret it. I tell you society will regret it! When Rome and Greece moved away from the arts and humanities, their civilization collapsed into a charnel house. We're headed for the Dark Ages young man," he said, shaking a foreboding finger at me.

"Do you think so?"

"Absolutely!" he exclaimed, throwing up his arms in frustration.

"I will be one person not responsible for civilization's collapse."

"What do you mean?"

"I'm a humanities major, but after graduation I'll likely beeline to the business world."

"Another student with his mouth on the teats of the golden calf," he sighed. "Roman patricians frowned upon men of commerce. They considered it obscene to actively pursue money-making."

"That's fine when you are born into a class that lives in villas with servants doing all your toil, not to mention having front row seats at the Coliseum," I retorted.

"I suppose there is some truth in that."

"Have you sought teaching positions at other universities?"

"Have applied to over two hundred colleges and universities, but no offers. A scholar of Latin and classics is as obsolete as a blacksmith. Mostly I support myself doing translations for the antiquities departments of museums and universities—when I can get the work, that is. And I blame the Church for my lack of occupation," he said with a tinge of bitterness.

"The Church?"

"Quite so. When the Vatican did away with the Latin Mass, it sealed the fate of that noble language. Priests no longer had to study Latin, and other professions followed suit. Doctors no longer wrote prescriptions in Latin; ergo, pharmacists no longer had to read Latin; law schools dropped Latin from their curricula, and so on and so forth. And when the day comes that the Cistercians stop chanting hymns in Latin, the beautiful language will die completely. 'Requiescat in pace,' gallant tongue. I suspect the angels no longer converse in Latin either," he added under his breath. "But as a personal tribute to the language of the Caesars I have arranged to have my headstone epitaph inscribed in Latin, albeit a simple phrase commemorating my simple life, so that in death I will have done my small part to keep Latin extant."

"You mentioned that you write?"

"In my spare time. It has been difficult trying to get settled in another career. You see, I had been an academic all my professional life. I have no skills that would recommend me for a career in business, and as far as manual labor I am not good with my hands and I have no mechanical ability. Had I lived 2,000 years ago I could have tutored Roman aristocracy, but in these present times I am a worthless commodity. But I am very excited about a collection of essays I am writing, and which I hope to have published someday. They have a classical style modeled on the letters of Seneca, whose brilliant writings were inspired by the severity of his times and personal misfortune."

Horace paused to take a gulp of beer, then quickly placed the back of his hand against his mouth to muffle a burp. He continued by saying: "When I taught at the university I expected to chair the classics department some day; indeed, Dean Chillingsworth, a fine scholar and antiquarian, had anointed me his successor. I saw myself becoming a provost, and maybe president of the university. But my dreams came tumbling down like the Walls of Jericho. I suppose there is a reason for everything happening as it does. Perhaps my essays will earn me posterity that teaching never would. Problem is I'll be long dead when the accolades start arriving. Have another beer?" Horace asked, when I drained the last drop from my bottle.

"No thank you."

My host swallowed the rest of his beer, and placed the empty mug aside. "Ah, that was good," he said with satisfaction. "Come, let me show you around the property."

I followed him through the book-lined hallway, passing a small book-lined bedroom and into a screened porch, and then out the back door which opened into a vegetable garden of squash, potato, lettuce, and cauliflower. Next to the furrowed garden was a small hothouse where hydroponic tomatoes grew.

"I sell my produce to local groceries," he said.

Beyond the garden lay a small vineyard, where I was surprised to see grapevines growing in the rocky soil. "I thought vines required fertile soil and a Mediterranean climate."

"Vines are quite adaptable and can thrive on terrain where little else can grow," he answered. "Let me show you the winery."

On the edge of the vineyard was a dilapidated wood barn. When Horace unlatched the door a strong smell of yeast burst upon me. Inside was a small winepress for crushing grapes, a fermentation tank, and several oaken casks where wine was aging. He dipped a fingertip into the fermentation tank, and licked the plum-colored liquid. "Still too sugary," he mumbled. "I started this little operation as a hobby, but I think it might turn into a profitable enterprise," he said proudly. "Last year was my first vintage," he added, as he removed a wine bottle from a shelf, uncorked it, and poured a couple of ounces into a glass. "Have a taste."

I took the glass from him and cautiously tasted the wine, believing anything concocted in this shack would taste like vinegar. But I was surprised by its pleasing flavor. "Not bad at all," I said.

"Its secret is the barn," he whispered, as if revealing a trade secret.

"The barn?"

"Yes, as the wine ferments it captures the mustiness of this old barn. And I age it in wood casks, where the wine 'breathes' better than if it were stored in steel containers used by most wineries nowadays. This is a true homemade wine. In fact, I'm labeling it Horace's Homemade Cabernet. Right now, I'm trying to market it as a table wine through a regional distributor."

I complimented Horace on his entrepreneurial spirit. "Contrary to what you've told me, it seems that you're making a successful transition from academia, and you certainly have more skills than what you give yourself credit for."

"Those are kind words, but everything you see here is still a small operation, and whether I shall define myself as a winemaker, farmer, writer, or whatever else, only time will tell. The future does scare me, I confess."

Before leaving the winery Horace presented me with the bottle as a gift. "Do you think if a monk were pictured on the label it might help my wine sales?" he asked.

I told him he should give it a try. He invited me to visit any time I wanted. As he escorted me from his property, the one-eyed Doberman ran up to us from out of the blue. "Good-bye Cyclops," I said to the dog as it came to rest beside its master.

"Antigonous, his name is Antigonous," Horace quickly corrected.

"Oh yes. I'm quite sorry," I said slapping my forehead, as I recalled the pinscher was named after some single-eyed fellow, but could not quite summon the name. In a gesture of goodwill I thought of patting the animal, but I checked myself when it dropped its huge jaw and displayed a mouth lined with razor canines. "The ugly beast could rip my arm off at the shoulder," I thought. Then I shook hands with Horace, thanked him for his hospitality, and bid him adieu. With wine bottle in hand I walked across the meadow, glancing over my shoulder now and then to assure myself that Antigonous was not following me. Then I entered the woods and headed back to The Timberhaus by the same way I had come.

Just before retiring that night it started to rain, so I decided to stay in the bunkhouse rather than sleep in the boat. But as the night progressed I became violently ill. I could not work next day and would have been fired had not Nick, who had witnessed my condition, vouched for my miserable state to Papa. That morning someone entered the stall where I lay, but the image was blurry as my head was throbbing, and my eyes weak from a restless night.

"Go away," I said in a feeble voice.

"Bryon!"

"Papa?" I answered weakly, as I squinted my eyes to gain focus.

The old man winced when he saw me. I must have looked like a newly-minted corpse. He stood solemnly at the foot of the mattress as I peered back with hollow, owl eyes over the bed sheet, that was pulled up to my chin like a shroud.

"What's happened to you?"

"Food poisoning," I replied.

"Nonsense!" He voided my excuse with a wave of his hand,

and turned his head away with disgust. "You have been drinking. Do you need doctor?"

"I just need sleep," I groaned.

"Then get your sleep, because you have a hard day's work to answer for tomorrow!"

That was Papa's way of conveying the good news that I would still have my job next day. Indeed, it was not food, but wine that poisoned my system—Horace's wine! Had he given me a bottle of pure arsenic I would have fared no worse. He had concocted a veritable witch's brew that he passed off as wine. As sick as I was, I willed myself to recover out of sheer desire to seek revenge against that madman. The night before I had drunk a glass of Horace's Homemade Cabernet, which tasted as good as the wine I sampled at his place earlier in the day. I imbibed slowly and had no adverse reaction to the wine at first; my body warmed slightly, and I enjoyed a tipsy feeling. Then I laid on the mattress, looking forward to a restful sleep under the relaxing influence of the cabernet. But ten minutes later I experienced a dreadful reaction. I felt a burning heat rise slowly from my lower body like mercury rising in a thermometer, that reached to the crown of my head. My face felt like it was on fire, and my body was as hot as a searing poker. Then the intense heat dissipated, only to re-kindle itself a short time later, and spread through my body with the same fury as before.

Next I fell into convulsive retching, followed by severe muscle spasms that caused me to contort and contract like a fish out of water. As I writhed in pain and suffered oscillating states of feverish heat and cold sweats, I thought I would either die or undergo a hideous metamorphosis like Dr Jekyll into Mr Hyde. Then the room began rotating slowly like a carousel, and then spun faster and faster until everything was a blur, and I felt myself being sucked into a whirling vortex of blackness. What I remembered next was my shoulders being shaken by a pair of hands trying to rouse me from my sleep. It was morning, and Nick had come to check on me after I failed to show up for kitchen duty. After describing my ailment to him, he informed Papa I was unable to get out of bed, who immediately investigated the state of my health.

XXII

Gunther could be best described as an unfinished product of nature. He was an eccentric thirty-year-old bachelor, who lived in a state of perpetual disorientation. He was unlike his father in every respect: Papa was active and assertive, Gunther was passive and lethargic; the elder was short and round, junior was medium height and thin; Papa had a shiny pate, Gunther had a crop of hair—to mention but a few of their contrasts. Most assumed that Gunther's twilight appearance was due to his drinking. It was not. Though he liked his bourbon, Gunther was just plain dull-witted. It was Gunther's good fortune to be born into a family business because he would always have a job, however menial; otherwise, he would never be able to support himself.

Gunther conducted the daily hay ride. At two o'clock each afternoon he drove a dilapidated 1940s truck up to the front of the commons. A dozen or so children would pile into the truck's flat bed, that was filled with hay and enclosed with high, wood-slat panels. Then Gunther would start the truck and, putting it in gear, it would jerk backward and then pitch forward. The truck always tilted precariously, like a storm-battered ship about to founder. Gunther drove recklessly and with as little caution as if he were transporting a dozen of Papa's pigs instead of children. Just before coming to the county road at the entrance to the resort, Gunther would abruptly turn off and drive helter-skelter across the pasture, leaving in his wake clouds of dust and the screams of terrified kids, punctuated by gunshot sounds of an engine backfiring.

During the twenty-minute ride children were bounced about on the bed of the truck, as Gunther thundered across dales and streams and woods. The ride ended at the commons where it began, with Gunther bringing the old truck to a screeching halt that pitched the children to the fore in a tangled heap. Then Gunther would detach one of the wood panels, and the children would tumble out—some laughing, some dizzy, some vomiting, and always covered with straw.

"We're going on a hay ride this afternoon," Tara said that morning at breakfast as I was removing a couple of empty plates from the girls' table.

"Gunther's hayride?" I asked incredulously.

"Yes."

"You're crazy."

"Why?" asked Carmen, who was dabbing her sausages with a fork.

"Gunther drives like a demon."

"That's what makes it fun," rejoined Monica.

"Come with us," insisted Diane.

"I would as soon be shot out of a cannon."

"Add some excitement to your life, busboy. You only live once," teased Diane.

"I choose to protect my one life as much as possible."

"You're a coward," added Tara.

"Cowards last longer. Besides, Gunther's truck should have been made into scrap years ago. It looks like something that hit a landmine during the Second World War."

"We won't have fun without you," Diane moaned, as I placed her empty juice glass and cereal bowl in the tray cart.

"Those are kind words Miss Rogan. But my advice to you fair maidens is to draft your wills before you embark on your next adventure." Then I wheeled my cart to the next table, where the couple seated there was signaling me to remove their empty bowls, as the waitress was waiting impatiently to serve their plates of ham and eggs.

It is those very things which I am resolute in not doing that I later change my mind, as if my resolve cracks under the strain of its own intensity. On the same day that I swore I would never mount a horse again, I was in the saddle that night. And so I changed my mind about the hayride.

Later that morning I went into the office to pick up my paycheck. "Guten morgen, Fraulein Heidi."

"Guten morgen, Herr Byron. How is it you are always the first to arrive for your check?" she asked, as she was feeding a sheet of paper into the typewriter.

"The more needy, the more greedy," I replied. Just then Gunther entered the office. "Hello Gunther."

He stared at me with a foggy look, expecting me to say something else. "Oh, hello…hello," he replied, when his tiny brain registered that I was merely greeting him. Then he sat at one of the desks and began typing very slowly with two index fingers.

"Here you are," said Heidi, handing me a check across the counter. "And sign your name here acknowledging you received it," pointing to a line in the account book.

As I was about to leave the notion struck me to ask Gunther: "Is it possible I might go on this afternoon's hayride?"

He looked up from the typewriter, pushing his glasses up the bridge of his nose. "Well…Papa usually doesn't allow employees," he said hesitantly. "Heidi, how many have signed up for this afternoon?"

"Nine."

"There is enough room for you," he said.

"Thanks Gunther!" Then I clicked my fingers, wheeled around on my heel, and went out the door.

"I don't believe what I'm seeing!" exclaimed Diane, when I surprised all by climbing into the rear bed of the truck. She, Tara, Carmen, and Monica were among the several riders settled snug into the pile of hay.

"It is not without trepidation that I undertake this venture," I replied as I shoe-horned myself between Monica and Diane. Indeed, as Gunther was setting the rear upright into place, I felt like a passenger watching the door close on an airplane that was missing one of its engines.

"You'll love it," Tara assured me as she tossed a tuft of straw in my face.

"The experience will be something to tell my grandchildren—if I survive."

The engine started, and the truck recoiled as Gunther shifted gears; a moment later the jalopy lunged forward and trundled along the gravel drive. The truck was so lopsided that I had to grasp the sideboards to prevent myself from rolling. Just before reaching the junction where the gravel drive meets the public road, Gunther swerved the truck sharply to the right. The truck teetered perilously, but managed to stay on its four wheels. Meanwhile, I had tumbled end-over-end slamming into the sideboards, where I wound up with my legs twisted backward like a yogi in meditation. I felt something move beneath me. A hand, followed by an arm, surfaced from the straw. Then I heard a muffled cry from Tara: "You're crushing me."

Suddenly the truck took a hard bounce, hurling me across the flat bed and headfirst at Carmen, who averted collision by quickly parting her legs allowing me to dive beneath her where I became buried in hay. But I could not free myself because Carmen was now sitting on top of me, and the rascal refused to budge despite my pleas. Suddenly, the truck veered and she slid off my back, and I emerged with a wad of straw hanging from my mouth. The truck gathered speed and rumbled across the pasture, tossing everyone about like leaves in a windstorm, as Gunther swerved left and right purposely hitting every bump. It was like being on an insane carnival ride, where the sheer terror inspires thrills and laughter. At first I was scared witless, as the rickety truck seemed ready to topple or break apart at any moment. But after a few minutes I realized that if this junker had not fallen apart yet it never would, and I began to enjoy the recklessness and craziness of the ride.

During the turbulence I landed atop Diane, and the length of our bodies were pressed flat against each other like pancakes. Our torsos were submersed in hay, and just as I felt her leg curling around me the truck veered sharply sending both of us flying across the bed, where we collided with other tumbling bodies. The hay had drifted into a tall heap right behind the cab of the truck, and everyone joined in contest to be first to conquer this mound of straw. We pushed and shoved and tugged at each other, but before anyone could claim it, a violent jolt from the truck scattered us like ten pins.

As the truck climbed an incline, the pile of hay collapsed covering us in an avalanche of straw. My head was the first to surface, then the redheads of Tara and Diane popped up like sprouting carrots, and so on until every head was accounted for. After excavating ourselves from the fodder, we erupted in a playful hay fight throwing amber tufts at each other, and creating a blizzard of straw. The ride was exhilarating lunacy from beginning to end. And when Gunther screeched the truck to a final stop in front of the commons, I regretted the ride was over. The rough and tumble trip left me dizzy, and when I alighted from the truck I staggered like a drunken sailor and toppled to the ground.

"You'll be dropping plates tonight, busboy," cried Carmen.

As I was lifting myself from the ground, I felt a fistful of hay shoved down the rear collar of my shirt. "I'll make you eat it, you little rogue!" I shouted at Tara. Then Monica lifted my shirt, brushed the straw from my back, and added an affectionate pat.

"Help him tuck his shirt into his pants," insisted Diane with a mischievous grin.

"No, no. A gentleman has his modesty," I answered, as I tucked in my tails. "I'm thirsty. I'm going to the recreation hall for lemonade. Who's coming with me?"

"I'm going swimming," said Carmen.

"Me too," seconded Tara.

But Diane and Monica remained with me. "We'll meet you at the pool in a few minutes," I said to the others.

"Bring us back a lemonade, too," said Carmen.

I was still wobbly from the hayride, so Diane and Monica buttressed me by linking my arms as we walked to the commons. "I feel more stable, ladies. I can manage on my own," whereupon they released their hold as we entered the recreation hall. The girls found a table as I ordered the beverages.

"Have you ladies concocted any more crazy adventures for the remainder of your stay?" I asked, as I set the tray of lemonade drinks on the table.

"We'll think of something," said Monica.

"And you'll be part of it," Diane rejoined.

I offered a toast. "To our health ladies—may it last despite our efforts to do otherwise." And then we clinked our glasses.

After finishing our drinks we walked to the pool. "Have you brought us lemonade?" asked Tara, who was wading waist-deep in the water.

"I have," I answered, as I set two paper cups on the side of the pool.

"Thank you, busboy," shouted Carmen who was about to dive into the water. She sprang from the board, somersaulted through the air and made a vertical dive, carving a parabola underwater before gliding to the surface, where she bounded effortlessly out of the water and onto the apron of the pool with the fluidness of a dolphin.

"You're quite an acrobat," I remarked.

She reached for the paper cup and took a gulp of lemonade. "Mmm…this is good."

She was wearing an apricot bikini that highlighted her soft, copper skin and revealed her fine, sensuous architecture. Sixteen and so inviting.

"Change your clothes and come swimming," said Tara.

"I'm exhausted from the hayride. In fact, I doubt if I'll have the strength to work this evening."

"You're an old man," said Diane.

"If you help me wash six hundred dishes tonight, I'll go swimming," I retorted.

"We should call you 'grandpa,'" added Monica.

"Why aren't you two duchesses in your swimsuits?" I countered.

Diane and Monica leaned toward each other from their chairs and exchanged a whisper.

"Let me in on your secret," I said.

Monica rose from her chair and stood face-to-face with me, with my back to the edge of the pool. "Do you like surprises?" she asked.

"Certainly."

A moment later she delivered a hard shove against my chest. I tottered on one leg and flapped my arms madly to regain my balance.

Then I let out a long roar, as I teetered over the edge and fell into the water.

"I have to work in these clothes tonight," I shouted at the pranksters after surfacing.

"They needed a washing," cried Diane. She and Monica were doubled over with laughter, my agitation adding to their amusement.

I waded to the rim of the pool where the two were standing, and with an upward sweep of my hand sent a wave of water onto their legs.

"You said you like surprises," said Monica. No sooner had she said this when Diane snuck from behind her, and pushed her unsuspecting accomplice into the pool. Then Diane cannonballed into the water and bedlam broke loose. The five of us splashed and dunked one another like a Jehovah Witness baptism gone wild. Everyone was locked in a zany free-for-all, and I had become the object of sport. Eight hands clawed at my shirt, and ripped it off my back. In a tug of war for the prize, the women reduced my shirt to shreds, like hyenas tearing apart a carcass.

"Grab his pants," cried Diane.

"You're a crazy pack of she-devils," I shouted. Indeed, the girls were going berserk, behaving like Amazons at a sorority party.

Monica held me in place by wrapping her arms around my naked chest, while Diane unfastened my buckle causing my bluejeans to slip below my waist. I gripped my pants as Diane tugged on the legs, and Carmen and Tara pulled off my sneakers. I felt like a shipwrecked sailor who had become victim to the cravings of impassioned Sirens. I was extremely embarrassed, and loving every bit of it.

"You have all gone mad!" I screamed.

"We're on fire!" barked Diane, as Monica tightened her hold on me.

"You've ripped the shirt off my back!"

"You look better without it," quipped Tara.

"Let go my pants!" I demanded.

"We want a trophy!" cried Monica.

"What are you doing?" a young girl shrilled, who had just arrived at the pool.

"We're stripping him!" shouted Carmen.

"Stripping him! Mama! Mama! Look what those women are doing to that man," she called to her mother, a fleshy woman who was lumbering toward the pool.

"Whas goin' on?" the fat woman asked.

"They're taking his pants off! Look!" the little girl shrieked.

"No look! Turn your back! It's a sin if you look," she snapped at her daughter, who was observing the episode with keen eyes. Then she set the towels she was holding on a chair, and plodded to the edge of the pool for closer inspection.

"Holy Mother of...What are youse doing?" she hollered.

"What's it look like we're doing, chubby!" shouted Diane, who was still tugging on my pants.

"Youse a bunch of tramps," she yelled at the molesters.

"Tramps have more fun," Carmen answered.

"You come outta that pool so I can slap your face!"

"If I come out of the pool it will be to toss you in it!" retorted Carmen, which brought laughter from the other girls.

"Say no more," I pleaded.

The insulted mother grew furious. Looking skyward and raising her fist, she petitioned Heaven with maledictions to strike Carmen dead. As the woman was invoking divine retribution, Carmen waded to within a few feet of where she was standing, and cupping her hands tossed water into the fat woman's face. The mother responded by hurling oaths at Carmen and the rest of us, pointing her fisted hand as if to guide her verbal salvos to their target, and threatening to have all of us thrown out of the resort. I used this distraction to refasten my pants, slip out of the pool, and escape to a bower of trees a short distance away. After venting her spleen the woman stomped away, taking her daughter by the hand. When she was out of sight I returned to the pool.

"Your antics have probably cost me my job. I'm history," I said irritably.

"You won't get fired. You're the best busboy in the Catskills," said Monica. She and Diane were now out of the pool, and straining water from their hair with combs.

"I'm changing into dry clothes. I'll see you at dinner—if I still have a job."

"Stay and dry yourself in the sun," suggested Diane.

"I'm leaving while I still have my trousers."

"We'll finish the job next time," taunted Tara.

XXIII

By the pricking of my thumbs,
Something wicked this way comes.
— Macbeth

Two days had passed since the hayride. Thoroughly depleted from my day's toil, I retired to the pond at ten p.m. So anxious was I for much needed rest, that my meager accommodations were never more welcoming—the pond could have been a marina in Monaco, and the rowboat a Sultan's yacht. With my exhaustion acting like an opiate I quickly fell asleep. But three hours later I awakened, feeling very uneasy and sensing that something was not right, as if I had a bad dream that I was unable to recall. I sat up and surveyed the dark landscape. I saw no one and nothing appeared amiss, yet I was still apprehensive. I got out of the boat, slipped on my jeans and sneakers, and set out to reconnoiter. I walked a short distance to a point halfway between the pond and a grove of birches, that forms the northern perimeter of the pasture. Then I walked back, going past the pond in the opposite direction, to a knoll overlooking a gentle slope that descends into open field. Not a soul was present, and all was quiet but for the pulsating sound of nighttime insects. Yet something was out there in the night, beyond my scope of vision but not beyond the reach of my intuition. I returned to the rowboat and laid down, and overpowered by the heavy night air quickly succumbed to asleep.

On the following night I awakened with a start around the same time as I had the night before. I was fraught with anxiety, suspecting some hostile presence was lurking in the shades of the night. I looked to my right and then to my left, behind me, and again to my right and again to my left, my head moving rapidly in all directions like a weathervane in a storm. Then I heard faint chanting in the distance. I could not determine if it were human voices, or if it were the sounds of the night, which mingling with a soft breeze seemed to mimic human tone. Then the chanting stopped. I ran to the knoll and kept a sharp ear for a minute, when the chanting resumed once more. The voices moved across the field, as if the chanters were in procession.

Through the tendrils of fog that hovered horizontally across the landscape, I spotted the heads and shoulders of five silhouetted figures moving in single file. Their muffled chants resembled the somber dirge of American Indians, and I wondered if I was witnessing the resurrected souls of Mohawks performing a nocturnal ritual. Then the wailing grew into a loud and wild chorus like a Grecian dithyramb, only to subside again into a low chant. I watched these phantoms from the netherworld, led by a being a head taller than the others, advance in my direction. Then they stopped, and in perfect tempo walked clockwise in a tight circle three times, and then three times counter-clockwise, and then sat on the ground. I take leave to say that when an experience is so surreal such as the one I was witnessing, the psyche mercifully arrests any inner terror by disengaging reality from one's consciousness as it did in my case, enabling me to sublimate my fear.

I moved closer, lying flat on the ridge of the hillock to avoid detection. The tall specter, who was apparently a chieftain, uttered a loud cry and the others answered in low refrain, but I could not discern what was said. Again he cried out, and the others responded as before. Then the tall one struck a match and lit a pipe. After drawing on it a few times he passed it to the others, who in turn drew puffs. These spirits had transformed themselves into bodily form, else how were they able to smoke? And I noticed that their forms gave off ground shadows, which the disembodied cannot produce.

When they finished smoking the five figures proceeded to higher ground. Approaching the ridge they moved into the full light of the moon, casting elongated shadows in my direction. As they climbed higher their lengthening shadows crept closer to me. The mental excitement of watching this eerie picture unfold, coupled with exhaustion from interrupted sleep, now took its toll. I was overcome with panic; these dreadful shadows were coming after me, and when they reached me would wrap around me like the tentacles of a monstrous octopus and strangle me. Closer they came while I remained frozen with terror, and just as they were about to reach me my vision gave way to a whirling blackness and I lost consciousness.

I was awakened by a ray of light. The sun had risen, lighting the hills in tawny brightness. My face and clothes were bedewed with morning moisture, and I was chilled to the bone from sleeping on bare soil. For a moment I was thrown into confusion not remembering how I had come to be where I was, but then the events of the night leaped in my mind. Was it a dream? Absolutely not! For I had awakened from the very spot where I had witnessed the supernatural hours earlier. Or could it be the spirits sensed my presence, and cast me into slumber to keep me from viewing their ritual?

I returned to the rowboat. It was now 6:30 by my watch. Grabbing my blanket and clothes, I went to the bunkhouse to take a warm shower and get ready for work. At the breakfast table I spoke to no one, my mind completely absorbed by the events of the night. I felt like Rip Van Winkle awakening into a new and changed world following a bewitching sleep. Certainly these mountains were as much enchanted today as when Washington Irving penned his Catskill tales. This most recent phenomenon had thrown me into mental chaos. As this maelstrom of confusion was churning in my troubled head, I reined in my runaway imagination by reminding myself that what I had seen was probably a band of vagabonds and nothing more. When the breakfast shift was finished, I told Nick I was awakened in the middle of the night by a chorus of chants, and asked if he had heard it too. He told me he had not, and suggested it was the product of my drinking too much beer before bedtime.

That night as I lay in the boat, my heightened emotions made me suspect of any sound—the rustle of branches, the croaking of frogs, and the flutter of night birds all conspired to sound like chanting voices. I tried to keep Churchill by my side for companionship, but the stubborn cat scratched his way out of my hold and fled into the night on his hunt, abandoning me to my fears. As my imagination wandered, I thought that if it were ghostly phantoms I had seen, they would pose less risk to me than humans; for while the dead may spook the living, it is mortals who inflict harm on one another. As I recalled macabre stories where satanic cults sacrificed innocent victims and drank their blood, the inhabitants from the underworld seemed far less threatening. But what if they weren't spirits, and in fact were blood-sucking mortals? I calmed myself by invoking the Almighty for His protection, and fervently reciting prayers that I had abandoned since childhood. Rescue mercifully arrived in the form of mental fatigue which closed my eyelids, and I slept soundly until seven in the morning, when I awakened fresh and unscathed from the chimeras of the night.

During the next few nights I slept tranquilly and undisturbed, my disquieting fears of the supernatural behind me, until I was awakened in the wee morning hours by the same chants. Curiosity impelled me to seek its source; fear kept me contained in the boat. The voices grew more distinct as they moved across the pasture and toward the hillock, from where I had made reconnaissance on that first night. In the distance I spotted the dark, vertical figure of the tall chieftain, emerging to his full height as he surmounted the ridge. Following him came another, and another, until there were five in all advancing in my direction.

Like a frightened child in a dark bedroom, I drew the blanket to the bridge of my nose with my fingers curled tightly around its edge. Closer they came, their chants growing louder as they proceeded in single file toward the boat. I slid flat into the hold of the boat and covered myself completely beneath the blanket. Next, I heard the press of feet on the soft grass, as this strange assembly passed within a couple of feet of where I lay. My heart throbbed, which in my elevated terror seemed loud enough for the intruders to hear. I pricked my ear to gauge how far they had moved past the rowboat, then I peeped from the blanket and saw them standing at the water's edge facing the pond. Their dark outlines resembled a grotesque candelabra, as the tall figure stood in the middle flanked on each side by his shorter companions in descending height. In silence they stood, as if meditating. Then the very tall one stretched his long, lanky arms above the water, and issued a solemn incantation in a tongue that sounded like gibberish.

Next he stretched out his long right leg, and placed his foot on the water's surface. The others did likewise. God in Heaven! Were they attempting to walk on water! But these were not spirits; they were flesh and blood, and certainly possessed by demons from whom they drew their sorcery. The tall one spoke again, but this time in plain English. I recognized the voice. Of course! It was Johannes! Mad Johannes! He stepped forward with the confidence that he was about to step on pavement, and then plunged waist-deep into the water. Immediately, the others checked themselves from stepping forward and stood motionless, each with his one leg still suspended in the air as Johannes went into a tirade, plashing the surface angrily with his long arms.

"It's your fault! It's all your fault!" he screamed at his followers, as they slowly descended their raised legs to the ground. "Were you sincere in your chants and thoughts the gods would have listened. But they won't listen to idiots like you! You're all a pack of morons!" whereupon he embarked on a raging tantrum, that continued for two or three minutes until his wrath was spent. Then he stood motionless and silent for about thirty seconds. "To hell with it," he said in disgust as he waded to dry ground. When one of the others dared to resume the bizarre chant, Johannes snapped at him: "Shut up, you damn fool!"

That which terrified me a short time earlier had turned into the most hilarious episode I had ever seen, as I observed the frustration of this odd group of pathetic characters. Johannes trudged back in the direction he had come, as the others sheepishly followed. As they neared the boat I slipped my head below the blanket, allowing a chink of space from which to see with one eye. Here was my opportunity to pay back these imbeciles for the fear and disruption they had caused me. When they had gone about ten yards past the boat, I issued a low, resonating growl.

"Did you hear that?" I heard one of them ask in an anxious voice.

"Sounded like a dog," another said.

"You have defiled sacred ground! Leave or perish!" I bellowed in a sepulchral tone.

"It is the voice of Rhadamanthus, the Judge of the Dead!" shouted Johannes in a terrified voice. "Restrain your anger, gracious god, for upon this soil our feet shall never again tread."

Then I heard the stamp of feet rush across the grassy ground. Peeking over the rim of the boat, I watched five figures speed like hounds across the pasture, and disappear into the folds of the rolling landscape. Though not able to walk on water, they were quite adept at fleeing on land. There are few satisfactions greater than extinguishing the gripping emotion of fear. No conqueror who ever subdued an entire continent could have felt greater victory than myself, for having vanquished the turmoil that beset me. I stretched to my full length in the boat and gazed at the stars, satisfied that my night would be free of further disturbance from those lunatics. What's more, Johannes was never again seen at The Timberhaus.

XXIV

Pressed into service means pressed out of shape.
— Robert Frost

"Have you heard the news?" Chris asked me with urgency. He was peering over his stall with his chin propped on the wood railing. I was lying on my mattress reading, and Churchill was licking the last drops of milk from his bowl.

"Tell me," I replied, without taking my eyes off the magazine.

"The President has just abolished all draft deferments for students."

"Impossible," I answered nonchalantly. Chris was daffy. I'm certain the fool had enough helium in his brain to levitate himself.

"It's true. I heard it on a news bulletin an hour ago," he insisted.

I dismissed his remark with a shrug.

"Go to hell!" he snapped. Churchill looked up from his bowl, as if the remark had been directed at him. This was a rare display of Chris's anger. Most times he never got upset, despite the many jibes thrown at him. I assumed his sluggish senses, like that of Fred's, were incapable of sustaining any ire.

Since the start of the war several years earlier, university students had been exempt from military induction, as the government felt that an educated population was as vital to national security as a standing military. Despite many changes in war policy the Administration had made over the years, academia remained untouched. Conscripting college students was just inconceivable. At a time of growing public hostility toward the war, the government's decision to draft college students would have surely incited the wrath of a nation already weary of the human and financial price of the conflict. What I later learned was that the President did not abolish deferments, but instead issued an order revamping the entire draft system, by which all men of military age—scholar or otherwise—would be eligible for military induction using a lottery system. Under this new system each day of the calendar year would be randomly drawn, determining a man's eligibility by the numerical order in which his birthday was picked. Those with birthdays that were selected early would be among the first drafted.

The President's order was in response to the growing number of young men fleeing to academia to avoid conscription. Colleges and universities were enrolling record numbers of students. Under the lottery system, the odds of being drafted would be based purely on chance. But what if my birthday came up early in the drawing? After coming within a year of graduation, I could be plucked from the classroom to fight a purposeless war. I always felt the Vietnam conflict was terribly wrong, and now loomed the real possibility that I could be drafted. I had been raised with the belief that it is a man's duty to serve his country in time of war, provided American liberty was at stake. Not the case in Vietnam, where young Americans were being killed to defend a corrupt Asian government. Yet many Americans, mostly older ones, believed it was one's duty to serve when called, regardless of the nature of the war. But history is fraught with lurid examples of how misguided patriotism almost destroyed the world; most notably in the 20th century when Germans, who failing to distinguish duty to their homeland from allegiance to a ruthless dictator, suffered total destruction of their nation.

At supper that evening, the kitchen was buzzing about the announcement the President had made that afternoon. "Is it true?" I asked Nick, who stood in front of me on the mess line.

He shook his head dejectedly.

The mood among everyone ranged from disbelief to anger, except for Otto. He wore a mocking grin, as he shoved the meal plates across the counter to the waiting line of workers; it was the closest expression to a smile I had ever seen on him. He was quietly delighting in the news that was upsetting all of us. When I picked up my plate of stew, he looked at me with a smirk that read: "You vill soon be gun fodder, you stinker!" I referred to Otto as the Fuhrer, because he reminded me how Hitler would have run a kitchen had the dictator ever chosen the culinary arts as his profession. Still, my dislike for him was tempered by sympathy. He spent his days in the hellish inferno of a kitchen, and in the evening he retreated to his cottage like a ghoul to his crypt. I never heard of Otto having a wife and family; he was a thoroughly miserable and misbegotten creature.

Discussion of the President's decision continued in the mess hall. "The President should be tarred and hung," demanded Chloe. Never lost for words, she rambled on without a break between sentences until she was out of breath, reminding me of a Celtic bagpipe which keeps playing until its air pouch is depleted. Then she sucked in air and continued her clacking: "Louie (her boyfriend) is halfway through college, and has spent thousands on his education. And now he could be yanked out of school and sent to fight in an Asian jungle. It's not fair, it's just not fair! After all, we're planning to get married after he graduates and have babies…"

"Louie will have a chance to father lots of babies with the mama-sans," interrupted Bruce.

"What's a mama-san?" asked Chloe, her voice narrowing to a squeak, as she was almost out of air from yapping.

"A mama-san is an Asian servant by day and a sex slave at night," he replied.

"You're despicable Bruce," Chloe shot back, as she fired a piece of her bread roll at him that she was about to put in her mouth. Bruce deflected the missile with his hand, which ricocheted through the air and into another worker's bowl.

"My cousin told me about the mama-sans," piped another waitress. "He served a year in Vietnam and said Saigon is absolute decadence. It's a tropical whorehouse."

"Sounds like my kind of place," said Bruce as he slurped his stew.

"I'd be proud to fight for my country," said Fred, who was sitting in the far corner. It was one of the rare times he joined the other workers for meals.

Bruce rose from the table and went over to Fred. "You'll never have the opportunity," he said, as he stood menacingly over the lame-brained busboy.

"Why not?" asked Fred nervously, as he raised a glass of water to his mouth.

Bruce grabbed the glass from his hand and replied, "Because you're a numbskull," and then poured the water on his head. Everyone erupted in laughter, and a terrified Fred ran out of the room. No one dared challenge Bruce on his treatment of Fred, lest they get a similar hair washing. Then again, no one cared because it was only Fred.

"Actually, it was never fair that college students should have been exempted from the draft," said Cindy, resuming the discussion in her raspy voice.

"It's not fair that anyone should get drafted," retorted Nick.

"What's unfair is that women have not been drafted," rejoined Bruce.

"Women can't fight wars!" Chloe hollered.

"If only women were to serve in the military, no wars would be fought," said Nelson. He was a tall, thin lad of seventeen who worked with Eric as a groundskeeper. He never mingled with the other help, and lived with his parents at their summer cottage nearby. His awkward and shy nature would give you the impression he was dumb, but I was told he was very bright, and attended an elite Jesuit high school in Manhattan.

"What ho, Nelson! You really can talk!" cried Tom. But Nelson never replied, and continued spooning the watery stew into his mouth. He had expended his weekly allotment of words with that comment.

"Nelson, you've come up with a novel idea," said Karen, one of the waitresses. "End war by creating a fighting force that's ill-fit to perform its function."

"I like that theory," said another waitress. "You should call it the Karen Principle."

"No. Name it the Nelson Hypotheses. After all, he sponsored the idea," replied Karen.

"But Karen refined and polished it," insisted Chloe.

"Call it the The Timberhaus Principle, to honor the site where great minds converged to deduce it," said Nick.

Just then Papa entered the room. "Hurry boys und girls. Hurry to your stations now. The guests are at their tables waiting for their dinner."

XXV

If it is divinely ordained that there should be wars among men, then we should be as slow to start a war and as quick to end it.
— CALLIAS, ATHENIAN AMBASSADOR

By 1972 a virus was sweeping the nation that was infecting millions. It was a virulent contagion as paralytic as the polio virus of the Fifties, which crippled and killed millions of children and adults. It was a virus not found under any taxonomical description, nor was it the focus of epidemiological investigation. Yet it was as debilitating as any plague or famine. The symptoms of its victims were weariness and apathy, and like any widespread epidemic it placed a heavy strain on the American psyche. It was the social paralysis of malaise, spawned from a costly and bloody war in Vietnam that was now in its eighth year. Just as sailors who are otherwise energized by rough seas grow lethargic from calm waters, the public grew weary when their passionate attempts to tack the misguided course of government became futile. When people are helpless to change their government's self-destructive policies in a foreign war, the rhythm of life loses its energy and social inertia sets in.

War debilitates and renders impotent powerful nations. Novelist Charlotte Bronte drew a dismal scene of English life in the years following the Napoleonic wars: "A venal, lord-and-king cursed nation full of helpless pauperism...put your head in at English cottage doors; get a glimpse of Famine crouched on black hearth stones..." And following World War II the British Empire collapsed to a fraction of its size, just like ancient empires that had tailspinned into decay from wars that exhausted their treasuries, and enfeebled their ability to provide for domestic needs.

The experience of World War II should have indicated that the US would never enter into war at least through the remainder of the century. But just as the First World War was "the war to end all wars," only to have a second world war erupt twenty years later, so now did Vietnam and the Korean War before it call men to arms once again.

Gibbon said that history is little more than the register of the crimes and follies of mankind, and Churchill echoed that sentiment when he said, "The history of man is war." Warfare has been so visceral to man's affairs that it can be argued eliminating war could only be accomplished by eliminating man. And the timely recurrence of war on the clock of civilization makes one ask if it is not an inescapable part of the human condition.

Yet Scripture gives hope that wars will end and man will eventually live in peace, as in Isaiah's prophecy that "swords shall be turned into plowshares." But, in fact, war originated when plowshares were turned into swords. In the 5th millennium BC, the development of copper smelting in Europe that led to the casting of plowshares, also provided the technology to manufacture battle axes, arrowheads, and spears. When the Bronze Age arrived in 2300 BC trade was flourishing throughout the Mediterranean, and the emerging merchant class found it necessary to build fortifications around their wealthy settlements to prevent incursions. A warrior class was born from this mercantile society, which introduced bronze swords, helmets, and breastplates. With the arrival of the Iron Age in 1000 BC population density led to the emergence of city-states, giving rise to government bureaucracies which, entrusted with protecting the social and economic welfare of the people, led to the formation of standardized armies which were the forerunners of modern militaries.

The source of world conflict has changed little throughout history. Blame it on the human social structure. Just turn to the ants as proof, as Darwin did. The famed evolutionist used warring ant colonies, with its social strata ascending from slave ants to the queen, as a parallel to human society which inevitably finds itself in perpetual conflict to protect its resources and preserve its social hierarchy. National prosperity requires protection of its wealth, but the same instruments for defense have been used to attack and subdue other nations. When a country grows strong enough to defend itself militarily, it inevitably flexes its might against less-muscled nations. To wit, the 17th century navy of England that was built to protect its maritime trade was eventually used to colonize and exploit other lands.

Meanwhile, war continues to raise its dragon's head, because lessons learned from the ravages of conflict are forgotten by succeeding generations. When cities are rebuilt concealing the scars of battle; and, when a new generation has not experienced the suffering of their parents, then society relaxes its vigilance and ignores events that will precipitate another crisis. Peace is seemingly an interim period for war to gain its second breath before starting anew. The growing magnitude of warfare and its apocalyptic toll on life in the 20th century has led adherents of eschatology to believe that events will lead to a war of unparalleled devastation, from which lasting peace will germinate from the ashes of destruction. Acting as an earthly purgatory, war will redeem mankind through its own blood and usher in a utopian world.

Despite Isaiah's optimism, war is inextricably woven into the human cloth. In *War and Peace,* Tolstoy ascribes the outbreak of the Napoleonic war to historical agents beyond the control of man, akin to a monkey riding on the back of a stampeding elephant: Having no choice but to be carried along and helpless to change its course. In short, Napoleon was the vector of unknown forces when he rose to power and conquered nations, the same forces which sealed his fate when he invaded Russia. Whether war is coded into man's genetics as Darwin suggested; or the result of inescapable historical forces as Tolstoy proposed; or a vehicle leading to the unfolding of an eschatological Divine Plan, the question that Americans were asking in 1972 was that which Montaigne had posed in the sixteenth century: How worthy is a cause that must sustain itself by the loss of millions of lives?

Stretching southward along the South China Sea, Vietnam, the US believed, was a key link in the formation of a Communist hegemony in southeast Asia that would imperil world stability. The United States' aim was to bolster South Vietnam's pro-Western government as a bulwark against communist aggression from North Vietnam, who wanted to conquer its estranged brethren. North Vietnam was led by Ho Chi Minh, a wisp of a man in his seventies, whom the Vietnamese affectionately called Uncle Ho for his peasant dress and simple lifestyle. The US believed Minh was a communist pawn of China, but in fact, Minh was a nationalist who wanted to reunite his divided country after a century of French rule. As a young man he went to Paris, not to study philosophy as had the founders of the Khmer Rouge who intellectualized the massacre of their fellow Cambodians; nor to study international law or government—not anything that provided the groundwork for liberating his countrymen. He studied in Paris to become a chef. But while there he met Vietnamese expatriates who wanted to liberate their country from colonial rule. At one time Ho desired to be an ally of the United States. During World War II he founded the Viet Minh, an independence organization which had assisted the American military by organizing a guerilla movement that helped defeat occupying Japanese forces. After the war he offered the United States rights to its naval base at Cam Ranh Bay, southeast Asia's most strategic port, if the US supported Vietnam's independence from France. The US promised that it would. But the US reneged on its agreement and supported France's sovereignty over Vietnam. Minh never forgave the Yanks for their betrayal.

In 1954, following a seven-year bloody war that followed in the wake of a nationalist uprising, France relinquished its one hundred-year control of Vietnam. But not before dividing the country and setting up a pro-Western government south of the 17th parallel, that was riddled with corruption and nepotism. Coinciding with the Vietnamese insurrection of the Fifties was the exaggerated threat of Communism being bandied about by American politicians, who instilled this fear into the public to get themselves elected to office. Accusing one another of being soft on Communism, if not an outright follower of this subversive ideology, was a common tactic which political mountebanks employed against each other. Then in the early Sixties American politicians sounded the clarion call to stop communist aggression abroad with military force before it reached American soil. By 1963 President Kennedy had dispatched 16,000 troops to Vietnam as "military advisers," to assist the South Vietnamese fight communists. French President Charles de Gaulle warned the United States to stay out of Vietnam, or risk getting drawn into a prolonged military engagement as his country had. But Kennedy did not listen. His strategy was not to remove any troops before the 1964 presidential election, lest he be labeled soft on Communism and lose reelection. But when an assassin ended Kennedy's life, his successor kept the troops intact.

In 1965 President Lyndon Johnson dispatched several infantry battalions to South Vietnam to extinguish a growing military brushfire with insurgents infiltrating from the North. Johnson thought that a strong show of military power was certain to scare the infiltrators, and in a few months the conflict would be over and US troops would return home. It was that simple. How could peasant rice farmers ever stand up to the most powerful military on earth? Allured by the prospect of quick victory and returning home as heroes, a new generation of untested American warriors rose to serve in Vietnam. A loyal but gullible public supported the US entry into the war, believing their country intended to suppress tyranny and defend freedom, and that our stay would be brief. But military objectives would clash with native culture, for when US troops arrived in Vietnam they became quickly disenchanted when they found little support from the people they were deployed to protect. Consequently, their military mission was compromised by their personal agenda to survive eighteen months of overseas duty and return home safely. Victory was no longer a priority.

America, though the beneficiary of centuries of history, believed she was immune from committing the folly of earlier nations and empires. Twenty-five hundred years ago during the Peloponnesian War, Nicias warned his fellow Athenians not to invade Sicily, a country of doubtful strategic importance and unfamiliar language and culture. And he warned the overconfident Athenians of the "unpredictable element" in war, that can reverse the fortunes of a powerful military. But Athens pursued its campaign, and their military and people suffered destruction. Likewise, Vietnam was of no strategic or economic value to the United States, and neither country had cultural ties. The United States made the fatal error by assuming the role of a modern Mohammed, using the point of a bayonet to convert an ancient people to a Western culture. They failed to grasp that the political system of a country is rooted in the ethos of its people and their traditions, which in ancient cultures has been layered into solid bedrock over the millennia. New political dogma can only replace former ones when social upheaval destroys its cultural foundation. "Freedom is not a fruit of every culture," said Montesquieu; and, neither can democracy be tilled into an ethnic soil where such political thought is not indigenous.

The Asians put up strong resistance. And the war became unsettling to many Americans, because the United States was not winning it. Heretofore, Americans had perceived war as yielding beneficial results for their country throughout her history. The Revolutionary War gained independence for the American colonies; the Indian wars had expanded US borders to the Pacific; the Civil War, the last war to have ravaged American soil, had long been distilled to folklore; and, our victory in World War II made heroes of our soldiers and resurrected our shattered economy. Ironically, the security to our nation that was to have been wrought by squashing communism in Vietnam triggered social unrest in the United States. Demonstrations swept across the country demanding a stop to the conflict, as more young men were shipped off to a foreign land to fight a worthless war that dragged on year after year.

The Vietnam War also ran up high social costs by diverting money from domestic programs, such as restoring roads and bridges in sore need of repair that were built during the Great Depression of the Thirties. Municipalities became under-funded, and in the wake of urban decline corporations relocated from major cities to other regions leaving high unemployment in its aftermath. But the war continued like a mutation that grew more resistant to efforts to contain it.

Outclassed heavily in military power, the North Vietnamese communists induced the Americans to meet them on an equal footing, much like the ancient Liparians when they squared-off in battle against the Estrucans. The Liparians engaged the Estrucans in sea battle who held a sizeable navy, while the Liparians possessed a meager fleet. In their first encounter the Liparians, rather than sending out its entire fleet and risk it being destroyed, engaged its enemy with only five triremes. The Estrucans could have crushed its smaller foe with a massive assault of sea power, but instead chose to meet them on a par, lest it be said they could not defeat an inferior force on equal terms. So they dispatched only five of its ships to the encounter. But the smaller opponent, evenly matched, was victorious in the sea battle; and, in their next encounter once more sent five ships which the Estrucans matched with the same number. Again the smaller navy prevailed, relying on craftsmanship and cunning. So with each encounter, David whittled away at Goliath's strength.

Likewise, when the North Vietnamese had to defend themselves against the most powerful military on earth, they did not take on the Americans *en masse* but fought them regionally. When hostilities would erupt in a province, the US responded by pouring in troops and dropping bombs for weeks, months, a year or longer until the fighting subsided. But no sooner would the US declare the region secure, than it would find new hostilities breaking out in another province. And so the Vietnamese liberation forces hop-scotched across the country with the Americans in pursuit, who believed they were winning the war province by province, only to discover renewed conflicts in regions where they had previously claimed victory. American generals educated at West Point were outwitted by peasant forces, who wore down the American fighting spirit by playing the simple game of hide-and-seek.

The Vietnam conflict heightened and American casualties rose. Washington was confounded that so many American soldiers were being killed fighting an inferior opponent. So, it turned to computer technology for a solution. After all, if a computer could land a man on the moon, could it not assist in winning a war by simulating battles and forecasting outcomes? Would that the American military had taken advice from Clausewitz, a man who never knew a computer. Two hundred years earlier this Prussian general wrote that warfare based on theory is fraught with uncertainty. He stressed that warfare is an intuitive art, and the best battle strategy is quickly nullified when the enemy does not cooperate with his opponent's mode of combat. I recall the story of a Roman soldier which underscores that principle. The soldier liked to exhibit his combat skills against a wood post, which he would jab with his spear and slash with his sword. When he asked Demonax the philosopher what he thought of his prowess, the latter replied, "They're fine, so long as you have a wooden opponent." The Vietnamese insurgents were not allowing themselves to be a whipping post by conducting a Western-style war as the Americans had expected. The "enemy" seldom wore military attire. He was entwined into the fabric of Vietnamese society. A farmer who started his day furrowing a field might be ambushing an American platoon that night.

The US approach was thoroughly impractical, violating the tenets of the art of warfare. It was fighting a limited war: Heavy bombing punctuated by truces, hoping to entice the enemy into suing for peace. But moderation, as Clausewitz stressed, is absurd. As the United States sought answers from the Computer Oracle, it neglected the human equation of war, notably the indomitable spirit within every man that manifests itself when one's liberty is at stake as it was for the Vietnamese. It was the indefatigable will of the Vietnamese that mocked computer logistics and stood up to overwhelming military power. Add to this the arrogance of the US military in underestimating their opponent, an arrogance which the ancient Greeks referred to as hubris—an insolent pride that would stir the wrath of the gods. It was hubris that destroyed Pharaoh's army in the Red Sea; doomed the Spanish Armada to a watery grave in the Atlantic; and, defeated Napoleon in his march to Moscow. Now, the US was to meet its nemesis in Vietnam. Years earlier I had an inkling of the "enemy's" resolve, that foreshadowed what lay in store for America. It was a hot summer afternoon in 1965 and I was in my kitchen sipping lemonade listening to the radio, when the broadcast was interrupted by a news bulletin reporting two hundred Viet Cong soldiers had just perished in a suicide attack on an American battalion. Tattooed like an epitaph across the chest of every Viet Cong body were the words: "Born in the North to die in the South." Even then, as a thirteen-year-old boy, I knew that the Vietnamese were willing to bleed themselves white to rid their country of foreign intrusion.

Long before war was theorized into an art or science, the crafters of ancient mythology understood that success lay in striking the enemy quickly to bring a swift conclusion to the conflict. In Greek legend Perseus was sent by the gods to kill Medusa, who was raising great havoc on earth. Medusa was a monster whose tresses were coiling snakes, and whose horrid sight turned men into stone. To achieve his task Perseus was furnished foot wings for speed; a helmet which made him invisible; and a shield and a mirror. When he found Medusa asleep he cut off her head, avoiding direct sight of her by looking at her reflection in the mirror.

The sixteenth century statesman-philosopher Francis Bacon extracted three maxims of warfare from this myth: The wings provided Perseus swiftness in action; the helmet made his mission clandestine; and, the shield gave him the protection of Providence. Bacon stated that there must be a "just and honorable cause for war," such as the overthrow of a tyrant, without which soldiers will not be motivated to fight. Perseus undertook the task because it would eliminate an evildoer and have a quick and successful end; one that would not be protracted and rack up enormous costs in lives and resources. In contrast, the US never defined a specific enemy in Vietnam. It was at odds with an ideology that could only be defeated by extirpating the millions who embraced it. And American soldiers had no enthusiasm fighting a bloody war to settle which dogma, Eastern or Western, was the better.

The US had an option in 1972 as in previous years to quickly end the war by withdrawing every American soldier from that country. It was a simple proposal. But humans, seemingly handicapped by an enigmatic element within their makeup, are more trusting of a journey through a maze rather than through a straight and simple path. Opponents of withdrawal claimed that if Americans abruptly left Asian soil, millions of Asians would be slaughtered by warring factions. But such carnage would only be the inevitable consequence of age-old ethnic hostilities which American presence had only deferred, but could never prevent. In the words of Clausewitz, "The passions which exist in war must already have a latent existence in the people."

When people take as absolute faith and without question what they hear from authority, it gives license to its leaders to abuse their power by manipulating facts, as did the United States when it concocted a bogus incident as a pretext to involve itself in Vietnam's civil war. The US involvement in Vietnam proved that despite an heroic history and benevolent constitution, any country is not immune to committing wanton destruction on the magnitude of a ruthless dictatorship. The Vietnamese landscape was being cratered by bombs, its crops defoliated, and its villages flattened. How could this have come to pass? The destruction went on because no one was to blame. No one to blame because those responsible for the havoc claimed they were merely passing on orders that had been passed on to them. Tolstoy explains it best through Prince Nekhlyudov in *Resurrection*. As Czarist rule is nearing its end in late 19th century Russia, the wealthy aristocrat visits St Petersburg to alert officials to the plight of the peasants and the cruelty of a barbaric penal system. But he meets with bureaucratic indifference because each official can plead that he was only following a chain of instructions to enforce the law. For example, the Czar gives orders to a regional governor to crack down on anarchists, who delegates that duty to a local magistrate, who in turn directs the police to make arrests, who then hand over the radicals to a prison warden. So if a peasant is incarcerated and left to rot in prison, the warden feels no sense of blame because it was the policeman who sent him the prisoner, and the policeman was only following a directive from higher powers to arrest subversives. In Vietnam, American soldiers would torch a rural village and casually puff on cigarettes as they watched women and children pour screaming from their burning hovels. They are simply following orders, and their commander who issued them is merely following instructions from a higher rank, as was each person before him going back to the President. And the President defends his military policy by claiming he had inherited the war from the previous President, and then cites support from the Senate who approved funding of the war. When no one can point to a guilty party, the groundwork for the most unimaginable atrocities is laid. When no conscience is stricken, the destruction continues. And the destruction continued because no one was to blame.

As I think of the devastating effects which the Vietnam War has had on the US, I reflect on the past when America was a different nation, and how it evolved from the time I was a boy into the country it is today. As a lad I was proud growing up in a secure and prosperous nation. I believed I could achieve anything in this land of opportunity, where there was a cornucopia of unlimited possibilities. There was even talk of sending men to the moon someday. Following World War II no nation was held in such high esteem throughout the world as was the United States. Never was there a nation in the twentieth century that countries wanted to emulate more than the US for its role in smashing tyranny, preserving liberty, and rebuilding countries obliterated by the most devastating war on the planet.

World War II was still fresh in the minds of Americans, as almost every family had a member in military service. At the Sunday dinner table and when relatives visited during the holidays, war stories were the theme of conversation in our home. And theaters were glutted with movies depicting American war heroics: Fighter planes in dogfights in the skies over Germany; intrepid American troops pouring out of trenches and fighting the enemy head-on; naval battles showing artillery shells fired from turrets and streaking like lightning through the sky. One of the most popular movies was made about the true story of five American brothers who served aboard the same ship and died together. They were the Sullivan boys—Albert, Frances, George, Joseph, and Madison, aged 20 to 28 years—who grew up in the Midwest and enlisted in the US Navy in 1942. They served aboard the USS Juneau, and they died together when their ship was torpedoed and sunk off the Solomon Islands that same year. Never in the twentieth century had a single family lost as many of its members in military service to the United States. But their names and sacrifice are all but forgotten. There is no national monument to their memory, nor does a holiday commemorate their names. And history books do not even afford them a footnote. The movie about their lives is shown no more, entombed in the Hollywood archives. Were it not for a museum honoring them in their hometown of Waterloo, Iowa, the heroism of the Sullivans would be fated to obscurity.

There was also another family that sent their sons, four of them, off to war. But unlike the Sullivans they survived. They were the Rutledge boys—my father and three uncles. At twenty-four years of age my father was drafted into the army at the start of World War II. Shortly thereafter his three brothers, Michael, Henry, and Patrick were also drafted. Michael served in the Pacific, where he survived a bullet wound from a Japanese sniper as his regiment stormed a beach in Guam.

Before being sent overseas my father was dating Marian, his future wife, whom he would marry just after the war ended. One evening my father told his fiancée that he had just learned his battalion was going away for three days of drills. Where? He did not know, but probably not far. The next day he and thousands of other soldiers boarded the *Queen Mary* at New York Harbor and sailed to England; he would not return home for three years. The *Queen Mary* was an English ocean liner that was impressed for military use to transport troops. Its luxurious interior was gutted to pack 15,000 human beings within its hull. The soldiers slept in hammocks arrayed smack against each other, with each soldier looking into the feet of the soldier next to him. The *Queen Mary* was the fastest ship on water, able to cross the Atlantic in three days, and could outrun German U boats. It zigzagged across the ocean avoiding a strait course, lest it become a target for torpedoes. My father recalled scary moments during the voyage when the ship would cut its engines to avoid being heard by enemy submarines, thought to be lurking in the waters. An awful, tomblike silence followed, more terrifying than the screams of howling demons, that might portend the blast of a torpedo ripping apart the steel hull and sending everyone aboard to Neptune's grave.

While in England my father witnessed the aerial bombardment of London by German A4 rockets or "buzz bombs." Launched from Peenemunde on the North Sea, the trajectory of the four-story rockets could be traced over the night skies of London by their buzzing sound, which would die out about thirty seconds before impact. Again that awful silence; unable to hear the final path of the rocket and not knowing where it would make its deadly strike. From England my father was transported to the Netherlands, then to Belgium, and was in Marseilles on the day when Allied troops attacked the beaches of

Normandy. I recall pictures of him in uniform taken in France, one of him sitting on an army cot sunk in mud. In each picture he wore the same weary expression of resignation, that spoke of the fading hope of ever returning home and seeing his loved ones again. The joyous news of Germany's surrender in 1945 was tempered with news that he and other soldiers would be shipped to the Pacific to finish off the war with Japan. It was estimated one million Americans and British would die trying to take the Land of the Rising Sun. He was given a medical examination and inoculated for smallpox, deemed fit for continued service, and was set to depart when word arrived that Japan had surrendered. President Truman had dropped the atomic bomb on Hiroshima and Nagasaki.

Nowadays, politicians speak of World War II veterans as patriots who were happy and honored to fight on foreign soil, and sacrifice their lives to preserve freedom for others. They paint a scene as if every soldier had a broad smile stamped on his face, as he hiked up the ship's gangplank with a fifty-pound duffel bag on his back to embark on a voyage from which he might never return. And that each soldier was willing to face death bravely, and should the battlefield be his graveyard, then the tearful mother and girlfriend whom he kissed goodbye on the dock would be more than compensated for their loss knowing their loved one died a hero. Such is the rhetoric politicians use in their panegyrics at Independence and Memorial Day celebrations. But it is nonsense. My father hated the war from the moment he boarded the Queen Mary until the time he set foot back on American soil. And millions of other veterans shared the same sentiment. What's more, he hated generals. "Generals wage war, but soldiers make peace," he told me. His patriotism was not displayed in a cheerful acceptance of military life; after all, he was robbed four years of his life and suffered hellish times. Rather, his patriotism was manifested by his valor and willingness to endure a loathsome situation. Civilization was rescued through the sacrifice of soldiers like my father and his brothers. Shortly after the war he married, bought a house, and raised his family. He has lived an honest and unpretentious life—the most noble that exists.

With the hostilities over, the spring of hope had sprouted, and the world was regenerating itself from the winter of apocalyptic destruction that had leveled Europe and much of the Far East. And in the United States an era of unprecedented economic growth was ushered in as returning veterans rebuilt a shattered economy. People were working again and factories roared with production. Swords became plowshares once more.

XXVI

Last night I had a dream that I was a butterfly. And when I awoke
I asked myself, 'am I a man who dreamt he was a butterfly,
or am I a butterfly dreaming I am a man.'

— Lao Tse

"I learned yesterday that my three years of college might be for naught," I said to Monica just as she joined me at poolside. "The President is modifying student deferments, and I could be drafted in a lottery."

"I had not heard that," she replied indifferently.

"If I'm drafted I won't serve," I added tersely. Silence followed as I stared at my submerged legs, shortened and bent by the water's refraction. Then I drew my legs out of the pool and stood up. "Let's get a soda," I suggested, taking Monica's hand as she rose to her feet. We headed to the vending machine which stood outside the office entrance, got two cold cans of cola, and then sat on a wood bench beneath the shade of a maple a short distance away. Monica had not spoken a word since we left the pool. I wanted to fume about the military draft, but I held my tongue because she didn't appear interested in hearing my gripe. I drew a long sip of soda as I watched a bumble bee moving in elliptical flight among the flowers. Then I said, "Tell me about yourself."

"It would take years."

"I'm patient."

"What would you like to know?"

"Have you a lover in Brooklyn?"

She drew back, embarrassed at my question. "How bold of you to ask."

"Do you?" I persisted.

"I broke up with a fellow last spring. We had been dating for a year."

"Was parting company difficult?"

Her face flashed a warning that I was encroaching on personal affairs. But her expression quickly lightened and she replied: "It was mutual. The fire had gone out of our romance. Not so much as a flicker was left. We had become the dullest couple. Yet when we first dated, he was a god to me. What is wrong with men? They are such impostors!"

"The problem with women is that they quickly place a man whom they like on a pedestal. When you elevate a man you miss the details. Keep him at eye level where you can judge him better. Furthermore, when a man fails to meet her glorified expectations, she becomes frustrated and discards him like an armless mannequin. It's only when a woman finds there are fewer men remaining from whom to choose, that she brings her expectations in line with reality."

"Men act the same way. And men are more mischievous and devious," she rebutted.

"Women prefer those kind of men."

"Nonsense."

"It's true. The weaker sex has a relish for reckless adventure. Some women would have a fling with the Devil just for the experience. That's why you read stories of death-row killers receiving hundreds of marriage proposals in the mail."

Monica's eyes bulged, and shook her head in affected annoyance.

"Have you always lived in Brooklyn?" I asked, shifting the topic.

"My family arrived there when I was five. I was born in Spain."

"Spain? How nice! Madrid, The Alhambra, bullfights, pretty señoritas on balconies being serenaded to."

"Spain was a prison to my family," she replied irritably. "My people are Basques."

"The folk from northern Spain fighting for independence, yes?"

"That's right. And for forty years that ruthless dictator Franco has tried to wipe out the Basques' quest for autonomy." Her breathing quickened, and there was rising emotion in her voice. "You have heard of Guernica?" she asked.

"Of course, the trashy painting that made Picasso famous."

"The *massacre* that took place there which inspired Picasso's painting," she sharply corrected.

"But Franco bombed Guernica because it was littered with communists and anarchists," I countered.

"Guernica is in Vizcaya, a province in northern Basque by the Bay of Biscay, where you will not find more devout Catholics anywhere!" she bristled. "The Basques are 5,000 years old, one of the oldest cultures in the world. We pre-date the arrival of Europeans, and were smelting ore when the Hebrews were still weaving baskets. Our language is not related to any other tongue. Scholars have never discovered, nor does our folklore hint from where we originated. If any people could claim to have sprouted from the soil, it is the Basque.

"Over the millennia my people have withstood invasions from Phoenicians, Romans, barbarians, and our most recent newcomer—the Spaniard. Foreign invaders have ruled us, but never conquered us; our culture and language have survived. But during the Spanish Civil War General Franco wanted to change that when he invited Hitler's Luftwaffe to bomb Guernica. My grandmother remembers that day. She was at the marketplace when she heard the drone of planes above the clouds, and then saw bombers dive like falcons from the sky. Buildings exploded everywhere, and after exhausting their bombs the Luftwaffe swooped low and strafed the streets with machine gun fire. Fifteen hundred men, women, and children were killed that day. Grandma lost her husband and a son."

Monica spoke of the destruction as if her grandmother's horror had been seared into her mind. "A fascist always has a pretext to justify his means. Although he prevented the communists from throwing Spain into anarchy during the Thirties and turn the Iberian peninsula into a satellite of the Soviet Union, Franco used the upheaval as an excuse to repress those who opposed him. He labeled the Basques as communists, and slaughtered with impunity. My grandmother said you can bomb a people night and day and destroy their towns and churches, but you cannot destroy their essence. Human nature becomes galvanized through hardship." She paused and lapsed into deep thought before adding, "But Marcel's death was senseless."

"Who is Marcel?"

She looked surprised, as if unaware that she had uttered his name. "Marcel is…was my cousin," she said in a strained voice. "He and his parents, my uncle and aunt, lived next door to my family. We were like brother and sister." Lowering her head she massaged her temples as if burdened by a headache. When she raised her head her eyes were misty. "He was murdered three years ago," she continued. "He was returning home one evening from classes at Iona; two thugs took his wallet and shot him dead. In one week he would have turned twenty years old.

"Marcel was a wonderful man. He loved life. There was nothing he would not do to help another person. Marcel was meant to live." Warm tears wetted her eyes and her lower lip quivered. "I had nightmares after his death. I thought I would lose my mind. I would see him running toward me calling my name. As he approached nearer his image would dissolve, but I could still hear him calling me and hear the sound of his approaching footsteps. I would answer, 'Yes Marcel, I can hear you, but where are you.' But he kept calling, 'Monica! Monica!' Then his voice turned to anguished shouts, and his footsteps echoed like explosions and I would wake up screaming." She cast her head down and wept, her long silky hair sliding off her shoulders and cloaking her face like a mourning veil. A long minute passed until she regained her composure, and then she continued: "The nightmares have gone, but he still visits me in his dreams. And they are the same dreams. I am looking out of the living room window of our house, and I see him drive past in his car and he waves to me. And in another dream the family is eating dinner, and Marcel appears at the table and I say, 'thank God you are alive Marcel. I only dreamt you were dead,' when suddenly I awaken and realize that the dream I took for reality was in reality a dream. And the strange thing is that in all these dreams I never see his face. It's as if the living are forbidden to look upon the dead."

"Remember that these are only dreams; fictional images that are manufactured in your mind," I assured her.

"When my grandmother lost her husband and son, they died as martyrs on their own soil. But Marcel's death was senseless. Ah, life is a vale of grief punctuated only by fleeting moments of happiness. I ask myself when, or if I ever marry, would I want to bring children into a hostile world? My mother always said when you lose hope Satan dances on his cloven hoofs for having claimed another victim." Then she looked at me with sodden eyes, and in a distressed whisper said, "But I've lost hope."

Until now Monica had erected an invisible barrier around her that kept familiarity at a distance. But this afternoon she decided it was time to communicate her feelings to me, at the expense of reliving personal tragedy.

"I still sense a strong Basque spirit etched within you."

"Life is so uncertain," she moaned.

"Very uncertain." Then I began rambling about the inequities in life, but I cut my monologue short because Monica appeared unimpressed; to her I was speaking platitudes. Then I resumed our discussion by saying, "You are going through a difficult passage in life. Two years ago I was at a very low point and so was my family, but it pales in comparison to what you and your family has gone through."

"What happened?"

"It was spring and I was finishing my first year at the university. My grades were poor, and I thought I was too dumb to be a university student. There are few things more frustrating than to be failing in academia, especially when one has worked so hard to get there. Moreover, I had emergency surgery, an appendectomy, just a few weeks before final exams. When I returned to classes I found myself light-years behind in my studies. I was in jeopardy of failing half my courses, and if I did I would lose my student deferment, and risk being drafted into the military. Two weeks remained before final examinations, so I studied until my head nearly cracked. I passed my courses, but just barely and was placed on academic probation. All I had to show for my first year at the university were low marks, and a six-inch purple scar on my lower abdomen.

"When things go badly it is natural to expect a reversal of misfortune. But only hard luck followed. I had been working part-time as a warehouse stockboy, but after my surgery I was unable to lift heavy loads and I lost my job. Nor could I find work elsewhere.

Dashed were my dreams of buying a car and driving to Jones Beach on summer days, where I would bronze my body and meet pretty girls. I spent most of that miserable, muggy summer moping around the house with not a jot to do, and no place to go. And at this same time my father's work hours were cut in half by his employer due to the bad economy. Money grew short, and mom was counting every dime. Anxiety reigned in our household: When would dad return to full-time work? How would the family survive? Would I be able to meet tuition payments for my studies?

"My father grew despondent. The family was under a terrific strain, and we got into spats over the most minor things. From the time I woke up in the morning until the night mercifully drew the day to a close, I wallowed in despair. Having neither occupation nor amusement, I spent the days thinking of everything that had gone awry in my life. I reflected on the four dismal years I had spent in high school, and my sour year at the university. I pronounced myself an abject failure, and saw no promise for the future.

"During the waning days of that summer I occupied my time in the neighborhood library, browsing through illustrated folios of Hawaii and other islands in the South Pacific. Paging through these books, I transported myself into a Gauguin world of Tahitian beaches with sugary sand and topless wahines. How I envied those copper-skinned natives living in tropical paradise having the blue Pacific as their playground. My sense of adventure was stirred, and I promised myself that one day I would enjoy such a life. So, I began to put my situation in perspective: Although I was going through a difficult phase, I promised myself that it would not last forever and that better times would emerge. Wallowing in abysmal misery was purposeless: I had to pull myself together. So, I decided to finish my studies and earn my degree come hell or high water. And as soon as I graduated I would reward myself by heading straight to the South Pacific, and live in a perfect world without crowded subways or fear of crime on the streets of New York.

"When I resumed college that fall, I applied myself in earnest to my studies. Meanwhile, my father had his hours restored and was back working full-time again. And now I'm a year away from graduating with honors. In retrospect, the summer of Seventy was a turning point. When there appeared to be no escape from my dilemma, I learned to grope through the gloom of my mind and find a path to a brighter future.

"Monica, take a look." I lifted my shirt, and with my finger traced a scar that was barely visible across my lower right abdomen. "The marks of my appendectomy have almost disappeared, yet it was once so deep and ugly that I thought it would never mend. When troubles come, as it does with frightening regularity, I look at that incision as a reminder that everything heals."

She remained silent as if waiting on my next word. But I had nothing else to add. Then she asked, "Do you still intend to plant yourself in the South Pacific after you graduate?"

"Unfortunately, paradise will have to wait. I've put too much effort into my studies not to apply what I've learned. I'll work for a few years, save my money, and then retire to the other side of the international dateline. And what a life that will be: Spending my days as a beachcomber drinking rum with a fishing line tied to my big toe, while she-natives in grass skirts fan me with palm fronds."

"Every guy I talk to has dreams just like yours. The Pacific islands will sink beneath the weight of every scalawag who wants to live there."

"And why not? Those savage maidens treat a man like a king. There, the dames aren't concerned about equality as they are in 'civilized' lands."

"You're a relic from the Dark Ages!"

"I'm a cave man. Pure Paleolithic."

"Be serious Byron. Are you really planning to throw your life away on a sand bar half-way around the world."

"Certainly."

"You'll die of alcoholism. Or boredom."

"Syphilis will get me first; it comes with the territory."

Monica shook her head. "How quickly you can move from being serious to absurd," she said drolly.

"I am a master at bathos. Perhaps I'm deceiving myself. But everyone needs a fantasy in order to cope."

My wisdom expended, I had no words left to say. An awkward silence descended. Monica leaned slightly towards me, her left leg crossing her right with arms folded and eyes fixed on the ground in a posture of guarded familiarity. She had related an unfortunate chapter in her life, but did my tale of personal hardship offer her empathy, or did she feel I belittled her sadness? Did I fill her soul with hope, or stuff her ears with gibberish? I gave her a tender squeeze on her thigh as I rose from the bench. "I must get ready for the dinner shift." And then I walked away. Several steps on I glanced over my shoulder at her. She had not budged, and remained in motionless melancholy.

XXVII

Hamlet: Do you see yonder cloud that's almost in shape of a camel?
Polonius: *By th'mass, and 'tis like a camel indeed.*
— Hamlet, Prince of Denmark

It was a majestic August day, marked by a warm breeze that carried the scent of the forest through the countryside. And above me the billowing clouds resembled vapory continents afloat in an ocean of blue sky. I could make out Australia and then Europe, where the boot of Italy drifted apart reshaping itself into the Isthmus of Panama which tenuously linked North and South America. And then the clouds became faces and figures – a dolphin's head, a kneeling woman, the profile of Abe Lincoln. And so the shifting clouds, like a mural in the sky, played with my imagination, until they formed Otto's nasty face and I abruptly abandoned my gazing.

It was too nice a day to spend its entirety at The Timberhaus, so right after lunch I headed out. I bicycled several miles past the outskirts of town, where the road wound and steepened around canyon walls until becoming too hazardous to negotiate. So, turning around I pedaled back to town, stopping at Willie's Café to devour a hamburger, fried potatoes, and a thick milkshake. Having rode nearly twenty miles I was sore in the buttocks and stiff in the thighs, so upon leaving the eatery I walked my bicycle through the remaining stretch of town to lubricate my joints and undo the stiffness. I must have been a merry sight indeed, walking as vertical as a penguin and grimacing with every step I took.

At the edge of town stood a modest pinewood church with a

gabled roof surmounted with a steeple, like one seen on postcards and wall calendars. On the front porch of the church were a pair of wooden arm chairs with cantilevered backs ideal for relaxing. Exhausted and sore, I parked my bicycle and ensconced myself in one of them. On the opposite side of the road lay open space, covered with a shawl of green velvet and embroidered with goldenrod, that spread to the distant hills. Such was the scenery I was admiring when I fell asleep. When I awakened I found a man sitting in the chair next to mine.

"Is the smoke bothering you?" he asked politely. He was about sixty and was holding a lit pipe.

"What time is it?" I asked excitedly. I feared I had slept for hours and missed the dinner shift, but my wristwatch assured me I had only dozed for twenty minutes. "Whew! I thought I had missed work," I said with relief.

"Do you work at one of the resorts?" he asked in a chipper voice.

"The Timberhaus."

"Dolores, our church organist, works there. Do you know her?"

"I do." She was one of the bookkeepers who assisted Heidi and was a nasty bitch.

"What's your name?" he asked, removing the pipe from his mouth.

"Byron."

"I'm Rev Hugh, church pastor." He was dressed casually, and not in cleric's attire.

"Please excuse me Pastor," I replied apologetically as I rose to my feet. "You must think me very bold. I had been bicycling all afternoon, and only wanted to rest a few minutes. I'll take my leave." I felt like Goldilocks having been discovered sleeping where she didn't belong.

"No, no, no. Sit and relax for as long as you like. I just came out to read the newspaper and blow smoke rings," he answered, with the stem of his pipe gritted on the edge of his mouth.

I slumped into the chair again for I was absolutely exhausted. "I've celebrated this beautiful day on my bicycle, but I've pedaled too many miles."

"It *is* a beautiful day. And it has been a beautiful summer. Just enough rain to keep the mountains green."

"It's been a miserable summer. I can't wait to get home," I said dejectedly.

"How unfortunate," he replied, as he lowered the newspaper and folded it on his lap. "I would think working at a resort would be fun."

"It's long hours with only one day off in seven. The working conditions are 19th century."

"Goodness." The cleric shook his head in dismay.

Then I rattled off to Rev Hugh the schlock I had to eat, the deplorable living conditions I had to suffer, and all of this compounded by the jerks whom I worked with. When I finished venting my frustration he told me that he had heard Papa ran a tight ship, but never imagined such conditions existed.

"Is there nothing profitable that you can reap from this summer?" he asked.

"Only that I will appreciate my bed more than ever when I return home."

"Ah, one day you will look back on your experience with fondness. Time dissolves misery."

"I doubt it." There was bitterness in my voice.

"Ah, but you will. You are young and do not enjoy the benefits of perspective as we older folks do."

I leaned toward him in my chair. "What do you mean?"

"When you return home and taste your mother's cooking and enjoy your first solid night's sleep in weeks, all the hardship you endured will dissipate like a bad dream. Right now you are too steeped in your immediate situation to see the reward of your toil."

"What reward?" I asked skeptically.

"The gratification of having endured loneliness and hardship that would have sent most young men packing after their first day."

"I hope you're right, Pastor." I leaned on my elbows and stared ahead at the open pasture whose tranquility teased my despair.

"How old are you Byron?"

"Twenty."

"Are you a student?"

I told him I was entering my final year at the university.

"You are at an interesting age. New chapters will be opening in your life very soon. When you graduate college you will become the steward of your life, and will be responsible for earning your own livelihood. Your life will be completely redefined. Happiness will no longer be interpreted by parties and poker games and sybaritic pleasures, but by the satisfaction of supporting yourself and loved ones. At times, life will seem very unfair as it does to you now. Obstacles will appear insurmountable, but with perseverance and fortitude you can overcome any impediment."

"I'm troubled about my future, pastor."

"Quite natural for a lad your age. Just do your best, and trust in the invisible hand that guides each of us."

"I've been tormented with 'what ifs?' What if I fail calculus? What if I get drafted? I think of so many hypotheticals ad nauseam. The irony is that I have ready solutions for other peoples' problems, but I can't find answers to my own uncertainties. For example, the other day I was consoling a girl my age who had lost a loved one. I advised her on how to deal with misfortune, and assured her that all grief passes. Would that I could heed the advice I give to others." I talked more about my apprehensions to Rev Hugh, who listened patiently. Then he replied with a single sentence, so profound in its simplicity that it carried the weight of a textbook:

"Do not fret about the future." The good minister paused to rekindle his pipe. Exhaling a puff of bluish smoke he continued: "To enjoy life in spite of its travails you must develop a personal philosophy, that will arm you against conflicts and console you in your troubles. What do you plan to do after graduation?"

"I'm tinkering with the idea of working in advertising, and concocting the best advertising copy on Madison Avenue that will sucker people into buying useless things."

The reverend smiled. "One of the cleverest advertisements I ever saw was in Alabama years ago. I had spent a year in the rural south ministering to tenant farmers. I was passing through a small town, and I spotted a marquee in front of a church that read: 'Most People in Hell Never Planned to Go There.' If that message didn't make people pause for reflection, I don't know what would."

"Maybe that's what churches need to fill their pews," I remarked.

"Fear of damnation?"

"No, advertising."

"The Word has flourished for two millennia on its own merit. A good product always sells."

"But it's not selling with my generation."

"Yes, and that concerns me."

"What's caused this change?" I asked.

"Among young people the Church is increasingly no longer a relevant and vital organ within society. Churches have been branded as charlatans for not providing solutions to social and economic ills. As religious institutions become distrusted, their dogmas are questioned: How could theologies dating back four thousand years be pertinent to the current era? After all, did not the prophecies and signs of wonder found in Scripture flourish at a time when most people were illiterate and superstition abounded? Had not many of the miracles and biblical origin of man been scientifically disproved? And why would an all-loving God threaten man with eternal damnation? Established religion, say the skeptics, is no longer applicable to the modern age. Answers are not to be found from the pulpit, but from university lecture halls and in secular literature. 'Eat from the Tree of Knowledge and your eyes will be opened,' said the serpent to Eve."

"Pastor, pardon my curiosity, but why did you choose the ministry?"

The prelate took a few meditative puffs on his pipe as he studied my question. "It seemed the natural course for me in the wake of previous roads traveled. In college I had considered several careers, none of them being the ministry. After graduating, I was swept into the war and spent the next three years as a naval officer in the Pacific. When the war ended I worked as a salesman for a large manufacturer. I earned good money, had prestige, and was promoted to a manager in the firm. But despite my success something was missing in my life. It was a dilemma for me, until I realized I had to define success on my own terms. Then it dawned on me that personal fulfillment would not come from material gain, but from helping others. Twenty years later I still think entering the ministry was the best choice I ever made."

The cleric radiated an incandescent harmony wrought from his compassion for others. Following a few moments of reflecting on his words, I turned to Rev Hugh and asked him something so irrelevant that as soon as the words dropped from my tongue I regretted having posed the question: "Pastor, is Latin the language of the angels?"

His pipe nearly slipped from his mouth, and he was seized with a petrified look. My face reddened with embarrassment for having reciprocated his wise counsel with such a stupid question. "Have you been talking to Horace?" he asked incredulously.

"Horace? The professor who lives alone in the hills?"

"So you know him! Who else would fill your brain with that silly notion!"

"He's bitter at the Church; holds it responsible for losing his professorship."

"Yes, yes I know. He's vigorously campaigning to revive Latin. He suggested that I offer my Sunday service in Latin, and has written letters to scores of clergymen to do likewise. He's an awful bother." Taking a puff on his pipe he added, "In a way I sympathize with Horace. Latin is a beautiful tongue, and though no longer spoken should still be studied, if only because it requires a student to use his brains."

"He darn near poisoned me with his…"

"Wine!" intercepted the pastor.

"Have you tasted it?"

"No! But he gave a bottle to my deacon and it nearly killed him! He wanted me to buy his wine for use during services, and hoped to eventually supply ceremonial wine to every church in the Catskills. I told him that his wine was snake venom, and if churches offered it to their congregations Christendom would be wiped out. He grew angry and declared that he drinks a glass every night at dinner. I told him if that's the case, he's the only one besides Rasputin who couldn't succumb to poisoning."

"He's thinking of picturing a monk on his wine label," I said.

"Lucifer would be more appropriate," rejoined the pastor who then broke out laughing. "I shouldn't talk like that about Horace. He's really an innocent sort. As long as he stays in the hills and doesn't push his poison on anyone, he won't cause any harm."

The afternoon was ebbing, and it was time that I return to The Timberhaus and leave good Pastor Hugh to his newspaper and smoke. I told him how happy I was to have chatted with him, for he was a wise and witty advisor, though not immune to being unnerved. He wished me success in school, and told me to remain steadfast during my remaining weeks at the resort. As I pedaled along the winding road, though still sore in my thighs, I was refreshed in spirit. How serendipitous that I should meet someone who provided me with words of encouragement when I most needed it.

XXVIII

If you have ever fallen on a rosebush and suffered the sharp prick of thorns in your flesh, such was my feeling when I awakened one morning after sleeping in the boat. The hull was badly weather-beaten, and splinters fastened to my arms and blanket during the night. So, after breakfast on this same morning, I set out to smooth the brittle wood with rasp, planer, and sandpaper I had borrowed from Gunther.

As I toiled in the sticky humidity, I noticed a person's shadow come up from behind and stretch across the ground in front of me. I turned around facing the sun, and saw a figure enclosed within a corona of yellow sunlight appearing like an apparition. Cupping my hands over my eyes like a binocular, I recognized Debra standing a few feet away.

"Are you fixing the boat?" she asked bashfully.

"I'm shaving the wood."

"Can I help you?"

"No thanks." Her expression turned doleful, so I immediately offered, "But maybe you could help me sand the wood? Would you like to do that?"

"Yes!" Her sapphire eyes brightened, and her face flushed with mirth.

Taking a sheet of sandpaper, I demonstrated how to apply it to the wood. She worked diligently as is the case with one of lesser faculties, who can focus on simple and repetitious chores which would weary a person of average intellect.

"You're doing excellent work," I told her. Indeed, she had done a fine job sanding the inner ribs and keel. My compliment left her smiling and open-mouthed, like a little child just given candy for good behavior.

"It's hot. Let's stop work," I suggested.

"Yes, it's hot," she repeated, as she wiped her beaded brow with the back of her hand, and then brushed the sawdust from her blouse and shorts. Two minutes passed without a word exchanged, as her mind slipped into limbo. Then she said, "I must finish cleaning the rooms. Bye, Byron," whereupon she skipped away. When she was some fifty yards from the pond, she broke into a run and shot across the field before disappearing over the knoll.

That night I dreamt that I lay in a field of green clover, where a lady suddenly appeared and kissed my forehead, and then fled into the morning mist. A moment later I awoke and thought I had caught the glimpse of a young woman running from the pond before vanishing into the pre-dawn darkness. I was not fully awake, and decided what I had seen was but the remnant of my fading dream. Next I heard a low "mee-ow" and found Churchill snuggled by my side. "Ah, 'twas you faithful friend licking my face. But in my dream you were a woman." Then I pulled the dew-covered blanket up to my chin and slept for another hour until daybreak.

The very next morning I awakened at dawn, and through blurred eyes I spotted the vague form of a girl disappearing through the curtain of willow branches. I rubbed my sockets to sharpen my vision, but she was out of view. Was I awake or was I dreaming? Was it possible to have the same dream two nights in a row? Or might it really be a phantom this time; a Mohawk squaw wrapping up her nightly haunt? But I'm certain this girl was dressed in bluejeans and not in deerskin. I jumped to the same conclusion about Johannes and his loony friends, but I still could not shake from my mind the ghostly legends of the Catskills. When I reached to my side to adjust my blanket, my hand clasped the stem of a red rose. Where did this flower come from? It could not have been carried by the wind, nor fallen from a vine for there were no rose bushes around. It had been placed purposely. But by whom? It had to be the girl whom I had just seen fleeing in my "dream." It was all very spooky.

Later that morning as I was washing the breakfast dishes, it dawned on me that the mystery visitor was Monica. Who else could it be? Only she and three others knew where I slept, and it was unlikely that Carmen, Tara, or Diane would have done it. She was playing a game to enhance her mystique, and using the rose as the basis for her plot. Were I to ask her if she had left the flower she would certainly deny it, and declare it absurd that I would even consider her doing that. Then Monica would have succeeded in having me admit my interest in her, by my suspecting that she had an interest in me. So, I decided to apply a bit of psychology to foil her childish prank.

That afternoon I joined the four equestrians at the corral, where I lingered with them before their trail ride began.

"There is a smell of roses in the air," I hinted.

"Smells like hay," countered Tara.

"I get a whiff of dung," said Carmen sniffing the air.

"I smell skunk," said Diane wrinkling her nose.

But Monica said nothing. Ah, much can be said for psychology when nothing is said. Now, I was certain it was she who had been to my boat!

When the girls left for their horseback ride, I went to the pond where a man was rowing with two little boys. I watched in amusement as the father had trouble navigating the rowboat, and it reminded me of when I first tried to plow the water with oars. When he finally managed to dock the boat, he looked as relieved as if he had just made landfall after being lost at sea.

"Phew, I'll never row again," he said wearily, as I steadied the boat while he and his sons stepped onto the wood platform.

"It takes practice," I sympathized.

"C'mon boys. Let's get ice cream."

"Daddy, I want to go back in the boat," protested the older boy. He was a chunky lad about eight, and had curly black hair.

"Daddy is tired, Randy."

"Take us out on the pond again," pined the younger brother. He was as thin as his brother was fat.

"Daddy has calluses on his hands from having rowed so much, Dommie."

"Let's go around once more," pleaded Randy.

"Daddy is beat. Now let's take a drive into town for ice cream," the father answered irritably.

"But daddy…" moaned little Dommie.

"Listen to me," answered the father in a rising voice. Then he placed his hands on his hips and shook his head in frustration. "Are you kids coming or not?"

"I don't want ice cream! I want to go in the boat!" answered Randy adamantly.

"Me, too!" rejoined his brother.

The father turned to me. "Do you know how to row that tub?"

"Of course."

He took out his wallet and withdrew a five-dollar bill. "Here. Take the kids out for half-an-hour. OK?"

"Sure, but I can't accept…"

He cut me off in mid-sentence. "Take it. Take it!" He shoved the bill into my hand. "Boys, this man—what's your name?"

"Byron."

"Byron is gonna take you out on the pond."

"Hoo-ray!" shouted his sons.

"Now you boys behave and obey Byron." Then the father turned to me: "I'm getting a cold beer. I'll see you later."

We had just cast off when little Dommie asked, "Are there any big fish in this pond?"

"Not any more. We caught all the sharks."

"There were sharks here?" asked Dommie. He fidgeted on his plank seat and spied a wary look around the pond.

"Lots of them," I replied.

"I thought sharks only lived in oceans," said the older brother skeptically.

"If you're a shark you can live anywhere you want," I answered. "But mermaids live in the pond now."

"Really!" the two boys exclaimed.

"Absolutely. I've seen them."

"Will we see them today?" asked Randy.

"They won't appear when people are around. They're shy."

"When did you see them?" asked Dommie excitedly.

"A couple of days ago. I was sitting under that tree by the dock, when I heard a large splash in the pond. I looked up from the book I was reading and saw a large fish tail sink beneath the surface. 'What a huge fish must be attached to that tail,' I thought. I could track the path of the fish by the ripple in the water as it swam just below the surface, until it reached that rock jutting out of the water in the center of the pond. Then I saw a pair of arms—woman's arms, long and slender—wrapping themselves around the rock, and moments later the head and shoulders of a young lady emerged from the surface. The fish tail I had seen was obviously a product of a wild imagination; someone had come to the pond for a swim and nothing more.

"Whoever she was then swam across the pond. I was amazed at what an excellent swimmer the lady was, for she swam effortlessly at a fast pace, yet never used her arms to stroke. Upon reaching that limestone overhang on the edge of the pond, she lifted herself out of the water and I could not believe my eyes—the woman was half-fish! Moments later she was joined on the limestone slab by two other mermaids, where the three laughed and talked and playfully splashed the water with their tails. They were creatures of remarkable beauty, with flowing, golden hair and fish scales that sparkled like aquamarine sequins."

"Sparkled like what?" asked Dommie, scratching his head.

"What were they saying?" asked Randy.

"Mermaids speak the language of Poseidon, a tongue unknown to humans."

"Tell us more," said Dommie anxiously.

"They appeared friendly, so I called to them and waved. But upon seeing me they panicked and slid from the rock and into the water; a moment later three fish tails rose vertically out of the water, and then sank beneath the surface. And I saw them no more."

"Why doesn't someone just dive into the pond and catch them?" asked Dommie.

"They enter the pond through subterranean passages that are impossible for any man to get to. No one has ever caught a mermaid. They are clever gals."

"You're lying to us," said Randy pointedly.

"If I am lying may a giant squid wrap its tentacles around me and drag me to the bottom of the pond."

"Are there giant squids in the pond?" asked Dommie nervously.

"Well if I lied, we'll soon find out," I replied cautiously. I rested on the oars and the boat glided to a stop. I feigned an apprehensive look, while the two boys looked anxiously over their shoulders and about the pond for any sign of a tentacled creature emerging from the surface. Thirty seconds of silence passed. "See boys, I was telling the truth. If I wasn't, you would hear me gurgling beneath the surface right now." And then I continued rowing.

When the father returned, his sons eagerly related my story to him. "Ain't no such things as mermaids," said their dad.

"But he *told* us," said Dommie.

I winked at the father.

"Well, maybe there are, who knows? Hey, thanks for minding the boys, Byron. Let's go fellas!"

I spent the remainder of the afternoon walking around the pond and thinking of Monica and the rose. Other women would express their intentions more openly, but Monica, being true to her stealthy nature, might be leaving me a scent to follow. I liked Monica, but her aloofness kept me at bay. What if her early morning visit was not meant as a prank, and the girl really liked me, too? Perhaps fate decreed her for me as a reward for my arduous summer. Just as these thoughts were lifting my feet off the ground, the gravitational pull of reality brought me back to earth. My infatuation with Monica was getting the better of me. But I needed to know where I stood with her. So I paid a visit to the cleaning witch.

Hilda kept a flower garden behind her cottage, that bloomed with yellows, purples, pinks, and reds. When she was not cleaning, she was doting on her flowers or "children" as she called them.

"Hello, Hilda."

She was on her knees breaking up soil with a hand spade. "Ah! You scare me!" she exclaimed, as she placed one hand over her heart and looked up.

"May I have a couple of roses?"

She got to her feet, screwed up her eye and asked, "How many?"

"Two."

"Two…OK, fifty cents."

"Fifty cents!"

"You think I toil in mine garden only for your pleasure?"

"Twenty-five cents."

"Okay, twenty five." She clipped me two red roses as I reached in my pocket for a coin. "Keep your money," she said as she handed me the flowers. "Now, tell me Byron, who is the lady?"

"What lady?"

"The lady you are giving the roses to."

"No lady," I answered, shrugging my shoulders.

"No lady! Hah!"

"Hilda?"

"What?"

"Have any girls asked you for roses in recent days?"

"None. Why you ask?"

"I was just curious. Thank you Hilda."

"Byron, you like Hilda's garden?"

"It's beautiful." And it really was.

"When I was a teenager I was an apprentice florist. I worked under the finest horticulturist in Germany. He taught me everything about flowers—cross-breeding, splicing, everything. I wanted to be a master florist, and dreamed of having mine own shop." She paused and a somberness eclipsed her gay expression. "Then the war came." Her eyes welled and her voice choked: "I must get back to work." Then she went down on her knees like a supplicant and resumed her gardening.

XXIX

Beneath its robe of joy, love carries a dagger.
— R. Mangan

The following afternoon I was standing at the pond's edge observing my image on the water, when another image joined mine.

"Debra, you always seem to appear from nowhere."

She giggled, taking pride in surprising me. "Are you taking the boat out?" she asked bashfully.

"I came here to read," I answered, holding up a volume of Herman Hesse that Heidi loaned me.

"Oh," she said with chagrin.

The girl's disappointment gave me guilt feelings. "On second thought, it is a nice afternoon for rowing. Would you like to go out on the pond with me?"

Her gloom vanished, her face brightened, and she nodded.

The boat was aground, and I pushed it to the water's edge. Debra got in, and shoving off from the rear I hopped in just as the boat slid into the water. She was thrilled. She contracted her shoulders and rubbed her elbows like an excited little girl. I rowed along the rim of the pond, and noticed Debra was mesmerized by the water's surface, as if it were a movie screen unfolding happy memories when she went boating with her father. After emerging from her daydream she asked, "Where will you go after the summer?"

"Back to college."

"College? I want to go to college."

"College is hard work," I responded.

"I like hard work. Hilda makes me work hard."

"Where will you go when summer ends?"

"Back to the farm. We raise chickens."

"It must be nice living on a farm."

"I hate it. I get very lonely. I want to go to college," she said firmly.

Then she opened her mouth as if to say something, but hesitated. Then she stared at me with a hollow expression and asked: "Do you have a girlfriend?"

Her question caught me off guard. "No…no, I don't have a girlfriend," I responded awkwardly. Her eyes glowed like two full moons, and a crooked smile beamed from her face at my response.

I rowed around the pond a couple of times more. Debra had fallen into reverie; she hummed and dipped her hand into the surface, straining the water through her fingers. Not another word was exchanged until I docked the boat. When we alighted she reached inside her handbag and took out a red rose. I was dumbstruck! Was it Debra who had been visiting me in my sleep? Her head was lowered as she stared at the rose, twirling it by the stem. She raised her eyes without lifting her head and handed me the rose. "I love you Byron," she said shyly.

I didn't know what to say. My God, the girl is in love with me! We stood in silence for a half-minute. And then I mumbled, "Thank you."

"Do you love me?" she asked in all innocence.

"The rose is very pretty. Thank you…thank you, Debra."

"Byron?" Her eyes pleaded for a response. An aggravated look swept over her face, as my troubled and confused expression exposed my feelings. She began pouting, and her chest throbbed with emotion. I reached out to hold her trembling hands, but she recoiled from me.

"Debra, I…I'm sorry. Please, don't be offended."

Then something in the distance caught her eye. A woman's voice rang out: "Debra, what are you doing?" I turned and saw a middle-aged woman walking toward us at a rapid stride.

"Ma…Mother," she stammered.

"Sweetheart, I've been searching everywhere for you this past hour," she said anxiously when she reached the dock. "Did you forget I was to take you to the dentist this afternoon? Why weren't you waiting for me outside the main office? I thought something terrible had happened to you."

"I'm afraid it's my fault. I took her rowing. It was my idea," I said. But her mother ignored me.

"Oh honey, you've been crying." She removed a kerchief from her purse and dabbed her daughter's eyes. "Has something upset you?" she asked, as she aimed a suspicious look at me.

"No mommy. Just sad the boat ride is over."

"Let's go, angel. The dentist is waiting."

As Debra was being whisked away, she glanced back at me; tears were flowing in currents down her cheeks. How I suffered for her. For a fleeting, precious moment she had basked in romance only to have her euphoria shattered, like a Gothic tale where a woman is turned back into a child by an enchantress.

"You look upset," said Nick, as I stepped inside the bunkhouse after returning from the pond. He was lying on the floor clad only in shorts, and sipping beer from a bottle. Snuggled next to him like a Persian cat was Cindy.

"I am upset."

"What's troubling you?"

"Don't ask," I said irritably.

"Aren't you touchy. By the way, who are those four girls who are always tagging along with you?"

"They're from Brooklyn. Up here for three weeks."

"I thought they might be your friends from back home."

"No. I've known them only a week, but they've taken a shine to me."

Just then Chris shuffled into the room. He had just awakened from a nap and was yawning.

"Go back to sleep, Chris," demanded Nick. He disliked Chris merely because everyone else disliked Chris.

"Why?"

"Because you're making me *yawn*," yawned Nick.

"Where have you been the last few nights?" Chris asked me.

"Camping in the woods," I replied.

"Nonsense. You've been flopping with those Brooklyn girls," quipped Nick.

"What girls?" asked Chris as he tucked his shirttails into his pants.

"Those four wenches that follow him like Pavlov's ducks," said Nick.

"Whose ducks?" Chris asked.

"Never mind," said Nick peevishly as he stroked Cindy's skinny thighs.

"A sip of beer?" purred Cindy. Nick handed her the bottle. She took a sip and handed it back to him. "All the waitresses are talking about you, Byron. They're wondering how you got those four girls under your spell," she squeaked.

"You're right, Cindy. It is a spell. At night I steal into the forest and make offerings to the woodland nymphs, who answer by casting enchantments on women while they're asleep," I said.

"What's a nymph?" she asked.

"A maiden fairy. The woods are filled with elves and fairies. They watch you, but you can't see them."

"That's only legend," said Cindy sarcastically.

"Legend? Have you never experienced the mysteries of the forest? Have you ever walked through the woods and heard the crunch of twigs as if someone were walking right behind you, but when you turn around no one is there. Or you suddenly hear a roaring wind racing through the forest that causes not a branch to sway or a leaf to stir?"

"He's scaring me," Cindy whispered to Nick. She looked frightened and curled closer to him.

"A lot of spooky things have happened to me at night in the woods," added Chris.

To which I replied: "As a matter of fact Christopher, one of the townsfolk told me he saw Chief Walk-on-the-Water last week."

"Who?" the three asked as one voice.

"The Chief is a 200-year-old Iroquois spirit. An eyewitness was walking along Hawkeye Creek around dusk, and he spotted him a short distance upstream. He saw the Indian walking on the surface of the water as if it were ice, and when he reached the opposite bank he vanished like a puff of smoke."

"Is that a fact!" said Chris excitedly.

"It is," I replied with a poker-straight face.

"I'm getting goose bumps. Give me another sip, Nick-baby," said Cindy.

"No Cindy." But she defiantly yanked the bottle from his hand, causing the remnant of beer to spill on both of them.

"You're a jerk!" he hollered at her. She looked ready to cry. The bottle rolled to the opposite side of the room spreading a lather of foam in its wake.

I used this interruption to go to my stall to gather my dirty clothes for laundering. Inside, Churchill was laying half-asleep on my mattress. He drowsily lifted his head, and opened one eye and then closed it as if to say, "I'm tired. Do what you've come to do and get out."

When I emerged with my bundle, I found Nick and Cindy locked again in each other's arms. The empty beer bottle lay in the corner, and the spilled grog filled the room with a stale odor.

XXX

So let this new disaster come.
It only makes one more.
— Homer

That night I had a dream which will always remain a haunting chimera. I dreamt that I was rowing on the pond, and Debra appeared on the shore with her arms laden with roses. Next I knew, she was sitting beside me in the boat, and in unspoken words conveyed her happiness to me. She was ebullient and her face was flawless, showing none of the signs of her palsy. It was a beautiful day; the sky was cerulean blue, and the Midas rays of the sun struck the pond waters gold. But suddenly, the sky darkened and the pond was transformed into a churning sea. I found myself alone in the boat, being tossed on the seething waters. And outside the boat standing atop the angry waves like a specter was Debra. Her expression was grave and her contorted lineaments reappeared, and the bouquet of roses in her arms had wilted into stems of thorns. Terror engulfed me. I struggled to awaken, but found myself locked in that state of nightmare from where I could not escape. I tried to scream but could not, desperately trying to utter just one scream that would shatter my subconscious and return me to the waking world. Finally I released a violent shout that woke me up. I sprang up in the boat. My brow was hot with sweat, and my heart pounded against my rib cage. What was it that had frightened me? I could remember nothing of the dreadful dream!

Like King Nebuchadnezzar of Babylon terrified by not knowing what he had dreamt, I thought about my disturbing dream when morning had arrived. How horrifying it must have been, causing my subconscious to repress any recollection of it! And my worst fear was having the terror of my previous night's sleep resurrected by suddenly remembering the details of the nightmare. Fortunately, I was off from work that day, affording me much needed distraction, as I had made prior plans to rendezvous with Danny. Later that morning I went to Brookhaven to meet him and his friend Linda, who worked in a nearby resort. There, the three of us hitched a ride on a truck along Route 19 to Hillview, where Linda's family lived. It is an historic hamlet founded before the Revolution, with a quaint town square famous for its public hangings in days of yore.

We joined several of Linda's friends at a restaurant and filled our guts with hamburgers and milkshakes. And later we sat on the green of the town square in the shade of maples and poplars, where Danny entertained us with his humorous rambling. He talked in great detail, taking thirty minutes to say what could be told in five. Though most of the time we couldn't keep track of what he was saying, it did not detract from our amusement, much like being able to appreciate an opera without understanding the words of the libretto. It was one of those rare and magical afternoons where time is suspended and life is harmonious.

I returned to The Timberhaus around four o'clock and retired to my stall to relax, where soon I would learn of an incident that triggered recall of my nightmare. A few others were lolling in the bunkhouse too, and I had not been there for more than a few minutes when Eric burst inside shouting: "Debra has drowned! They just dragged her out of the pond!" Had it been anyone else broadcasting this news other than a nut like Eric, I would have believed it; nor was there any reaction from the others, except for one worker who told Eric to shut up. But he shouted again, this time with an intensity dismissing any notion that he was joking. "She's dead! She's drowned! I swear to it! Come see!"

I catapulted from my mattress, sending Churchill who was laying on my chest, through the air and over the partition into the next stall. I raced with the others from the bunkhouse to the pond where a growing crowd was gathering.

Through a gap in the thick circle of onlookers, I saw Debra lying prone on the ground with outstretched arms. Undertones of "Is she alive? Is she dead?" circulated through the crowd. Then a voice shouted, "Let her through!" The circle opened allowing a woman carrying a small medical bag to pass. She knelt beside Debra and checked her pulse for vital signs of life, and then turning the unconscious girl on her stomach administered vigorous pumping with both her hands on Debra's back. A hush descended upon the spectators. Debra coughed and a gush of watery vomit spilled from her mouth. Sighs of relief swept through the crowd, with many making the Sign of the Cross in prayer. Men and women wept alike, and the names of the saints were openly invoked to ask mercy on the girl. Then Debra fell into a coughing spasm and her eyes blinked. She was alive! At this point Papa, Otto, and Hilda arrived, just as the distant siren of an approaching ambulance could be heard.

"Mein Gott, mein Gott! What has happened!" clacked Hilda, as the crowd parted to let her and the others through.

"She's alive," answered the woman who had brought the girl back to life. This Good Samaritan was a guest at the resort and a nurse by profession, I later learned.

"How has this happened? Who is responsible?" cried Papa. There was alarm in his voice and anguish on his face.

The ambulance had arrived. Debra, unconscious, had an oxygen mask placed over her mouth, and was strapped into a stretcher by medics in white jackets, who then placed her into the emergency vehicle. Papa, Hilda, and the woman who had resuscitated Debra also got into the ambulance; the rear doors were shut behind them, and the vehicle sped off with its siren wailing through the cloud of dust that it left in its wake.

A father and his teenage son had discovered Debra floating face down in the water only minutes before I had heard the news. The boy raced to the office to notify the management, shouting word of the accident to everyone along the way, Eric among them. Within minutes half of the resort's guests had converged on the pond. At dinner the mess hall was whirring with talk about that afternoon's incident, but there was still no word on Debra's condition. And there was speculation that Debra had attempted suicide.

"She could not have fallen from the boat, because it was tied to the dock," said one of the waitresses who had been at the scene.

"And what was she doing in the water fully-clothed?" asked another.

It had not occurred to me that the poor girl had attempted to drown herself, but now that appeared to be a reasonable possibility. Suicide—an act that is so final, so complete; the total destruction of one's own self. To be one's own executioner. As that dreadful word suicide floated in my head, the dream in all its vividness that I had from the night before burst into my mind. It was a premonition of Debra's death! She entered my dream to say farewell! This meant, of course, that Debra would not survive; perhaps, she was already dead!

Suddenly, I was thrown into a mental void where everything and everyone around me dissolved. While in my oblivion I relived my last meeting with Debra at the pond the day before, and how happy she was when I took her out in the boat. And then she gave me the rose and confessed her love to me, and how her brief flirtation with romance ended in bitterness. Then I snapped out of my limbo, and found myself back in the crowded and noisy mess hall. I felt weak and faint.

"Are you feeling alright?" asked Chris. He was sitting opposite me at the table, and noticed my pallor.

"Byron, you're as white as a sheet," another remarked, which drew the focus of everyone else on me.

I raised myself feebly from the table. The room fell silent. "What's wrong with him? He's ready to collapse!" I heard voices say as I walked dazed and confused from the room. I was assigned to bussing tables that evening, but I don't remember much. I was sleepwalking, somehow able to perform my duties without being conscious of what I was doing.

When I got off duty I walked through the grounds, trying to sort a blizzard of thoughts raging in my mind. In the dream Debra had that look of absolute hopelessness and grief that only the grave could resolve. A demon screamed in my tormented head that I had driven the girl to drown herself. I was certain she was dead, for a dream with so haunting a message could not lie. Debra had visited me in my sleep. Would she enter my sleep again and speak to me from the grave? Would my nights that were a haven of peaceful repose from days of arduous work become a nightmarish hell that would plunge me into insanity? When Monica described the nightmares following her cousin's death, I dismissed her dreams as nothing but figments of her imagination. How easy it is to counsel another's fear; but when someone tries to be one's own doctor, he is lost for a remedy. Dreams—the phenomenon that ushers us into an enigmatic realm that is as frightening as it is benign. One moment we find ourselves atop the tallest peak infused with happiness as we watch the world below, when suddenly we find ourselves locked within four walls, not knowing how we got there or if we will ever get out. Dreams can summon joyful episodes and reunite us with old friends; or, recall a painful experience that reopens emotional wounds.

I went into the recreation hall, and seeing Heidi asked her if she had any news on Debra. She had not, nor had Papa returned from the hospital, I was told. Then I called the hospital but was informed only next of kin could be given information on a patient, nor could they locate Mr Rudiger. I left the commons and wandered forlornly over to the stables, and then turned and walked back. Around ten o'clock I spotted Papa and Hilda alighting from a car and walking toward the office. I was about one hundred yards away; one hundred yards from hearing dreadful news. I began to tremble and my legs turned rubbery as I tried to catch up with them.

Heidi was hurrying out of the lobby just as I was walking in. "Oh, there you are; I was sent to look for you." There was urgency in her voice.

"What about Debra?" I asked in a frail tone. Suddenly, everything went into slow motion. A lifetime could have passed in the moment I waited for Heidi's answer. I watched her lips as they formed a response, and it seemed an eternity until the words fell from her mouth.

"Debra is alive. She will be fine."

My knees buckled and I clutched her arm for support. "What's wrong?" she cried out.

"I…I'm OK," I answered breathlessly as I regained my balance.

"Papa is back, and wants to see you in his office right now. Right *now*. Byron, can you hear me? Are you well?"

"Yes, yes, I heard you," for I had been mumbling to myself. My heart fluttered, and I tried to steady my legs as I headed to the office.

"Come in," I heard Papa's low, guttural voice say when I knocked on the door. The old man was pacing slowly back and forth, and distress was etched on his brow. Hilda was there, too; he spoke something in German to her whereupon she filed silently from the room. Then he motioned for me to sit, as he seated himself behind his desk.

"Debra is alive…"

"I just heard." There was a quaver in my voice.

"…und doctors expect her to be up und about in a few days."

"Thank God."

Papa looked upward as if contemplating what he would say next. Then he sank his head into the bowl of his hands and slowly raised it, dragging his fingertips down his wrinkled cheeks. "You und Debra were friends?"

"I knew her."

"You took her rowing on the pond a couple times, yes?"

"Yes sir."

"Did you do or say anything to upset that poor girl?"

"Of course not."

He slammed the palm of his hand down on the desk like a gavel. "And you were to meet her at the pond this afternoon!" he thundered, as his expression flashed to a tempest.

"No sir! I had no such plan." I was astonished by the question, and my tone convinced him I was telling the truth.

Papa's aspect lightened after his momentary cloudburst. "My dear boy, I believe you." His voice was now soft and conciliatory. Then he placed his hand against his forehead, and slowly shook his head. "Ah, this has been so upsetting. I met Debra's mama at the hospital, und she believes her daughter was expecting you to meet her at the pond this afternoon. Her mama told me Debra was in love with you. Und when you did not come, she grow upset und try to kill herself."

My head dropped into my lap and I began weeping.

"My boy, I have spoken unkindly. Everyone is saddened by what happened. But thank God she is alive." A minute passed while I tried to conquer my emotions. Papa then rose from his desk and gripped my shoulder. "Are you alright?" he asked sympathetically.

"I'm fine," I answered, as I smeared my tears across my cheeks with the back of my hand. When I looked up I saw tears collecting in Papa's eyes as well.

"Go now, Byron," he said weakly.

XXXI

Who cannot wonder at this harmony of things, at this symphony of nature which seems to will the well-being of the world?
— Cicero

After leaving the office I wandered aimlessly outside to settle my nerves. The night was tranquil, and a crescent moon hung in the sky like the ear of God eavesdropping on the earth below. When I heard Debra would live, the crushing anxiety and fear from a short time earlier began dissipating, but the intensity of that turmoil had left me with a deep emotional wound. After roaming for twenty minutes I walked to the pool and sat at its edge, observing the reflection of the stars on its surface. Then I heard footsteps and saw a figure approaching in the dark. My heart raced and a crippling fear engulfed my body. Maybe Debra had *just* died, and this was her spirit seeking revenge like the ghost of Hamlet's father.

"Byron?"

"Monica?" I asked in a panicked tone.

"Did I frighten you?" She issued from the darkness and into the glow of the pool lights.

"A bit."

She sat beside me on the apron of the pool. "You look pale and ashen. Are you ill?"

"I'm exhausted."

"Did you hear about the girl who nearly drowned this afternoon—the cleaning girl? Do you know her?"

"Debra the cleaning girl; yes, I know her. But she will recover. Where are the others?" I asked changing the subject.

"In the recreation hall. Aren't you going to ask about our trip to Howe Caverns?"

"Oh...yes...How was it?" I was lost in thought.

"Fantastic. We took a boat ride on an underground river. It frightened Tara. She kept asking the tour guide if the rocks might cave in."

"Were you looking for me just now?" I asked.

"No, I was only wandering about."

"Let's go for a walk," I suggested. We left the pool and walked along a trail that cuts the pasture and leads to the foothills.

"You are very quiet. Something is bothering you," said Monica pointedly. I had not spoken a word for several minutes during our stroll. "What is wrong?" she asked impatiently after I gave no reply.

I drew a long sigh, then I asked: "If a person, despite his good intentions, caused another great harm, is he culpable in any way?"

My question caught her off guard. "I...I don't know. It depends on what the person's motive was. Why would you ask me that?"

"Generally speaking, if good were intended but injury resulted, can the person who meant well be blamed?"

"Without knowing the circumstances, I can't say. Have you hurt someone?"

"Not intentionally."

"Who?"

"Debra, the girl who drowned."

She stopped and placed her hand over her mouth to stifle a gasp. "Tell me, tell me what happened Byron."

And I did. I told Monica everything about my meeting Debra the day before, her tearful departure with her mother, and my conversation with Papa.

"I don't see how you could be at fault," she replied compassionately.

"Yet I blame myself."

"You have been through hell and back. But tomorrow you will feel better," she assured me.

Having walked over a mile we reached the terminus of the trail. "The others may be wondering where you are. We should return," I offered.

"Let them wonder; the night is young," she answered, dismissing my concern. Then she slowly scanned the dark hills that rose before us in silhouette, and spotting a ledge projecting from the hillside suggested we sit there and observe the night.

From atop the shelf that rose about thirty feet above the base, the Catskill landscape lay before us cloaked in raven blackness, and above us the heavenly prairie, fertile with stars, hinted of infinite galaxies within the eternal cosmos. The night sky was beautiful and serene, belying the ongoing silent upheaval where celestial bodies are continually rent by stellar explosions. But when viewed from a telescopic distance the universe appears undisturbed, like those pictures taken from the moon revealing our planet as a gem of sapphire, free of conflict and quarrel. Just as distance in space transforms a muddle of stars into orderly constellations, perhaps the passage of time would crystallize my present anguish into a benign remembrance of an event that was now so troubling to my soul.

"I wonder if harbored in that milky cluster might exist a civilization like ours, where some tormented being might be peering into the night at this moment searching for an answer to his turmoil."

"And might he be sitting with a woman on a hillside?" asked Monica as she snuggled beside me.

The portals of our eyes met. At that moment she became everything to me—all of creation capsulized into a single human being. We kissed and curled ourselves into a passionate embrace.

"No, you mustn't," she said, checking my advancements. Then she slid out of my hold and straightened her blouse.

"I thought Monica was crazy about me!" I chuckled as I glided my fingers through her silky hair.

She gave me her typical noncommittal look that she wore like a veil to conceal her feelings. Then she replied sotto voce, "Do you think so, handsome?"

"I hope you are."

"I like you Byron. I really do. But Diane is the one who is crazy about you."

"How intriguing! I've been part of a triangle all this time. For some reason romance is enhanced when it has a geometrical aspect."

"Clever line. Euclid would be proud."

We embraced again, but she abbreviated my kisses by turning her head and whispering: "It's time to go."

Neither of us spoke as we walked back to the resort. Hand in hand we strolled in blissful silence, our thoughts in mutual harmony. When we reached the commons we stopped and kissed once more.

"Let's join the others," she said, taking my hand. But I did not budge, and when she pulled my arm to its length she stopped and rewound herself back into my arms.

"Sweetheart, it's been an exhausting day for me. I should retire," I answered.

She gazed into my eyes and replied, "Keep me in your dreams, and may they always be happy ones." Then she stamped a quick kiss on my lips and ran toward the recreation hall, where rock 'n roll music was blaring within. I went to the bunkhouse to retrieve my blanket and sweater, and as I walked to the pond I thought what an unusual day this had been; marked first with tragedy, then trepidation, and lastly romance—a three-act Greek drama in reverse.

XXXII

When a man is in the grip of difficulties he should say,
'there may be pleasure in the memory of
even these events one day.'
— Seneca

Two days after Debra's near fatal accident, Heidi came to me in the dining room where I was cleaning tables following the afternoon lunch. "Stop what you're doing and come to the office," she said with necessity.

"Now?" I asked.

"Please."

"What about this?" I pointed to my unfinished business.

"Leave it. Come quickly," she insisted, as she grabbed the damp cloth from my hand and tossed it on a table.

Two thoughts surfaced: I was about to be fired, or there was bad news from home. Outside, the sheriff's car was parked in front of the office.

"What is he doing here?" Heidi did not answer, but continued walking briskly ahead of me. She escorted me into Papa's office, then immediately left closing the door behind her. Papa was sitting at his desk, his head sunk between his shoulders, and standing behind him was the sheriff. My attention was focused on the lawman—his arms folded, his expression grim, and his metal badge throwing off a glint from the ceiling light—such that I did not notice the woman sitting just a few feet away.

"This is Mrs Martin, Debra's mother," Papa said. She was sitting on the edge of her chair with her eyes cast down, and both hands clutching a handbag that lay on her lap.

My heart began to thump. Would I be arrested? If so, for what? Debra's accident? The sheriff stepped from behind Papa's desk and approached me. I lowered my head to avoid his eyes. "Have a seat, youngster," pointing to a chair in front of the desk. The sheriff then sat himself on the corner of the desk, planting one foot on the floor and straddling his other leg across the edge.

"Byron, tell me about your relationship with Debra," he said directing his eyes to mine.

"Relationship!" I shouted as if I had been stuck by a pin, for the question assumed Debra and I were more than just friends.

"Or should I say your friendship with her," he replied in an apologetic tone.

"How is Debra?" I asked with a check in my voice as I glanced at Mrs Martin from the tail of my eye.

"She's recovering," the sheriff answered. "How did your friendship begin with Debra?"

I looked up and my eyes met Papa's heavy gaze. Immediately I averted my head. I felt that my voice would crack and I hesitated reply. "Why are you asking me these questions?"

"The sheriff's office is opening a disquisition into Debra's accident. And I'd like you to assist me by answering a few questions," he said politely.

"Please answer the sheriff, Byron," Papa added.

"It began as any other acquaintance at The Timberhaus," I replied in a throaty voice.

"Be more specific, young man," the sheriff broke in.

"We smiled at each other whenever we met; we engaged in brief chats."

"And you went boating together," he quickly returned.

"Yes."

"So you invited her to come boating," he said.

"No, she asked to join me," I replied. A sigh of disgust arose from Mrs Martin. The sheriff raised his hand to stop the grieving mother from any comment.

"How often did the two of you row on the pond?" he asked.

"Twice."

The sheriff stroked his graying mustache. "Did you ever induce the girl into romantic behavior?"

His voice turned authoritative, and our discussion was turning into an interrogation. Just as I felt my composure would fail, I answered firmly: "Absolutely not!" I looked defiantly at the sheriff, then at Papa, next at Mrs Martin, and then back at the sheriff. The boldness of my reply startled everyone. I spoke further, relating to the sheriff what I had told Papa the evening of the accident; and of the few times I met Debra at the pond; how she helped me sand the boat; and how cheerful our companionship was. "She enjoyed our get-togethers and reminisced about the happy times when her late father had taken her rowing. I was her friend, but I did not know how deep an impression I had made on her until that afternoon. It was our last meeting. She tossed me a rose, a red rose. And then she said," here I paused to stem my rising emotion, "she said 'I love you, Byron.'"

Emotion enveloped the room and Mrs Martin burst into tears. The sheriff, who was an acquaintance of the woman, crouched beside her and took her hand in his.

"Sheriff Wilson. Do you have any more questions for Byron?" asked Papa in a weary voice, who himself looked on the verge of tears.

"No sir," the sheriff replied, as he consoled the weeping mother.

Papa looked at me and motioned to the door. I rose slowly to my feet and left.

XXXIII

The main guest house at Brookhaven is an arthritic wood-frame structure, that tilts slightly on its foundation from years of accumulated settlement. And on this Wednesday afternoon a week after Debra's drowning, intermittent drops of rainwater fell like tears from its shingle roof following a morning downpour. The building was the personification of melancholy, and it was on the porch of this jaded building where Danny was waiting. When he saw me drive up he leaped across the balustrade, and ran down the sloping lawn toward the car like an excited puppy greeting its master.

"Good to see you, lad," he said in his lilting brogue as I stepped from the car. Then he looked over the automobile with a critical eye. "And who did you steal this from?"

It was a 1949 DeSoto that Giuseppe Roncalli loaned to me for the day. Giuseppe and his wife, both in their seventies, were a kind couple staying that week at The Timberhaus, where they had been coming for the past twenty-five summers. The Roncallis lived in The Bronx, and Giuseppe still worked as a cobbler in the same shop on Pelham Parkway for over fifty years. Giuseppe liked me, and in the course of my conversation with him the day before when I complained having no car on my day off, he offered me his DeSoto provided I "drive-a careful and no wrecka his baby." I had not seen Danny in nearly a fortnight. I telephoned him the day before to tell him I was able to borrow a car to drive to the lake. We both had off, and he jumped at the opportunity to join me.

"If this car were any older it would need a horse to pull it," Danny added.

"Don't worry. It will get us to where we want to go."

"Are you really set on going to the lake?" he asked.

"Wasn't that our plan?" Cooper Lake was ten miles away. It had an historic water mill and hiking trails, and was where Danny and I planned to recreate for the afternoon.

"I thought we might go to Earltown instead."

"Earltown? Why would we go there?" I asked impatiently.

"Beth and Peggy must report to the welfare department once a month, and they're scheduled for a meeting today at twelve thirty. They told me they would pay you the $20 transportation allowance that the county gives them; otherwise they'll take a taxi."

"I'll do it!" It was equivalent to two day's pay at The Timberhaus. Furthermore, the drive is scenic and I had heard Earltown is a pretty village.

"Good lad. The lake won't evaporate and can wait for another day; besides, 'tis just a water hole where the ducks pee. I'll tell the girls right now." Then he sped across the lawn and disappeared around the building. Two minutes later he returned with Beth and Peggy. The two girls looked sullen and apprehensive.

"Here's twenty dollars," was all that Beth said as she handed me the money. Then she and her sister took their seats in the rear of the car.

The girls barely spoke during the ride, and then only by whispering to each other. The forty minute drive wended through a soothing landscape of cordial hills, furrowed cornfields, and sunlit meadows. It was as if time had frozen, not a billboard or a light post marked the road; only an occasional passing vehicle on the two-lane road hinted of the twentieth century. Danny sat slumped in the front seat with his hands folded behind his head, gazing at the countryside through the windshield. But Beth and Peggy did not notice the beauty moving past them on the road. Their doleful expressions, captured in the rear view mirror, spoke of fear and apprehension. They were wards of the government, and today might learn that they were being assigned to new guardians. They did not enjoy freedom as others did; they were chattel and could be uprooted and sent from one foster family to another, as would a slave from master to master.

"Here it is," said Beth, pointing to a domed courthouse when we reached the town square. "The welfare agency is inside." I stopped the car in front of the building. "It will probably take an hour," mumbled Beth as she and Peggy alighted from the car.

I parked the De Soto under the shady canopy of elms that lined the street. Then Danny and I set out to stroll the village. The town square consisted of Georgian-style brick buildings arranged as a quadrangle, mimicking New England town layouts which were adopted by hamlets springing up in the New York wilderness in the late 18th century. Inlaid into the quadrangle was a park where cobblestone paths converged diagonally to its center, and here set atop a six-foot granite pedestal stood a bronze statue of Thomas Earl, town founder. The statue was heavily oxidized giving Mr Earl a greenish complexion, and his hair had a heavy dose of white from pigeon droppings. A gaggle of teenage boys and girls lingered at the statue, puffing on cigarettes and listening to music from a portable radio. And on the park benches sat elderly folk reading newspapers and watching squirrels, as they scampered across the grounds and spiraled up the trunks of maple trees.

As we walked past the village stores and offices, we found a barber playing checkers with a friend on a bench in front of his shop, as two townsfolk stood watching their moves. Next door, a tailor worked his sewing machine from just inside his shop window. And at the corner hardware store wheelbarrows, lawn mowers, and garden tools were displayed along the sidewalk. Across the narrow street on the opposite corner was the newspaper office of the *Earltown Gazette*. Next to it was a lawyer's office, and next to the barrister was a jewelry and pawn shop where "Levi Isaacs, Proprietor," offered "Quick Cash for Jewelry and Watches." And on the corner was a pharmacy and soda fountain where Danny and I stopped for a root beer. The jingle of tiny bells above the door announced our entrance, as we headed to the swivel stools at the counter. Our waitress greeted us with a wide smile; she was a plump woman with large breasts that strained the shoulder straps of her white apron. I asked her to bring us a pair of root beers.

"'Tis a pretty town, but there's nothing to do here," observed Danny. "The young people must be bored witless," he added, pointing to a group of teens outside who were loitering at the corner.

"Boredom is designed for youth," I answered. I had instant flashbacks to my own dog days a few weeks earlier before coming to the Catskills.

"'Tis true. Youth is spent nine dreadful months each year in the classroom, followed by a boring summer waiting for school to re-open. A pitiful cycle, indeed."

"Indeed," I echoed.

"Can I get you fellas anything else?" the waitress asked as she set our sodas on the counter.

"No thank you," I answered.

Danny drew a long sip of root beer through his straw. Then he said, "Life is unfair when you're young. On the other hand it must be terrible to be old. Old-timers have little to do except to wait for the Grim Reaper. People work hard all their lives, in order to have money to enjoy themselves when they retire. But by then they're either too old to enjoy life, or else they have only a few years left before they're tucked into the soil."

"Irishman, you are too young to dwell on such things."

"But someday I *will* be old," he retorted.

"So will I. And so will everyone else who rides out their life span. The only alternative to old age is to die young. I'll choose the former."

"Not a day passes without my thinking about it," he said glumly.

"Think about what?"

"Dying," he groaned.

I thought he was joking. Danny stared straight ahead locked in deep thought, as he idly rotated his drinking straw between two fingers. But he was serious. "Ever since I was old enough to grasp the concept of death, not a day has lapsed without the notion stirring in my brain."

"I find it incredible that a young man in excellent health could entertain such an idea. Have you had a brush with death, or maybe lost a loved one?"

"No, no lad. I just *told* you I have always thought about it. I don't know why—maybe I was conceived with it. It's my first thought when I awaken, and the last thing on my mind before falling asleep."

"Is it that you fear what awaits you on the other side?"

"No. It's not knowing when death occurs," he replied.

"I don't understand."

"I'm a creature of science. I view life scientifically, not religiously. When a person dies, is he really dead? A post mortem may pronounce him dead, but is his mind still alive and can his body still feel sensation?"

"The mind is immortal and eternal; at bodily death it enters a spiritual realm," I retorted.

"I'm not talking about consciousness in the afterlife," he countered.

"I've never known a corpse who could laugh or cry," I said light-heartedly.

"But maybe a corpse would like to scream 'get me out of this tomb!' Do we really know if the mind passes into spirit? Or does consciousness remain within the body? Think about that lad. Think of being conscious at your own funeral."

"I would rather not. Nor should you. Thinking of such macabre ideas will drive you mad. Leave such matters to the theologians." To inject levity into the conversation I added: "Perhaps you should consider becoming a Moslem; their Koran says that when they die they enter Paradise, where they are served by seventy virgins."

"Would that it were true, lad," sighed the bartender.

"It is certainly more juicy than the traditional view of Heaven. George Bernard Shaw remarked that having to listen to harps and singing angels all the time would be quite boring."

Danny forced a weak smile.

"And how about the ancient Babylonians who worshipped Baal. To earn salvation every virgin had to congregate outside the Gates of Ishtar and prostitute herself to any passerby. Imagine the lucky tourist who undertook the task of being an obliging missionary."

But my humor failed to change Danny's mood; he remained sunk in his morbid and neurotic thoughts. But he snapped out of his musing when the jolly waitress asked him if he wanted another root beer.

"No thank you, doll," Danny answered with a cheery smile that gave no hint of his inner unrest.

"What brings you fellas to town?" she asked in a pleasant

voice, tempered with the innate mistrust that small town folk have of strangers.

"Just passing through on a day-drive," I replied.

When she left I mentioned to Danny that visitors like ourselves might be perceived as threats to this tradition-bound community, where American flags hang from porches, church bells toll the hour, and every store is closed on Sunday.

"A threat to their tradition!" he retorted incredulously. "The only tradition I've seen here are lazy teenagers and old people feeding pigeons."

Danny drained the root beer from his glass, I paid the waitress, and we left. We turned the corner and walked down the block, which brought us outside the quadrangle and into the town's residential quarter. Here, two and three-story frame houses with gabled roofs and wide verandas reclined in front of broad green lawns that spread to a maple-lined street.

As we strolled past the homes, Danny was uncommonly quiet. He tapped the sidewalk with a bramble in tempo with his footsteps, and seemed immersed in personal turmoil. There was another person behind the mask. Beneath his smile lay an underlying moroseness; his humor was but an antidote to his inner demons. We returned to the car to wait for the girls. A few minutes later Beth and Peggy emerged from the courthouse. Their eyes were red from crying.

"I'm afraid to ask them what happened," Danny whispered to me as the sisters approached.

I opened the rear door of the car for the girls. And as I was about to start the ignition I suggested we picnic at the park as I had rolls, cold cuts, and soda which I had brought for Cooper Lake. The girls agreed. I removed a plastic storage chest from the trunk of the car, and the four of us went across the street to the park where we spread a blanket. As I was about to pass out the food, the girls burst into sobs. It took a few minutes for them to regain their composure, and then they explained that the welfare department was reviewing a custody request by their parents, and that it was possible each of them might wind up living with a different parent. Their mother had undergone successful rehabilitation for alcoholism and was pronounced "dry"; and their laggard father had returned to the area after a long absence, had found a job, and wanted his daughters back. But the girls wanted nothing to do with their parents. On the other hand if their parents were not granted custodianship, both girls would be assigned to a foster family when the summer ended.

"I can't live like a bohemian. It's like living in a circus troupe—moving here, moving there. I'm running away," said Beth defiantly.

"Me too," added her sister.

"Things will work out," assured Danny, as he poured soda into paper cups and handed them to the girls.

"How will they!" snapped Beth.

"They will. Every problem has a solution. *Every* problem. Trust me girls." Danny put on his mask again; he who was so pessimistic a short time earlier was now the eternal optimist, dispensing wisdom and advice like a sage.

"It's easy to be rosy about another's future," replied Beth cynically.

"I propose delaying this discussion 'til after lunch," I said softly. "Ham or bologna on your roll?"

"Bologna," answered Beth.

"Ham," mumbled her sister.

The girls barely touched their food. They were twin portraits of despair—benumbed with hopelessness, and eyes cast down to avoid facing a world of gnawing uncertainty. Then Peggy's portrait changed to alarm when someone caught her attention.

"Beth, look who just arrived," said her sister with a tremor in her voice.

"Oh, no!" gasped Beth, who was suddenly seized with fright.

I looked in the direction where Beth's eyes were fixed and saw a tough-looking youth swagger into the park, where he joined the group of teens assembled around Thomas Earl's statue. He had not been chatting long with his friends when he spotted Beth and called out to her, but Beth pretended not to hear. Then he came over to us.

"Hello Beth, what brings you and little sister back to town?" he asked smartly.

"Leave me alone, Jimmy," she answered firmly without looking at him.

"Is that any way to greet an old boyfriend?" he sneered. Then he crouched to his knees, coming eye-level with Beth who refused to meet his bold stare. "Let's kiss and be friends again," he offered, as he drew his fingers through Beth's hair.

"Don't bother me!" She recoiled and gave him a sharp slap on his invading hand.

Momentarily stunned by Beth's reaction, the ruffian then vented his anger on her.

"You are a —!" he shouted in Beth's face, finishing his sentence with an obscenity.

Danny shot to his feet and launched a verbal assault. "Foul-mouthed hooligan! Crawl back to your hole!" he hollered.

"Watch your language, you skinny mutt!" the bully shot back, as he moved toward Danny with his fists clenched. Beth tried to block his path, but the thug shoved her aside.

"Your tongue should be torched, and don't be pushing that girl, you snake," the little bartender said sharply.

"Is that so leprechaun!" shouted Jimmy, who moved so close to Danny's face that the tips of their noses almost touched.

"Aye, 'tis so! You're an overgrown baby who has never left your mother's breast!" The Dubliner neither flinched nor blinked an eye in front of the goon who loomed above him.

The hoodlum's face ignited with rage, and fire was kindled in his eyes. But little Danny gave no hint of fear, and was more resolute than ever.

"Apologize or I'll—"

"Or you'll do what?" retorted Danny, cutting him off.

"I'll kick your..."

"You'll kick nothing," snapped Danny defiantly.

The brute answered by thumping Danny on his shoulders, who responded by thumping him back. Meanwhile, I rose to my feet to intervene if necessary. Then I noticed a perplexed expression flash across the bully's face which read: "What if this little guy did possess the physical wherewithal to back up his cockiness?" The confrontation was akin to the roaring lion and the whip-wielding trainer; Danny was the trainer who had to remain dauntless or risk being devoured. So the rogue decided to cut his losses and retreated slowly in backward steps, while casting vicious looks at Danny and Beth. Then he reared around and stomped out of the park.

"He could have ripped you in half," said Beth, as she threw her arms around Danny and hugged him.

Danny wore a smile so broad that his face widened twofold. A short time earlier he had been as dismal as a rainy day in Dublin, and now he was bright and cheerful from his triumph. "Aye you're right, he could have halved me into two Dannys, that's for sure. But I used a bit of psychology on him, putting enough doubt into his small brain that I just might be as tough as my words."

The bleakness of the two girls had vanished, and both were now buoyant from having seen the scamp vanquished.

"Now that the weasel has been slain, let's finish our lunch and see a movie," I suggested. "*Kung-Fu Carnage* is playing at the theater. It starts at 2:30, that's a half-hour from now." I remembered seeing the show time on the marquee, when Danny and I had been walking the town. I thought the movie would be a good diversion for the girls as there was little else to do. The picture was an action-loaded thriller that had been very popular among movie-goers that summer. It featured an heroic karate expert who tracked down villains and brought them to justice by beating them to death.

The others agreed to my proposal. After finishing lunch we left the park, and headed to the theater a few blocks away. The movie was laden with violence, and the most brutal scenes were filmed in slow motion to enhance its graphic aspect. It had no plot whatsoever but the girls loved it, while Danny and I thought it so stupid as to be entertaining. And the movie did leave its impression on young viewers. After the performance several youngsters were reenacting scenes from the movie, by belting each other with karate chops and leg kicks as they left the theater.

"'Tis no wonder you Yanks be killing each other," remarked Danny, as he watched the kids trade kicks and blows.

It was now 4:00. We returned to the car and drove back to East Durham, so that the girls would not be late for work.

XXXIV

"Are you going to the campfire tonight?" Carmen shouted from her bicycle when she spotted me leaving the recreation hall. Every Tuesday night a campfire and sing-a-long was held in a grove alongside the stream.

"I will be there," I replied. "And I'll swipe a bag of marshmallows from the kitchen to bring."

"Don't bother. We have enough marshmallows to build a snowman," she answered as she glided by. Then she raised herself from the seat of the bicycle and pumped hard on the pedals, as she sped past the main gate and onto the public road.

There were about a hundred people at the campfire, mostly teenagers and parents with small children. It was a beautiful, moonless night with the stars flickering like votives across a sable sky. The acrid smoke from the blazing brushwood created a musky aroma, and the pulsating heat of the fire was a warm blanket against the nippy air. No greater fellowship exists among people than when they are united in campfire song. Italians, being great lovers of lyric, broke into melodious jingle as they swayed left and right to the accompaniment of a concertina. And there is something about a campfire that evokes the primeval past, when our prehistoric forebears used the open fire as the focal point of communal ritual. There is a hypnotic, mystical element of fire that subdues the mind and stimulates the subconscious, as it must have done to the ancients during pagan rites who augured events from its flames.

"Is it my imagination or do you see how the singing seems to orchestrate the movement of the flames," remarked Monica, who was sitting beside me.

"I do see a correlation," I replied. Indeed, the flames rose higher as the singing reached a crescendo, perhaps attributed to the exhalation from rising voices that fanned the flames, and then fell as the voices lowered.

"Byron," said Monica nudging me with her elbow, "do you know that young man sitting by himself behind the crowd?"

I raised my head and spotted Fred, my boyhood acquaintance introduced earlier in this story. He was sitting on a tree stump separated from everyone else. "That's Fred. He does odd jobs around the resort."

"This afternoon at lunch he was bussing our table and hadn't a clue as to what he was doing. He went from table to table in a daze and the waitresses were ready to choke him. I had barely touched my food when he reached for my plate. I had to snap it from his hand before he put it in the cart."

"Believe it or not, he's from my neighborhood. I've known Fred since I was a kid. He's an imbecile."

"Oh, you shouldn't talk like that about people," she said in mild reproof.

In the middle of a lively song, Diane and Tara abruptly rose and left. They were gone some time, and just as I was about to look for them Tara returned. She was daubing the rims of her eyes, swollen with tears.

"Are you OK, Tara?" I inquired consolingly. I assumed she and Diane had had an argument.

She sniffled, then gestured she was alright.

"Where is your sister?"

She answered by pointing to a copse of trees several yards away.

I went to the thicket, where I found Diane sitting on a fallen timber looking skyward. I watched her from behind a tree, peeking over a branch and not sure if I should interrupt her. I walked toward her, and when she saw me she turned her head away. She had been weeping.

"What's wrong?" I asked softly as I sat beside her.

She murmured something that I did not understand, and then placed her head into her hands. I put my arm around her shoulder; she sank her head into my chest, and then broke into convulsive sobs. Her grief was intense, and I was at a loss as to what was distressing her. After a couple of minutes her weeping stopped, but she remained clung to me with her hands gripping my shoulders. Then she slowly lifted her head, as if awakening from a sleep. Her face was rinsed from crying, and her locks were matted across her dampened forehead and cheeks. She wiped the corner of each eye with a fingertip, and then drew back the moistened strands of hair over her shoulders.

"I'm sorry…I'm sorry. I lost control of myself," she said in a halting voice. Then she sat upright and edged away, opening a small berth between us.

"What's happened, Diane?"

She drew a deep breath. "The song. When they started singing that song—it was my father's favorite. Every year since Tara and I were little he accompanied us to the campfire. There was so much gaiety then. Only last year he was here with us singing spiritedly in his strong tenor voice. We had so much fun. Now he is gone. Nothing will ever be the same. Nothing will ever be as good as it was."

"I've said that many times as well. But I keep reminding myself that I have lived but a fraction of my years, and many good things await me. I hope."

"And many cruel things, too. When my father suddenly died last year, my life turned upside down; it was as if the world slipped off its axis. I've been left with a foreboding of insecurity that anything might go awry at any time. I'm most fearful when things run smoothly, because that's when the unexpected happens. My father was a good man." She paused and dropped her head; then in a plaintive whisper asked, "Why did he die?"

"That's a question you'll be asking yourself for a long time. And no one has ever come up with a suitable explanation as to why someone so dear to us can be suddenly taken away. Unfortunately, it's beyond our human intellect to understand. I've never lost a parent, but I've witnessed the grief of friends who have. Physical loss is so permanent. As certain a fact that each of us will die, it is still incomprehensible that the only life we have ever known will eventually be extinguished forever."

I placed my arm around her and drew her to my side. "Diane, do you believe your father still exists—not in human form, of course—and that he might be here with you right now?"

She looked at me anxiously and asked, "Do you think he is?"

"I think so. People who have lost loved ones have told me that they can still perceive their presence, as if a sixth sense can feel the pulse of the unseen. I'm not talking about a séance, but a genuine spiritual companionship."

She looked at me quizzically. "But how can we know that?"

"Well, consider that a person can detect rain on a bright, clear day because of subtle changes in body pressure and temperature. And that animals can sense the slightest movements below the earth's crust just before an earthquake strikes. If physical senses can perceive what can't be seen, then we cannot dismiss that our mental faculties are capable of detecting spiritual phenomena. I truly believe our consciousness is linked to a higher consciousness." Diane appeared a bit baffled and was about to say something, but didn't. So, I continued:

"Perhaps I'm sounding too metaphysical, but..."

"Sounding too what?" she asked.

"Let me put it this way. Even if you doubt your father's spiritual presence, he is still present in you and your sister. You are his physical legacy. He brought you into the world to be happy and successful. You love your father, so you must do everything to make him proud of you as if he were alive. But he is still alive, residing in a realm closer to you than you can ever fathom."

An expression of relief crossed her face, as if she had awakened to some tremendous truth. She rose to her feet and wiped her eyes, feeling more confident and composed.

I stood up and extended my hand. "Come, let's join the others."

Taking her hand in mine we returned to the campfire, and for the next two hours we sang until our voices were hoarse. Finally the blaze dwindled to glowing embers, and the crowd dissembled. I walked the four ladies back to the cottage, bid them goodnight, and gave Diane and Tara a parting hug.

XXXV

The monuments of wit survive the monuments of power.
— Francis Bacon

"Hello!" I cried out to Monica and the girls. I had just left the scullery following lunch and was heading to the bunkhouse to shower, as they were walking toward the shuffleboard court.

"Did you sleep well?" asked Diane.

"Like a bear hibernating. And let me say that the creatures of the night are much quieter than the creatures of the bunkhouse," I replied, as I uncapped the bottle of cola I had in my hand. I had just gotten off kitchen duty and my throat was drier than sandpaper. In a single gulp I almost emptied the entire bottle. Then I wiped my lips with my forearm and said, "It must reach 110 degrees by the dishwasher. It's like working in the coal room of a steamship. And what might your plans be this afternoon, ladies?"

The girls looked glum and answered with a shrug of their shoulders. A lingering morning fog had reduced the landscape to a cheerless monochrome, which reflected the mood of the girls.

"Nothing in particular. It's too chilly to go swimming, and we're not planning to go horseback riding," answered Diane.

"It's either shuffleboard or tying a noose around our necks," added Carmen.

Suddenly an idea percolated, so I offered this suggestion: "A few days ago I discovered a waterfall about a fifteen minute hike from here that empties into a swimming hole. And beside it lies a vacant cabin tucked in a forest glade, where there are rope swings and hammocks suspended from boughs. It's a great place to relax and have fun. I think I'll head up there right after I shower. Care to tag along?"

The girls looked at each other, and nodded in agreement. "Good, I'll check back with you in twenty minutes." After scrubbing the grime from my body and hair, I changed into my shorts and grabbed a beach towel. Then I rejoined the girls and the five of us began our trek upstream.

The fog had lifted and a strong sun emerged when we reached the falls. Lack of rain in recent days had trimmed the falls to a thin sheet of water, which poured from an overhang some fifteen feet above a natural pool. Hedging the falls were layers of terraced slate that provided a staircase to the ledge from where we leaped, as the pool was deep enough to allow us to jump without touching bottom. We had a feast in the water. Each of us cannonballed recklessly into the pool, barely missing crashing into one another by mere inches. At times I found myself pulled beneath the surface by my ankle, and no sooner did I rise to the surface when one of the girls would dunk my head below again. The pool had a diameter of some twenty feet, and Tara had the notion that we create a whirlpool. So, around and around we swam along the circumference, until we created an eddy of significant strength that propelled us into a whirl. And whenever the swirling motion began to ebb, we immediately renewed the rotation, until we made ourselves dizzy from the gyrating current.

After our frolic in the water Carmen and Tara took to the swings, gently pumping their legs, while myself and the others reclined on hammocks with the warm sun massaging our faces. Then an idea stuck! It occurred to me that this would be an ideal setting for story-telling. I rolled off the hammock, and beckoned the girls to gather in a circle with me on a soft, sunlit patch of ground in the grove.

"Good women, our gathering here on this beautiful summer's day summons to mind Boccaccio's *The Decameron,* a collection of wonderful stories narrated by ten young ladies and gentlemen, while taking refuge in the Italian countryside from the ravages of the Black Death. Back-dropped against the 14th century pestilence that was decimating Europe's population, they lived idyllically for ten days amusing themselves with stories of misfortune and comedy, sprinkled with characters from all avenues of life.

"Their only rule was that they were to leave behind their woes and grief and enjoy one another's camaraderie through the magical balm of recounting tales. Six hundred years later we are assembled here in the Catskills, and I propose that we continue that fine tradition by each telling a story, and as we are five in number, let us call our gathering 'The Pentameron.' Each of us has been wounded by personal sorrow or tragedy handed to us by life. Indeed, the near-fatal drowning of a young lady recently is still fresh in our minds. So I ask that our only rule be that we set aside our troubles this afternoon and be gay and merry, and entertain ourselves with tales of wit and humor."

The girls readily adopted my proposal, and without hesitation Monica offered the first story:

"I, too, have read *The Decameron*, and I recall that each story-teller prefaced his tale with a hint of what irony or suspense would unfold. Using that format let me begin by saying that sometimes we are disappointed when we pray to the Almighty and our petitions go unanswered, causing us to regret the time spent in humble supplication to the Heavenly Benevolence who appears to have ignored us. But sometimes it happens that a prayer is answered with such unexpected results, that not having prayed at all might have been the wiser course.

"Lucy McGwinn hailed from an upright and religious family in Brooklyn, and because of her good rearing she practiced her Christian faith by kneeling in prayer every night before bed, and never missing Sunday worship. This was commendable behavior for a twenty-four-year-old lady, as most maidens her age give little thought to religion and the salvation of their souls. Yet Lucy was not a prude; she had an active social life, but no matter how late she and her girlfriends caroused Manhattan's Saturday night spots, she never missed services at Glad Tidings Church on Sunday morning. She even sang in the choir, having a liquid soprano voice worthy of a seraphim.

"In judging her looks it depended on which half of her body you appraised. Lucy best attracted men when she sat at a table, where only her northern hemisphere was visible. She had a beautiful face with large green eyes, a fine nose and mouth, and flowing auburn hair. Her shoulders were magnificently rounded, her waist was slim, and her slender arms terminated into delicate, soft hands. But her beauty ended at her waistline. Her lower region was in stark contrast to her upper anatomy; it was as if her southern sphere was grafted from another's body. She had an enormous buttocks that stuck out like a Kalahari, where the women of that African tribe are able to carry their children on their backsides. Her disproportionate anatomy, while detracting from her otherwise handsome features, did not render her entirely displeasing, for men were able to overlook her unfortunate abnormality and derive pleasure from her other parts. Yet it did hinder her from enjoying a lasting relationship, because every man she dated would in time become less forgiving of her hindquarters.

"When a teenager, Lucy often came home from school in tears because of classmates poking fun at her huge backside. Fed up with the taunts his daughter was receiving from other children, Lucy's father devised a plan to turn his daughter's burden into a blessing. So one day he brought her to the Brooklyn Museum where a replica of Venus de Milo was on exhibit. In the gallery where Venus was displayed, a dozen or more people stood breathless gazing at the armless statue.

"'That is one of the most famous sculptures in all of ancient art,' her father explained. 'It depicts the Greek goddess of love and beauty. Look honey, look at the facial expressions of the visitors; they are absolutely amazed by that woman without arms. They don't see her as deformed. In fact, they are overwhelmed by the soft curves and harmony of her body, that breathes life and motion into the marble. And sweetheart, you will always be a goddess to me.'

"Lucy was ebullient, and from that moment she was convinced that her derriere was nothing to be ashamed of; maybe even to be proud of. And she thought perhaps someday a sculptor would immortalize her nude body in stone, and museum-goers would be as much awestruck by her plump rump as they would by an armless torso. However, her father's quick fix solved one problem only to give rise to a much larger one, i.e. Lucy's newly found confidence gave her little incentive to prune the size of her buttocks, something she would regret when she got older. What daddy should have done was force his 'little darling' to do rigorous exercise, and sear her fat butt with a branding iron every time she was caught eating candy.

"Now in her twenties, Lucy had a real dilemma. For a solution she appealed to the Almighty to unite her with an understanding man, who would be able to reconcile her imperfect anatomy with her other fine attributes, and appreciate her as a loving and caring woman. There is someone for everyone she always heard her mother say, and she believed there was a special man in her life out there waiting for her. Each night she prayed in earnest, and at Sunday services she sang with purpose and fervor, making certain she caught the ear of He who hears everything. Within a fortnight her prayers were answered!

"It happened that one evening after coming home from work feeling depressed, she began brooding over her loveless life; so, to take her mind off her woes, she escaped her lonely apartment and dined at a nearby restaurant. When she finished dinner and was ready to leave, a sudden, heavy downpour delayed her departure, so she lingered in the restaurant lobby for the rain to lighten before going to her car. She was waiting perhaps ten minutes when a tall, handsome gentleman entered through the front doors, folded his umbrella, and headed to a telephone booth in the lobby where he searched for coins in his raincoat pocket.

"Unable to find change to make his call, and there being no one else in the lobby but Lucy, he approached her and politely asked if she could redeem his dollar bill; whereupon, Lucy eagerly accommodated this fine-looking man by opening her purse and giving him change in quarters and dimes. He warmly thanked her, and then made his call. After a brief phone conversation he lingered in the lobby for the storm to subside, and broke ground for conversation with Lucy by commenting on the severity of the storm. They chatted for a few minutes, and as the gentleman—Raymond was his name—had to be on his way, he offered Lucy the protection of his umbrella to her car. So the two left the restaurant together walking shoulder-to-shoulder beneath an umbrella through the parking lot. Before entering her car Lucy thanked him for his courtesy, and to her great thrill Raymond asked her if she would like to meet him at a later date, where the two could get better acquainted. Lucy fumbled through her purse for a pen, and scribbled her phone number on a piece of paper which Raymond slipped into his pocket. Then he gave her a wink of his eye, and bid her have a safe drive home.

"Lucy returned to her apartment in as opposite a mood as when she had left. She was ecstatic! The timely answer to her prayers was a blessed omen that this man may be the one ordained for her by Providence. But not once that evening did she bend a knee and thank God for prayers answered, so preoccupied was she with matters of the flesh. Her hormones, dormant during many months of unwanted chastity, were now awakened and engulfed her body with delightful sensuality as the drought appeared to be near its end. It was three a.m. when she fell asleep.

"The following evening Lucy kept an anxious vigil beside her telephone like a mother with a sick infant, expecting a call from Raymond. Whenever the phone rang she answered it with a spirited 'hello!' thinking it was he calling. But when the caller turned out to be a girlfriend or a relative her voice dropped and she cut short the conversation, so as to free the phone line should Romeo be trying to contact her. But Raymond never called that evening, and Lucy went to bed feeling like a bride who had been stood up at the altar. But the following evening Raymond did call her, and the sound of his voice almost levitated her off the floor. They arranged to rendezvous at a coffee house the next day, and after the phone conversation a very happy Lucy jumped in the air and clicked her heels, and danced for joy like David before the Ark of the Covenant.

"Over coffee the following evening Lucy found Raymond to be as intelligent and polite as he was handsome, with a good job and a promising future. He was a university graduate and new to New York, having moved from Cleveland only six months earlier to take a job as a junior officer in a bank. The following Saturday the two met for dinner. In a nutshell Lucy had the best Saturday night of her life. Raymond treated her to a romantic dinner at a seafood restaurant in Sheepshead Bay, and he made her laugh with his witty humor. More importantly to Lucy, she had been treated with respect, for unlike some rascals she had dated, Raymond did not coax her into giving him dessert in return for having bought her dinner. When she returned to her apartment that night, Lucy was so elated that she flung off her shoes and did cartwheels across the living room floor.

"Thereafter, Lucy and Raymond began dating regularly, and within a short time were together nearly every evening. Because she believed that Raymond was to be the special man in her life, she tested his character by stalling any sensuality and purposely delayed his entry into her inner sanctum. To her satisfaction Raymond exercised proper forbearance, never forcing her into the boudoir, although at times she knew he was itching to consummate their relationship. But after a few weeks Lucy rewarded his patience by letting down the drawbridge, raising the portcullis, and allowing him to plunder her fortress.

"Raymond was a sheer barbarian in the bedroom. His sexual drive was like lake waters harnessed by a dam, that when opened by sluice gates burst into roaring, raging torrents. Each night he put Lucy into orbit with his kisses and invasions, until her eyes spun in her head and her tongue hung out of her mouth, before both collapsed into sleep from splendid exhaustion. But by the pink light of dawn the lovebirds were awake and at it again. Within the space of a month Lucy had to replace her bed mattress twice.

"Lucy, though a faithful lover still remained a lover of her faith, and never allowed her amorous escapades to conflict with Sunday worship. She made certain that Raymond had his hammer back inside his tool box on the Sabbath morn, in order for her to be dressed and out the door in time for ten o'clock services. Raymond had been a lapsed Christian for some years, and to her credit she persuaded him to go to church with her. Never a devout person, Raymond attended church only to please Lucy rather than pay homage to the Lord, because to him preserving the pleasures of the flesh was more important than preparing his soul for salvation.

"Lucy wanted to win Raymond as a husband. Indeed, Lucy expected him to ask for her hand in marriage very soon. Raymond truly liked the girl, but preferred her as his whore. Like any intense relationship at first, the flames of passion eventually cooled and

Raymond saw Lucy in a new light. He could not see himself spending his life with her for the same reason as those suitors who courted Lucy before him: she was a fine woman to ride in the dark, but who would ever have a bride whose derriere could fill two chairs. And whose anatomy would their children inherit? The thought of having babies whose butts were too big for diapers made him cringe. Lucy peppered her stud with questions like: 'Do you intend to be a bachelor forever? Wouldn't you like to have a progeny to carry on your name?' But Raymond sidestepped these questions as artfully as a politician. Irritated by his evasiveness, Lucy put the brakes on Raymond's carnal privileges. When once he tilled her garden every night, now he could only sow his seed once a week.

"I should mention that Lucy had a nice apartment located in a fine neighborhood, whereas Raymond had been living in an old building in a deteriorating section of town. At the time he met Lucy he was planning to move into better surroundings, but since he was at Lucy's pad every night, he accepted her invitation to shack-up with her and gave up his meager apartment. Raymond had been enjoying the best of two worlds, having a comfortable place to live with no rent to pay and a warm body at night. But this convenient lifestyle was now in jeopardy. Lucy did not intend to house a stud; she wanted a husband and hoped that their living together would bring herself and Raymond to the altar. A woman like Lucy who was intensely focused in her relationship could also be intensely emotional. Lucy had a temper, and Raymond had witnessed a few of her flare-ups. And if she ever discovered Raymond's true intentions, she would have tossed his clothes out the window and booted him out the door. So Raymond devised a plan.

"One evening when Raymond found Lucy sullen and withdrawn, he said to her: 'Sweetheart, I am well aware that you would like to see us joined in marriage, and am equally aware how frustrated you become when I avoid the topic. But there is a reason for my being equivocal on this issue, and I will tell you why.'

"'Tell me,' she replied curtly.

"'First, let me say that ever since you encouraged me to attend church with you, I feel I have become a better person. Communal worship has brought us together as a couple, and has given me a spirituality that was sorely lacking during the many years I neglected my religion. Perhaps you have noticed that with each passing Sunday I sing my hymns louder and pray more devoutly during services. Heretofore, whenever I went to a bookstore it was to browse through magazines featuring scantily-clad women, but now I make a beeline to books on religion and morality. I have gained a new outlook on life, and am blessed with a woman who I have considered marrying and sharing the rest of my life with.'

"Lucy became radiant upon hearing this, and was about to throw her arms around Raymond when he stopped her and continued by saying: 'But the other day after work when I was alone in church—I have not told you, but on some evenings I go to church to mediate for a few minutes—I had an epiphany!'

"'What happened!' exclaimed Lucy.

"'It was nothing short of a divine revelation. Then and there it became apparent that I had a higher calling.'

"'A higher calling to what?' asked Lucy anxiously.

"'I am going to become a monk.'

"'A monk!' the girl shouted incredulously.

"'Yes, Lucy. And I am forever grateful to you for putting me on the path to sanctity.'

"Lucy's face blanched white at this stunning news. 'You're joking, aren't you?' Her voice was as dry as a biscuit. But Raymond's sober look was enough to convince her that he was not.

"For Lucy this was a test of faith as great as Abraham's, when he was asked to sacrifice his only son Isaac. Now the Lord was taking from her the husband for whom she had prayed. Her benevolent God had reverted to the vindictive Jehovah of the Old Testament. For the next few minutes she was silent, digesting what she had just heard. Gradually, the light returned to her dazed eyes, and she appeared to have regained her composure when suddenly she threw her arms upward and screamed: 'Is there a God in Heaven!' Then she reached for a crystal candy bowl lying on the coffee table and hurled it across the room, where it hit the wall and smashed into pieces.

"'Get out of my apartment! Leave this instant!' she roared like a tigress.

"Raymond rose from the sofa and calmly replied: 'A servant of the Lord must be prepared to suffer in His name. Tonight the cold ground will be my bed and a rock will be my pillow. Farewell Lucy and God bless you.'

"But as soon as the door closed behind him, she called him back and tearfully asked him to excuse her fit of madness. Then taking him by the hand she led him inside where they sat and talked. Raymond was exceptionally polite but firm, and told her that his decision to go monk was final. And he gently admonished her for disputing God's wisdom, for it was not for her to challenge the will of the Almighty. Raymond told Lucy that it would be a couple of months before he entered the monastery; until such time he would partake in a religious initiation, whereby much of his evenings would be spent with the Abbott and other clergy, who would counsel him and offer him spiritual guidance in preparation for the solitary life. Of course, he knew his decision meant that he must find another place to live, which was no small chore being that apartments were so scarce and rents so high, but he told her that the temporary inconveniences of this life mattered little compared to the riches that await the faithful in Heaven. When this clever rascal finished talking, poor Lucy cried profusely and felt like the most selfish girl ever conceived. To make amends she told Raymond that he was welcome to remain in her apartment, for however difficult it was for her to accept God's plan, she would never do anything to frustrate his spiritual calling.

"During his period of 'religious transformation' Raymond was having a grand time, while an unsuspecting Lucy remained alone almost every evening, often grumbling that her life was more akin to a monk's than a monk himself. On many nights Raymond did not return to Lucy's apartment at all; his alibi was that he had been performing charitable work in which he befriended lonely strangers and offered them companionship. And there was much truth to this, for he had been 'converting' lonesome women whom he met in cocktail lounges to the joys of the bedroom.

"After several weeks it came time for Raymond to leave, and he gathered his belongings from Lucy's apartment. In his solemn farewell Raymond told Lucy that her good deed of hospitality to him would not go unrequited, for he was fully confident that the Lord would reward her with a wonderful husband. A tearful and heart-struck Lucy wanted to know where she could write to him or even visit him, but Raymond told her that he had just learned from his superior that he was being dispatched to a cloistered monastery in the Egyptian desert, where communication with the outside world was forbidden. In fact, Raymond had rented an apartment on the other side of town, that he would be sharing with a college girl whom he had met during a night of debauchery at a sorority party.

"Thus ends my tale of this unfortunate woman who, after apparently having received the answer to her prayers, seemed to have been betrayed by prayer itself. Perhaps there are events in life that a woman or man is capable of shaping himself, rather than dragging God in as a marriage broker, who in His inscrutable way knows what is best for everyone. And when He answers our prayers with a 'No!' we may find ourselves better off as a result."

All of us applauded Monica's story. "You have told an excellent tale, and one which challenges our wits to tell one as entertaining. Now pass the baton to another, Monica. Who among us will be next?" I asked.

Diane spoke up. "I have one that I'm certain you will enjoy." And without further hesitation she began:

"I have heard there is much friction between doctors and nurses, and anyone who has ever worked in a hospital knows this is true. Ironically, there exists between these two groups in the healing profession an open wound that will never heal. Some nurses choose their profession in hope of catching a doctor for a husband, and when they aren't successful in netting a big fish, they sour of their job and abhor its gruesome tasks. Doctors, on the other hand, view nurses as wanting to marry them only for their money and prestige, and not having to bother to work another day in their lives. Nurses accuse doctors of being sidetracked by the huge sums they earn, putting money over the welfare of their patients. And nurses resent having to do the dirty work, while doctors strut like proud cocks through hospital corridors ordering them around like servants. Such are the roots of enmity between Hippocrates and Florence Nightingale.

"Having concluded the preamble to my story I now introduce a playful doctor and a spiteful nurse, and how their mutual dislike plays out a very amusing tale. Dr Goodlay was an intelligent and dashing gynecologist, who at the beginning of his medical career had only the best interests of his patients in mind. But as time passed he succumbed to temptation and became more involved with his female patients, especially young and pretty ones, than was appropriate. In fact, he turned into such a knave that he ran his medical practice like a harem. When examining a patient he would arouse her sensuality by degrees; first, by softly poking his fingers here and there about her private parts as part of his diagnosis, then gliding his fingers tenderly across her nether region, all which time he acted thoroughly professional asking her if she felt any pain or discomfort. And when she would respond with a blissful sigh he would reach inside his pants, withdrawing his hard and stiff instrument and administer the pleasing injection.

"Goodlay's nurse was a spinster named Miss Loveless who had both a romantic crush and hatred for the doctor, the latter feeling resulting from her not getting from him what he had been giving many of his patients. She sizzled with jealousy and indignation whenever she heard giggles and sighs coming from inside Goodlay's examination room. Were it not for the nurse's dream of one day getting into bed with Goodlay, she would have reported his antics to the medical board and have him stripped of his license. But Goodlay had no intention of seducing his nurse. She had ordinary looks and was ten years older, and he would have fired her had he not feared the consequences of her vindictiveness.

"One day, while having spent the morning brooding over a long 'dry spell' of many years, Nurse Loveless fell into a black mood. But out of the abyss of her despair, there flashed an idea for a plan that would give Goodlay his comeuppance, and allow her to achieve her dream of having a romance with him.

"It was standard procedure in Goodlay's office that whenever anyone was admitted for a physical examination, the nurse would administer routine tests which included drawing a sample drop of blood from the patient's finger. That day there was a patient scheduled for an exam who visited Goodlay every month for her 'annual' check-up. Nurse Loveless despised this woman for having everything that she lacked—youth, good looks, and a glorious body. When the patient, Lisa Libido, arrived, Loveless sampled her blood and then mailed the specimen to a lab for testing.

"Whenever a lab report was mailed back to Goodlay's office, it was the nurse's job to open and read it, and chart the findings on the patient's medical record before giving it to Goodlay for review. A couple of days later Miss Libido's results were returned from the lab, showing that her tests were fine. As Loveless was entering this data on the patient's record, she set her plan in motion: 'Here is the opportunity I've longed for. I'll teach Dr Stiff-Bone a lesson he rightly deserves.' And then she forged Miss Libido's lab results to show that the syphilis virus was detected in her blood. When she showed the falsified report to Goodlay, his face turned as white as chalk.

"To prevent Miss Libido being told that she was 'infected,' Nurse Loveless pretended to Goodlay that she had already informed his patient of the results, and recommended her to a clinic of social disease for immediate treatment. Thus, Goodlay was relieved that his lover would receive prompt medical attention without his having to confront her, while Libido would never know anything about the ruse. A couple of weeks later when Lisa called the doctor's office to schedule her monthly check-up, Nurse Loveless told her firmly that the doctor would only see her on an annual basis, and recommended she call back in a year. Lisa Libido immediately suspected that Goodlay wanted to end their relationship, and in an angry voice told the nurse she would find another gynecologist and hung-up.

"For weeks Goodlay was visibly upset, fearing he himself had contracted the lethal virus, but scared to undergo a blood test lest his fears be confirmed. Loveless delighted in the doctor's private anxiety, as well as how her trick had caused him the added anguish of having to keep his belt buckled. Meanwhile, Nurse Loveless, who always wanted to get into bed with Goodlay, felt the opportunity was now ripe. 'Goodlay would like nothing more than to infect me out of pure spite,' she thought. Indeed, her assumption was correct, and Goodlay began making overtures to his nurse. Soon, Loveless found her name added to the long registry of Goodlay's seductions.

"As doctor and nurse lay together, Loveless took great joy in the fruits of her chicanery, while Goodlay consoled himself that he may be infecting a woman he utterly despised. For several months as this romance of revenge continued, Goodlay dosed himself with penicillin, dreading the prospect of being infected and fearing news of it would leak to the medical community and ruin his reputation. But when none of the tokens of the dreaded disease appeared, Goodlay wondered that he might not be infected after all. He had himself tested, and discovered his worst fear had been completely unfounded.

"He was ecstatic over the news, his joy being somewhat tempered by his having had to prostitute himself to Nurse Loveless for what turned out to be a worthless endeavor. Goodlay immediately severed his affair with his nurse and was ready to fire her, for he suspected it was she who had authored the entire charade. But he heard from within himself a voice of reason that whispered this was an experience from which a valuable lesson could be learned. Reflecting on his past behavior, he realized that eventually each person must bear the consequences of his misconduct.

"The hatred that he harbored toward Loveless for her deceit, gradually turned into a grudging respect for bringing to light his own depravity, and he blamed himself for underestimating the cleverness of this woman. So he retained his nurse, deciding he could not fault her for craving the pleasures of the flesh like any other woman. But more importantly she served as a harsh reminder that if he resumed his scurrilous conduct with his patients, he could certainly become a victim of the dreaded malady which for months he feared he had contracted.

"Henceforth, he cleaned up his act and conducted himself respectfully. But even virtue has its price. Heretofore he had enjoyed a booming gynecological practice, but now business nose-dived, since many of his patients whom he had 'pleasured' no longer patronized him for lack of the sensual treatment they were accustomed to receiving."

No sooner had Diane finished her comic tale when her sister, whose expression hinted of an amusing story to follow, immediately began:

"It is a fact that between two sisters, however much they love each other, there often exists a rivalry that continues throughout their lives. The younger sister, I being one, is jealous because the older sibling gets things before she does. For example, when the younger sister is home alone on Saturday nights, the other sister is on a date with her boyfriend; while the younger sister is still riding a bicycle, the older sister is driving a car; and, if by early adulthood the two sisters are unmarried, each is trying to beat the other to the altar.

"My story concerns two sisters, and how one of them proved that intelligence and beauty is no match to craftiness when it comes to winning a man. Jane was twenty and Jill was seventeen, and though only three years separated them from birth, they were light-years apart in most other respects. Jane had a good brain and was very pretty, while Jill was modest in both intellect and looks. Jane was receiving straight A's at the university where she was studying chemistry, while her sister was struggling to graduate from high school.

"Because of her mental and physical attributes Jane never lacked a suitor, while her sister was lucky if she ever got a second look from a man. Selfish by nature and conceited about her fine looks, Jane enjoyed stringing a man along, and when she grew bored with a boyfriend she would discard him like a useless toy. At this time Jane was dating a handsome university student who was head over heels with her. Marco, Jane's beau, was anxious to get from her what every man expects to get from a woman, but Jane was holding back—not so much that she did not enjoy the pleasures of the flesh, but she occasionally teased a man by refusing to nourish his appetite. Had it been any other woman Marco would have folded his cards and abandoned his relationship, but he did not want to relinquish a woman as pretty as Jane, even though the odds of striking gold with her grew more remote as their relationship continued.

"Younger sister Jill, sensing Marco's unfulfilled desires, positioned herself to fill the void created by her un-obliging sister. Despite her plain looks, Jill exuded a warmth that most men found pleasing. This was an advantage she had over her sister who, relying solely on her beauty to attract a man, lacked a personality needed to sustain a relationship. When Marco arrived at the girls' house to pick up Jane, Jill would greet him with a strong hug and kiss on the cheek, and tell him how nice he looked. Marco was flattered by Jill's compliments, and started paying more attention to her. He found excuses to visit the sisters' house more frequently, where he would linger to chat with Jill.

"Jane resented the attention her boyfriend was showing her sister. When Marco arrived for a date, he and Jill would sit on the couch and gab, and almost forget about the movie he and Jane had planned to see. Indeed, Jane would have to grab him by the ear and lead him out of the house. Jane harshly rebuked Jill for her intrusions, but Jill continued her advances on Marco unabated, for she was quite eager to seduce him.

"Marco used the feud between the two sisters as his wild card, hoping that this competition would induce Jane to surrender herself to him. It finally dawned on Jane that unless she gave Marco that which her good looks and body were made for, then she might wind up forfeiting him to little sister. So she decided to satisfy her beau's yearnings. Sensing that her sister was preparing to consummate her relationship, Jill had to contrive a way of preventing this from happening for she was in love with Marco.

"On the following weekend the girls' parents were leaving town to visit relatives, and Jane invited Marco to spend the night with her when her parents were away. Jill learned of this tryst one evening when she had her ear pressed against the bedroom wall and overheard her sister's phone conversation with him.

"Their parents were leaving Saturday morning, and that same evening Jill had plans to attend a slumber party at a girlfriend's house, allowing Jane to have the house to herself where she and Marco could romp like dogs in heat until daybreak. Jill had to devise a way of foiling this affair. A myriad of ideas raced through her mind, among them persuading her parents not to leave town, as she had done once as a young child when her parents were planning to take a weekend trip without her, and leaving her instead with a spinster aunt whom she detested. Jill had made up a story that in a dream she had seen the house burn down, as her aunt tried to douse the flames with a garden hose. Her parents, stunned by the vivid detail of their daughter's 'dream,' took it as an omen and cancelled their travel plans. But she did not think that ruse would work again. She thought of feigning illness just before leaving for her party to ruin her sister's amorous adventure, but that would only cause Marco and Jane to postpone their tryst to another place and time. She had to do something what would not only wreck her sister's relationship with Marco, but win him as her lover. So, she began piecing together various scenarios like one fumbling with a jigsaw puzzle, until the right pieces fit and a clear picture unfolded. Suddenly, Jill remembered overhearing Jane tell Marco to come to the house under cover of darkness at ten p.m., and to leave his car at a public park a few blocks away in order not to leave any clue of his presence. And then like prairie lightning an idea flashed into her head.

"When Saturday evening arrived Jill, with pillow and pajamas stuffed in a shopping bag, bid her sister goodbye at six o'clock and headed to her girlfriend's slumber party, less than a ten-minute walk away. Meanwhile, Jane's plans—as she had told Jill—was to spend a quiet evening alone in the house reading a book. Around nine thirty while at her friend's house, Jill pretended she had a skull-splitting headache and left the party. She immediately headed back to her own house where, without making her return known to her sister, quietly dropped off the belongings she had taken to the party on the side porch, and then walked to the park to intercept Marco.

"Jill had been lingering at the park a short time, when she recognized Marco's car pull into the parking lot. She watched from a distance as he alighted from his sedan, and walked across the greenway toward the other end of the park. Meanwhile, Jill took a shortcut through an arbor of trees without being seen and emerged onto a walkway, where she came upon Marco who was approaching from the opposite direction. Marco, however, so preoccupied with the nocturnal feast awaiting him, did not notice Jill when the two passed each other until Jill called to him.

"'Is that you, Marco?'

"Marco recognized Jill's voice and stopped in his tracks. 'What are you doing here!'

"'I was about to ask you the same,' Jill replied coyly. 'What a coincidence that we should run into each other. And what brings you out here tonight Mister Marco?'

"Marco was growing very uneasy, for he wondered how he would ever get to Jane's house without Jill finding out. 'It…it is such a nice evening that I decided to park my car and stroll through the grounds,' Marco replied fumbling for words, while checking the time on his watch.

"'I had to leave a party this evening because I was not feeling well, so I came here for a walk and fresh air. No use having two sick people in the house tonight,' Jill said matter-of-factly.

"'What do you mean?' asked Marco anxiously.

"'My parents just came home unexpectedly this evening. Mom took ill.'

"'Your parents are home!' the astonished man exclaimed. 'But I just talked to…' He was about to blurt out that he had just talked to her sister over the phone only a half-hour earlier, when Jane confirmed that all was clear for him to come over.

"'Mom and dad returned not more than fifteen minutes ago,' replied Jill, who was clearly enjoying Marco's agitation. 'Did you say you had just talked to someone?' she added.

"'No…no. I didn't speak to anyone,' Marco said in a shaken voice.

"'Since we're both here for a stroll, would you care if I join you, Marco?'

"Marco equivocated for a few moments before reluctantly obliging her, and the two began walking side by side along the meandering path. He was in a daze, not from the sting of Cupid's arrow, but from the blow of Thor's hammer. Jill tried her best to coax conversation from Marco who was paying no attention to her, such had the frustration and disappointment from lost romance muddled his mind.

"After ten minutes the fog that had wreathed his head began dissipating, and he broke out of his gloom. When Jill observed Marco's spirits were improving, she complimented him on the smart style of his clothes, and he quickly brightened under the glow of Jill's flattery. Marco always enjoyed Jill's company as I have mentioned, and as the two walked in step he realized that the sensual excitement that had been building for days in anticipation of spending the night with Jane, was now redirected toward Jill.

"They had been walking for some time when Marco pointed to a park bench sequestered in the shadow of a tree, and he asked Jill if she wouldn't mind relaxing there with him for a few minutes. When they sat down Jill snuggled beside Marco, and in no time at all the two were anointing each other with kisses. In the course of their passion they rolled off the bench, and onto the soft grass where Jill undid her straps and Marco his belt; and there Jill felt the joy of a man for the first time. The couple lay together for some while, observed only by the blinking eyes of an owl perched on an overhead branch, whose muffled hoots played in refrain to Jill's sensuous sighs.

"Ladies and gentleman, need I say that Marco's relationship with Jane was over forever. Kaput! The next day Jane telephoned Marco at his house and gave him an earful for having stood her up. Marco could not manage to get in a word as Jane ranted with curses; and, it quickly dawned on him of the trick Jill had played. But what excuse could he offer? None! For the truth would damn him if he told Jane why he never showed up.

"Marco was not angry at Jill; indeed, he marveled at her ingenuity. For many months thereafter, Jill's parents noted how frequently their daughter was receiving invitations to slumber parties, but attributed it to their daughter's popularity and thought nothing more about it. But when Jill left her parent's house on Saturday nights, the pillow she was carrying soon found its way into the back seat of Marco's car, where she and her beau enjoyed many happy hours in the throes of love-making."

When Tara concluded her fine story of romantic irony, it was now Carmen's turn to assume the role of raconteur.

"I will preamble my story by postulating that the more attractive a woman is in wits and looks, the more difficulty she has finding a good man. Many men are proud, but pride is the child of insecurity. When a proud man meets a smart and pretty woman, their relationship eventually sours because he becomes envious of the very assets which had attracted him to her.

"The heroine of my tale is a woman near the pinnacle of beauty and intelligence; consequently, her choice of eligible bachelors were few, because the pool of compatible men shrinks in proportion to a woman's attributes. In other words: the finer the jewel, the fewer who can afford it. For her to have a broader menu of suitors, she would have to disguise some of her beauty and brains, but this was no more possible than to pass off gold as copper. Intelligence is manifested in so many facets of one's personality that however one tries to suppress it, it will always find its way to the surface. So too it is with beauty, which is accented and complemented by intelligence."

"Enough of philosophy, Carmen. On with your story, and make it lustful: otherwise 'get thee to a nunnery,'" interrupted Monica.

Carmen answered by scooping a handful of dry grass and tossing it in her sister's face. Then she continued:

"Donna was blessed with marvelous intellect and looks. She was like a portrait painted so flawlessly, that the figure acquires a surreal aspect because it shows no hint of imperfection, and as such appears more divine than human. This lady was twenty-seven, and was the unhappy victim of the male inferiority syndrome known as 'she is too good for me,' an all-too common dilemma which beauties find themselves in. When a man did have the courage to ask her out, he would abandon her after a few dates, assuming Donna would eventually drop him for another man. Donna had grown so discouraged that she wondered if foaming from the mouth and buck teeth might give her a better chance of finding and keeping a man. At times, she looked forlornly in the mirror and asked her beautiful face: 'Are you a blessing or a curse?'

"Donna's pessimism was reinforced whenever she saw a handsome man with an ugly witch or a fat woman, and wondered why a man would be attracted to such a thing. She concluded that some men find a woman's deficiencies appealing, either out of a warped sympathy or because their own personal appearance shines brighter against their partner's physical drawbacks.

"Mindful of the saying 'even blemishes may have their charm,' Donna decided to contrive a handicap for herself. She considered crossing her eyes or walking with a limp, but decided that these faults were too severe. She needed an impediment that would endear her to a suitor. One evening while at the grocery, she heard a young woman with a mild lisp talking to a store clerk. The lisp actually added to the lady's charm, much as some foreign accents do, so Donna decided to go that route. She practiced rolling her R's into W's, and S's into 'th,' so that Friday sounded Fwi-day, listen was lith-en, and so on.

"One Saturday afternoon at the shopping mall Donna was eating lunch alone in the food court, when a very good-looking man about her age sat at a table next to her and started a conversation. They chatted for an hour, all the time she with a lisp, and they agreed to have dinner together the following night. Their dinner went well, and Donna and Kent began dating regularly. Donna quickly grew madly in love with this man, but after a few weeks she became anxious because it was at this stage in her previous relationships when she and her former boyfriends parted company. She did not want to be burned again.

"One evening Donna was with Kent in his apartment, and as the two were cuddled together on the divan he said to her: 'Sweetheart, you know that I have the sincerest interest in you, and anything I say to you would never be meant to harm or insult you. What might be considered a flaw in another woman, is an absolute virtue in you. With that said, I must tell you that I absolutely love your lisp. It gives you an appeal unlike that of any other woman.'

"Donna now realized that her experiment had worked, for with her impediment she had hooked Kent. But it dawned on her how his feelings might change when it came time for her to abandon her lisp, as she longed to return to her normal speech pattern. Then Donna answered: 'I'm so relieved hearing that, because I was worried that my lith was bothering you. As cute as it may sound to you, I will sound cuter without it, so I plan to undergo speech thewa-pee.'

"'Don't you dare,' objected Kent. 'Without your lisp you would not be the woman whom I have come to love and adore.' Donna was now in a pickle and she had only herself to blame. She had disguised herself to Kent, and now she was stuck wearing the costume. Yet she could no longer deceive her beloved, and if Kent did not love her for who she really was, then it was not true love after all. Because of his objection, Donna no longer had the option of gradually erasing her lisp by pretending to use therapy. But she had another idea. She remembered reading stories of people who had experienced sudden and severe emotional trauma, and though not sustaining any physical injury, had their faculties stricken in such way that they lost their speech, even their sight. Conversely, mental trauma might also reverse a psychosomatic disorder. With this psychological phenomenon in mind, she decided to contrive a story about witnessing a shocking event that caused spontaneous loss of her lisp.

"Donna considered telling Kent that she had seen a horrible accident: A man falling from a rooftop and splattering like an egg on the pavement, but decided the tale was too revolting. But her clever head quickly devised another psychological plot. She had heard that a stutter or other speech impediment is sometimes rooted in sexual deprivation, and that sexual gratification could rid a person of his verbal affliction.

"Donna had not slept with Kent yet, choosing to test her boyfriend's discipline and patience like Lucy, the character in Monica's story. But the night was nearing when she and Kent would consummate their love, and she would use that romantic opportunity to eradicate her 'impediment.' The next weekend the two bedded together, and enjoyed a night of unabated lust. The following morning Kent remarked with astonishment: 'It's gone! Your adorable lisp has disappeared!'

"'By gosh you're right! See that, I just said 'right' instead of 'wight'! Donna exclaimed. 'Can it be that I'm forever relieved of that embarrassing defect which you found so adorable?'

"Kent was truly in love with Donna, and her comment made him ashamed for having admired a fault which caused pain to his sweetheart—or so he thought. He was deeply apologetic, and Donna was extremely moved by his words. Thereafter, she never lisped and was as happy as could be. She allowed her brilliance and wit to shine, which endeared her even more to Kent who felt himself galvanized into a better man through Donna's attributes. Their relationship prospered, and within a year they were joined as husband and wife, and now enjoy the most enviable gift that life can bestow—a happy marriage."

After we applauded the fine ending to Carmen's tale, four pairs of female eyes focused on me to hear the story that would complete our Pentameron. Despite the girls having no inhibitions in relating their explicit tales, I still felt awkward telling a bawdy story in front of them: "Ladies, men are more adept at telling dirty jokes than stories of romance; furthermore, I feel especially handicapped after hearing your wonderfully entertaining tales, for I must plead that my fragile imagination can hardly match your excellent wit."

"If ever a man could excite a woman with a juicy story it is thou," shouted Carmen.

"Set our hormones on fire with something spicy and dirty, and don't worry that your audience is female," added Diane.

"We're all sluts!" rejoined Tara, whose comment was cheered by the others.

With that encouragement from my audience I began: "It is a known truth that older men are attracted to younger ladies, because they want to re-live their youth. To sleep with a woman half his age doubles a man's ego, and he sees himself no longer growing older but growing better. But for a man to accomplish this conquest he must use a bit of cunning, and oftentimes discovers that the best path to seducing a young girl is through the girl's mother.

"Ronald was thirty-five years old, single, dashing, and had a good income. One afternoon while playing tennis with a friend, he met Sandy who was playing at the court next to his. Ronald invited Sandy and her girlfriend to play a doubles match together, and from that Saturday afternoon Ronald and Sandy became weekend tennis partners.

"Sandy was an attractive divorcee, ten years older than Ronald, and had an eighteen-year-old daughter. Their friendship soon turned intimate, but because of their age difference neither expected to have a permanent relationship with each other. Instead, it was an affair of convenience: Sandy had a stud; Ronald had a mare; and, each had a tennis partner.

"When Ronald first met Sandy's daughter, he thought Judy was the cutest thing he ever saw and ripe fruit for plucking. And when Judy saw Ronald she was love-struck, and immediately forgot her crush on her high school English teacher. Not only was Ronald the male who filled the gap of an absent father, but he was the shining prince of her fantasies.

"Sandy and Judy always enjoyed a close relationship, and mother and daughter did many things together. Ronald capitalized on their affinity by insisting Judy be included in almost all of his and Sandy's activities, like going to the movies, dining out, or attending a ball game. Indeed, the only time Sandy and Ronald were alone together was in bed, and even then he fantasized he was under the sheets with Judy—Sandy merely being a physical proxy for her daughter.

"Ronald lavished much attention on Judy, and any other mother with a grain of sense would have been highly suspicious of his behavior; but Sandy was a naïve person and extremely grateful to Ronald for his interest in her only child. Ronald could not wait to puncture Judy's seal of virtue and bring her to womanhood, but he knew he had to move cautiously. Eighteen is a whimsical age for girls: One day they are sinners, the next day saints. And though Judy was head-over-heels for him, Ronald was not sure how willing she was to let him plunge into her crevice, because of mixed signals he was receiving from her. For example, most evenings the three would snuggle together on the living room couch watching television, with Ronald ensconced between mother and daughter, his arms draping their shoulders, and their heads resting on his chest. But whenever Sandy rose from the couch, say to answer the telephone, Judy would slip from Ronald's arm and slide a couple of feet down the couch. But Ronald's luck would soon change.

"One Sunday afternoon the trio went to the beach, and Judy wore a string bikini that would turn the head of a blind man. While Sandy was sunning on the sand, Ronald and Judy went into the water where Judy teased him by splashing him and grabbing his legs, and every time Ronald was about to grab her she darted away with the speed of a dolphin. This game of 'catch me if you can' ended when Ronald said, 'Judy, hop on my back and I'll take you for a ride.' Immediately she leaped on his back, and rode piggyback through the water with her arms locked around his chest and her legs curled like a python around his torso. Then he told her it was her turn to tow him through the water, so she let him mount her back and fasten his arms and legs around her. Then he delighted the sexy urchin by tickling her and squeezing her sides, and before long there was not a region of her body that his roving hands had not explored.

"That evening back in Sandy's house as the three were nestled together viewing television, Ronald counted himself the happiest of men for he had a virgin on his menu, and soon he could brag of having seduced both a mother and her daughter in tandem. At one point when Sandy left to go to the bathroom, Ronald and Judy quickly embraced and tickled each other's tonsils with their tongues. Ronald was feverish for sex and he told Judy he wanted her that night. But Judy equivocated saying 'yes' and 'no' and 'maybe.' Ronald summoned every romantic word in his lexicon to persuade her, and thought he was on the verge of convincing her when just then Sandy returned to the living room and said that she was retiring to bed. Of course, Ronald had no choice but to return with Sandy to her bedroom, while Judy remained watching television.

"Ronald was in bed only a short time when he told Sandy he wanted to fetch a glass of water from the kitchen and, dressed in his robe, made a beeline to the living room instead. With the sweetest words he could muster in his baritone voice he again appealed to Judy, but the young tart refused him. So Ronald returned like a defeated warrior to bed, as his opportunity for conquest would have to wait.

"Ronald's business took him out of town for the next few days, and on his return he had supper at Sandy's house. At the table Judy flirted with Ronald, tapping her foot against his leg, and slowly drawing a six-inch pickle in and out of her mouth. As Judy fiddled her food with her fork, she mentioned that boys at school were suggesting promiscuous behavior to her, but she assured her mother that she would not cheapen herself like other girls. Then the little scamp winked at Ronald, and swore to her mother that she would carry her virtue into her wedding night. Sandy beamed with pride upon hearing this, while Ronald almost spit out his asparagus. Because of her flirtations and suggestive gestures at the table, Ronald was sure that Judy wanted him; so, at the first opportunity after dinner Ronald asked Judy if he could sneak into her bedroom that night, but again she put him off.

"A few weeks passed and Ronald still had not plundered the treasure trove he sought so much. Judy still remained very affectionate toward him, but continued delaying the grand event by weaving excuses. Ronald now felt like a middle-aged fool, allowing a young jade to string him along. It dawned on him that since Judy knew she could have him at any time, there was no urgency on her part to fulfill his desires. And he shuddered to think if Judy was sincere when she promised her mother she would 'save it' for her wedding night. Nevertheless, he would not abandon his quest.

"As these shenanigans were unfolding, another person would soon enter the scene who would unwittingly play a decisive role in this story. Sandy's mother was coming to town for her annual visit. This was one week of the year that Judy dreaded, because she absolutely despised the old hag. Grandma was sixty-nine and criticized Judy for everything—her clothes, her friends, the food she ate, the music she listened to. And she always addressed her granddaughter as Judith, a name that Judy hated. But what irritated the girl most was when her grandmother kissed her, because she had very foul breath as is the case of an old woman with false teeth. Indeed, Judy would rather drink her own urine than kiss grandma.

"Upon her grandmother's arrival, Judy fell into a glum mood and began reflecting on her conduct. She felt guilty for betraying her mother's trust, and realized the great and irreparable damage that would result between mother and daughter if she ever consummated her affair with Ronald. And the more she thought about this, the more her shining prince seemed like an evil ogre. Her guilt stoked feelings of resentment and revenge against the person who had driven a wedge between herself and her mom. So, she began thinking of a plan to get even with Ronald.

"Sandy's mother had been widowed many years, and though age had dimmed her lust to a weak-glowing ember, grandma still had enough sexual spark despite decades having passed since her grotto hosted a man. One evening after work Ronald dropped by Sandy's house for dinner. Ronald was amused by Sandy's mother because the old woman flirted with him, a trait—and the only trait—she shared with her granddaughter. Following the meal, Judy invited Ronald to play backgammon with her outside on the patio. While the two were alone Judy told him that she wanted him that night. Ronald's heart beat wildly as she lewdly described her desire for him, and that she would lose her mind if he did not satisfy her craving. So overwhelmed was he by this unexpected but welcome acquiescence by Judy, that he thought he would faint.

"Because grandma was visiting, Ronald had not planned to spend the night; as Sandy knew her mother would be insulted by her sleeping with a man while she was a guest in her daughter's house. So Judy arranged for Ronald to slip back into the house after midnight through the rear door, which would be unlocked. At nine o'clock that evening Ronald bid goodnight to Sandy and her mother, went home for a couple of hours, and then drove back to Sandy's neighborhood at half-past midnight, parking his car around the corner from her house. He entered the house through the rear, and as he tiptoed upstairs his brow began to sweat and his knees buckled in anticipation of the moment he had been praying for. But little did Ronald know of the surprise awaiting him. You see, before retiring Judy asked her grandmother if she would switch bedrooms with her, pretending that the pollen wafting into her room from the trees outside her window was causing her to sniffle and sneeze. So grandma took Judy's bedroom located right off the upper landing of the staircase, and Judy took the guestroom down the hall.

"Ronald gently turned the knob, and the bedroom door opened. Peeking into the dark room, he saw a figure beneath the bed sheet laying on her side with her face tucked into the pillow. After surveying the room from corner to corner, he quietly stepped inside closing the door after him. Meanwhile, Judy, who had been watching from the end of the hallway, moved as stealthily as a cat toward the room Ronald had just entered, and quietly posted herself outside the door.

"As Ronald moved toward the bed he said in a low voice, 'Sweetheart, I'm here,' but the only reply he heard were muffled snores. The bed was positioned below the window and smack against the wall, and it was toward this side that grandma lay, so Ronald could only approach the bed from the opposite side facing grandma's back. Ronald sat on the edge of the mattress, softly touched her shoulder and cooed, 'Psst, psst. Wake up, sweetie. Sir Lancelot is here, and ready to woo thee with his Excalibur.' But the person beneath the sheets kept snoring away. Then he rubbed her shoulder and whispered in her ear, 'Don't play games, honey. I know you're awake,' but grandma did not awaken.

"Since Ronald had no reason to suspect that the person in bed was anyone but Judy, and because his excitement was rising to full throttle, he paid no attention that the woman's hair was a completely different texture and length than Judy's. Ronald flung off his clothes, slipped under the bed sheet, and started wetting grandma's neck and shoulders with kisses while massaging her flesh with an affectionate hand. Just as he was getting ready to whack her anvil with his hammer, the old lady emitted a couple of snorts as she was roused from her sleep. She rolled from her side and onto her back and raised her head off the pillow, where the moonlight streaming through the window caught her features, allowing Ronald to plainly see who he was fondling and kissing.

"Granny sprang upward in bed and placed both hands over her mouth, too terrified to scream; while Ronald, frozen with shock, just stared at her. Ten excruciating seconds passed before he was able to mutter, 'Judy, I thought…but you're not. Oh my God, oh my God…' As he stumbled with his words, Judy's grandmother recognized the intruder, and quickly putting two and two together realized the prank her granddaughter had played. Seeing that Ronald was frightened out of his wits, her terror quickly evaporated, giving way to a wondrous rekindling of sensuality that she had not known for years.

"As Ronald was about to flee her bed, she grabbed firm hold of his manhood and said: 'Finish the job you came here to do, or I'll scream bloody rape.' Ronald was absolutely terrified, not to mention in great pain, and in a few fleeting moments he had to decide which of the two punishments were lesser: Being led out of the house in handcuffs for attempted rapine, or laying this old hag. So he chose the latter. For the next hour Ronald underwent the greatest humiliation of his life, while Judy—observing everything through a slight gap in the door—enjoyed the best show of her life, which was certain to be the toast of any dinner conversation for many years to come. Grandma's breath, as Judy had known, was truly foul, and Ronald was absolutely nauseated from rolling his tongue inside a mouth of toothless gums, for the old lady always removed her dentures before bedtime.

"When Ronald was finally relieved of his penance he felt like an old man, while grandmother felt like a young girl. After dressing he quickly fled the house, and never saw Sandy or Judy again. He fell into a depression for many months, during which his sword never left its scabbard. But Ronald did achieve one of his objectives on that fateful night, for his goal was to lay both a mother and her daughter. And that he accomplished, though not in the order of generations so desired."

The ladies issued a round of congratulations for my amusing tale; Diane feeling bad for the penance Ron had to endure, while Monica insisted that the rogue deserved what he had gotten, but all the ladies agreeing that a lecher like Ron would be a terrific date. Tara declared this last story was the best, but in tasteful humility I acknowledged that each of us was worthy of a laurel wreath for our creative yarns. And it was agreed that our storytelling had elevated our spirits and provided an excellent catharsis, purging any qualms that had been distracting us from enjoying the day.

I had forgotten about the time, and when I checked my watch it was already half-past four! "Ladies, unfortunately it's time for me to escape pre-Renaissance Italy and return to the toil of a 20th century scullery."

Then the five of us rose to our feet and departed from the grove, by way of the footpath which brought us there.

XXXVI

Except for the summer of 1959 when they vacationed in Italy, Ernie Galliano and his family had not missed a summer at The Timberhaus in twenty-two years. Ernie was an out-going and loud-mouthed man who wanted to be the center of attention everywhere. Ursula was Ernie's wife. She was a husky woman with large limbs, and at six feet stood a head taller than her husband. To complement her masculine proportions she walked with a heavy step, and a lit cigarette always dangled from her lower lip.

The couple had two daughters who were ten years apart, with age not being the least of the differences between the sisters. Denise was in her late twenties, and was divorced with two young boys. She was fine-figured and very pretty, and I thought it odd that so charming a lady did not have a husband. She was fortunate not to have taken after either of her parents, benefiting from a genetic quirk that spared her the drawbacks of momma and poppa. Frances or Fran, the younger daughter, was seventeen years old and a replica of her mother. Being true to her inheritance she had her father's boisterousness and her mother's size, and we jokingly referred to her as Fran the Man. Her parents were overprotective, which retarded her maturity and kept her a little girl locked inside a large woman's body. In a word, Fran was a jerk.

Fran had a crush on Bruce. She was enraptured by his cowboy toughness and downright meanness. There is something in bad men that some women find appealing. They are lured to them like forbidden fruit, drawn by the temptation to confront the brute within the man, or in Fran's case to assert her independence and erase her image of being a goody-goody. But Bruce hated Fran, thought her a nuisance—which she was—and only put up with her because she cleaned the bunkhouse as a favor to him. To her credit she was an excellent housekeeper. She swept the floor, scoured the thick black encrustations from the kitchen sink so that its white enamel shone, and scrubbed the latrine of its greenish slime and mold. Bruce was often rude to Fran, but that never bothered the silly girl who felt his abuse was more than offset by the privilege of being in his company.

Also visiting The Timberhaus that summer was a sixteen-year-old vixen, Liz Polanski. Liz had known Fran from previous summers at The Timberhaus, and it was only because of their long acquaintance that Liz tolerated the big, bothersome girl. She was very pretty, and with her dark hair and exotic eyes had the aspect of a temptress. A notorious flirt, her single intention that summer was to sacrifice herself at the Altar of Hymen. Liz tailed Bruce like his shadow. Bruce saw women only as lustful objects of pleasure, and Liz wanted to have fun, so the two were ideally matched. Liz was in the bunkhouse every evening cuddled beside Bruce, who freely squeezed her parts which made her laugh, and she relished every moment of his invasions.

Bruce and Tom enjoyed the freedom of riding the open land, but they were bored at The Timberhaus. Their pay was miserable, and they were tired of taking families on trail rides three times a day. They wanted larger pastures, so the two decided they would seek work as ranch hands in Texas after the summer. But they needed money for their trip, and had none.

"Will you take me to Texas?" purred Liz, as she rubbed her nose against Bruce's cheek.

"Of course, babe. In fact, I'll buy us a ranch," answered Bruce as he took a swig of beer from the bottle.

"Ooo, wonderful," giggled Liz. "Ouch! Stop that you naughty boy," gently slapping his roaming hand.

"The Big Bruce Ranch will be the most famous in Texas. I'll throw Saturday night dances and Sunday barbecues. I'll have 10,000 acres with 10,000 steer. And I'll breed Arabian horses."

"I can't wait to go there," said Liz in a Texas drawl as she massaged Bruce's shoulders.

"Neither can I," rejoined Fran excitedly.

Bruce looked at Fran and motioned to her with his finger to come closer. The big girl plopped on her knees in front of the wrangler. "What do you want cowboy?" she asked excitedly.

Bruce placed his thumb over the lip of the beer bottle and shook it, and then pointing the bottle at Fran released his thumb, sending a jet of foamy beer into Fran's face. Everyone erupted in laughter. The shock that the silly girl received from such an unexpected insult was both pitiful and hilarious. It was like watching someone slip and fly in the air; the episode is so funny that we ignore how the person feels when he falls to the ground with a thud. For the first time Fran became enraged. She broke into tears and stormed from the bunkhouse, cursing Bruce as she left.

"If she ever follows us to Texas, I'll brand her backside and roast her on a spit," bellowed Bruce.

When the laughter died, Tom, who was sitting in the corner drinking ale, shouted: "Bruce-man! It's nice that Durham Savings will lend us the money for our Texas adventure."

"There's not enough money in Durham Savings' vault to pay for a third-class ride to Texas in a cattle car. It's where children deposit their glass jars of pennies. But if you want to be bank robbers, I suppose it's as good a starting point as any," Eric interjected.

"Who said anything about robbing a bank!" demanded Bruce.

"You and Tom have been talking about it the last couple of days," answered Eric.

"Mind your business!" snapped Bruce.

"I'm only offering you sound advice, Jesse James. Begin small and work your way up the ladder of notoriety."

"I'll smash your face if you give me any more advice," returned Bruce.

Eric stared at Bruce with a cock-eyed, besotted look. "Is that so, cowboy? Well the price of marijuana and mescaline has just doubled starting today."

It was from Eric whom Bruce and Tom got their drugs.

XXXVII

Every child begins the world again.
— Thoreau

On Monday morning of the following week there was a heavy downpour, with sheets of water so thick it seemed glue was suspended from the sky leaving the air very muggy; and by afternoon the humidity equaled the temperature which hovered at 90 degrees. But in the scullery the mercury soared to 110, where the hellish steam evaporates grease and grime from dirty plates, and then condenses it into an oily film that attaches to the clothes and flesh. By the time I had finished my shift, my arms and face and neck were veneered with grime. After work I went to the pond where I stripped to the waist and doused myself with water, vigorously rubbing my skin until I had wiped the scum from every pore. Then I dunked my soiled shirt into the water and wrung it out.

After washing, I tipped the boat sideways to drain it of rainwater that had collected inside the hull, and then pushed it beneath the canopy of the weeping willow. I hung my shirt over the side of the boat to dry, removed my sneakers, slipped a cushion into the hull, and then laid in the boat to nap. The pale yellow of filtered sunlight spilled through the branches and onto my face. My eyelids grew heavy, and the drone of bees became fainter until all was silent. Soon, I was fast asleep. In my sleep I heard a soft cooing in my ear, and thought Churchill had come to lie beside me and join me in my dream. Then I was pulled from my sleep when I felt a tugging on my toes, and a moment later my sock was off my foot. I raised my drowsy head and found a little boy, a baby about two years old, sitting cross-legged by my feet! He looked at me with the one sock dangling in his tiny hand

and said: "Take of your tocks!" Then with a couple of firm yanks he pulled the other sock off.

I felt like I was stranded on Lilliput and glanced around to see if I had been overtaken and tethered by other little people, but I saw none except this beautiful child with big round, blue eyes. My shirt, now dry, had been spread neatly across my chest like a tablecloth. As soon as I removed it, the tot protested and pointed his finger at me: "Go seep! Go seep!" meaning I should go back to sleep. During my nap the toddler had placed the shirt over me just as a mother places a blanket over a sleeping babe. The tyke had taken it upon himself to keep watch over me as I slept.

"What's your name little man?"

Taking his thumb out of his mouth he said, "Jamie," and then promptly returned his thumb to his mouth.

"Where is mommy and daddy, Jamie?"

He pointed to the hillock beyond where the cottages lay.

"Did you run away from mommy and daddy?"

Jamie shook his head indicating "yes," then he shook his head indicating "no" in the typical inconsistency of a child. I was absolutely enervated by the heat and wanted to go back to sleep, but I couldn't leave the baby on his own. His parents were certainly looking for him, and if left unattended he might wander into the pond and drown.

"Come here, Jamie." I extended my arms and he crawled along the length of my body, coming to rest on my chest with his short, chubby legs tucked one inside the other like a baby Buddha. Then I grabbed his sides and held him aloft. He laughed as he flapped his hands like a bird, nudged from the nest for the first time. And then I set him outside the boat. But the feisty tot immediately scrambled to get inside, hooking his tiny fingers onto the rim as he tried to hoist himself back into the hull.

"You are a handful, Jamie." I picked him up and set him on the ground again, and then I got out of the boat.

"In! In!" he pouted, and then he scurried to the rear of the boat and tried pushing from the stern to launch the boat into the water.

"No Jamie. No boat. We look for mommy and daddy."

The little boy looked around. "Where mommy and daddy?"

"Mommy and daddy looking for *you*, Jamie." I slipped on my shirt and socks, and suddenly Jamie darted toward the pond. "No Jamie! Stop!" The sloping ground hastened his momentum, and I was sure he would not be able to stop himself from plunging into the water. But just as he reached the edge, he broke his stride and came to an abrupt halt.

"Jamie, you're a naughty boy!"

"Fish! Fish!" He pointed to the water as I picked him up and carried him back to the boat, where I placed him inside as I laced my sneakers.

"Let's find mommy and daddy." I lifted him out of the boat, and taking his little hand in mine we walked toward the hillock, but he broke away and raced ahead. Then he veered to the right and scrambled toward the pond, but I quickly intercepted him. Lifting him off the ground with his legs swinging in the air, I set him down facing the hillock. "Run Jamie! Run!" As he sped toward the hill, a young woman emerged from over its top.

The toddler rushed toward his mother, whereupon she collected her little boy in her arms and hugged and kissed him. "Where were you, angel?" Jamie thrust out his little arm pointing to the pond.

I explained to the mother how I had found him, or rather how the baby found me, and she laughed when I told her he had removed my socks and laid my shirt over me.

"That's because when I set him down for a nap I take off his socks and cover him. And I think it's time for his nap right now," she said, kissing his forehead and tiny nose as Jamie struggled to break out of her arms.

"I think Jamie wants to go rowing."

"No Jamie, we must go. It's time for your nap," she said affectionately.

The baby shook his head defiantly and pointing to the pond shouted, "wa-ta, wa-ta." Then he began crying.

"I can take both of you on a quick cruise," I offered.

"I'm sorry to trouble you, but this little sailor isn't giving me any other option."

I slid the boat down to the water's edge, and the three of us got in. Jamie sat on his mother's lap and was absolutely fascinated by the watery world as I rowed around the pond. Within a couple of minutes he was fast asleep in his mother's hold. I brought the boat aground, and the boy's mother thanked me for being so kind to her little one. With the baby nestled in her arms, she walked across the field in the direction of the cottages and disappeared over the hill. Babies have an inspiring innocence. They live each moment, captivated by the simplest things. Who is more happy than a baby, as each day brings new wonders and yesterday is forgotten. Alas, how many yesterdays I wish I could forget. Then I resumed my nap in the boat and slept for two hours.

XXXVIII

A remnant of medieval times that has successfully stitched itself into the American landscape is the county fair. In days of yore merchants, farmers, and artisans gathered for several days at certain times of the year in open-air stalls and tents to auction livestock, sell textiles, and engage in miscellaneous trade. Commerce was mixed with carnival as minstrels, actors, acrobats, and jugglers entertained merchants and craftsmen. As centuries passed, society evolved more efficient modes of commerce through stock exchanges and mercantile houses, with the result that fairs became less a commercial emporium and more a festive atmosphere as they are known today.

During the third week of every August, a cow pasture ten miles outside East Durham becomes the site of the Schoharie County Fair. On a midweek night I attended the fair along with Danny, the four Brooklyn girls, Beth, and Peggy. From clapboard booths vendors hawked souvenirs, and children threw darts at targets to win prizes. A man on stilts dressed as Uncle Sam walked among the crowd, and children and adults watched in awe as a man wearing a turban exhaled jets of fire while another man juggled knives. Inside a tented pavilion a beauty pageant was underway to select the Queen of the Fair, and looming large like a rotating disk against the ebony sky was a Ferris wheel dressed in orange lights.

The focal point of the night was the outdoor stage, where a band was entertaining a growing crowd with bluegrass music. I love bluegrass for it has a unique and ingenious harmony that centers around the fiddle, which played in lively and alternating rhythms creates a contrapuntal melody that deceives the ear into thinking one fiddle is doing the work of two or more. With the mere touch of the bow on the strings, the band's fiddler made his instrument sing. The spirited music brought many dancers to their feet. Couples locked arms and spun around and around held in balance by the centrifugal force of their whirling, and then would let go of each other and fly like haywire satellites into the arms of other partners. I danced like a dervish for twenty minutes without stop; my clothes were drenched with sweat, and when I did rest I felt an exhilarating exhaustion.

"I doubt I'll have the strength to get up in the morning," I said to Danny as I plopped on a chair next to him.

"Me too, lad; me too." His soaked shirt was unbuttoned to the waist and his chest was palpitating from exertion. "Beth and Peggy are having a grand time tonight. The poor girls have been wretched all week, and were talking about running away. And I've no doubt they will if they're forced to be split like Solomon's baby between two parents."

"Which leaves us with only one thing to do," I said.

"And what is that?" asked Danny, as he swiped his hand across his wet brow.

"You marry Beth, and I'll wed her sister. We'll make decent ladies out of them after all."

"You're as mad as a bitch in heat," laughed Danny slapping my knee. "And here come our future brides now." The two sisters had just quit dancing and were laughing and swaying like drunken sailors, both clinging to each other to keep from falling. Beth dropped herself on Danny's lap and Peggy threw herself on mine.

"Who were those fellas you were dancing with?" asked Danny, as he bounced his knees up and down giving Beth a ride.

"Who knows? Who cares?" answered Beth, as she pillowed her head on his shoulder and closed her eyes.

A few minutes later the music stopped and Diane, Monica, Carmen, and Tara joined us. Peggy made no attempt to quit my lap; she stared absently into space with eyes glazed from exhaustion, while Beth remained slumped in Danny's hold.

We left at one a.m. when the fairgrounds closed, and our party of eight crammed into the DeSoto sedan I had borrowed again from Giuseppe Roncalli. I had driven only three miles when the car suddenly wobbled and veered to the right, nearly causing me to lose control of the steering. I brought the car to a stop on the shoulder of the road and discovered the front right tire had blown. With the car headlights turned off we were surrounded in pitch blackness, and without a flashlight I had only the flame of Danny's cigarette lighter with which to inspect the tire.

"It's as flat as a beaver's tail," I said to Danny, as the two of us examined the tire that lay like melted rubber on the ground.

"Aye lad. Let's slap on the spare tire and get this car rolling. Ladies, we'll be out of here in no time a 'toll," assured the bartender.

I removed the spare tire and the tire jack from the car's trunk. After jacking the front of the car a few inches off the ground, I attempted to remove with the tire wrench the lug nuts that held the front wheel in place. But the nuts would not budge.

"Let me try," offered Danny, as he handed me the flame and I handed him the wrench. Gripping the wrench tightly and with heels dug into the ground, he yanked on each lug nut without result. "Hercules could not loosen these damn things," he said in frustration. Then he slammed the wrench to the ground in disgust. The lug nuts were deeply imbedded into the wheel having been driven in by a riveter, and would probably require a riveter to remove them.

Together we tried to tackle the obstinate nuts. With Danny gripping the lower part of the wrench and my hands firm on the upper part—and Diane holding the flame—we yanked with all our might on one of the hexagonal nuts. But our multiple effort only multiplied our dilemma. As we gritted our teeth and threw every ounce of energy into trying to free the nut, the iron wrench began to bow under the strain. Suddenly the wrench socket slipped from the nut, throwing both of us off balance and flat on our backs. This sudden jerk caused the jack stand to slip from its metal base, and the front wheel of the car to smack into the ground with a thud, with Danny's left foot barely escaping from being crushed. The ladies screamed and Danny, in momentary shock, grabbed his foot to assure himself it was still attached. Then he began shouting hysterically, unleashing a stream of oaths and curses. After collecting his wits Danny announced what each of us were well aware of: "We're stranded!"

Our only hope lay in being picked up by a passing motorist. But half-an-hour had already elapsed without a car being seen.

"We may be stuck here until daybreak," said Carmen despondently.

"We should have gone on horseback," said Diane. "Horses don't get flat tires."

"But horses get broken legs. And it's easier to change a flat than mend a fetlock," said Tara innocently, not getting the gist of her sister's sarcasm.

Our situation was bleak. It was three miles to the nearest phone, but whom could we call for assistance? No taxis were running at that hour, and we could not contact anyone at The Timberhaus or Brookhaven because their offices were closed. We had two choices: Either wait until daybreak for help, or walk seven miles in complete darkness to Brookhaven. But none of us wanted to greet the rising sun by waiting all night in the chilly, open air; and the girls were too exhausted to trek several miles. So Danny decided that he would walk to Brookhaven, awaken Elijah the cook, and return with him to pick us up. But I and the ladies protested that it would not be safe for him to journey alone in the night, where bears and wildcats roamed the hillsides. I insisted on accompanying him but he strongly objected, arguing that two men could not leave half-a-dozen women stranded on the road at that hour.

As we were mulling over our quandary, the glare of headlights appeared in the distance. Here was hope of rescue, and we all gathered alongside the road ready to hail the approaching car or truck. The vehicle, which seemed to be a good distance away judging by the faint shine of its lights, was upon us in no time at all. And what had been a weak beam of headlights moments earlier, was now a dazzling brightness that came at us like a fireball. What followed was a loud noise of an engine, a passing blur, and a strong wind shear that nearly knocked us off our feet. Whatever it was that sped past us was then quickly swallowed into the night.

"What was that!" shouted the astonished girls in a single breath.

My immediate impression was that it could not have been a truck or car, for any vehicle traveling that fast could not have stayed on the road.

"T'was a rocket zoomed by!" exclaimed Danny.

"It was a spaceship! It was a spaceship!" shouted Tara, as she jumped up and down like a pogo stick. "Aliens have landed!"

As incredulous as was Tara's suggestion, it awoke a shared thought among us that perhaps we had witnessed an inter-galactic phenomenon. During the last several years, the media was saturating the public with bogus sightings of spacecraft, and interviews with people claiming to have been abducted by little men with green complexions and encephalitic heads. This was merely a desperate attempt by newspapers and television to boost their circulation, but in the aftermath of this hype a handful of whacks still remained convinced that outer-terrestrial beings had reached earth and were living among us. Yet what I had just seen sent a fleeting thought through me that perhaps there was a kernel of truth to this foolishness. As we were lively discussing among ourselves what had just blasted by us, a double beam of light reappeared on the road coming from the opposite direction.

"It's the aliens!" shouted Carmen excitedly.

"They're coming back for us!" trumpeted Tara, who sounded excited about meeting her first space creature.

The beam, moving at incredible speed, appeared to slow as it came closer, and just as it was closing in on us the still night was rent by a deafening screech of brakes. What had been a blurred streak came into focus as a jalopy of a car skidding across the road, where it spun around twice before coming to a stop.

"Sakes alive! Is that you Stubby!" cried Danny.

Stubby answered by sticking his huge head out of the cab and belting out a loud, goofy laugh.

"Was it you who shot by a minute ago?" I shouted.

"Yep, that was me!" boomed Stubby proudly. A duet of groans rose from Tara and Carmen, whose hope of an interplanetary encounter had abruptly ended.

"Had you drove any faster, you would have gone into orbit!" exclaimed Danny.

"We thought a spaceship landed," said Tara.

"A spaceship! A spaceship!" shouted Stubby as he burst into asinine laughter.

"He's a crazy ass," Danny mumbled to me.

"You're a godsend, Stubby. Pull your car over and drive us back to Brookhaven," said Beth.

Stubby swerved his car onto the shoulder right behind the disabled sedan. "What a time to get a flat," he said as he stepped from his car. "Do you have a spare tire?"

I explained our futile attempt at changing the tire. Stubby took a flashlight from his car and inspected the wheel. Then he handed the light to Danny, took the wrench in his huge hands, and began yanking. Within the flashlight's cone of light I could see Stubby's face turn beet-red, and the veins in his neck bulge under the strain, but none of the lug nuts would budge despite his furious effort.

"You're right. It's no use," Stubby said as he dropped the wrench to the ground. "Okay! Everyone into the car!" he shouted.

Were it not for the extremity of our situation, none of us would ever dare ride in a car driven by Stubby. We squeezed ourselves into the front and back seats, sitting on each other's laps so as to fit eight extra bodies where there was only room for four. Stubby sped the car into the night, tearing up the road behind him and negotiating blind turns with reckless abandon. He drove like Phaethon who, stealing the sun god Phoebus' chariot, rode so fast and reckless across the sky the earth was set ablaze.

But we reached Brookhaven safely where Stubby deposited Danny and the two waitresses, before driving onto The Timberhaus where he dropped off me and the others at two thirty. After a few hours sleep I called a mechanic in town at six in the morning, who picked me up in his tow truck and together we drove to the abandoned car. The flat tire was mended in no time at all. I paid the mechanic seven dollars, and had the car back in front of Mr Roncalli's cottage by seven thirty. Having not yet awakened, Giuseppe never learned of his "bambino's" misadventure.

XXXIX

Civilizations decline, not necessarily through some colossal criminality, but from multitudinous cases of petty betrayal or individual neglect.
— Thomas Carlyle.

"Well Byron, I guess you're heading off to gallivant with your Brooklyn beauties?" Ellen asked, as we were leaving the dining room following the lunch shift.

"Can you blame women for wanting to be around me?"

"Tell me, which are better: brunettes or redheads?"

"Now how would I possibly know?" I replied coyly.

"Who would ever take you for a stud," she responded, giving me a friendly shove on the shoulder.

"It's not that kind of relationship," I protested meekly as we parked ourselves on a bench.

"Really? Girls don't tail a guy like that unless the stallion gives them a good ride." Before I could mouth a reply she changed the topic: "You're a nice guy Byron, but you should be more sociable. Many of the other workers think you're too stand-offish."

"I prefer the term 'noble detachment'; besides, I work with a lot of crazies."

"But crazy people are fun," she retorted as she lit a cigarette.

Ellen was very affable and at twenty-three was the oldest waitress. She was from the area—a hick who lived with her aunt. She was not attractive; indeed, her visage was somewhat gross. But she often joked about not being good-looking, as if to disarm criticism of herself. Yet if a woman could be both ugly and appealing, Ellen would qualify. Looking at Ellen was like gazing at a picture referred by psychologists as reversible configuration, whereby two alternating images appear out of the same picture, like the classic drawing of a woman's profile which can be perceived either as being a young lady or an old hag. Ellen had a drooping lower lip that hung from her mouth like a disfigurement, but as the eye became accustomed to seeing it, it took on a sensual quality. A small growth was attached to the lobe of her left ear, and another on the side of her nose. And her lower teeth were crooked. But if she were walking ahead of you on a sidewalk with her back turned she would make a striking appearance, with her finely shaped body and legs and long silky hair cascading off her shoulders. But once you saw her face you would declare she was an ugly portrait attached to a beautiful sculpture. It was these contrasting elements of flaw and comeliness that made her unique.

As facial attractiveness, or lack of it, makes a first impression, Ellen found it impossible to get a man to appreciate her other physical attributes. I had heard from a waitress that when Ellen was with her girlfriends (who themselves were not pretty), her ugliness actually made them appear good-looking in the eyes of men. The waitress went on to say that it was very frustrating for Ellen when she went with friends to parties or taverns on Friday nights. As the evening wore on her girlfriends would pair-off with young men, and she would find herself alone in a corner watching the others dance or sit cradled in the laps of their new-found flames. So Ellen decided to take up with God; she started going to church. She was not at all devout, but believed churchgoers were sympathetic people who would be more accepting of her, especially young, unmarried men.

The story goes that she attended a Methodist service one Sunday and spotted a handsome man sitting in a pew by himself. She mustered her courage to sit next to him and gave him a smile, which he acknowledged by lowering his head and sliding several feet away from her. Ellen stomped out of the church and would have nothing to do with Methodists thereafter. So she opted to attend a Lutheran church hoping to find members of that denomination more personable. But the results were no different. Then she attended Episcopal, Catholic, and Presbyterian services using the same strategy, only to frighten young men out of church, if not out of their faith.

Unhappy girl—not being able to find compassion and understanding in a House of God left her very distraught.

Like many unattractive women with unsatisfied lust, Ellen flirted with promiscuity. She would do anything to seduce a man, provided she could find a man to seduce; and this she managed to accomplish every New Year's eve, but on New Year's eve only. She would nab a man at a party who was blind drunk willing to satisfy her carnality for the night, but come morning the sober man realized that the lady he vaguely remembered from the night before was not wearing a party mask after all. New Year's was bittersweet for Ellen, for on the day she awakened with a man was also the beginning of a year-long drought.

During our chat Ellen talked about her personal situation. "I suppose I'll be wearing an apron and serving greasy food for the rest of my life. I lasted six weeks in college; the classroom was a prison. I confess that at times I feel like a misfit because many girls my age have graduated from college and are pursuing careers. A generation ago waiting tables would not be considered too much beneath a woman's station, because few women had careers. Guests ask me, 'What are you studying? When will you graduate?' And when I tell them I do this for a living they assume I'm missing a couple of chromosomes. But I'm enjoying myself and am relatively content."

I observed an older gentleman sitting on a bench next to ours, who occasionally lifted his head from the newspaper he was reading and cocked his ear to our conversation. At times he would nod as if approving what he heard; other times, he would shrug his shoulders as if to disagree. He impressed me as an odd man, not unlike the old-timers who sit on park benches all day and feed pigeons.

"It brings to mind a story about my uncle," she continued. "He went to college after the War, first in our family to graduate from college. Very bright chap. Was a civil engineer for many years, building roads and bridges. He worked hard, very hard. When one project was finished, another one was always waiting for him. Never had time for a wife or family. If he didn't devote all his time to his job, he would lose it; hence, his dilemma. Then one morning he never showed up for work. He was missing for a week, when one evening he appeared at our house disheveled and unshaven. He told us he hated life and wished he were dead. That was ten years ago, and since then he has worked odd-jobs—pick and shovel work, mowing lawns, tending bar—earning just enough to keep him off skid row. My father can't understand why his brother's life flipped upside-down. But it's easy to see why. He resented his education and occupation and all the money he earned because it enslaved him. It stole his life away. To him, success was worthless, like the chest of gold coins Robinson Crusoe retrieved from the shipwreck that was of no value to him on a deserted island."

"Your uncle made the error by not becoming a bum first, and then an engineer."

Ellen looked at me, tilting her head sideways as if puzzled.

"Had he taken time off after graduation and bummed around for a year, he would have appreciated his career. But he allowed himself to burn so low, that not a trace of the wick was left to reignite himself. One morning you'll wake up and decide to chuck the apron and go to college and become…become…"

"A somebody," she replied, finishing my sentence with a tone of resentment.

"I'm not implying that you are a nobody, sweetie."

Her expression lightened. "No harm done honey." She took a puff on her cigarette and then asked, "How many kids your parents have?"

"Three."

"I'm one of seven. But the days of large families are over. Young couples now have more money to divert themselves with material things. What would have been child three and four are now replaced with two expensive sedans. Kids just get in the way of our selfish lifestyles." She paused watching the curl of smoke rise from her cigarette. "Television commercials convince us to buy more gadgets. Americans accumulate things like a sultan collecting concubines. But at least the horny sultan invests in babies that his whores manufacture. We Americans fill our homes with extravagant trash. Ah, the trappings of success. Someday I hope to find a rich sucker who will marry me," she said, tapping her knee against mine.

"And raise seven children?"

"No! Drain him of all he's worth and then divorce him. Isn't that the American way? I need another cigarette," she said extinguishing the one that had burned to its filter, and pulling a fresh one from her apron pocket which she quickly lit. "You remind me of my cousin. He's the same age as you. Attends college, and studies hard; oh, but he is so dull. He used to be very humorous but has suppressed it, because he thinks levity will thwart his chances of becoming successful. The witty comedian has turned into a boring stoic. My advice to you Byron is stop camouflaging your humor. I've seen your funny side; for example, last week when you imitated Papa calling his dogs in a thick German accent. Myself and others heard the voice in the kitchen, really believing it was Papa about to send his mongrels after us. You should air-out your humor more often." She exhaled a jet of smoke and rose to her feet. "Got to run, sweetheart."

When Ellen left, the man who had been eavesdropping on our conversation placed aside the newspaper he was reading, folded his arms across his chest, and stared straight ahead as if in thoughtful reflection.

"Pardon sir, may I borrow the sports section to read?" I had not seen a newspaper in a few days.

"Take it. I'm finished with it," he said politely as he extended the newspaper to me.

I took the paper and returned to my bench. After scanning the sports I turned to the front page where the headline read, "American Casualties Climb as Viet Cong Continue Offensive." Beneath was a photo of the President at a press conference, back-dropped by a wall map of southeast Asia. "When will this war end?" I asked myself.

Hearing my remark the gentleman rejoined, "There is much bad news in the world. At least the sports pages don't bring tragedy."

"Except when my baseball team has lost five games in a row," I countered. "I get piqued when my favorite team doesn't play well. It's a silly attitude when weighed against what's happening in this world, like this crazy war."

"War is nasty. Millions perish; millions more are displaced," he replied.

"The irony is that while in high school I decided I would make the military my career. My plan was to graduate from college and become an officer in the Air Force. I would travel the world, wear a fancy uniform festooned with medals, and be addressed as 'Sir.' Then this conflict broke out. War is an unwelcome interruption to a military career."

"I was a young man in Italy during World War II and I witnessed much destruction and suffering."

"I'm surprised war has not extinguished civilization by now."

"Simple arithmetic. More people are born to replace those who have been killed," he said.

"This Asian war is causing a lot of division, and at times it seems the framework of society is collapsing. War is by far the most destructive force on earth."

Upon hearing my remark he raised his finger like an exclamation mark and then replied: "Ah, you are wrong my friend! With all of its destructiveness, war has ceded its infamous title to a silent crisis, which threatens to erase more people from the globe than the most terrible war." Then he looked at me with wide, dark eyes expecting me to guess what crisis he was referring to.

I replied with a puzzled look that transmitted, "what are you talking about?"

"The greatest threat to society is a widespread phenomena that is becoming more and more acceptable; once the exception, but now the rule. It is destroying lives, splintering families, and a generation from now we will see its horrific consequences. And yet this greatest destroyer is *legal*," he said.

Again he issued a look encouraging me to decipher what this greatest menace was. I felt like Oedipus being challenged by the Sphinx to solve her riddle. I shook my head.

"Divorce," he replied.

"Divorce has always been around."

"True, marriages have always broken up. But divorce was never as common as it is now. What used to be a rarity is now an epidemic. But now, not only has its stigma been removed, it's considered 'in vogue.' Watch television and you see so-called marriage experts encouraging couples to divorce if either partner has a simple flaw. Their message is not to waste your life with someone who doesn't make you happy all the time. Start fresh with a new spouse. The first marriage is merely a testing ground, not a permanent relationship. Look out only for yourself. They are anointing selfishness a virtue. Several years ago my youngest daughter moved to California where she lived for a year. Every man she met, and every woman she knew of her age were divorced. In her letters to me she lamented that you weren't a Californian unless you were divorced; it was like a right of passage. Marriage was a game that you played to fail."

"How long have you been married?" I asked.

"Thirty-nine years. And I got married at the worst time when Italy and the rest of the world was in economic collapse. I had children at the worst time; we barely had enough to eat. I was an Italian at the worst time; Mussolini got us into war, and my country was destroyed. But my marriage lasted, and my five children survived, and Italy is back on her feet. Historians will credit world leaders for bringing peace and rebuilding nations after World War II. But the real credit belongs to the 'fools'—the average man and woman who got married and had babies at the 'wrong time'; who were too unselfish to dessert their families during the hardest of times; and, who perpetuated a new generation that enjoys the fruits of our sacrifice.

"Nowadays, half of all marriages fall apart. Most children are now reared by only one parent. If a child doesn't have mama and papa to raise him, he won't be raised well. It's like a farmer trying to raise crops on fertile soil, but without water. A child will not learn discipline and have respect for others. He has a greater chance of getting into trouble with the law, and becoming a burden to society." He paused to garner his thoughts, and then continued by saying, "The animal kingdom always knew what we humans haven't fully understood."

"Which is?"

"Give me your ear. Listen." Then he angled himself closer as if to share a big secret. "The North American timber wolf mates with the same partner for life. Why you think?"

"Don't know."

"Ah, but the timber wolf knows. The wolf, I figure, isn't monogamous out of any high sense of morals. I'm sure the wolf lusts for other she-wolves and would like to hanky-panky. But he doesn't. Why?"

I shrugged my shoulders.

"Because his survival is at stake. The wolf knows that it takes two parents to raise its cubs. The mother teaches and disciplines her young; the father protects and provides food. If the papa strays, the young will not learn survival skills and perish. Then the species is doomed. Another example is the African lion. Vicious and powerful, yet so misunderstood. The male lion keeps the species intact by doing the opposite of what you think it should do—by killing the young. It wins a lioness by killing her mate. And then it will kill her cubs. And why do you think he kills the little, defenseless cubs? Because he's a brute? No. Because he will mate with the lioness whose offspring he destroyed, and raise his own pride so that the bloodline will not be sullied by half-kin. The lion knows that siblings who have a different parent run the risk of interbreeding with other blended prides, which would lead to sterility and the species would become extinct. I don't exaggerate when I say Western society is risking extinction. If husband and wife don't stay together the family collapses. If divorce and re-marriage continue and family lineages become diluted with half-brothers and sisters, then in not many generations from now our descendants will be marrying distant relations unbeknownst to them. Offspring will be born feeble like members of royalty, and mankind will be a sorry lot.

"There are reasons why divorce had been taboo for a millennia until recently. And why women were expected to subordinate their will and ambition for the sake of the family. It is because each generation is responsible for engendering the next generation to ensure the passage of customs and culture, and that responsibility cannot be altered by selfish ambitions. What's more, family planning agencies are bent on eradicating Western births like a virus. It is considered reproachable for parents to have more than two children nowadays. Young couples are inundated with the popular hysteria that children only pollute the earth and sack its resources, and threaten to deny them the material luxuries which their parents never enjoyed because they raised large families.

"I have witnessed the havoc of war. But it pales in comparison to the destructiveness of broken marriages. War sweeps over a continent like a raging fire over a forest. But a forest resurrects itself because its roots are fixed to the soil, which serve as the foundation for a new forest. But divorce uproots society where in many cases it cannot replenish itself. People get upset when war demonstrators torch the American flag. But no one gives a second thought when a marriage contract is burned, and that is what happens when a husband and wife break-up. Now, you tell me: which two hold a nation together, family or flag?"

The answer was obvious. "Family, of course."

"Yes, family, family!" he repeated, satisfied we were in agreement. Then he asked: "Do you know much about Roman history?"

"A fair amount. I'm studying classics in college."

"Ah, that's good. Unlike many Americans who only know ancient Rome from what they see in the movies: Gladiators clubbing one another and Christians being thrown to lions, yes?"

I smiled, and admitted he was right.

"Americans should look to the Romans for inspiration. Ancient Rome is a touchstone for our current times. Of course, I very proud for America to have adopted me, but forgive me for saying this," he cupped his hand by the side of his mouth so as not to be overheard, "Americans are very stupid."

"Stupid enough to land men on the moon?"

But Angelo (he mentioned his name) replied, "Ah, Americans can do marvelous things with science especially when their scientists are German, but in many cases they fail to get the basics right. Doing correct the simple things is the sign of a stable culture. If cavemen didn't get right a simple thing like the flint arrowhead, we no be here, yes? Now, before I talk about the Romans I want to say something about the moon landing; it's good you brought that up. After reaching the moon Americans were saying, 'If we can land men on the moon, we can do anything.' I always have trouble with that statement."

"Because?"

"Because when a society believes it can do anything, then man takes the place of God. Who needs God? What can God give that technology cannot? Man becomes the author of every solution. Now, compare the excitement of the lunar landing with that of Columbus's landfall on the Americas. When Columbus discovered the New World, he credited the Supreme Creator for his success. In his captain's log and letters he wrote that the Lord had inspired him to undertake his enterprise, and he thanked God for being able to survive storms, threats of mutiny, and hostile cannibals. And on the island of Cuba on Christmas Day he founded the first European settlement. Did he name the settlement after himself? No. Or after the Queen of Spain? No. He called it La Navidad, The Nativity. And after crossing the Atlantic on his return voyage, he anchored in the Azores at the island of Santa Maria. He didn't run through the streets shouting, 'I can do anything! I am a hero!' The first thing he did was offer prayer and thanks in the town's church for his safe return. Now back to Rome," he continued as he slapped both hands on his knees. "Ever hear of Cicero?"

"Cicero! He was the reason why I dropped Latin after my second year in high school. I was up until midnight translating his speeches."

"Oh, so you know about Rome's greatest orator," he remarked proudly.

"Of course. But it's been a while since I read him."

"Well, let me pinch your brain and refresh you. Many are the reasons for Cicero's greatness, not the least being that he was a skeptic. He decried people who believed the first thing that caught their ears. He would have been disgusted with the 'free press' in America. With so many newspapers and television and radio stations, Americans have the opportunity to hear more lies than truth. The media has cultivated such a false impression of authenticity that people accept anything they read or hear as being scripted on Mt Sinai."

He raised his head and stroked his chin with a forefinger, as if deciding what to say next. Then he proceeded: "Rome's greatest leaders made the welfare of the people a priority. They viewed their accomplishments as merely the fulfillment of one's civic responsibility. They were like *silent thunder*, where the clap is noiseless but forceful—a reverberation that cannot be heard but is felt in the legacy of their achievements, as well as in their defeats." Then Angelo posed a couple of questions: "Would you refuse a bag of gold for a pot of boiling vegetables? Would you sell all of your possessions to obtain the liberty of prisoners? Let me tell you about a couple of interesting fellows who did just that. First is Manius Curius. He lived in the 3rd century BC, and his great military exploits saved Italy from invasion. He was a humble man, and right after rescuing his country he hung up his shield and spear, and retired to the peace and security of his farm. One evening he was relaxing outside his cottage, watching the sunset as his dinner of turnips boiled over a wood fire, when all of sudden he was approached by ambassadors from Samos, an island in the Aegean Sea. They held up a bag of gold and offered it to him to enlist his support. But he told them a meal of turnips was more satisfying to him and turned them away.

"And during the Punic Wars—the wars Rome had with Carthage—two Roman generals stand out as shining examples of character not from their victories, but from their defeats. Fabius Maximus, after being defeated by Hannibal, sold his estates in order to pay for the liberty of his soldiers taken prisoner. In a later conflict when Marcus Regulus was captured by the Carthaginians, he was sent to Rome on conditional release to negotiate a treaty and an exchange of prisoners. Now when he arrived in Rome he informed the senate of his mission, but instead of requesting that the senators negotiate he advised them to do the exact opposite. 'Do not give into the demands of Hannibal!' he insisted. Though he could have broken the terms of his release and stayed in Rome, he returned to Carthage knowing what his fate would be. He gave Hannibal a flat 'NO' right to his face. So Hannibal had him executed. Now, eh… sorry, your name again?"

"Byron."

"Byron, you have been very patient listening to me. But I cannot finish without telling you about my favorite Roman. Not to tell you about him would be like ending a play without the final act, yes?"

"By all means. Please continue."

"Grazie, grazie. Sertorius strikes a chord in me because his life is so poignant for current times, when America is embroiled in war and losing the respect of other nations. Sertorius was a commander of exemplary integrity who understood the calamity of war following his first venture into battle. It was when the Teutons attacked the

Romans at the river Arausio in Gaul, leaving 80,000 Romans dead and Sertorius severely wounded. That devastating experience taught him that it was better to subdue a foe by winning their respect rather than by force of arms. As a commander Sertorius was known for treating fairly all who came under his rule, and showing mercy to those he defeated in battle. And as his reputation grew rival tribes welcomed his governance, rather than his having to subjugate them.

"I have talked enough, Byron. Now I must go find the Missus. She is probably wondering where I am. Got to make the lady happy if I want to reach anniversary Forty. Take care of yourself my boy, and study hard."

"Thank you Angelo. It was nice chatting."

He rose to his feet, stretched his arms over his head, and slowly walked toward the guest cottages.

I was sorry when our conversation was over. At first I listened to Angelo merely out of deference. But I was soon intrigued by his thoughts and opinions, as he was able to detect subtleties and explain their significance which even a university instructor might dismiss as being too trivial to consider. He had a natural intelligence; one that was nurtured not in the lecture rooms of a university, but within the classroom of his mind, by tapping his faculties and finding within a treasure trove of perspective and ideas.

XL

When the Gauls laid waste Rome, they found the senators clothed in their robes, seated with stern tranquility in their curule chairs; in this manner they suffered death without resistance.

— Livy

But I think Angelo was a bit too generous in his appraisal of ancient Rome. The Roman Empire was not without its debaucheries, corruption, and conspiracies. Mark Antony engaged in drinking bouts, love affairs, and racked up enormous debt; Plutarch describes his days spent sleeping off debauches and wandering about with befuddled wits. Tiberius was a distinguished military commander and tribune, and courteous to a fault. But when he became emperor of Rome he engaged in lecherous pleasures and committed barbarous acts. The Roman biographer Suetonius writes he had young couples copulate before him to excite his waning passions, and after torturing his victims he had them thrown off cliffs. And early in his career Julius Caesar extorted money to pay off debts; resorted to bribery to win votes; brought false charges of treason against his rivals; and once plotted to overthrow the government by attacking the Senate House.

At its worst Rome was governed by narcissists like Claudius who erected magnificent monuments to himself, assassinated his rivals, and depleted public coffers with lavish public shows like gladiatorial combats, chariot races, and circuses. And when the treasury ran dry he imposed heavy taxes on farmers and merchants, and invaded the neighboring lands of Germans and Gauls, plundering their towns and exacting annual tribute from them in gold and silver to bankroll his extravagance.

But at its best Rome was led by statesmen of devotion and

humility like Cato, who took as much gratification toiling on his farm stripped to the waist, as he did ruling Rome garbed in consular robes. They did not isolate themselves from whom they served as politicians do today, who choose to barricade themselves from their constituency as if they were an invading army of Vandals ready for the slaughter. Rather, they kept a pulse on public sentiment by rubbing shoulders with the common man in the market place and at festivals, and as spectators at the Games. And though not immune to greed, Romans cautioned against the pursuit of money as an end unto itself, because lust for wealth diverted a person from productive and intellectual endeavors. For how would the Roman Empire as we know it ever have arisen if the great architects, writers, and sculptors forsook their genius to chase after personal fortune. In its place would be born a culture of indolence and greed, spawning no better than an artisan society. Throughout their history, good and bad, Romans scripted a manual of survival that has instructed man on the consequences of vice and the rewards of virtue.

Rome's influence is still visible in our architecture, and in the Latin phrases etched in entablatures of government buildings; Rome is evident in stone and mortar but not in the hearts of legislators. Although bestowed with the rich inheritance of Roman jurisprudence, our lawmakers have soiled the stewardship bequeathed to them by subordinating Roman ideals to that of personal glory. Once elected, they begin laying the groundwork for their own memorials, from statues in the rotundas of public buildings to avenues bearing their names. They are obsessed with promoting their own legacies lest their names vanish in oblivion. But monuments of stone erode with time, erasing the names and memory for whom they were erected. Lasting monuments to good governance are the enriching intangibles of liberty and freedom, that remain inscribed forever in the conscience of future generations.

It is in the abyss of national crises where Reason resides, waiting patiently to be summoned to rally sagging spirits. What America sorely lacked in 1972 was leadership that would ignite its kinetic energy to raise itself from the doldrums, and reinstate its respect among other nations. During troubled times when a nation is in disarray, there sometimes sprouts above the tumult a philosopher, or wise man, who brings rationality amid chaos, offering the consolation that however severely injured civilization is, its wounds are never fatal. When the Roman Empire was torn asunder by the sadistic rule of Caligula and Nero in the 1st century, the statesman Seneca wrote inspiring letters while in exile, which later generations have drawn upon for confidence in tumultuous times. When war ripped apart Europe in the sixth century, the scholar and fallen statesman Boethius wrote of attaining happiness while in prison awaiting execution. And in the fifteenth century when Europe was once again severed by political and social unrest, the Dutch cleric Thomas à Kempis wrote how good comes out of evil based on an inscrutable blueprint drawn up by the Divine Architect. An exile, a condemned man, and a monk used the turmoil of their respective ages from which to extract a balm to soothe broken spirits in a hostile world.

Who in this current age, I wonder, will recycle our troubles into hope and galvanize society with common sense? Alas, "common sense is not so common." Do not look to a man of great wealth or political power, as such a person is typically a product of steadfast convention. Most likely it will be some sap mired in anguish and adversity, who out of the poverty of his spirit finds enlightenment and sheds fresh ideas and hope to the world. The past has provided Voltaire, Locke, Paine and others when the organs of society needed regeneration. But what if these inspired minds, like the Great Pyramids, are a beauty of bygone eras never to be replicated?

XLI

"What have you got tucked underneath your arm?" asked Diane.

"Have you forgotten about the blanket you loaned me?" I said as I handed her the Afghan.

"Oh my God! My mother would lock me out of the house if I returned without it."

I thanked her for its use, and told her that management had grudgingly given me a couple of old blankets, so tattered and worn that you wouldn't wrap a corpse in, but it was better than nothing. It was eleven a.m. and the girls were gathered outside the recreation hall with their suitcases. In a few minutes one of the guests would drive them to the bus depot, bringing to conclusion their Timberhaus vacation. We chatted about the zany times we shared; the girls regretting how fast their three weeks went and wishing the summer were longer, while I felt the summer couldn't end quickly enough. As we were exchanging addresses, Monica separated herself and walked some thirty feet to a bench tucked within a leafy bower, where she stood with her back turned and arms folded giving me a subtle summons for private conversation. I walked over and sat on the bench.

"If you've come here to meditate, I hope I'm not disturbing you."

She raised her eyes from the ground, and in her typical reticence responded with only a smile.

"You and the girls were a godsend. My spirits had been at the low-water mark until you arrived."

"We learned a little about each other." Then she sat beside me, crossing one leg over the other.

"I want to see you again."

"You'll be busy with your studies when you get home."

"Quite busy."

"As will I."

"Too busy to see a movie or go for a stroll in Prospect Park?"

"Last night I was thinking about us," she said as she lowered her gaze.

"And?"

"It was a wonderful time we had together."

"Every reason to continue our friendship."

"But I want to put our friendship in its proper setting."

"Meaning?"

"Well, let me give you an example. A few months ago I got together with several high school friends I had not seen since graduation. It was a wonderful reunion, and we talked about the good times. But my high school days have their place in time as do the boys and girls I knew then. My friends have moved on, and have met new friends in college and at work just as I have. Our tastes have changed; our expectations are different. It was great to reminisce with them and I still count them as the finest people I have known, but they're not part of my world anymore. And I want to put our acquaintance in its proper perspective, Byron. Let's remember these weeks when two strangers became friends, enjoyed themselves, and helped each other by sharing intimate thoughts."

Monica was talking like someone reading from a script—so little spontaneity; never a word out of place; everything in its proper order just like her friendships, memories, and experiences. I glanced down and wasn't even aware we had been holding hands, until I felt the squeeze of her palm against mine.

"He's here! He's here!" shouted Carmen. The driver had just pulled his car up.

"I'll expect a Christmas card from you," I said as we rose to our feet.

"You'll find one in your mailbox." Then she placed a tender kiss my cheek.

I helped the girls load their suitcases into the trunk of the car, and then we engaged in a final round of hugs. As they drove off, their waving arms dangled from the open windows until the car was lost from view. I would miss the girls, but was certain to see them again before the year was out. Or would I? Suddenly a surge of doubt swept over me that negated my hopefulness. There was an element of finality in their departure; the manner of their protracted waving as they drove away suggested that this was a last farewell.

The next morning as I was wrapping up the breakfast shift, I received an unexpected caller.

"Did you sleep well last night, Byron?"

I looked up from where I was crouched, placing the last stack of plates into the lower cupboard. Standing over me was Papa, with thumbs hooked on his suspender straps that stretched like longitude lines over his globe-like belly.

"Yes...yes, quite well," I replied, startled by his sudden appearance. Why would he ask me that? Could it be...?

"The attic is comfortable, yes?"

"What attic?"

"Come, come, my dear boy. I found you sleeping in the storage attic last night."

I had taken refuge from a heavy thunderstorm the night before in the attic of the recreation hall, where old furniture is stored including a bed. "The reason I slept there..."

"No bother to explain, Byron," he interrupted. "I don't blame you for not sleeping in the bunkhouse. Now come with me und I show you your new quarters."

I rose to my feet and followed him outside the kitchen, where we boarded his little tractor and drove a short distance beyond the guest chalets to a crumbling one-bedroom cottage. Stored inside the bedroom were brooms, mops, mirrors, and picture frames, but the bed was in decent shape and there was a chest of drawers where I could store my possessions. It was a dump, but at least I had a roof over my head.

"Take care of your new home," shouted Papa above the loud, chugging sound of the tractor motor as he drove off.

I wasted no time in moving my belongings from the bunkhouse.

No more sleeping under the stars, or having to shower in the rat shack. But like other times at The Timberhaus, good news was short-lived. That night I was not long in bed when I heard the tapping of tiny feet on the floor. Turning on the light I found several mice scurrying about, with more squeezing in beneath the bedroom door. They were a bold pack of rodents, defying even Churchill, as they zigzagged for ten minutes through the room in a game of "catch us if you can," until finally escaping through cracks in the floor. I stuffed a towel beneath the door to prevent their re-entry and returned to bed. But a few minutes later they found their way inside the walls and ceiling, where their scratching sound kept me awake most of the night. This was my first and last time sleeping in the cottage. The following night I was back in the boat. But this hovel was a safe place to keep my clothes and personals, and it had a private shower, albeit without hot water. And it was where Churchill had shelter and could enjoy an occasional mouse meal.

XLII

One evening, a couple of days later, I walked over to the shuffle board court where teenagers congregated every night to get acquainted, smoke cigarettes, and swap tales. On this humid evening several teens—guests and workers alike—were gathered here and among them was Cliff, an occasional visitor to The Timberhaus whose family had a summer home a few miles away. He sported a thick mustache and bushy side-whiskers, making him look older than his eighteen years. Cliff was a notorious braggart whose bombast knew no bounds. He had Liz seated on his lap, and was boasting to her that he was a black belt in karate. Then he described to all who were present an incident that had occurred a few months earlier, when he claimed to have beaten-up a half-dozen Puerto Ricans who had attempted to rob him.

"I had just gotten off the subway and was walking along Pelham Road, when I spot three ruffians walking toward me. Just as we were about to pass on the sidewalk, one of them stops and asks me if I have a cigarette. Before I could answer his two buddies jumped me, but I was able to flip them off my back with no trouble at all. Suddenly, out of nowhere, three more hoods appear. Before I knew it one has his arm wrapped around my throat, while another drills his fist into my stomach. Then in a quick maneuver I plow my elbow into the chest of the guy trying to strangle me, and before his buddy can throw another punch I grab his arm, twist it, and then I kick him in the groin. Let me describe what happened next." Cliff bounded to his feet to re-enact the scene but forgot about Liz, who had slipped from his lap and fallen to the ground on her butt.

"Now I find myself encircled by six toughs, each with a switch-blade drawn. They're madder than hell, and cursing me in Spanish. The circle of doom grows tighter as they tiptoe closer, twirling their knives like batons. I wait as they come nearer; then I jump four feet into the air, kick out my legs hitting two in the face, and send their teeth flying out of their mouths like popcorn as they crash to the ground."

"Four feet in the air?" asked Liz in astonishment, who had not yet picked herself off the ground.

"Yes, four feet."

"Let me see you jump that high," she asked, as her eyes widened with fascination.

"Later, when I finish my story," Cliff replied impatiently. "Four thugs are left. They're acting more cautious because they see how able I can defend myself, but they're still intent on carving me up like a Thanksgiving turkey. One darts toward me, slicing the air with his knife and then quickly steps back; another does the same, each in rotation like a grotesque ballet as they try to distract and unnerve me."

"What happened next?" asked Liz with flaming curiosity.

"Listen to this," continued Cliff. "I..."

"Is Fran here?" a husky voice called out. It was Ernie Galliano.

"Here I am daddy!" Fran answered.

Notwithstanding Fran's complete lack of femininity, Mr Galliano had a Sicilian suspicion of his daughter's virtue, believing it was always at risk and should be protected like a mummy's treasure. And that risk grew greater after sundown.

Ernie Galliano took a heavy drag on his cigarette and then exhaled. Taking Fran aside he said in a gentle, fatherly voice: "Your mother and I have been worried about you. Why didn't you tell us where you were?"

"I'm sorry daddy," replied Ernie's little girl who stood head and shoulders over him.

"Say goodnight to your friends, darling," he said in a paternal voice.

"Just a few minutes more, daddy? I'm listening to a good story. Please?"

"Very well, angel. But don't keep your mother and I waiting up for you." Then he kissed his cherub on the cheek and left.

"Tell us the rest of your story, Cliff," Fran said eagerly as she plopped herself on the bench where she had been sitting, much to the dismay of the others who wished she had left with her dad.

Cliff shot an irritable look at Fran for having been interrupted, but continued in an energetic voice: "The hoodlums are moving in for the kill, so I pivot my left foot like this," he said illustrating the stance, "and swing my other foot counter-clockwise into the face of one of them; then I pirouette and switch legs kicking the next bugger, until everyone of them is lying flat on the pavement with heads looking like smashed pumpkins."

"Did you kill them?" I asked dryly.

"I don't think so," he replied nonchalantly.

"What did you do next?" asked Liz with excitement.

"I continued my stroll as if nothing had happened."

"I like a guy who's rough and tough," cooed Liz as she gripped his thigh for support and raised herself off the ground, where she had been laying since being tossed from Cliff's lap.

"In tough neighborhoods I command respect like Tarzan in the jungle," Cliff replied with cocky confidence.

"Cliff, anyone who believes anything you say is as stupid as you," mocked Chris as he glanced at gullible Liz, who was too shallow to take offense at his indirect reference to her.

"I'll rip your tongue out so you'll grunt like a caveman," snapped Cliff.

"What would you want with another tongue? To talk back to yourself?" retorted Chris with sarcastic calm.

Cliff threw his arms up in disgust. "You are all a bunch of morons. These mountains are filled with hillbilly idiots. I can't wait to start classes at Princeton this fall. There I can associate with people of my own intellect."

"You're attending Princeton!" exclaimed Liz, as she drew in her breath in astonishment.

Cliff nodded modestly as he slid his hands into his pockets and lowered his head in an air of fake humility.

"You must be very smart!" she added.

"I won a scholarship. And I'll be playing on their football team."

"My goodness. A scholar and an athlete," chimed Chris sardonically.

"Strong mind, strong body," returned Cliff. "In high school I was captain of the wrestling and football teams. And I graduated with the highest academic grades in school history."

"What will you be studying at Princeton?" asked Liz, who was completely captured by Cliff's tale.

"Theater. I plan a career in cinema. In fact, I almost bypassed college to make my movie debut."

"A movie debut!" ejaculated Liz.

"I was offered the role of the bodyguard in *Oil Slick,* the suspenseful mystery about the assassination of a wealthy oil sheik that erupts the world into chaos."

"I never heard of that movie," said Liz somewhat puzzled.

"It's not due for release until December," he answered.

"Cliff, you're a megalomaniac," interrupted Stu. He was a skinny, acne-faced buddy of Chris's.

"What's a mega…megla whatever you call it?" inquired Liz.

"It's a person who lives in fantasy land," replied Stu.

"I can teach you good manners very quickly," shot back Cliff in an accelerated voice. A duel of words followed, quickly giving way to a heated exchange. Others began bantering him to apply his martial arts on Stu. Cliff kept glancing at Liz for support but her impression of him was rapidly melting, and instead of offering encouragement she glared at him as one who realized she had been made a fool of.

"With a single blow I can nutcracker each of your heads," he said to everyone in a voice quaking with anger.

"Why don't you?" challenged one.

"I would be violating the ancient and venerable codes of karate if I did. The sensei teaches that the student of karate is never an aggressor."

"Sensei who?" asked Liz.

"Sensei, or master," retorted Cliff.

"Go ahead and hit me with a karate chop. I promise never to tell the master," said another as the others laughed.

Cliff scowled at his jeering audience, his hands formed in tight fists as if trying to squeeze the rage from his body. He turned to Liz: "I'm leaving, let's go babe."

But Liz pretended not to hear him.

"Liz, let's go," he repeated in an aggravated voice that set his facial muscles twitching.

Liz shrugged. Cliff placed his arm around her shoulder and spoke in a low voice. "Let's drive into town, sweetie."

"I don't think so, Cliff," she said lifting his arm off her shoulders.

"You're not staying here with these clowns, are you?" he asked heatedly.

"These clowns are my friends," she replied irritably. Liz's expression was akin to a holographic print, which viewed from different angles offers different images; so, the look on her face now diffused disappointment, anger, frustration, and insult. Within a few minutes her hero had turned into a goat.

"Suit yourself!" Then he reared back his foot and kicked the ground, sending a shrapnel of pebbles into the air. With head hung low he did not see John approaching and bumped him, spilling beer from the can John was holding. Then he cursed John for being in his way.

"What's the matter with that guy?" shouted John in disbelief as the martial arts master stomped away.

"Be glad he's gone," answered one of the teenagers.

With John were two girls from his high school, who had decided to join a farming community in Vermont rather than return to school in fall. They were urging John to go with them but he refused, telling the girls he wanted to finish high school and attend college, as he wanted to be a lawyer. It was a ludicrous notion because John was brick-dumb, who spent most his evenings drinking like a brewmeister and getting high on marijuana.

"John, we will farm vegetables and raise poultry."

"I can't Sue. I can't. Besides, communes have become passé."

"But John, it's the way people are meant to live. We have the opportunity to return to the lifestyle of American pioneers and Indians who tilled the soil, cared for the earth, and lived in harmony with nature. When people abandoned farms, we became a greedy nation that has led to crime and war."

"Sue, I have another…" punctuating his sentence with a gastric burp, "I have another mission in life." Then he took a gulp of beer.

"Your mission should be to heal the earth whose skin has been scarred by land developers and whose resources are being leeched by oil companies."

"I'm going to be a lawyer; a country lawyer like Abe Lincoln who defended the rights of the poor."

"Abe Lincoln wasn't always a country lawyer. He made very good money as a corporate attorney for the Illinois Central Railroad," interrupted Jake, one of the groundskeepers.

"You don't know what you're talking about," returned John.

"I certainly do. Two summers ago I visited Lincoln's home in Springfield, Illinois. He lived in a fashionable two-story Colonial with parlors and guest rooms."

"Impossible! Lincoln was dirt poor!" snapped John.

"Only if you believe American folklore. He was quite prosperous. And when you finish law school, you'll owe so much money for your education that you'll be as poor as the people you plan to defend."

"I'll get scholarships," answered John. Then he tilted back his head, and raising the beer can over his lips took a deep quaff. Moments later a rumbling could be heard from his stomach, which literally began to swell from the interaction of the grog with his intestinal juices. Next came a volcanic belch of Vesuvian proportion right into Sue's face. After recovering from the momentary stun of John's eruption, everyone broke out in laughter except Sue who did her best to contain her displeasure. John offered no apology for his shameless manners and most ladies would have slapped his face; but Sue was infatuated with the slob and would think no less of him had he vomited on her lap.

"John," continued Sue gently stroking his knee, "our commune numbers thirty people and is growing. Young people from all strata of life are joining communes. All of us are equals regardless of income or family background. We will change the world. In twenty years there will no longer be social classes, or families, or governments as they exist now. Man will live cooperatively. No longer will the earth be the playground for generals and their wars, the clergy no longer will be allowed to spread their divisive dogmas, and..."

"What divisive dogmas?" a listener interrupted.

"Religion confuses the masses with its different creeds. And religion has been the cause of every war," answered Sue assertively.

"Let's all be atheists and live happily ever after," answered another sarcastically.

"With one belief, we would be of one mind and one purpose," replied Sue.

"What is that one belief?" asked Liz, who had all but recovered from her chagrin.

"The belief that no one should force another person to do what he doesn't want to do."

"I like the idea of doing anything I want to," said Chris in agreement.

"It's called chaos," voiced another.

"It's called freedom," rejoined Sue.

"If Thomas Jefferson had your ideas, we would now be living in the Stone Age," injected one of the teens.

"At least cave men had a sense of community and preserved the earth's resources," countered Sue.

"Living in a cave would be fun," said Chris whom no one was listening to.

"If we don't mine the planet's wealth, we would have no choice but to live as cave dwellers," offered a dissenting voice.

"John, give it some thought. Don't become part of a system that perpetuates injustice," pleaded Sue.

"I want to change the system by working through it," said John as he guzzled more beer.

"It's too corrupt to change. Our system is like a patient dying of cancer. It will succumb to its own malignancy, but in its place a new and better order will arise that will be beneficial to all and detrimental to none."

"Think so?" asked John indifferently, whose main concern was running out of beer.

"Positively! After all, mankind controls events and creates the future."

"Nature controls events." Heads turned to see where that unfamiliar voice came from. A middle-aged man puffing on a cigar who no one had noticed, rose from a bench on the opposite side of the shuffleboard court and approached us.

"Who are you?" Sue asked.

"My name is Carl." I recognized him. He and his family were lodging at The Timberhaus, and I had serviced his table.

"Man controls events," Sue answered sharply.

"Does he?" challenged the visitor.

"Of course. For better or for worse, the shape of this world is of man's doing," insisted Sue.

"Really?" said Carl in a condescending tone. "Although we like to believe we are in the driver's seat, it is often nature that initiates change."

"What are you talking about?" John asked. He then opened another can of beer, whereupon foam spouted along the rim which he vacuumed with his lips before taking a gulp.

"I'll give you a couple of examples," replied Carl. "Nature appointed an errant asteroid to strike the earth and wipe out the dinosaur. And in the 14th century the Bubonic Plague eliminated two-thirds of Europe's population."

"What is your point?" Sue asked impatiently. She appeared uncomfortably disarmed by the facts the man used to support his opinion.

Carl continued: "In each example nature precipitated events that provided the momentum for change. In the first case a cosmic collision killed-off ancient forms of life, paving the way for eventual human evolution. In the next example humankind was nearly wiped out by disease; but man's near demise also led to a severe labor shortage, leading to the collapse of servile social classes that were replaced by more democratic systems."

"Are you a philosopher, mister?" asked Sue rudely.

"I'm a high school teacher. And in my years of teaching I've found that a problem of youth is their lack of perspective. If young people flipped the pages back and studied earlier eras, they would appreciate how we got to where we are. You won't change the world by fencing yourself off from it on a commune. There was a reason why people left their farms and moved to the cities and factories. Our forebears who tilled the soil knew the earth could be very moody during times of drought, and flood, and pestilence."

"The man is right," one girl chimed in.

"The teacher makes sense," echoed another, as an undertone of agreement circulated among the group.

The instructor, visibly pleased from the approval of his listeners, glanced at his watch and said, "Got to check on the wife and kids." And then he left.

Our group was soon joined by other workers who wandered in. Meanwhile, John was still talking to his two lady friends, his social idealism fueled by yet another can of beer; Fran was annoying everyone with her silliness; Liz found another lap to sit on; a girl was dancing on the court with a shuffleboard stick as her partner, and so on.

As this motley socializing was going on Ernie Galliano reappeared and approached his daughter, who was sitting on a bench with a few others. She did not notice him because she was occupied telling a joke that no one was listening to. Then, with a wide turn of his right arm he belted his daughter's face with an open palm. The impact set off a loud pop like a firecracker, causing every head to turn. I caught Fran's stunned expression, that moment of shock just before her brain registered what had happened.

"Go to your room this instant, young lady! And don't keep your father waiting a second longer!" Galliano roared.

Holding both hands to her cheeks, Fran had that horrified look you would find in Munch's woodcarving *The Scream*. Then she broke into violent sobbing.

"Did you hear me Frances!" he roared, as he raised his backhand ready to deliver another strike.

The pathetic creature, fearing another blow, shielded her head with her arms. "Daddy, no! Please daddy, no!" she gasped hysterically. Then her father grabbed her upper arm and yanked her off the bench, hauling the screaming and trembling girl away with him like the Devil carrying off a terrified soul.

I was appalled. Everyone was astonished by what they had just seen. There was a minute of dead silence, followed by a low murmur of each asking the other if what they had just witnessed was real. It was incomprehensible that a father would inflict such pain and humiliation on his daughter.

Then someone spoke out: "Did you see that? He almost took off her head!"

"My father is nasty, but he would never do anything like that to me," Sue said.

"Mr Galliano is a beast," said Liz angrily.

"So is his daughter. Fran deserved a good slug," countered John, whose comment set the tone for the warped humor to follow.

"I agree. The girl is an idiot," piped another.

The initial shock of what everyone had seen quickly unfolded into a black comedy. The attack by father on daughter was so unbelievable as to be ludicrous, almost comical, like a cartoon character who elicits laughter when he is beaten and bruised.

"I wish I could see that again," said Chris excitedly.

"Fran can take a punch; I'll give her credit for that. Anyone else would be sprawled on the ground," one was heard saying.

"Her fat head saved her; anyone else would be dead meat," rejoined Sue.

A few others who had just filtered in were greeted by news of the spectacle they had just missed.

"I would have given anything to have seen that!" shouted one of the latecomers.

"You should have seen him clout her," said John, demonstrating how Galliano reared his arm back and fired a hand salvo into his daughter's face.

"We should get her dad to drag her back here and whack her again. That was really something!" said another.

"The poor girl will be so humiliated she'll never want to be seen in daylight again," said Liz, the sole voice of sympathy.

"Good. She should only emerge at night, like a vampire bat, sparing civilization her company," retorted another.

The barbs and jokes grew crueler. Any sympathetic comment about Fran was quickly countered with sarcasm. I walked away and retired for the evening.

The following afternoon I saw Fran walking around the pond. She was the image of dejection; her head was hung low, as she languidly swished a reed along the water's surface. When she spotted me she ran off like a frightened doe. I never saw her again. She did not appear with her family for meals, and rumor was she was still being punished. But I believe she cloistered herself because she was too disgraced to be seen. On Saturday Ernie Galliano checked his family out ending their two-week stay, and returned home to the Bronx.

XLIII

We are kept keen on the grindstone of pain and necessity.
— H.G. Wells

It was the middle of August, approaching the hot days of Indian summer, when the season marshals its strength for its final blast of heat. On a muggy afternoon with sweat pasted to my flesh and the buzz of mosquitoes filling the air, I took refuge in the shade and coolness of a stream. Walking barefoot on the smooth gray stones in the shallow water, I headed upstream in the same direction that took me to Horace's cabin. As the chill of the ankle-deep water cooled me, easing my body from the oppressive heat, my worries were revived for when the stress of the body subsides, the troubles of the mind emerge and vice-versa.

Pessimism engulfed me, and the Hobbesian reality dawned on me that life was cold and brutish. I was not enjoying life as a young man ought, and was even growing negative toward my proudest goal—graduating from college. In less than two weeks I would return to classes and face the most difficult courses of my curricula—calculus, physics, developmental psychology and the like, and I envisioned a year of poor grades and finishing my university days on a sour note. I was enduring a laborious summer, and when it ended next week I would have only a weekend to relax before tackling the arduous academic year ahead. And I was worried about being drafted into military service before graduating, given recent revisions to conscription policy, and the President's escalation of the war in Vietnam. On the other hand if I were spared from the army and did graduate, I would embark on a career right away allowing me no respite after sixteen years of academic grind.

Onward I trekked under the labor of disturbing thoughts. How

I envied the tiny minnows dashing through the water, whose little brains are not encumbered by an intellect like man that burdens him with worry. At the halfway point of my walk the stream elbowed, blocking further view of the watercourse. When I rounded the bend who should I find sitting on the bank's edge and only a short distance away but Otto, with his baggy trousers rolled up to his knees and his feet in the water.

The chef was startled by my sudden appearance. He yanked his feet out of the water and looked nervously around as if contemplating flight. I felt as awkward as ever and wondered if I should ignore him or greet him. I slowly passed giving him a wide berth as I would a bear, and from the tail of my eye I saw him slowly lower his legs back into the water. But acting on impulse I turned and said: "Hello Otto." No sooner had the words left my lips that I wanted to kick myself for having greeted the kraut.

"Hello Byron," he answered uneasily. I was surprised that Otto even knew my name. He fidgeted awkwardly, and the cap which he was holding slipped from his grasp and fell into the stream. He leaped to his feet and shouted something in German to the floating cap as if reprimanding it for mutiny.

I retrieved the cap from the water. It was a filthy and tattered piece of headwear, and left a greasy film on the surface. Otto was extremely grateful when I handed it to him. "Thank you! Thank you very much!" he boomed, as he examined the soaking cap as if it were a jewel recovered, and showed as much affection for it as a boy would for his teddy bear. Then he set the cap gently on the ground to dry, and sat down. But the cook's cheer quickly changed to visible agitation; he appeared to struggle with how to respond to my favor, as if any token of gratitude would betray his stern reputation. His lips moved, but no words were forged. My lingering only seemed to increase his distress, so I left and continued upstream. But I had only gone a short distance when Otto called me.

"Byron! Byron! Come here my boy!"

I walked back very sheepishly, uncertain of what to expect. He reached into a paper bag and pulled out an apple. "Here, young man," he said handing me the fruit.

"Thank you," I replied faintly. I could not understand this man who had always been a raging demon, but now acted like a benevolent uncle.

"It's very hot today, yes?" he said as he pulled a soiled handkerchief from his pocket and patted his forehead. He was now friendly and relaxed.

"Yes, it is." I bit into the apple; it was very tart and caused my eyes to wince.

"I like to sit by the stream; it reminds me of my boyhood," Otto began. "On summer days my brothers and I would sit in the shade along the water's edge and fish for trout. Those were happy days." Then he took a deep breath and exhaled. "When I was your age I worked very hard. Only on Sunday, the Sabbath, did I rest. My generation had no spare time for fun and rowdiness like today's kids," he said in a rising tone of disapproval. And then he grumbled about today's youth being spoiled and bratty, and how hard labor kept a man from growing old. He seemed poised to give me a full blown lecture, but quickly controlled himself and continued his boyhood reflections.

"I and my brothers worked on a dairy farm, which had been in our family for generations. We lived in a large house of quarried stone built by a forebear two hundred years earlier. And in our ancestral house were born I and my brothers and sisters—eight of us—as were our father and his father before him and so on back." Then he looked at me apprehensively with an expression that read, "Why am I telling you this?"

"Continue on," I said encouragingly.

"A stream flowed through our farm, with each spring carrying the fresh melt of winter snows. I called it Chameleon Stream because its waters changed color during the day. When the sun rose above the mountain ridge the waters took on a pale blush, and as the day unfolded it mimicked the ultramarine hue of the sky. With passing clouds it sombered to slate gray and then quickly cheered to azure. Late in the day the rays of the retiring sun burnished the waters bronze, and as daylight waned would deepen to indigo, and then at night turn to inky black. My eldest brother Helmut was to inherit the farm, but instead he went to Heidelberg to study. He was a brilliant scholar; very brilliant. While at the university he wrote philosophical essays. He would have been a great professor.

"It was a time when Germany was trying to define itself as a people and establish its ethos. In the 1920s and '30s we were a shattered nation, adrift in the sea of a geo-political storm as Helmut liked to say. We were a people of many ideological stripes—radicals, Marxists, free-thinkers, liberals, conservatives, monarchists, anarchists, and so on. We were slowly recovering from a war that had decimated us, and for the first time in centuries we were without a Kaiser. 'How shall we be governed? What is our future?' Such were the questions that echoed the sentiment of my people. Such were the questions Helmut sought to answer."

I was amazed by Otto's depth and clarity. He was a completely different person from the kitchen tyrant I knew. He did not face me as he spoke, but stared straight ahead as if in a trance, re-living the era he was describing.

"My other brother Klaus was between me and Helmut in years. He studied medicine in Berlin. With both my brothers pursuing their respective professions and my papa suffering from tuberculosis, the stewardship of the farm was left to me. That was good. I was never a man of books. The outdoors were my classroom; I hunted and fished. At the time I did not understand all the fuss about government and politics, when there were millions of people with no food in their bellies. The solution to our national nightmare was simple: Our survival depended on what we could harvest from the earth. Hard work would provide sustenance; hunger would be cured; and, the masses would prosper. The intelligentsia are vital to every society but pondering abstracts won't feed people; it is the farmers who put food on the table." Then speaking aside Otto added: "But people overlook practical solutions and listen to politicians instead.

"And then came the Second World War. My brothers were ordered to the Russian front and never returned. My mama and papa and all my sisters died in the aerial bombings. Our farm was destroyed and our home was reduced to rubble. And I am the only remnant, spared by Fate to tell the horrible tragedy of my beloved family. By 1945

Germany was in ruins and enemy troops were converging on the country from all sides. I was conscripted during the final months of the war, when Germany was in retreat and gasping its last breath. I, and many thousands like me, were handed rifle and helmet and thrown into the heat of battle without *any* training whatsoever. My infantry unit found itself desperately maintaining a line of defense against the advancing Allied forces. We were under continual bombardment. The stench of sulfur and death filled the air. Everywhere the land lay under a pall of mustard haze from bombing, turning day and night into seamless murkiness.

"And then there was this terrible explosion. The ground came loose beneath my feet, and I found myself being hurtled through the air. Debris and bodies were blown all around me, yet everything moved in slow motion. It seemed I was tumbling for an eternity, and I thought I was dead and flying into the netherworld. Next, I remembered drifting in and out of consciousness and being borne on the back of another, who put salve to my wounds and water to my lips. I was blinded and too weak to speak, but I knew I was in the care of some guardian angel who was carrying me many miles to safety and nursing me back to life.

"When I regained full consciousness I found myself lying prone on the bare earth. As my blurred vision slowly gained focus, the scramble of objects became sorted into a picture of blue sky and puffy clouds seen through an opening in the treetops directly above. Then suddenly popping into this vertical frame was the round face of a young soldier looking down at me.

"'Can you talk?'" he asked benignly.

"'Who are you?'" I replied weakly.

"'I am Corporal Rudiger,'" he answered.

"And that is how I met Papa, the man who rescued me from the battlefield and bore me on his back for three days until we reached safety. In the wake of tragedy is spawned many heroes, like Papa, who though never decorated for valor, was as heroic as any general or field marshal."

Otto paused. His Adam's apple shivered vertically in his throat, and his voice cracked when he tried to speak. His eyes welled and

I thought he would cry. He drew in a deep breath and struggled to regain his composure. Then he lowered his head with thumbs pressed against his temples, the picture of silent anguish.

I felt it improper to remain. Otto was a proud man and observing his distress was adding to his pain. I rose to my feet and said softly, "I will go now." And then I continued on, but only for a short distance when I looked back. Otto had not moved a muscle, still locked in his mournful pose. As I walked I ruminated on this almost surreal encounter with the chef. I was astounded by his story, and by the complexity of this man. What had prompted this very private person to reveal to me a chapter of his past, which I am certain he had disclosed to very few others. Otto had spoken on impulse. And it is during spontaneous conversation when a person reveals most about himself, for he lowers his guard and relaxes his inhibitions, enabling him to purge painful memories.

Ten minutes further into my journey the steam bifurcated, so I chose to bear left. After advancing fifty yards the stream had dried to a footpath and the brush grew thicker, such that I had to navigate through low-hanging shoots. Soon I spotted dappled sunlight ahead, indicating I was approaching a clearing. I had just pushed a leafy bramble out of my way, when I burst into glaring sunlight blinding me as to what lay directly ahead. Stepping forward I plummeted downward and in a moment I was in free-fall, heading into a water basin some fifteen feet below. I hit the water standing without sounding bottom before rising to the surface. It happened so quickly that I was both shocked and exhilarated from having survived the unexpected drop. I looked up and discovered I had slipped off a dry waterfall. Had there been a rushing sound of water to alert me of the falls I would have avoided the plunge, but only trickles of water drooled from the waterfall's ledge. Yet the basin was filled to its brim, likely fed by a subterranean spring. A hundred feet away lay a cabin and I realized this was the spot of the Pentameron tales, and the basin was the same one where the girls and I had romped that afternoon.

In soaking clothes I eased my body against the sloping limestone walls, submerged to my neck in cold water that oozed from my flesh the sweat from a muggy afternoon. All was quiet—no rustle of leaves, nor sigh of breeze; no twitter of birds, nor croaking of frogs. Complete silence. A large turtle appeared on the rim of the basin, protruded its wrinkled neck, and stared at me. Then it withdrew its head inside its carapace as if to nap. Nature and its creatures were taking a siesta. In the reposing silence I reflected on my qualms and compared them to Otto's heavy cross, which he carried with him everyday of his life. Unfortunately, there is no panacea to life's problems, other than the fortitude to face whatever life throws at us. But I was quickly distracted from my cares when, just as I arched my right leg above the surface, a butterfly came to rest on my bended knee. It slowly opened and closed its diaphanous wings before taking flight and disappearing into the brush. Thus, a momentary visit by this simple insect enabled me to divert my mind to more cheerful thoughts.

XLIV

An act of kindness done at the right moment
has a power to dispel old grievances.
— Thucydides

The following evening at half-past the hour of eight I was relaxing in the lobby of the recreation hall, where inside the band was setting up stage and guests were dribbling in for the nightly dance. Then a bunch of rowdies led by Tom and Bruce stormed in, planting themselves on the couches and chairs, and making as much noise as a herd of cattle during round-up. So, I left and went outside to look for another spot to while away the time. I roved aimlessly for a quarter-hour under the canopy of a Van Gough starry sky, until it struck me to head to the hillside where I had gone with Monica that evening in the aftermath of Debra's drowning. It was there that my burdened soul was unweighed while gazing into the infinite night sky, whose vastness whittled my fears to insignificance.

Fifteen minutes later I arrived at the hill, and just when I had surmounted the ledge, I spotted the silhouetted figure of a man sitting on the jutting shelf where Monica and I had sat. He was resting his chin on the knuckles of his fist, as he peered into the night. Was it Horace? His cabin was but a mile away. The head moved, bringing a sordid profile into view that was none other than Fred! Disgust swept through my body. I worked hard all day, and was looking forward to a quiet evening of relaxation only to encounter this sorry creature. Fred withdrew his fist from his chin and sank his face into his hands. Then he raised his head, turning it slowly back and forth in mimic of despondency. Even in silhouette the tormented condition of this misbegotten creature was apparent; he lifted his head heavenward as if to beseech the Divine, and then dropped his head dejectedly because God did not answer. As Fred mimed his one-act play of despair, I observed the silent turmoil that was stirring within his troubled soul. I walked slowly toward him, the snap of loose stones beneath my tread startling him from his thoughts.

"Who's there?" he asked, as he swiveled sideways facing my direction.

Suddenly I felt something strange, something odd yet overwhelming. Fred had become transfigured! Incredibly, I felt looming within me a tremendous respect for him. Fred was as much a human being as any other man; he had dreams, aspirations, fears, trials, dilemmas. But more than most men he had higher hurdles and bolder obstacles to overcome. He was a tragic figure trying desperately to break the Promethean chains that bound him to a servile existence. Yet there was a noble stoicism in this pitiful character, that enabled him to endure day after day abject loneliness and ridicule from an intolerant world.

"Who's there?" he repeated, his voice mixed with fear and surprise when I didn't answer immediately.

"Fred, it's me," I answered sheepishly.

"What do you want?" His voice now shook with trepidation as he dismounted the ledge and dropped back a few feet. He did not recognize my voice, nor did he realize that he was backing perilously close to the steep side of the bluff.

"Watch your step, Fred."

"Byron?"

"Yes, it's Byron," I answered as I came closer.

Fred panicked. My sudden appearance on this remote spot on this dark night, coupled with Fred's apprehension that most people only aimed to harm him, led him to back-step in retreat causing him to lose his footing on the scree. He pedaled frantically to gain foothold to avoid toppling over the edge.

"Grab the branch!" I shouted.

He clutched an overhead branch, and propelled himself forward onto stable ground. My heart nearly came up through my throat within the span of those terrifying seconds when Fred nearly took a fatal plunge. Fred sank to his knees in exhaustion like a boxer who was floored. He looked up wearily at me and asked, "What do you want?" His voice was hoarse and he panted heavily.

I stepped back, overcome with the lamentable sight of Fred looking as defeated as any human being could. But his pathetic look suddenly changed to a steely, defiant glare. "What–do–you–want!" he demanded, with an imperious tone so uncharacteristic of him.

Seeing Fred in this pitiful condition was the culmination of years of emotional scars which others had lashed on him. Others? Was I not one who had abused him, too? "Look at this sad creature," a voice within said, "and witness the handiwork of your mistreatment. See how your words can flay like a whip." Then I uttered something I thought I would never hear myself say: "I…I want to be your friend."

Still kneeling, Fred fell forward on his hands and dropped his head. I waited for him to catch his breath and regain his composure. Then I extended my hand. "Grab hold." He wrapped his skinny fingers around my wrist and I hoisted him to his feet. "That was quite a feat. How you kept yourself from falling off the bluff was amazing," I said. Fred truly had shown impressive footwork and agility as he rebounded to safety.

"So you want to be my friend," he said, elasticizing his words into a sneer as his chest heaved with emotion. "Haven't I heard that from you before? Do you want to borrow money? I have none to give. Do you want to extract a favor from me that once given, you'll toss me aside like a broken toy? Yes, I remember those times when you wanted to be my friend! While other boys would shun me, it was you with the warm heart who befriended me—only to betray the confidence I had in you. I bore the taunts and insults of nasty schoolmates, but at least they didn't have the guile and pretense to be anyone else but the abusive punks they were. But you were the cruelest of all; the hypocrite that you were and always will be. So what do you want from me now, Byron? I have only that rock," he said pointing to the ledge, "where I came to enjoy peace and quiet. If you want to sit there, take it. I'm leaving."

Fred overwhelmed me with the punch and conviction of his words. He spoke with a bitter eloquence spawned from years of frustration and resentment. During our boyhood Fred always wanted to be my friend. While other children would have nothing to do with him, I would be his friend when it was to my advantage, and string him along only to lead him to greater disappointment. I recall how Fred's father went out of his way to secure companions for his hopeless son. One summer day I ran into Mr Madera who suggested it would be nice if Fred and I got together, and invited me to join his family that Saturday at Jones's Beach. I accepted and spent the day swimming in the ocean, going on rides in the amusement park, and eating as many franks and hamburgers as my stomach could hold and which Mr Madera could pay for. But when Fred called on me the next day, I told my mother to tell him I was not at home. Another time on a hot afternoon I was very bored and wanted to see a movie, but had no money. So I visited Fred; we went to a local theater where he paid for my admission, the popcorn, and the soda. Another time a few friends and myself wanted to go bowling, but again no money. So I asked Fred to join us who, though unable to lift a bowling ball, agreed to come and paid for everyone. There were other instances when I used Fred as a "friend for a day." My mother was enraged at my behavior towards him. "If you like him so much, adopt him," I would reply curtly to her. I was cruel; indeed, I took pleasure in being cruel. But at fourteen years of age my personality was still embryonic, and I lacked the maturity to understand the pain that I was inflicting upon him.

"My father had repeatedly warned me never to have anything to do with you," continued Fred. "'Byron is using you,' he often said to me. I despised him for saying that, convinced he wanted to deprive me of the one friend that I ever had. But I wouldn't accept the truth. I believed the lie: That there was at least one person in the world who liked me, and you were the one person who wouldn't betray my trust.

"Of all the foolish things I've ever done in my life, it is what occurred several weeks ago and I hate myself for it. When I first saw you here, I was in disbelief. Byron from Flushing! The remote possibility of our crossing paths in so unlikely a place immediately convinced me that our re-acquaintance must have a purpose. In an instant the bitterness from years earlier vanished, and I believed fortune had steered us into each other, intending that we would develop as adults a good friendship which we never had in our youth. Yes, we would become inseparable buddies as I had wanted it to be when we were boys. But I curse myself for having entertained such naïve optimism, thinking there could ever be a reconciliation between us."

It's true that when Fred spotted me for the first time at The Timberhaus, his heart leaped; when I saw him, my heart sank. I, the only person whom he ever trusted, would once again disappoint him. For several minutes not a word was exchanged between us. He stood like a sentry with his arms folded, staring out into the blackness of the night. Then I spoke: "I meant it when I said I want to be your friend."

Without looking at me he answered calmly, "I won't fall for that line again." Then he turned and walked past me.

"You're mistaken, Fred." But he ignored me.

I followed him on the narrow footpath descending from the precipice, and when we reached the open field I walked in stride with his quick steps, offering words of reconciliation but he censured me with his silence. After a few minutes he slowed his gait and mumbled a few words. And then we began talking. At first his conversation was very guarded, trying to avoid sociability. But after a few minutes the icy tension between us thawed, and we reminisced about the old days and discussed our future plans.

He told me he had been working odd jobs since leaving high school. His father had died and his mother and siblings were living in Florida, where he was heading that winter to work in the citrus groves. His aim was to save money to build a cabin in the Catskills, and learn to farm and fish. He would coach a children's baseball team, teach Sunday school, and on he talked fueled by the interest I was showing in his plans. I was struck by his enthusiasm. And I realized how, through an act of kindness, the demoralized spirit of another could be quickly resurrected.

Caught up in conversation we lost track of time, having talked for two hours as we wandered through the nighttime pasture. Before parting company I remembered that Fred and I had once attended a baseball game as boys at Shea Stadium, and suggested to him that we see another game there in October before the playing season ended. And I insisted he join my family for a Sunday dinner before he headed south. He was elated at my invitation.

As I walked back to the pond that evening I thought of our separate paths in life. I was returning to the university, while Fred would be a migrant laborer in south Florida. One year from now I would be graduated and professionally employed, while Fred would be doing seasonal work. But if a man lives honorably, however hapless he is, who can fault him? Whose scale reflects the true measurement of a man? Respectability shines no less in a person with meager abilities, than it does in the powerful and gifted. In a materialistic world where men are judged by education and wealth, Fred is a failure. But failures can be heroic. A twenty-year-old Polish seaman, broke and depressed, shot himself in the chest. But Joseph Conrad survived and became one of the greatest writers in English literature. In 1854 a seven-year-old American boy, partially deaf from the effects of scarlet fever, was tossed out of school for being too difficult to manage; Thomas Edison never set foot in a classroom again, but went on to become the greatest inventor. How true the words of the Apostle: "To shame the wise, God has chosen what the world counts weakness."

XLV

The wind rolled devouring fire high to the roof;
The flames leaped over it
And the hot fumes rioted to the sky.
— Virgil, "The Aeneid"

Two nights after meeting Fred, pandemonium erupted in the bunkhouse. At 11:00 p.m. I stepped out of the packed and stuffy recreation hall for fresh air, where I had spent the evening listening to a country music band. As I was mulling about I picked up the faint cry of howls coming from the vicinity of the bunkhouse. As I walked toward the shack to investigate, the shouting grew more distinct and sharper as the music from the hall receded in the background. It sounded like a devil's orgy, filled with primal screaming and hideous laughter. Rising above this lunatic opera, Tom could be heard howling like a rabid animal.

When I reached the embankment overlooking the bunkhouse, Tom was knocking out the plywood walls of the shack with a large wood club. Scraps of wood went flying while several others hurled beer bottles at the framework, letting out whooping cheers as the bottles smashed into pieces. In no time at all the rat house was reduced to its bare studs. Then Tom struck a corner wall stud knocking it out of place, causing the adjoining studs to collapse like dominoes and the rusted metal roof to come crashing down, belching a huge cloud of dust that carried with it a strong stale and musty odor.

Next, Tom lit a bramble and tossed it onto the pancaked ramshackle. The torch slid beneath the pile and settled at the bottom, burning as a low, incandescent flame until it suddenly combusted the dry and rotted wood into a tinder box. Tongues of flames shot out from beneath the flattened roof that quickly enveloped the remains of the shack. A chorus of insane yells arose, cheering the hungry flames that licked voraciously at the crumpled heap.

"The fools will burn down the entire resort," I thought. I ran to the public phone on the front porch of the office and called the fire department. As I pleaded for them to hurry, I watched the flames grow larger, throwing its red glow on the surrounding trees. I thought of awakening Papa; but no, I did not want to face his questions about a fire I had not started. Besides, the old man would panic and there was nothing he could do to stop the damage. Minutes later sirens and bells resounded across the hills, and soon a half-dozen firemen were dousing the flames which miraculously had not spread beyond the wreckage.

The clamor of the fire truck brought out scores of guests. But the fire was quickly extinguished and the crowd dispersed. When Papa arrived the bunkhouse was a smoldering ruin. He was barefoot and shirtless, and his large belly drooped over the waist of his pants held up by suspenders. His reaction was a pantomime of disbelief, anger, and resignation—he placed his hands on the side of his head, then he threw his arms outward, and finally dropped his arms to his sides and shook his head in dismay. Next morning I visited the site of the fire. The junk house was now a patty of melted tin and charred wood. If ever arson deserved praise it was the fire that destroyed that despicable structure.

"Who set fire to the bunkhouse!" roared Papa when he stormed into the mess hall next morning as the workers were eating breakfast. All heads looked up, but no one answered. "Who set that fire last night!" he thundered again as he punched the air with his fist.

"It wasn't me," Tom answered casually.

"It was not you, eh?" returned Papa. "Then tell me Mr Tom, who did set it?"

"I haven't a clue, Papa," said Tom without looking up from his plate.

Papa's face turned crimson. Hearing the person he was most suspicious of deny that he knew anything of the fire was more than Papa's rattled nerves could bear. He was on the verge of exploding, as he wiped his hand down his forehead and over his face as if trying to erase his anger and restrain himself. Tom and Bruce told Papa that they had been at a friend's house overnight, and only knew of the fire that morning when they returned to find the bunkhouse blackened ember.

"Nonsense!" growled Papa after hearing their alibi. Then he went to each table and pointing an accusing finger in the face of each worker shouted: "Und you, Eric! Und you, Nick! Und you, Byron! Und you…und you…" But each of us just shook his head.

"So, everyone was away last night und no one saw nothing, ja?"

No one answered.

"Then it was the tooth fairy who set the bunkhouse ablaze," the old man added sarcastically.

"One of the greaseballs probably tossed a lit cigarette into the place," said Bruce.

"A cigarette! This fire was no accident! Und don't refer to mine guests as greaseballs! Many guests reported shouting und noise near the bunkhouse just before the fire broke out. Papa built that house with his own hands many years ago," he thundered while holding out his chubby, gnarled hands as if exhibiting a pair of tools. "Now, find another shelter. Live with the pigs for all I care." Then he wheeled around and stomped from the mess hall.

"The pigs live better than us," grumbled Tom.

Later that day Nick recounted to me what had happened the night before: "There were a dozen of us in the bunkhouse that included rowdy friends of Eric and Bruce. Everyone was popping pills and drinking, and Bruce and Tom were swallowing amphetamines like candy. Bruce had that horrid, monstrous look of a psychotic, and seemed bent on destruction. By late evening everything went haywire. Tom went berserk, and we began smashing bottles. As stoned as we were most of us had enough faculty left to grab our possessions, sensing the house was doomed. And I had just flown the shack with possessions in hand seconds before it collapsed. The next thing I knew the place was in flames."

Fortunately, all my belongings were safely stashed in the cottage Papa had given me. As to where the workers would now lodge, most were local kids who would live at home. The others would either sleep in their cars or in the hay loft of the barn.

XLVI

I bicycled to Brookhaven on the afternoon following the torching of the bunkhouse, planning to share news of the previous night's excitement with Danny. But as soon as I entered the lounge he began unleashing his outburst. "She's a crazy lass, an absolute idiot!" exclaimed Danny slamming his fist on the bar counter. "Just the other day she was whining that it was impossible to find a decent man, saying there was nothing but rabble to choose from. 'Advise me, Danny. Please advise me,' she implored. So I had a heartfelt talk with her for two hours, giving her all the advantage of my wisdom. Afterwards, she told me how grateful she was and kissed me on the cheek, and I said to myself, 'what a thoughtful, sincere girl.'"

Danny was beside himself as he then related to me how Beth had just reconciled with Jimmy, the brute whom Danny had almost come to blows with in Earltown Park on the day the girls had been to the welfare agency. Jimmy had visited Beth two days ago, whereupon the two mended fences and rekindled their old romance.

"The girl is loony," Danny said, tapping the side of his head with his finger.

"She is only seventeen. Girls that age don't know their own minds."

"She made a complete arse of me. When she and Jimmy returned the other night after gallivanting all day they were feeling very high, laughing and shouting their lungs out. Lucky for them that Mrs Van was dead drunk and didn't hear them, or both their heads would be hanging next to that guy," pointing to the deer's head mounted on the wall behind the bar. "Before yesterday I was truly concerned about Beth, but now I could care less if she slept with Frankenstein and had his baby."

I listened as Danny continued to vent his frustration. When he wound down I told him that Beth's infatuation was a passing fancy, and it would not be long before she returned to her senses and ditched the jerk. It was time for me to leave, so I left the lounge and hopped on my bicycle. As I was cycling from Brookhaven I met Beth on the road. She did not notice me until I called her, and even then she did not recognize me right away. Her eyes were bloodshot and her hair was tousled. She looked as debauched as a Greek maiden during the Feast of Bacchanalia.

"What have you been up to?" I asked.

"I've been partying for the last couple of nights," she yawned.

"With whom?"

"An old boyfriend." Then she wrapped her arms around herself as if embracing a lover.

"How is your sister?" I asked changing the topic.

"Huh?"

"How is Peggy?"

"Oh, that bitch. I haven't talked to her in three days."

I told Beth I would visit her soon, and then peddled away. But I had not gone far when an afterthought occurred. So, back I turned and caught up to her: "I'm off the day after tomorrow. What say we go out for ice cream sodas after your lunch shift."

"That would be nice, but I have plans."

"Plans?"

"Yes, with my sweetheart," she sighed. Her eyes were swimming at the thought of him—Jimmy, of course. Without saying another word I mounted my bike and sped off.

As I coasted downhill to the main road, I recalled what Danny had said to me earlier in the summer about Beth looking for a husband to free herself from the bonds of foster parentage. I knew she was upset over the prospect that the county might force her to live with one of her parents. But if Beth were to run off and marry that thug, she would only deepen her dilemma. She was like someone caught in quicksand, desperate enough to grasp a boa constrictor dangling from a branch to keep herself from sinking.

Peggy's face was gullied with tears, and the orbs of her eyes red from sobbing. She was sitting on the porch steps of Barrett's Ice Cream Parlor, where I ran into her the following night when I was in town. "Beth is going to run away with that despicable hoodlum," she said dejectedly to me.

"When?"

"Sometime before the Labor Day holiday. She is determined not to live with mom."

"Your mother has been given custody of…"

"Both of us."

"Have you talked to your sister?"

"If I say anything to her she tells me to shut up. Beth has changed overnight. She has been bitten by that vampire and is under his influence. Jimmy has complete control of her." Then she sank her face into the bowl of her hands and poured fresh tears.

"Will you live with your mother?"

"Never!" she barked.

"Where will you go?"

"Who knows? Any place is better than home," she said with a cracking voice.

"You would be making a mistake as worse as your sister's. Both of you—"

"Don't lecture me," she snapped.

"There are things which everyone would like to escape. But we must confront our problems, no matter how painful they are."

"Hell would be better than my present situation," she said in a sunken tone.

"Perhaps if you appealed to County Welfare they might find a caring foster family who—"

"There are *no* caring foster families!" she answered tartly. "Legal guardians could care less about their wards. They are not family!"

I said no more and left the porch. It would be futile to offer further advice. It reasons that if a person cannot figure out the obvious consequences of her actions, no amount of counsel will help. Beth and Peggy were human shipwrecks pinned to the wheel of misfortune, and doomed to repeat the failures of their parents.

XLVII

"And what brings you here today," I asked with surprise looking up from my magazine. There was Danny appearing out of thin air and standing before me where I was sitting in the recreation hall, enjoying *National Geographic* with an afternoon brew.

"I knew I would find you here sipping on a beer," he said as we shook hands.

"How did you get here?"

"With this," he said as he raised his right thumb. "I hitched a ride."

"Tell me, what's new with Beth and Peggy?" Ten days had passed since I spoke to Peggy, and I had not heard any more news about her and Beth.

"I have plenty to tell you. Beth has eloped," he said as he sat down at the table.

My ears refused to believe what I had just heard. "With Jimmy?"

Andy nodded. "Mrs Van flew into a mad rage when she learned that Beth had run away with Jimmy. But there is lots more to this story." Then he related to me all that had happened.

A week from last Thursday at two in the morning, Danny said he heard a knock at Beth's door. Then he heard Beth and a man talking inside her room, and a short time later he saw Beth leaving the cottage with suitcase in hand accompanied by Jimmy. A minute later he heard a car roar away into the night. "I stood frozen at my window, not believing what I was seeing," continued Danny. "I regret not having run out and clubbed that bum."

Danny further described how later that morning he was woken

up by a huge ruckus in Beth's room. The door to her room was wide open, and inside Mrs Van was ransacking the place in a drunken fury; overturning the bed mattress, tearing apart sheets, and pulling out drawers. "'Mrs Van! What is going on!' I shouted at the crazy woman.

"'What is going on? This is what's going on!' she shouted back to me as she shoved Beth's note under my nose. It read 'Goodbye Dame Van. Rot in hell. Beth.'

"Just then Peggy arrived at the scene. She had been gone all night—God knows where—and knew nothing of what had happened. Mrs Van sprang at her like a tiger and grabbed her by the hair. 'Tell me! Tell me you wretch! Where did your sister go!' she screamed, as she wrung the poor girl's head back and forth like a child trying to rip apart a doll. Peggy was in shock not only by the physical abuse, but by learning for the first time that her sister had suddenly left.

"If I hadn't restrained Mrs Van, she would have certainly strangled Peggy. And I told her that if she touched the girl again I would summon the police. She listened to me and left the room. Meanwhile, Peggy was hysterical and crying. When I finally calmed her down, I told her that I had seen her sister run off with Jimmy and showed her Beth's note." Danny, consumed with emotion in recounting this episode, stopped to compose himself as he was on the verge of hyperventilating. Then he resumed by saying: "Peggy was distraught over her sister's abandoning her and said she would run away too, for she could not bear another minute at Brookhaven. After having witnessed Mrs Van's assault, I agreed that the girl was no longer safe here. And as I was convinced she would run away—she said she would rather live on wild berries and sleep in the woods—I decided to find her safe refuge.

"There is an abandoned cabin not far away where I found shelter for Peggy, and where I brought her food that I swiped from the kitchen. When Frau Van discovered her gone, she told me angrily that she could care less about the girl, and hoped she would never come back. But I was certain Mrs Van would report her missing to the police, which would mean the cops would be questioning me and scouring the area for Peggy, not to mention the fine stew I would be in if they found I had abetted her escape. So I asked the old lady if she had informed the authorities.

"'The police!' she yells back at me. 'The police have better things to do than to hunt for that Jezebel. And don't get involved in business that doesn't concern you. Is that understood, Daniel!'

"What a relief it was to hear that. Never was a nasty reply ever more welcome. Obviously, Mrs Van would have plenty to worry about if the police were called in. The finger would be pointed at her for assaulting Peggy, and her mistreatment would come to light. Furthermore, Van enjoys getting those guardianship payments each week from the county, and those stipends would stop as soon as it was learned Peggy was missing."

"Is Peggy still in the cabin?" I asked. But Danny just continued with his narrative.

"A couple of days pass, and Peggy is still holed up in her hiding place. She's looking absolutely desperate, having no choice but to remain in that shack and dwell on the prospect of having no place to go or anyone to turn to. On this one afternoon when I brought her a couple of sandwiches, I delivered to her a letter that had come in the morning mail. It had no return address, but I suspected it was from her sister.

"That evening when I came to check on her, I found her in a stupor. She was glassy-eyed and slumped in a rattan chair on the cabin porch, clinging to the letter that I had given her earlier that day. When I saw her in this pitiful state I knew the letter she had received was from Beth, informing her what I suspected had happened. Beth had eloped with Jimmy. Sure, wasn't I right when I said she would marry any jerk who proposed to her."

Danny resumed by saying that Beth and Jimmy had run off to Maryland and were married in a civil ceremony, as the law there allows couples under eighteen years of age to wed. The newlyweds would live in Virginia where Jimmy has a brother. Rather than announcing the joyful tidings of a marriage, the tone of Beth's letter was a rambling scorn for life. Beth castigated her parents for denying her a proper upbringing, and lashed out at Mrs Van, the county welfare department, and former foster families for their mistreatment of her. In a sense it was akin to a suicide note, blasting out against an unkind world before throwing her life away in a marriage that was doomed, and adding her name to the lengthening scroll of family tragedy. Meanwhile, Peggy was foundering on the shoals of uncertainty.

"I told her that I would do everything I could for her," Danny continued, "and tenderly assured her that her sister still loved her and that every thorny situation can be resolved. Then I remembered an elderly couple who live on a farm about ten miles away. Mr Anderson and his wife occasionally drop by the lounge for a drink, and once had me to their place for dinner. They are the grandest couple I ever met. So, I called Mr Anderson that evening and explained Peggy's situation to him, and I asked if he would take the girl at his farm. At first he wouldn't agree due to the legal gamble he and his wife would be taking. But I implored him to accept her, underscoring Peggy's desperation and her determination to run away. Mr Anderson was very sympathetic for he was aware of Mrs Van's storied madness, yet he was still reluctant to get involved. But he said he would discuss the matter with his wife. A few hours later he telephoned me and had a change of mind. He agreed to accept Peggy for a couple of days, after which the girl must agree to report to the welfare agency to find a suitable foster family.

"When I told Peggy of the arrangement she adamantly refused to cooperate, insisting that she would never again live in a foster home. I told her that the Andersons were very kind, and staying with them for three or four days would allow her time to relax and get her situation into perspective. And then if she were still unhappy, I would not stop her from fleeing. Peggy agreed, although reluctantly. At eleven o'clock next morning I escorted Peggy from the old cabin to a bridge-crossing a half-mile away, where Mr Anderson was waiting in his truck to pick her up.

"But the following morning there was an unexpected twist. Mr Anderson, without Peggy's knowledge, called the welfare agency informing them they had given shelter to Peggy in the aftermath of Mrs. Van's assault. The couple was determined to help Peggy, but recognizing the heavy liability they were incurring by harboring a runaway, the Andersons wanted to work with the law with the aim of gaining custody of the girl. A caseworker was dispatched a few hours later to the Anderson residence to interview the couple and Peggy, who was terrified and felt betrayed, thinking the welfare agency had come to take her away. Peggy, choked with tears, told the caseworker what had happened between herself and Mrs Van, and that a co-worker had witnessed the incident. That same afternoon the caseworker visited Mrs Van, whom she found half-crocked on vodka. Van was unintelligible and hostile, and told the caseworker she would strangle Peggy if she saw her. The next day the Andersons were granted temporary custody of Peggy, following a brief hearing at the welfare agency in Earltown."

Danny told me that shortly thereafter Mrs Van wrote a deranged letter to Mr Anderson and his wife, denouncing Peggy as a vile creature and thief who would bring ruin to their home. But Peggy and the Andersons have proved an excellent match. Peggy thinks the world of Mrs Anderson, who has given her a loving home where she can lead a normal life. She is slowly placing the past behind her, and is expressing optimism about her future. Yet Peggy has lingering apprehension as memories of past disappointments are fresh in her mind. She fears the béte noire—a welfare agent who might come knocking at any time and take her from her happy home.

When Danny finished his story I thought how perilous life is for many teens. Youth is built upon many tiers of failure. And it is these failures which the young in their naiveté believe will lead to a fruitless life. Suicide, crime, addiction—and in Beth's case running away to marry—are products of a juvenile pessimism when teenagers believe there are no options left to improve their situation. Despite her crisis Beth's situation was neither impossible nor irreparable. She had but one year to wait before reaching the legal age of majority, and then could start life anew on her own. But desperation drives a person to rash acts which are filled with a lifetime of regrets.

Ironically, experts in the field of behavioral science make prisoners of their own theories those whom they try to help. Psychologists tell us that children who have been abused, neglected, or have suffered other dysfunctional trauma become severely handicapped in their socialization: The process wherein acceptable behavioral patterns are developed. And these self-styled wizards claim that their personalities become so irreparably damaged that they will never conform to society, just as a paralytic will never walk. And their views are widely embraced by a gullible public and acquiescent academia. But the behaviorists deceive us when they ignore that within every person is implanted indelible traits, which dictate throughout life one's temperament, ambitions, passions, and other characteristics which make up one's unique persona. While adversity affects our attitude, it cannot change our nature; our essence is immutable. It is our inner strength—that indestructible vertebrae which keeps us spiritually erect—which defines our being and enables us to surmount incredible obstacles. We are, borrowing from Invictus, "the captains of our fortune."

"I wish the news was better, but at least I was able to salvage Peggy," Danny concluded.

Then we left the hall together, and relaxed by the pool until it was time for him to leave and me to start my shift.

XLVIII

Men were most happy in former ages,
Content with the yield of fertile fields,
And not ruined by indolent luxury.
— Boethius

An early morning rainfall enlivened the air with the fragrance of sassafras and witch hazel, providing a soothing tonic for my lungs as I cycled into town. It was my day off and I was in need of a brisk bicycle ride to expend my frustration, after receiving the disturbing news of Beth and Peggy. When I reached East Durham I turned off the highway and onto a byroad, where I bicycled for some distance until descending into a dell where I stopped to rest. Relaxing on a patch of soft earth, I laid my back against a granite slab while sucking on a long blade of grass, and absorbed the serene quiet broken only by the staccato taps of a woodpecker, announcing to nature in its Morse code that a stranger was in the midst. As I surveyed the quiet vista it was like gazing at a painting out of the Hudson Valley school with its colors and shadows, framing a friendly landscape of modest hills, birches, and rivulets. How ironic, I thought, that the serenity I was enjoying is rooted in ancient turbulence, where beauteous formations were wrought by seismic upheaval that carved bucolic vales, and by tempests which fed rivers and lakes. After a brief rest I hopped on the bicycle and pedaled a few miles more passing cow fields and farmhouses, and crossing narrow wooden bridges that traversed shallow, pristine streams. Where the winding road opened into a broad meadow I had now rode about ten miles and decided to turn back, but my retreat was stopped when my ear picked up the drowsy, tympanic beat of a drum. The sound grew more distinct as I cycled in its direction, and coming closer I could hear the accompaniment of guitars and banjos. The road curved around a circuit of trees bringing into view a pasture where thirty or so people were gathered in bohemian dress, some singing ballads. When they saw me approaching, several of them raised their hands signaling me to join them.

"Welcome to the Elysian Fields," greeted a man waving a thyrsus. He was about my age, with wiry red hair and a wineskin pouch dangling from a shoulder strap. "Join our circle for fun and entertainment, won't you?"

I dismounted the bicycle and walked up to him.

"My name is Bacchus," he said as he patted my shoulder.

I told him mine.

"Make yourself at home. Care for any?" he asked pointing to his wineskin. I declined, whereupon he raised the nozzle above his mouth and squirted a stream of red wine down his throat in the manner of an Andalusian shepherd.

I wandered through the assembly, greeted by smiles and hellos. A pretty young lady wearing a serrated fawn skin inserted a rose petal over my ear. She had long, black hair with a lustrous sheen parted in the center, which accented the symmetry of her features. "I'm Eros," she said.

"An unusual name," I remarked.

"Eros is the Greek goddess of love-making and procreation," she replied with a tease in her eye. "You have entered the Elysian Fields, a name taken from the abode of idyllic happiness in Greek mythology, where the good are sent when they die. We all live in harmony, and have abandoned our given names and adopted those of Greek and Roman legend."

"Would that chap over there playing the flute be Pan?"

"Sakadas," she corrected.

"Eros, can I assume that the behavior and personalities of those in this community match the mythical characters whose names they have adopted?"

"You catch on quickly," she said in a playful taunt.

Eros must be the Elysian whore who puts smiles on young men's faces, I thought. Yet this woodland nymph looked more like a pastor's daughter than a heathen slut. "Do you mind if I stroll through the grounds?" I asked.

She responded with a sweep of her arm indicating I could wander as I pleased.

The encampment was comprised of several tents, similar in design to the Mongolian yurt, with each accommodating about four people. A fellow strumming a lyre who referred to himself as Apollo invited me inside one of these octagonal huts. Patterned rugs lay scattered on a canvas floor, and in the center lay a fire pit, spotlighted by an oblique ray of sunlight pouring through a rooftop portal which ventilated rising smoke. He explained that a farmer was allowing them use of his twenty acres in exchange for their tending vegetables and clearing brush. And like vassals on a medieval fief, they could keep a percentage of the farm yield for their sustenance.

This commune, like the one which John's lady friend wanted him to join, was one of the remaining vestiges of communal living which littered the American countryside during the late Sixties. Idealistic youths believed that sharing property would counter avarice and end poverty, thus ridding the nation of social ills and inequality which had festered since the Industrial Revolution. Their aim was to end the industrial rape of Mother Earth by returning to an agrarian economy and live off the bounty of the land. Ironically, many who engaged in this social experiment were from well-heeled families, who benefited from the industrialization which they wanted to reverse. But Utopia was short-lived; poor hygiene and reckless behavior wrought diseases like hepatitis. And struggling with the absence of modern amenities brought home the reality that an anachronistic subculture taken from the nineteenth century cannot exist in the contemporary age.

Upon exiting the hut the air was rent by the crash of cymbals, attended by the clap of a Phrygian drum, which signaled that a play was about to begin. The community gathered in a semicircle before a low, wood platform that served as a stage. The play recounted in a humorous vein the fiery relationship between Juno and her husband Zeus, the Supreme god of Greco-Roman mythology whose philandering caused great vexation to his wife.

The performance opened when a young lady took to the stage and announced in a resonating voice: "I am Juno, wife and sister to Zeus, the father of the gods who reigns over heaven and earth from his throne on Mount Olympus. Yes, the all-powerful Zeus who can alter the course of nature. But how does that reckless lecher use his power? By scouring the earth for pretty maidens to seduce! The scoundrel has littered the Grecian countryside with his bastards, and only the other day he was up to his tricks again. He plundered Io, innocent daughter of Inachrus, as she was returning from the stream of Peneus, and then turned her into a heifer to disguise his crime. Now Io's father is beside himself with anguish, knowing that his daughter can only marry a bull and his grandchildren will be cattle. Not a day passes without Mercury bringing me news of my husband's villainy. The poets mock me as 'scowling Juno,' but if they wore my sandals for a day they would strum a different tune on their lyres. And how boring it is cooped up in this ethereal mansion where everywhere is shiny and bright, and everything made of gold."

The actress wearily sat on a chair and cast down her head, when another actor wearing a round, saw-tooth cap and wings on his ankles raced in breathlessly, proclaiming as he bent to one knee: "Oh, queen of Olympus and wife of mighty Zeus, protectress of…"

"Shut up Mercury and get to your point," she snapped at the panting messenger.

"The great Zeus, son of Cronos, has been sowing his seed again in virgin pastures," announced Mercury in an alarmed voice.

"I know, I know," said Juno dismissing him with a wave of her hand. Just then a stout, bearded man with curled locks appeared, stretching his arms and yawning.

"Welcome back, Zeus," greeted Juno sarcastically. "How exhausted you look. Has chasing the woodland nymphs of Maenalus all night left you fatigued?"

"I had affairs to settle in Crete," he answered sheepishly.

"Affairs indeed! The huntress Diana is furious! You de-flowered one of her virgins, and she's let all the Mediterranean know about it!" stormed Juno.

"Diana is a miserable bitch. I have a mind to turn that lesbian into a goat."

The marital dispute was suddenly interrupted when Pallas Athena, daughter of Zeus, ascended the stage.

"Mercury, how dandy to see you! Tell me courier, have you communicated my message to Calypso to release Odysseus whom she has held captive as her stud?"

"I have colossal news for you, goddess," replied the winged-footed messenger in heavy words as he was still recovering his breath. "I have recently returned from the island Ogygia where I conveyed to Calypso that the illustrious Odysseus, son of Laertes, must be put at liberty at once and return to his wife Penelope. Odysseus is now on his way to Ithaca."

"Many a man would love to spend the rest of his days with beautiful Calypso, being fed ambrosia and nectar from her bed," said Zeus. "Tell me errand boy, how did she react when learning she had to surrender her stallion?"

"As you would expect a strumpet to react when confronted with the curse of chastity. She told Odysseus that if he preferred to return to his dull wife, and watch her weave shawls and be henpecked all day instead of remaining with her, then he must find his own way off the island. Leading him to a forest of alders, she handed him a bronze axe and told him to chop away, whereupon he crafted himself a fine vessel from fallen timbers which he now navigates in calm sea waters."

No sooner had Mercury finished his account when a distressed look registered upon Athena. "Father! Father Zeus!" shouted Pallas Athena with alarm, as she peered into the distance with the look of a clairvoyant. "Poseidon has tomented the sea and is delivering a huge, angry wave that is rushing toward Odysseus. Alas, it has smashed into his boat and the raging water has swallowed him beneath the surface. He is doomed! And I have been the author of his misfortune, having instigated his departure from the island where he had been safe, albeit the play-toy of that goddess-whore."

"Fret not, daughter of Zeus!" cried Mercury, standing tip-toed with hands in front of his eyes telescoping his vision. "I can see that Odysseus has recovered his boat, and Poseidon's wrath has been checked by the goddess Leucothoe who has risen from the sea to comfort him."

"That snot should mind her own affairs!" snapped Pallas. "Let her comfort the dolphins and other sea creatures, but leave Odysseus alone!"

"Alone for you, jealous daughter of Zeus," quipped Juno.

"My only design for Odysseus is that he return safely to Ithaca and be reunited with his loyal spouse," sighed Pallas.

"Do you think Penelope cares a jot about Odysseus? She's been entertaining suitors these nine years in his absence."

"Cease your slander, Juno," said Zeus sternly. "Penelope has been a most faithful wife."

"Hmm, perhaps that is true husband; otherwise, she would have been your concubine by now," sneered Juno as she turned and stomped away. Then immediately ascending the stage came a freckle-faced man strumming a lyre and wearing an acanthus leaf crown, who announced in a wistful voice:

"I am Orpheus, the mirthless minstrel who until late was known for the happy harmony of my chords, but now I strum a mournful dirge for Eurydice my bride, who died not once but twice—the first time by the will of Fate; the second through her husband's folly. So deep was my distress over her death that I recently journeyed to the Underworld to see her, but only suffered a redoubling of my grief. Transported by Charon the ferryman across the river Styx, I arrived among the dead and sang my plaintive song which so moved Persephone, queen of Hades, that she allowed me to guide Eurydice out of the Underworld and return her as a mortal among the living. But upon breaking the condition that I should not turn around while leading her out of the depths of gloom, my bride fell back into the dark chasm never again to see the light of the world."

"O doleful poet, will you mourn Eurydice forever?" asked Pallas Athena. "Have a drink from the waters of Lethe and erase the memory of your loss," she said extending him a goblet. But the poet rejected her offer with a frown. So Zeus' daughter continued: "Temper the loss of your wife with the freedom of being a bachelor. Now sing me a lively tune and I'll dance a jig to lighten your heart."

"O goddess, how callous are your remarks!" snapped the widower. "If I wanted to be merry, I could summon all of Diana's nymphs to dance for me by merely plucking a few strings." Then Orpheus strummed his lyre and began a grieving lyric.

No sooner had he finished his elegiac when a petite blonde-haired lady, appareled as a woodland nymph in a short skirt cut high on her right hip and a single strap across one shoulder, sprang onto the stage shouting: "No tune from your lyre would ever get me to dance for you! You poets use your rhyming tales to deceive, when you depict nymphs running through sylvan woods engaging in wanton behavior with horny men. Would that it were true! Your epics herald the feats of fearless warriors, but courage fails these sissies when they see a naked woman. These muscular combatants will single-handedly chase an entire army, but flee from a nymph. Despite my beauty I have not lain with man or demigod in ages. My tender flesh will petrify to stone if not soon caressed by the limbs of a man," she sighed as she folded her arms across her breast, with each hand stroking the upper arm of the other. Then raising her head and extending her arms skyward she shouted, "Phoebus, you who pursued Daphne and got nothing for your chase, pursue me and I'll willingly yield as your captive! Neptune, you who raped lovely Caenis, come out of the ocean depths and take pleasure in my grotto!"

Following the desperate pleas of the nymph, Juno turned to Zeus and pointing to the pixie scoffed, "Here's a lady you've overlooked."

Juno's remark brought laughter from the audience, whereupon the actors slowly withdrew from the stage as a tall man with a prominent jaw and dressed in ancient warrior garb ascended the platform. Drawing a sword from his scabbard, he raised it vertically above his head and proclaimed in a booming voice, "I am Mars, god of War. Once again I have been awakened from my repose as nations engage in futile combat. The valleys which in peaceful times produced abundant crops and vines, are now laid waste and dyed crimson with the blood of fallen soldiers. Villages are leveled; temples are destroyed; and, other sacrileges are committed which anger the gods. Famine and epidemic has spread through the land; and the cheers that exhorted young men to victory as they marched off to battle have now turned to cries of lamentation for the death and destruction which does not cease. In the temples burnt sacrifices are offered to propitiate me to stop the carnage which I am accused of having caused. 'Mars,' they implore, 'why have you sown enmity among nations? Has not your appetite for bloodshed been satiated with the deaths of tens of thousands? Bring quickly the final act of this tragedy, and close the curtain on this ruin and havoc.'

"But it was not by my decree to turn prosperous cities into graveyards. It was not I who planted war into the minds of your monarchs and leaders. Rather, it was the devises of your rulers to ignite conflict in order to swell their coffers with spoils, and reap fame by subduing other nations. Alas, the monstrous Cyclops who despised the gods and consumed the flesh of men is alive today among tyrannical autocrats, who devour men in the machine of their marauding armies. Yet, I have sent you omens in hope that you would end your self-destruction. When war broke out between Athens and Sparta I released Plague from her Grove of Pestilence to spread epidemic across the land, thinking the warring people would halt their conflict and turn their efforts toward wiping out disease. But Athens listened to silver-tongued Pericles instead, who urged them to pursue combat and so intensified a curable hostility into a savage war lasting over twenty years. I have foiled battles by ordering the sun to eclipse at noon turning day into night. I have checked the spread of massacre from reaching foreign shores by ordering Neptune to agitate the seas and send huge waves to swallow your triremes. Still, arrogant nations have ignored my portents until they realize they are being subdued by the very instrument with which they conquered—the sword. And now they beg the gods for divine intervention to stop the consequences of their folly."

At this point in the Warrior god's monologue, seven women dressed in black gowns and wearing black veils rose to the stage and stood in a horizontal line behind the speaker. Their arms, visible only from below the elbows, were thin and bony. Each was holding a rapier and their fingers were dyed as if dipped in blood. They were hideous looking, like those who would greet the damned at the Gates of Hell. In low, dreary voices they began to hum a mournful tune in refrain to Mars's speech which continued:

"Will you mortals never reside in amity? Can you not relax to the liquid melody of the flute instead of marching to the blast of a trumpet. Rather, you listen to your rulers who incite you to abandon your plow, and take up the shield and spear and sow hostility among nations where friendship and hospitality once existed. You sense the thrill and glory of battle as your priests offer libations to the gods for victory, and your oracles predict military success. By all appearances Providence stands firmly in your corner, willing to smite the enemy who blocks your way. But defeat comes nonetheless. The well-wishers who sang paeans to regiments of young men as they filed out of their villages to join their brigades, later watch in painful silence the procession of biers bearing their fallen returning home for burial. The panegyrics which exhorted young men to gain heroism on the battlefield, are now replaced by funeral obsequies and the chants of dirges. Have you not learned anything from the tales and legends of your ancestors, which relate the horrors of war and the fate of its instigators? Yet you commit the same folly. Now poets, take up your stylus and record in cheerless verse the unhappy times of yet another generation." Having finished his oration to the responding applause of the audience, the actor sheathed his sword and exited the stage. Then one of the women in black stepped forward and began to speak, while the veiled ladies behind her swayed from right to left in somber, metrical movement to her grim words:

"We are the Seven Furies, avengers of bloodshed. The criminal who sneaks upon his prey and kills them, then wipes the blood from his blade to conceal the evidence cannot hide his crime from the gods. The mother who kills her infant and buries it in a nameless grave shall face reckoning for her atrocity. And the conqueror who marches through foreign lands, cutting a swath of death and destruction in his path, shall not justify his carnage in the name of liberation when his only goal was for personal fortune.

"Were you to journey to Hades you would find great nobles in that Kingdom of Decay, who in their mortal lives wore robes of Tyrian purple and crowns encrusted with diamonds, but now languish in darkness emitting perpetual groans for sacrificing innocent lives. The ghosts of their victims cry to us for justice. Let no man believe that his crimes will go unrequited, for there is no transgression of which we are not apprised. We, the Seven Sisters of Vengeance, have a thirst for revenge that can never be quenched."

The speaker then stepped back into line with the other Sisters, and the seven slowly exited the stage. The audience was benumbed by the electrifying presentation they had just heard. And if any among them had not believed in Hell beforehand, would not likely dismiss its existence now.

After a brief intermission the play continued, lampooning characters from Greek and Latin antiquity. But gathering clouds quickly darkened the landscape and a heavy rain put an end to the performance, as if the gods were retaliating for being mocked. Actors and audience quickly dispersed to their huts, where I took shelter in one of them and acquainted myself with several members of the community. I asked them if they intended to spend the rest of their lives in this commune. They responded that they would always live in a communal setting, and believed communes would flourish just as Christian monasteries did at the start of the second millennium in 1000 A.D. And a few were planning to visit India and Nepal to acquire "enhanced spirituality."

"Katmandu will bring me closer to God," said Phaon, an effeminate chap who wore an open vest over his bare, hairless chest. "There the clouds crown the mountain peaks like a divine wreath, a 'shekinah.'"

"A what?"

"Shekinah—illuminating cloud of divine presence."

"Why can't this 'shekinah' be found on a cloudy day in the Catskills?"

"Because the Catskills are spiritually polluted."

"With what?"

"With summer vacationers who come to eat like gluttons, drink like Vikings, and foul the air with their cars. But Katmandu is suffused with piety, emanating from the prayers and chants of lamas living in cliffside monasteries."

We chatted a bit more until the rain lightened, whereupon I thanked my hosts for their hospitality and bid them adieu. Then I headed back to The Timberhaus, cycling through a countryside that was contaminated by families known as summer vacationers.

XLIX

Why did I rob banks? Because that's where the money is.
— WILLIE SUTTON 1901-1980.

"What time did the robbery happen?"

"This morning. Just after opening for business."

"What robbery?" I interrupted. I had just finished washing the breakfast dishes, and entered the empty dining room to sip on a cup of coffee. There I caught Marcie and Gwen's conversation as the two were folding linen napkins and setting them in stacks.

"Durham Bank was robbed," replied Marcie without looking up from her folding.

"Who robbed it?" I asked eagerly. My thoughts flashed to the conversation Bruce and Tom had weeks earlier about getting a "loan" from Durham Bank.

"Three men. They ran off with $9,000 and conked the bank manager on the head," said Marcie.

"Mr Ellsworth? Was he hurt badly?"

"A small lump on the head. He'll just be wearing a larger hat size for a while," she answered.

"How did you learn about this?"

"From Gunther. He heard the news when he was in town this morning."

"I have a hundred dollars in that bank," I said.

"You *had* a hundred dollars; the robbers took all the cash," said Gwen.

"I'll get it back. Deposits are insured, half-wit."

"Better than having no wit at all," she quipped. Gwen was a

good-humored 18-year-old whom I often jousted with, and quick with her answers.

"Gunther said that Papa is in a dither because he has his business account with the bank," injected Marcie. "When I asked Gunther if our paychecks might be delayed he grew agitated and said, 'No! No! Of course not!' And then he slipped away without saying another word."

"I'll bet you're right," replied Gwen. "By the time the bank straightens out its books the season will be over, and all us workers will have left without getting our final week's pay."

"I wonder if Papa will bother to send us our checks after we're gone," added Marcie.

"He has to, it's the law," I piped.

"Do you hear this guy," remarked Marcie rolling her eyes half-circle. "When it affects workers, Papa cares no more about the law than the food he makes us eat."

It seemed as if the gods were conspiring against me. To prevent my money from being stolen I made weekly bank deposits, and then the bank is robbed. And with the resort closing next week, it was quite possible I would not get my paycheck, not to mention when I would be able to withdraw my savings.

"You were about to say something?" Gwen asked me, observing my expression.

"No...no," I answered distractedly. But I was on the verge of asking them if they had seen Bruce or Tom or Eric that morning for none had showed up at breakfast, though it was not uncommon for them to miss a meal. I had a suspicion that the girls might guess I suspected the trio were involved in the heist by asking their whereabouts, leading them to think I had foreknowledge of the crime. Tom was reckless and dumb: A lemming who would follow Bruce off the edge of a cliff, and to whom a bank robbery was just a way of having fun. Eric was drug-crazed and bordering on schizophrenia where reality and illusion are one. But Bruce was a despicable knave; he had an evil star and an inborn virulence, and I suspected it was he who had clubbed Thomas Ellsworth.

"What are you mumbling?" asked Marcie.

"Nothing, nothing," I answered testily, not even aware of my muttering.

"You're upset about your hundred bucks. Don't worry honey, you'll get your money," assured Gwen, giving me a confident pat on the knee.

"I'm not worrying about the money," I said in a deflated voice. I rose slowly from the chair, took a last sip of coffee, and left.

But I *was* worried about my money, and the thought of losing it was kindling my anger. So I decided to confront the two cowboys and ask them where they were this morning. I headed directly to the stables where I found Tom grooming a palfrey, and Bruce filling a horse trough with a water hose. Their backs were turned and they did not see me at the entrance, but suddenly my courage failed. I was set to leave when the palfrey whinnied and stirred. The two wranglers turned around.

"Hello!" I called awkwardly. The two glanced at each other and then looked at me.

"What brings you here, Rick-man?" croaked Tom, as he resumed applying short, brisk strokes to the hindquarters of the horse.

"I, I'm looking for Gunther. I was told he might be here."

"Haven't seen him. Have you Bruce-man?"

"Uh-uh," grunted Bruce.

I said nothing more and walked away.

Bruce and his buddy Tom were "eggs of the night"—parentless; the former raised by a grandmother, the other in an orphanage. And without having had the affinity of family life, they never conformed to social norms. They were rebels who rejected society's laws because each refused to be dictated by another's rules. If they broke a law they did not feel they were doing wrong, rather the two felt they were wronged by laws which inhibited their freedom.

As I walked across the hoof-cloddy soil back to the recreation area I tried to sort out this situation. If Tom and Bruce had robbed the bank they would have fled the area. But on the other hand their conspicuous absence would make them suspects. Yet if they committed the robbery, how could they have managed to flee in broad daylight and return to the resort without attracting notice? Perhaps

I was jumping to conclusions. Had I taken out of context Tom's comment about getting a loan from Durham Savings as his intention to rob the bank? But during that same conversation in the bunkhouse, Bruce was infuriated by Eric's remark that he and Tom had boasted of robbing a bank. And the timing of the robbery, which coincided with the end of summer and the wranglers' planned departure for Texas, tipped the scales toward their guilt. Tom and Bruce could be waiting for nightfall to escape under the cover of darkness. If so, little time was left to report what I knew to the sheriff. But what was there to tell the lawman other than my suspicions?

At lunchtime, the mess room buzzed with talk of the bank theft. Police roadblocks had been set up everywhere between Durham and the New York State Thruway. Everyone agreed that the drowsy town was overdue for excitement. And rumor that none of us would get our paychecks added to the sensation.

"What is all this noise?" boomed Tom. He and Bruce had just barged into the mess room with their plates heaped with gravied pork and bread.

"Durham Bank was robbed this morning," squeaked Cindy.

"What is this world coming to!" exclaimed Tom in a satiric tone. "It's a good thing we keep our money in our boots, eh Bruce-man?"

"Yeah," said Bruce, just before shoveling a slice of greasy pork into his mouth. As he munched he drew out a sliver of fat from between his teeth and dropped it on his plate.

Tom and Bruce showed no reaction to news of the robbery, asking no questions and unconcerned about hearing any details on it. They acted no differently than at other times; Tom joked with the waitresses, while Bruce gobbled his food like an ogre. But I noticed that Chris appeared subdued and was in deep thought. He leaned his head on his hand, while lightly tapping a spoon against his soup bowl.

The current of chatter was abruptly broken when Papa stormed into the mess room: "Where is Eric! Where is that lazy good-for-nothing!" he shouted as his scowling eyes scanned every face.

"Haven't seen him," a few answered, while others shrugged their shoulders. Then Papa turned on his heel like a drill sergeant and stomped from the room.

After eating a ghastly lunch of last year's pigs, burnt rice, and soup that tasted like salt water, I wheeled my bus cart into the dining hall where news was circulating among the tables that a car belonging to one of the guests had been stolen. The story went like this: Vito and Gina Gossalini returned from town the night before and parked their car in the lot directly behind the recreation center. Then they went inside the hall, where they danced tarantellas and polkas until closing. Afterwards, the Gossalinis walked the short distance back to their cottage, leaving the car where they had parked it. They did not discover their auto missing until morning, when Vito went to fetch a bowling ball he had left inside the rear trunk.

Vito could not believe his car was gone. At first he wondered if he may have parked it elsewhere. He rushed back to the cottage to consult his wife, who assured Vito that he had parked the car in that lot. The couple took tremendous pride in their auto, as it was a new and expensive import; and for the childless Gossalinis the theft was the equivalent of a kidnapping. Gina ran with Vito back to the lot, only to find the sad truth ratified by the empty spot where their car had been.

General opinion was that the stolen car was linked to the bank robbery, and I believed Tom and Bruce used the car in their getaway. Eric had not been seen at all that day, and my hunch was that he had either fled in the car or dumped it. What puzzled me was how Tom and Bruce got back to The Timberhaus, for they would not have risked being seen driving a car stolen from the place they were returning to.

At mid-afternoon I spotted Chris standing among the tall timbers which line the banks of the creek. He was alone and leaning against a tree while puffing a cigarette with intensity.

"Your mother would be furious if she caught you smoking." He did not see me, and my remark startled him just as he had inhaled on the cigarette, which sent him into a paroxysm of coughing. His face turned brick red, and it was only after I administered several whacks to his upper back that he was able to regain his breath. "I recommend chewing gum instead," I suggested.

He looked at me in earnest and spoke: "Promise not to tell anyone what I tell you now."

"I promise."

He looked around as if suspecting the trees might have ears. "I think…I'm almost sure…" A long pause followed. His face blanched and his breathing raced.

"Go ahead," I said reassuringly.

"I-think-they-robbed-the-bank," he blurted so fast that the sentence came out like one word.

"Who did?"

"Huh?"

"Who did?" I asked again.

Chris looked at me from the corner of his eye, and in a low stutter answered: "B-Bruce, T-Tom, and…and Eric."

"How did you come to know this?" I asked calmly.

"I heard them talking about it."

"When?"

"A few weeks ago. But I thought they were rambling from too many beers." He was referring to the same conversation I had overheard.

"If they did rob the bank, why haven't they fled?" I asked.

"They're probably waiting until the dust settles."

"And the money?"

"They have likely hid it, or maybe Eric has it. I don't know."

"Then you know what you must do."

"What?" he asked anxiously.

"Inform the sheriff."

"Absolutely not!"

"It is your duty," I said plainly.

"Bruce will kill me if I do!"

"Probably."

"Oh gosh," he moaned, looking on the verge of tears. "I can't. I can't," he added while nervously raking his fingers through his hair.

"You must."

"And if I don't?" he asked bitterly.

"Then I will tell the sheriff."

"You promised not to repeat a word!"

"You should not have trusted me."

Chris slumped against the tree and turned the side of his face into the bark. "I need time to think this over," he said dismally.

"I will leave you to your conscience, young man. Goodbye." And I walked away. I empathized with Chris's distress, yet I took a warped pleasure in teasing him and making light of his quandary. It was my way of easing my own anxiety over this sticky situation. After all, every drama has its comic relief.

L

But next morning the mutual dilemma shared by Chris and myself was resolved when Eric was arrested. In his flight he had terrorized an apple orchard, driving the Gossalini's car like a maniac through rows of trees where he slammed into tree ladders, and left several apple pickers dangling from branches like human fruit. In a nearby backwoods he abandoned the car and then set out on foot. A short time later he was picked up by a sheriff's deputy, who had been dispatched to the area to investigate the panic at the orchard. The rascal denied having driven any car, insisting he was out on a morning walk. But Eric's crazed look and his loss to explain how he had strayed thirty miles from The Timberhaus fueled the suspicion of the lawman, who searched Eric and found on him the keys to the Gossalini's car. An hour later Eric was in jail, and spilling to the sheriff the roles which he, Bruce, and Tom had played in the bank theft.

By ten o'clock a team of sheriff's deputies arrived at The Timberhaus and surrounded the stable where inside Tom and Bruce were outfitting their horses. When the lawmen announced themselves, Tom jumped on his palfrey and bolted from the stable, high-jumping the circle of deputies and hurdling the corral fence. It was said that Tom was laughing as he made his escape and shouted to the deputies: "You stupid sons of whores will never catch me." It was a scene that rivaled any found in a cowboy movie. The rocky and rolling terrain prevented the deputies from giving chase in their cars; they could only watch helplessly, and in awe, at the remarkable horsemanship of the young scalawag as he quickly disappeared across the countryside as if on winged Pegasus. Meanwhile, Bruce was apprehended after a brief but futile struggle with the deputies, who wrestled the brute to the ground and clapped him in handcuffs.

According to what Eric told the sheriff, after robbing the bank the trio drove in the stolen car to a remote wooded area a few miles from town, where Tom and Bruce had tethered their horses earlier that morning. The wranglers then fled on horseback with the loot, while Eric drove off to dump the car. Where Eric had gone with the car over the next twenty-four hours until the time of his apprehension, no one knew; not even Eric could remember. Somewhere in the woods Tom and Bruce hid the stolen money for later retrieval, and then rode back to The Timberhaus as if they had been on their morning gallop.

But Bruce vehemently denied any part in the robbery. When he and Eric were brought before Ellsworth and the three bank clerks, all of them agreed that the stature and the clothing of the accused matched those of two of the robbers. But exact identification could not be made because the robbers had worn face masks. The situation was further complicated because the stolen money was missing. Although Eric knew the loot was hidden, he did not know where it had been stashed. Only Bruce and Tom knew that. But Tom had fled and Bruce was not talking. Eric and Bruce were charged and held for robbery, and an arrest warrant was issued for Tom as an auxiliary. But the sheriff knew that he had to recover the money, if he were to have any hope of securing a criminal indictment from the district attorney. Up to this point the only known crime committed was auto theft, for which Eric alone was charged.

The Gossalini's joy of learning that their car had been recovered was tempered by news that it had received considerable scrapes and dents from Eric's kamikaze driving. News quickly spread of Bruce's arrest and Tom's escape, stirring excitement among the guests some of whom, scenting an opportunity for heroism, offered to assist in searching for Tom. But Sheriff Wilson rejected their offers.

The sheriff questioned all the workers for clues. Chris, Cindy, and Nick admitted that they had heard Tom and Bruce talk of robbing a bank, but thought at the time it was only boasting brought on by drinking. And no one could shed light as to where Tom might have fled. As for myself I told the sheriff that I rarely spoke to the accused robbers, which was true, but denied ever having heard them discuss plans to rob a bank, which was false. I had mixed feelings concealing from the sheriff all that I had heard. But since other workers had already informed him of the culprits' boast of robbing a bank, my admission to prior knowledge of a possible robbery would not bring the sheriff additional clues. Furthermore, I would be returning to classes soon, and did not want to be bogged down as a witness in a criminal case that would divert me from my studies.

But what two-legged creatures could not solve, four-legged animals did. The sheriff brought in a pack of bloodhounds, who after scenting Bruce's clothing and personal possessions, were let loose along the probable route that Bruce and Tom would have rode on the morning of the robbery. Within two hours the hounds had found the stolen loot stashed in a saddle satchel belonging to Bruce and hidden inside a tree hollow. Bruce's fingerprints were found on the satchel, thus corroborating Eric's story.

What else need I say about the bank robbery? Durham Savings re-opened for business the day after the theft, and before leaving The Timberhaus I withdrew my hundred dollars with interest. I said farewell to Thomas Ellsworth, who was wearing a small bandage on the back of his head where he had been whacked. Eric and Bruce were arraigned and transported to an Albany jail to await trial; and Tom was still on the loose, perhaps hiding with friends or sleeping under the stars.

LI

There is some pleasure in being on board a ship battered by storms when one is certain of not perishing.

— Pascal

Bowing to Earth for yet another day in its endless orbit, the squinting sun had just thrown out its last ray of light as it dropped below the spine of the western highlands, leaving the countryside in a melting, golden afterglow. It was Saturday evening, the second of September, and the final weekend of the summer season at The Timberhaus and all the Catskill resorts. The day after tomorrow the region would be dispeopled of vacationers, and nature would retake dominion over its woodlands and hills undisturbed by the clamor of visitors. Animals of the forests would begin stockpiling for the coming winter, and birds would start their southward retreat.

My mind was relaxed and untroubled on this tranquil evening. As if a wizard's curse had been broken, the mountains were no longer a prison fortress, but had returned to that endearing Catskill landscape I had embraced as a boy. The beleaguering fear and anxiety which engulfed me during most of the summer had dissipated, for they were nothing more than harmless concoctions of an excited mind. I looked back on the great disappointment and shock that greeted me on the first night I arrived at The Timberhaus, and the ensuing weeks of toil, frustration, and loneliness. It was a chaotic summer, or so I thought. I had to navigate through my dilemmas without the aid of a guiding North Star. Most times I felt my situation was akin to wandering through a hedgerow maze in an English garden, where I found myself lost in a labyrinth of lanes and no way to get out. I took wrong turns, backed up, and charted other paths until I found an exit from my predicaments. And I accomplished this by squaring myself to the challenges which each day presented. But upon reflection the challenges which loomed as mountains, were really only trifles. It was the dwarf I had to battle, not the giant.

Next morning I awakened with the joy of a sailor who had just arrived at port after several weeks at sea. Tomorrow I would be home where I would pick up the rest of my life's voyage with my summer adventure in its wake. No more sleeping in this boat! I stripped the rowboat of the padding and blankets for the final time, tossed the oars into the hull, and then pushed it into the pond. "Farewell, my friend!" I shouted as the craft glided slowly across the water. Then I headed to the chalet to wash myself and get ready for work. I began my last day at The Timberhaus as I had begun my first—in the kitchen. Papa must have felt life had been too easy for me of late bussing tables, and as penalty for requesting early liberty—I was leaving one day before the resort closed—he assigned me to the scullery. This final day was no different from those previous. The kitchen was as steamy as the Amazon, and for lunch I ate pig meat and drank sour milk. But today's inconveniences were trivial. The flames of Purgatory were dwindling, and salvation loomed when at two o'clock I would be rid of this slavish work forever, and later head home on a bus to be reunited with my family and enjoy a hearty dinner with them that night. I was in a wonderful mood and all the workers were gay and jubilant and looking forward to going home this weekend, most having not seen their families in three months. Only a few employees like myself were leaving today, as the rest would work through tomorrow when the resort would close at noon on Monday, Labor Day, and begin its hibernation until next summer.

When I stacked the last lunch plate on the kitchen shelf I whooped a cry of ecstasy and flung my soiled apron in the air, where it floated in eerie descent from the ceiling like a ghost and into my arms. Then I rolled it in a ball and stuffed it in the canvas laundry crib, as happy to be rid of it as a prisoner his uniform on the day of his release. Otto gave me an odd look, and then shook his head grinning, but said not a word. He, too, was in good spirits; it was the only day I did not see him scowl or hear him shout in the kitchen.

I was meeting Danny that afternoon. He was leaving Brookhaven tomorrow, and then would head to Brooklyn to visit relatives before flying home to Dublin. At two thirty a jalopy roared into the resort and screeched to a halt in front of the commons. This was immediately followed by the car motor backfiring several times and steam pouring from beneath the engine hood, resembling an angry bull venting puffs of vapor from its nostrils. Danny alighted from the car looking ashen.

"God's sake, Stubby! Will you ever drive without trying to break the sound barrier!" Danny screamed. But Stubby merely laughed at Danny's irritation.

"Glad to see you, good friend!" I cried as I trotted over to greet the Irishman.

"Well lad, will you be sad parting company with this place?" he asked as we shook hands.

"As sad as an inmate leaving an asylum. But I feel great. And you? After tomorrow you need never suffer Mrs Van again."

"After tomorrow I will have poured my last drink. No more tending bar for me!" he said, slicing the air with a downward sweep of his hand. "T'was the most miserable summer of my life."

"Yet we each survived it," I replied.

"Aye, that we did, that we did."

"Let's go inside for a beer," I offered. "Are you coming, Stubby?"

"Nah. I gotta check the car before it blows up. The radiator needs water."

Inside the recreation hall Angela was working the snack bar. "I'm in mourning. Tomorrow The Timberhaus will be a ghost town," she sighed as she handed us two cold bottles of beer. "Will you be back next year, Byron?"

"Next year I graduate," I said proudly.

"Wonderful! No, no, it's on the house," she said waving off the money I was handing her for the beer. Angela was getting married in October, and we wished each other happiness and success.

Danny and I planted ourselves at a table, clicked our bottles, and raised a toast of "slainte!" (cheers). Danny took a gulp, and smacked his lips. "A few days from now I will be in rainy Dublin, and never have I looked so forward to nasty weather," he said nostalgically.

"And tonight I will be feasting on roast turkey with all the trimmings, and sleeping in a *real* bed," I said. Mom wrote me earlier in the week describing the "welcome home" dinner awaiting me.

Danny hunched over the table, and in a low voice said, "There is a young lady who I'm itchin' to see when I get home."

"A girlfriend?"

"Not exactly. But I'm hoping to start a relationship with her. I met her a few weeks before I left for the States."

"Has she written you?"

He hesitated. "Only once, at the start of summer. And I've darn near ruined my summer thinking about her. She's on my mind all the time. And the weird thing is I hardly know her."

"Have you dated her?"

"We're just acquaintances. Odd as it may sound, I was afraid that if I dated her I might get romantically attached to her."

"What's wrong with that?" I asked incredulously.

"Because I would be tempted to cancel my trip to the States and I didn't want that to happen. But I'm absolutely crazy about her," emphasizing his point with a slap on the table. "And I'm worried that she may not want to date me when I get back." He dropped his chin into his palm and looked at me from beneath his brow with eyes that begged for an answer.

I scratched my head. "I'm no Solomon, but my advice is when you return home, ask her out. If she refuses, find another."

Danny appeared dismayed when I suggested that his dream woman could be replaced by someone else. "I suppose that's what I'll have to do," he said resignedly.

After polishing off our beers we went outside, where I parted company with the Dubliner for the final time. "Drop me a letter when you get back," I said.

"I shall. And I expect a letter from you as well. And If you ever visit Dublin, you'll have a place to stay. I'll show you around. 'Tis a charmin' town. 'In Dublin's fair city, where the girls are so pretty…'" His ditty was interrupted by a car honk. "I got to go; Stubby is getting impatient."

"Have a safe trip."

"If I survive Stubby's driving, crossing the Atlantic will be the least of my concern. Take care of yourself lad."

We shook hands and hugged. Then Danny scurried to the waiting car.

"Okay! I'm coming! I'm coming!" he shouted. Stubby was blasting the horn like a baby playing with a toy. Danny had gotten only one leg into the car when Stubby drove off. There was panic on Danny's face as he struggled to close the door and keep himself from being ejected as the car spun around and left in a thunderous roar, leaving a swirling funnel of dust in its track. Moments later the jalopy was out of sight.

The day was moving quickly and I had still not packed, so I hastened to the cottage to shower and change my clothes. I emptied my belongings from the drawers, shaking each garment to make sure no mouse or insects were hidden within to become a stowaway in my suitcase. I wore the same outfit on the day when I arrived at The Timberhaus, which I had not worn since. My shirt and slacks now hung loose and baggy; I had lost weight but my body was lean and firm from weeks of hard activity. Next, I checked the corners of the musty room and looked underneath the bed to see if I had left any possessions. Then with suitcase in hand, I closed the door after me and went to the office to pick up my paycheck, thanks to the bloodhounds who having found the stolen cash would allow me to leave with money in my pocket.

"Heidi, I will be leaving in an hour and I have a few goodbyes to make. Can I leave my luggage here," I asked as she handed me my check.

"Yes, but don't forget to pick it up," she returned.

"I feel like pulling your ears for such a remark! I'm as likely to forget my suitcase as I would forget that I'm leaving today," I joked. She grabbed a pencil from her desk and tossed it at me, which I intercepted before it struck. "Thanks for the souvenir."

I returned to the cottage to look for Churchill, where he planted stakes after the bunkhouse was destroyed. I was concerned because I had not seen him since yesterday afternoon, and the bowl of milk I had left for him in the room was untouched. It was quite unlike the cat, for he was as fond of milk as a babe at suck. What a pity it would be not to cuddle my companion one last time. I walked back to the commons calling, "Churchill! Churchill!" but without result. Next I searched behind the kitchen where, beside the shed, I heard a rumbling inside one of the trash cans. The can teetered and then fell on its side, spilling garbage on the ground and with it a cat holding a bony mackerel in his mouth.

"Churchill!"

The cat looked dumbstruck, and I sensed he was embarrassed that I found him scavenging. He deposited the fish on the ground and then licked his paws and groomed his coat to make himself presentable, and then walked toward me in slow, measured steps. I put out my hands to receive him, but he drew back as if I were a stranger. Then I dropped to a crouch and clicked my fingers. "Churchill, I've been worried sick about you, and you won't even let me touch you. Come, come to me boy."

The temperamental feline approached me, sat on his haunches, and purred as I stroked his furry coat. "I'm leaving, Churchill. I won't see you again my friend."

He answered with a "mee-ow."

"You knew I was leaving today, didn't you? You cats have such fine instinct," I said as I caressed his chin. "And now you have returned to your roots, to the garbage pails where I first discovered you."

Churchill cocked his head and gazed at me with his discerning green eyes. Then he rose on all fours, arched his back, and with a long, sonorous "mee-ow" bade farewell. Next, he picked up the spiny mackerel in his mouth, bounded atop the wood picket-fence, and tip-toed across its narrow ridge.

Cats are not devoted to their masters as dogs are. They are aloof and independent. And Churchill was no different. He was not unfaithful, but merely loyal to his nature. How foolish it is to judge animals within the context of human behavior. We deceive ourselves by assigning them human attributes, and expecting them to react as people would. Churchill was letting me know that he was not my pet anymore than I was his, and that our mutual friendship was over and we each had to go about our own business. I watched him as he continued along the ridge, and when he reached the end of the fence he turned and looked at me as if to say: "Why are you staring at me? Go, you have a bus to catch." Then he jumped to the ground and disappeared into the tall rye grass of the open field.

As I was about to return to the office to retrieve my suitcase, it occurred to me to pay a quick visit to Otto. Ever since my encounter with Otto at the stream a couple of weeks earlier, neither of us had ever alluded to our chance meeting. It remained business as usual and Otto remained as cantankerous as ever. But he was in good humor on this day and I wanted to part company with him on a friendly note. I entered the kitchen through the backdoor, and found him in the pantry where he was eyeballing shelves of canned foods and check-listing the items.

"Hello Otto," I said from the pantry threshold.

He turned and was surprised to see me. "Yes, what do you want?" he asked awkwardly as he turned back to face the shelves.

"I'm leaving, and I've come to say goodbye."

"Yes...well, goodbye," he replied addressing a row of preservatives.

"It was nice working with you, Otto," I politely lied.

"Hmm. That's good. Now, permit me to finish taking inventory. I have much to do." His voice was cordial but a bit uneasy.

"Have a nice autumn," I replied despondently.

"And you as well, Byron."

I believe Otto never forgave himself for having divulged so much of himself to me on that hot afternoon by the stream. He was a solitary man, and I was probably only one of a few people who had penetrated his private world. To him I was an uncomfortable reminder of that highly personal conversation, when he related to me his tragic past and shattered dreams.

It was near time to leave. In my final hour at The Timberhaus I had been snubbed by a cat and slighted by a cook and the sooner I was rid of this place, the better. When I returned to the office to pick up my suitcase, I asked Heidi if she had seen Fred.

"I haven't seen him today at all."

"I won't have a chance to say goodbye to him."

"I'll tell Fred you were looking for him," she said.

"Better yet, have you a sheet of paper? I'll leave him a note." Heidi gave me paper and an envelope, and I scribbled a brief goodbye to Fred, reminding him that the invitation to join my family for dinner still stood.

"I'll make sure he gets this," Heidi said when I handed her the envelope.

At four thirty Gunther drove me to the bus depot in his station wagon. During the brief ride he asked me what my plans were now that summer was over. He had asked me this same question numerous times during the season, and each time I told him I would be returning to college. And now, as before, he remarked, "I didn't know you were a student." The man was a veritable dunce.

When we arrived at the depot I had no sooner stepped out of the car when he drove away, not waiting for me to retrieve my belongings from the rear of the wagon.

"Stop! Stop! My suitcase!" I screamed, running after the car. Hearing my desperate cry, Gunther hit the brakes and apologized for the "oversight."

The depot was a flimsy shelter consisting of a long, wood bench with a three-sided lattice enclosure standing adjacent to Harry's Dry Goods Store. The late afternoon was solemnly still and quiet, as if grieving the passing of summer.

LII

A happy family is but an earlier Heaven.
— George Bernard Shaw

The bus arrived ten minutes early. It was half-full and most of the passengers were French-speaking en route from Montreal. As the bus was ahead of schedule it would not depart for several minutes, allowing the driver and some of the passengers to stretch their legs outside and smoke. I took my seat and closed my eyes. In my mind I drew a picture of being with my family that evening, and having so many stories to tell them. "I'm going home, I'm going home," I repeated silently like a mantra. Right after the passengers returned to their seats I heard a minor commotion outside. Then stepping inside the bus the driver called: "Is there a Byron on board?"

I glanced at the other passengers, but found no one else answering to the name. I hesitated to reply, somewhat apprehensive as to why I was being summoned. "I'm here," I answered sheepishly.

"You have visitors."

I went to the fore of the bus and could not believe who I saw—gathered outside the door were Chloe, Chris, Cindy, Nick, and John!

"Why didn't you tell us you were leaving today?" squeaked Chloe, as she surprised me with a hug.

"Well, I…I…assumed…thought everyone knew," I said tripping over my words. "And I was so busy this morning I just didn't get a chance to finish my good-byes."

"By a stroke of good timing we met Gunther, and he told us he had just dropped you off at the depot," said John.

"So we made a wild dash to catch you before your bus left," added Chris.

"Und they make me drive like a madman to get here." Emerging through the knot of well-wishers was Papa himself.

"Papa!" I exclaimed.

"Best of luck to you my boy," he said patting me on the shoulder.

"We spotted Papa getting into his truck and we asked him for a ride," said Chloe excitedly.

"It was nice of you all to come," I said with emotion.

The bus driver started the motor, and those remaining passengers lingering outside began to board. "Oh, oh, time is up. It was so great to see you all. Thank you. Thank you so much!" I said. And then in a spontaneous burst I kissed the ladies' cheeks and bear-hugged the men, except Papa who had receded into the background and watched everything with amusement. I stepped onto the platform of the bus and waved and said goodbye, and as the door was closing I heard Papa say, "Okay, boys und girls, I treat you all to ice cream sodas!"

When I looked down the aisle, I realized I had been the focus of attention among the Canadians. They had been giraffing their necks over each other's shoulders, peering out the windows in curiosity. As I walked to my seat they exchanged smiling nods of approval and "eh biens" to each other, satisfied at the outcome of the surprise farewell.

As the bus meandered through the docile hills with strobes of sunlight breaking through columns of pine trees, I grew maudlin about my Catskill summer as I ruminated on the people I had met and the situations I had encountered. This was a season that would have no sequel: Never would I see again those who saw me off on the bus; never would I work a summer job anymore. But in a few hours I would be reunited with that treasure which only a couple of months earlier I had taken for granted—my home and family.

I slept during most of the three-hour ride, briefly awakening when the bus stopped in Poughkeepsie and Nyack to pick up more passengers. I awoke again when the bus rattled and bounced as its tires took on pot-holes, announcing arrival in The Bronx. A few minutes later the vertical bluffs of northern Manhattan appeared on my right, rising from the Harlem River; and to my left high-rise apartments overlooked windowless tenements and rotting store-fronts. Vehicles from converging parkways slowed traffic for twenty minutes. When the bottleneck opened the bus continued southward into Manhattan along the West Side Highway, until arriving at the Port Authority bus terminal.

The terminal is an enormous harbor where buses arrive and depart from all parts of the country. The bus slowly proceeded past scores of bus stalls, until pulling into its assigned slot where the passengers disembarked. My mother was there waiting for me as I stepped off the bus.

"You look great!" she said as she embraced and kissed me. Then mom stepped back and looked me over: "But you've lost weight!"

"A few pounds. Where is dad?"

"He's in the car. We couldn't find a parking space, so he's orbiting the bus terminal. Let's not keep him waiting."

Outside, we spotted dad rounding the corner of Tenth Avenue and signaled to him. No sooner had he stopped the car when taxis began blaring their horns.

"The New York Symphony is welcoming you," said my father amid the deafening honks as I entered the car.

As we drove across town on 42nd Street, my eyes were drawn upward by the precipitous heights of the buildings. It seemed impossible that Manhattan and the Catskills could share the same planet—the former with its pinnacles of skyscrapers and human congestion; the latter with its benign mountains and open space. Night was descending on the city as we crossed over the East River on the 59th Street Bridge heading into Queens, with the dark waters below reflecting the Manhattan lights as an inverted skyline on its surface. Twenty minutes later the car turned onto our street, and we pulled into our driveway.

"Landfall!" I cried.

"It's the same old neighborhood. Nothing has changed," said my mother.

Nothing has changed, yet everything looks different, I thought.

Inside, the aroma of baked turkey filled the house. Vegetables were simmering on the stove, and my sister Lynn was tossing salad in the kitchen.

"Welcome home, Byron!" She set the salad spoons on the table, wiped her hands on her apron, and hugged me.

"How was Europe?"

"Terrific! Was I surprised when mom told me you were working in the Catskills. How were the mountains?"

I drew a deep breath. "I have lots to tell. By the way, where is little brother?"

"He's in Oyster Bay for the weekend. Tommy Keogh's family invited him to their summer cottage. He'll be back tomorrow night."

"Is everything ready?" asked my mother.

"I just have to carve the bird," my sister answered.

As the ladies fussed in the kitchen, I freshened myself in the bathroom. When I came out a carved, ten-pound turkey and platters of vegetables were set on the dining table.

"Thanksgiving in September!" I boomed, rubbing the palms of my hands. As I was about to stab a slice of turkey my mother blocked my fork.

"Not yet. Let's say a prayer of thanks first," she said. Four heads bowed as mom thanked the Almighty for her son and daughter's safe return from their summer adventures. No sooner had "Amen" left my lips, when I attacked the turkey and mashed potatoes. I began eating fast and furiously, stuffing my mouth until my cheeks ballooned. But I had not gone very far in my meal when an odd thing occurred. As hungry as I was I could not eat any more of this delicious repast. I was not used to eating good food. For two months I lived on a prisoner's diet, and my stomach would need time to readjust to a palatable meal. I played with the food, swirling the creamy potatoes with my fork, and knocking the peas around my plate like marbles.

"Eat your dinner," said my father.

"The food is excellent—" I began to say.

"Then eat it," interrupted my mother, somewhat irritated that I was mediocre on the dinner she and my sister had taken such effort to prepare.

"But I can't swallow any more food." And I explained why.

"The same thing happened to me when I was discharged from

the military," said my father. "After three years of army food, I couldn't eat the first meal I had back home. My mother, God rest her soul, had gone to great lengths to cook an excellent dinner for me, and I could barely touch a morsel of it."

"Did you behave yourself while you were away? I know how young folk like to carouse and drink," said my mother.

"That reminds me. Dad, I brought back a fifth of Johnnie Walker for you."

My father suspended the fork of potatoes he was about to place in his mouth. "Why did you do that?" he asked with surprise. "I don't drink Scotch."

So I told him how I had acquired the whisky. My father drank whisky only during Thanksgiving and Christmas, and the bottles he had were holiday gifts which he kept unopened until the following year, when he passed them off as holiday presents to friends and relatives. For example, a few years ago my parents were entertaining relatives at our house for Christmas, and cousin Jerry presented my father with a quart of bourbon. The following year we were invited to Jerry's house for Christmas dinner and my father gave him the same bottle as a gift, forgetting whom he had received it from. In fact, the bottle had never been taken out of its original box, and when Jerry saw it a look of "déjà vu" flushed across his face.

I pushed aside my plate; I could not eat any more. The moist slices of untouched turkey with its golden brown edges, and the gravied potatoes, carrots, and peas—a meal I would have traded ten years of my life for at The Timberhaus—would be tomorrow's leftovers. After dinner mom and Lynn returned to the kitchen to prepare desert, while my father and I adjourned to the living room. I slumped in a wingback chair, overcome with drowsiness. "I'm exhausted dad; I have two months sleep to catch up with." Suddenly a familiar voice called out from the corner of the room.

"Where's Byron? Where's Byron?"

"Captain! I completely forgot about you!" It was our talking parakeet. I opened the bird cage and Captain hopped onto my finger. I drew him up to my face, where he nibbled on the tip of my nose. "Not too hard," I said.

"Not too hard," he repeated. Then he hopped from my finger and onto my shoulder where he nibbled on my shirt collar.

"You received several postcards while you were away," my father said. "Mom, where are Byron's cards?"

"In the top drawer of the secretary," she hollered from the kitchen. I opened the drawer and found several postcards addressed to me.

"I have three cards from Bill. He sent one from Paris, and here's another from Paris; gosh, he must really like 'Paree,' and here's one from Frankfort."

"Have you seen my card from London?" asked Lynn who had just entered the living room.

"Yes, here it is." I read it aloud: "'Byron, having a bloody good time in London. Visited Buckingham Palace and had tea with the Queen. Heading north to Edinburg tomorrow. Cheers!'"

"It's pronounced 'Edin-boro,'" corrected Lynn.

"Did you like Scotland?"

"Yes, and I have a hundred bonnie photos to show you."

"Aye, I'll look at 'em ta-marra, lassie. I'm a wee bit weak in the eyes," I said with a burr. I continued shuffling through the postcards. "How about that! Justin was in Spain. Sent a card from Barcelona. Odd, he never mentioned about traveling this summer. He must have written this with his left foot; I can't make out a single word he wrote." I tilted the card sideways trying to decipher his script, but it was no more understandable than hieroglyphics.

Captain hopped on my wrist and grabbed the edge of the postcard with his beak, yanking it out of my hand. "Can you understand his writing, Captain?" The parakeet then hopped on my lap and began gnawing the card. "Stop, Captain." I gently pulled the card from him, then he flew atop my head.

"What's this? Hawaii?" The next postcard pictured a narrow waterfall pouring out of a cavity in a rugged green mountainside. "Oh, it's Puerto Rico. Who sent this? Becky. Becky? No, it can't be."

"I recall seeing that card. Who is she?" my mother inquired, as she entered the living room carrying a tray of tea cups and chocolate cookies.

"Remember the Becky from high school who I took to her prom?"

"The girl with fat legs?" asked mom as she set the tray on the coffee table.

"She did *not* have fat legs. But yes, the same."

"I had forgotten her name. Wasn't her father a policeman?"

"A fireman," I corrected. "Haven't heard from her since high school. And now she sends greetings from San Juan. Listen to this: 'Me and a few friends are here for a week of motor biking and scuba diving. Great beaches, beautiful scenery. Adios!' After three years she decides to contact me. Can't figure her out."

"What happened between the two of you?" asked my father as he stirred cream into his tea.

"I took her to her prom. Had a very fine evening, too. But the following Monday at school she completely ignored me. I felt so betrayed. Didn't speak another word to me until just before graduation. She wished me good luck and told me to keep in touch. But I never did. Why would I?"

"The poor girl is probably agonizing over you, Byron. Call her up and put her out of her misery," said Lynn.

"Perhaps I should. What do you think Captain, should I call her?"

"Captain, pretty bird. Captain, pretty bird," the parakeet answered.

"Thank you, sister." I took the cup and saucer from her and placed it on my lap. As I sipped my tea mom brought me to date on the latest neighborhood gossip, starting with Leo Monzoni's quarrel with Moe Walder arising from jealousy over Walder's Cadillac sedan.

"There was always bad blood between those two," my mother began. "Moe's new Caddy was parked in his driveway and as usual had the rear extend over the sidewalk, so any passerby would have to step into the street to go around it. He does it purposely so people will notice his expensive car. Leo was passing by walking his collie, and purposely let the dog squirt on the car fender. Moe stormed out of his house and threatened to run over Leo's dog, and then a loud argument followed. And just last Saturday old Mrs Stevens burst out of her house wielding a skillet, and threatened to crown Mr Banks because the smoke from his backyard barbecue was drifting into her house."

"Mrs Stevens is loony," I remarked.

"The poor woman is 82 years old; what can you expect? And Banks threatened to roast her on a spit."

"Banks is a jerk and would probably do it," my father added.

There were other neighborhood feuds. Mom related how Murphy's lawn sprinkler was spraying water into his neighbor's bedroom window; another neighbor's dog dug up another neighbor's tulip garden; and Billy Jones drove a baseball through Mrs Sand's plate glass window. Now my mother is as fine a woman you can find anywhere; in my eyes she has no equal. But like most homemakers, she finds few things more amusing than a fracas among neighbors. It provides a purgative for the house-bound wife, by which she vicariously vents her own frustration through others' disputes. Whenever a squabble erupts between neighbors on our street, a raised horizontal slat can be seen on a window-blind framing a housewife's peeking eye. Indeed, nothing upsets my mother more than coming home from a day of shopping and learning she had missed a big argument while she was out. "Why do I miss all the action?" she would moan.

"Byron, Byron! Did you hear what I just said?" my mother asked, after observing that I was not listening to her last tidbit of neighborhood news.

"What? What did you say?" I had been staring into my tea cup and my mind was drifting off.

"Never mind. It's no use talking if you're not paying attention," she said impatiently.

"He's tired mom; he's had a long day," said my father without lifting his eyes from the newspaper he was reading.

"Please forgive me mom, I didn't mean to be rude. I appreciate all the work you've done to make my evening enjoyable, but I'm exhausted." In fact I was completely spent. The evening was passing quickly and it was approaching eleven. "It's time I retire," I yawned. Captain, who was still perched on the crown of my head, scrambled to my brow from where he clung upside down looking into my face. I looked at him with upturned eyes: "It's your bedtime, too." I slipped my forefinger under his feet, and then transferred him to my sister's finger, as it was Lynn's duty each night to return him to his cage.

"Kiss me goodnight, Captain." I squeezed my nose against the thin metal bars of the cage and let him nibble my nose.

"Goodnight baby," he said. Then he let out a shrill whistle.

I bid my family goodnight with hugs and kisses, and promised to tell them all about my summer adventure the next day.

LIII

Then came the hour when sleep...the Heaven's gift,
Comes graciously to greet weary mankind.
— HOMER

Upstairs, my bedroom was the same as when I had left it. Several weeks earlier I had languished here in crippling monotony. But what had been a penitentiary cell before my departure was now a welcome sight—four walls for privacy, a closet to hang my clothes, a ceiling light, a radio clock on the night table, *and* a bed. The moment I had been looking forward to ever since the night I arrived at The Timberhaus had been realized at last.

Once in bed, I dug my heels into the mattress and embraced the pillow like a lover. I expected Morpheus to send me into blissful sleep right away, but such was not the case. Just as I would have to get used to eating good food again, I would have to get used to a comfortable bed. I laid on my right side, and then on my left; I curled into a ball, and then lay flat; I propped my pillow to raise my head, I flattened my pillow to lower my head. This contorting and turning lasted some ten minutes until I exhausted myself into tranquil repose. I gazed through the bedroom window which framed the September night like a portrait, as a pumpkin-colored moon hung low in the sky and the backyard trees swayed gently to a late summer breeze. I reflected on what a wonderful day it had been. The surprise send-off at the bus depot had lifted my spirits, and erased any lingering bitterness from my Timberhaus experience. And the happy reunion with my family was a fitting closure to a memorable season, notwithstanding its trials and ordeals. For once reunited with my loved ones and returned to the comfort of my home, of what matter were the difficulties I had to endure.

But as I began dozing a gnawing turmoil sprang from within, turning me back from the threshold of peaceful slumber. Not knowing the cause of my agitation made it more disquieting. I sat up in bed and pulled my knees up to my chin, and then came the disturbing realization that my summer paled in comparison to that of my friends, who had either journeyed across the Atlantic or traveled to the Caribbean, while I had ventured only 150 miles from home. The postcards taunted me with the reminder that others had been to parts of the world and enjoyed wider adventures. As I dwelt on this my summer experience began to sour. Had I really accomplished much after all? Was all my hard work and nights slept under the sky worth it? I fretted on this for several minutes when a benevolent inner voice spoke: "Why are you upset? Do not compare yourself to what others have done or enjoyed. Be content with your own gains." Then my qualms vanished, and my mind was at ease.

I closed my eyes and quickly fell asleep, finding myself floating through Stygian darkness where nothing could be seen, yet sensing I was in a realm of infinite vastness. Emerging through this ether of blackness came odd, scattered shapes like the jumbled patterns seen in a kaleidoscope. Then these fragmented shapes coalesced into a single template from which issued the familiar faces of summer, not as a common portrait, but in singular sequence with each face molded from the one before it. Although each image appeared for only a moment, I could recall the tale of every person in vivid detail as if I had gazed on their faces for hours.

Monica first appeared staring at me with her sublime, inscrutable expression. Then Monica changed into Diane, whose charming smile belied the deep grief for her beloved father. Diane became freckle-faced Tara, who in turn became Carmen wearing the alluring look of juvenile charm. Faces came and faces went. Danny had a merry look that suddenly turned dour, as if he had just remembered his fixation on death; Papa appeared, his face rigid and stern from continuous toil and disdain of pleasure. His features shifted into grim-faced Otto, who wore his misery like a hair shirt to constantly remind himself of past anguish. Otto dissolved into Hildegarde, the cleaning lady whose life had also been shattered by war, and whose only remnant of a horticulture profession lay in the tiny rose garden that she cultivated behind her cottage. The wizened Hilda melded into angel-faced baby Jamie, whose bubbling, bright eyes dismissed the world's worries with the unqualified enthusiasm that a toddler has for life. The faces scrolled onward in this eerie tableau: Bruce, staring coldly with his malevolent dead-eyed glare; the deranged look of Eric; the benign Pastor Hugh; the brilliant and bewildered look of Horace; the scrupulous bearing of Thomas Ellsworth; the daffy mien of Stubby. And then she came, looking at me with electric-blue eyes encased in a contorted and melancholy expression. Debra appeared so vivid and so haunting. Her image lingered and would not disappear; it was though she was etched inside my eyelids. Smile to me Debra, please smile. But her expression remained unchanged. Pitiful, unfortunate girl. She squeezed every drop from her meager faculties in her courageous but futile attempt to surmount her handicap, and achieve the aspirations of other girls her age. But what had come of her effort?

Slowly her picture faded into the depths of my subconscious. And then I woke up. I got out of bed, and went to the window. All was quiet, nothing stirred. Suddenly a flash of lightning streaked across the sky followed by another flash. Yet no clap of thunder was heard. A "silent thunder," recalling the words of Angelo. The lights in all the neighboring homes were off, except for the two-story house that lay behind our rear yard. The windows on the ground floor were still lit, but then—one by one—each row of window lights winked out. Then the bedroom lights on the second floor were turned on as its occupants got ready to retire. The house was a sprawling Tudor that occupied two lots and had a swimming pool. It was referred to as the "rich people's house," because a wealthy couple used to live there with their two servants. The house had been built during the Twenties before the Great Depression, when the surrounding area was still parks and trees.

Before they sold their house ten years ago the former owners were rarely seen, except when they threw lavish poolside parties a couple of times a year. As a boy I used to peer at the festivities through the tall, thick hedge bushes that margined our yards. Women wore stylish gowns and men wore tuxedos, and a string quartet played chamber music. It was like a scene from the pages of *The Great Gatsby.* How nice to be wealthy, I thought. Maybe I, too, would be rich someday and live in a house just like that. There was rumor that the master of the house was a show business executive, and that movie and theater stars had been guests at his house. But the only people seen regularly on the grounds were its caretakers, Lucas and his wife Annabelle, a sweet, elderly couple who every evening walked the owners' dogs through the neighborhood. The couple who now owned the house were obviously well-to-do, but they too were seldom seen and no one knew who they were.

I laid down again and stared out the window. Darkness had melded the tall treetops into the outline of a mountain ridge silhouetted against the night sky. I dozed off, and in my sleep I could see the view from my bedroom as if I were still awake. Then the backyard loomed as a Catskill vista, and I sensed myself racing across moonlit pastures toward a distant mountain which, as I moved faster and faster, grew larger and more distant. Then the mountain became a floating island, and on its peaks and slopes were nested the great landmarks of the world. There was Notre Dame Cathedral, and perched just above it on a slope were the ruins of Angkor Wat, and next to it stretched the serpentine length of China's Great Wall. "At last I have seen the world, and can brag to everyone about my travels," I told myself. Then I found myself scaling the mountain walls attempting to reach the moon, but as I climbed the mountain sank deeper into the water until I found myself standing in a shallow stream, the mountain having disappeared beneath my feet.

It was pitch dark and I was very frightened; I started to flee for I felt in terrible danger. I raced along the stream for miles and miles through impenetrable blackness, but the trek was endless and I sensed an evil, undefined force following me which I knew would kill me if it caught me. Just then the stream turned into my neighborhood street, and I found myself running toward my house. Now I was safe. No evil could follow me here. Standing on the front stoop of the house were my parents. "You're late for dinner," my mother said. "I just got back from the Catskills," I answered. And again I awakened.

I thought I had slept for hours, but by the clock on the nightstand I was asleep only half-an-hour. But now I was thoroughly relaxed, as the dream had purged my subliminal anxieties. And with this tranquility there sprang from the wilderness of my mind an illumination—akin to the Zen state of "satori" or unexplainable enlightenment—that all was well. Staring at the ceiling, I watched the room slowly lose definition as the moonlight retreated and darkness crept down the walls. As slumber advanced everything around me began to dissolve. No longer could I feel the press of my body on the mattress, or the pillow beneath my head; nor hear the creak of swaying boughs, or feel the soft breeze of the night. A profound and peaceful sleep embraced me and ended my long day, bringing a close to my twentieth summer: The summer of Seventy-Two.

66414908R00236

Made in the USA
San Bernardino, CA
13 January 2018